# A FAMILY MATTER

*Also by Nigel Rees*

The Newsmakers
Talent

# A FAMILY MATTER

Nigel Rees

**HEADLINE**

First published in 1989
by HEADLINE BOOK PUBLISHING PLC

British Library Cataloguing in Publication Data

Rees, Nigel, *1944–*
A family matter.
I. Title
823'.914 [F]

ISBN 0–7472–0137–4

Typeset in 11/12¼ pt Plantin
by Colset Private Limited, Singapore

Printed and bound in Great Britain by
Richard Clay Ltd, Bungay, Suffolk

HEADLINE BOOK PUBLISHING PLC
Headline House
79 Great Titchfield Street
London W1P 7FN

To S.M.B.
with love

# ACKNOWLEDGEMENTS

The owners of Althorp, Broadlands, Burghley House, Highclere Castle, Ince Blundell Hall and Sudeley Castle will discover that certain features until now considered unique to their properties can also be found at Castle Cansdale. However, let me make it plain that Castle Cansdale is not based on any of the above-named stately homes. Nor is it my intention, in any way, to draw comparisons between their owners and the Hooke family.

I am indebted to Michael Fullerlove of Wiggin & Co., Cheltenham, for providing me with the kind of legal advice which Hugo Hooke and his family could have done with.

# The Hooke Family

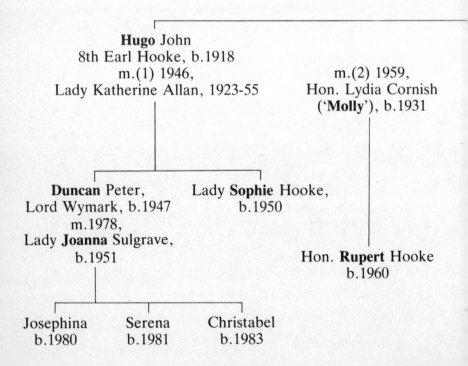

Andrew John
4th Earl Hooke, 1810-66
('The Bachelor Earl')

Robert Hugo
5th Earl Hooke, 1815-80
m.1850, Lady Elizabeth Cavendish,
1821-68 (no issue)

**Hugo** John
8th Earl Hooke, b.1918
m.(1) 1946,
Lady Katherine Allan, 1923-55

m.(2) 1959,
Hon. Lydia Cornish
('**Molly**'), b.1931

**Duncan** Peter,
Lord Wymark, b.1947
m.1978,
Lady **Joanna** Sulgrave,
b.1951

Lady **Sophie** Hooke,
b.1950

Hon. **Rupert** Hooke
b.1960

Josephina
b.1980

Serena
b.1981

Christabel
b.1983

```
                              ┐
                    Hon. Arthur Hooke
                        1817-70
                        m.1839
                 Hon. Constance Walsh, 1820-51
                              │
            ┌─────────────────┴─────────────┐
        Albert Hector                    2 sons
    6th Earl Hooke, 1850-1912          3 daughters
      m.1895, Lady Kitty Peel
    ('Countess Kitty'), 1879-1926
                  │
        ┌─────────┴─────────────┐
     Richard Giles          2 daughters
 7th Earl Hooke, 1899-1943
        m.1917
 Hon. Marjorie Pinnington, b.1899
          │
 ┌────────┴──────────────────────┐
     Hon. Alec Hooke          Lady Alice Hooke,
        b.1920                   1925-29
 m.1958, Countess Farbiszewski,
      b.1933 (marr. diss.)
```

# PROLOGUE

SICILY, AUGUST 1938. The only sound that could be heard as the open-top tourer entered Calatafimi was of the white-sided rubber tyres rolling over the rock. Nothing else stirred in the burning heat of the middle of the day. If there were any residents in the town – and there must have been, of course – they were all shadily indoors. The streets were deserted, the shutters up. Not even a dog lay sprawled in the dust.

The silence unsettled the three young Englishmen in the Alvis. As they motored slowly through the small town they did not speak, merely stared at the houses, looking for signs of life. Nothing came back to them from behind the brown peeling shutters.

The tubby driver mopped his neck with a handkerchief and half turned to his two companions seated behind him.

'Drive on, eh?'

The lankier of these companions was resting his forearm on top of the door. His distinctive nose gave him an air of superiority. His fair hair flopped handsomely. He wore a white shirt and cricket flannels. The passenger next to him, though only a year or two younger, seemed more of a schoolboy. He wore glasses, looked more studious and clutched a copy of *Baedeker* to his knees.

'I should think so, Toby,' said the fair-haired one.

'It's Sunday every day in Calatafimi,' added the bespectacled boy, carefully enunciating each syllable of the place name. He grinned at his brother, who hardly responded.

The Alvis continued on its way. In time they were once more in the parched countryside, the alien motor whipping up clouds of white dust in the primitive landscape. Very occasionally, a man wearing dark clothes – tanned, roughly-shaven, peasant-looking – would stop by the roadside and turn as the foreigners drove by, his face impassive, not comprehending what the visitors came to find in his country.

1

The Englishmen knew, or thought they did. Sicily was the last stop on a grand tour of Europe. They had driven first to Germany, rampant with Hitlerism, where the British Prime Minister was about to fly with peace proposals; then down to Switzerland and across the border into Italy: Venice, Florence, Rome, Naples – Mussolini's Italy now. Then finally, a few days before this, the ferry had carried them across the Straits of Messina into Sicily.

They were staying at a large hotel, La Torre, in Palermo and were making forays each day into the forbidding countryside. Today was the last of their trips. Tomorrow they would begin the long drive home to England.

'Soon be there,' said Alec, the studious, bespectacled one, his shock of dark hair damp with perspiration; the clothes he wore were more suited to a northerly clime.

'You'd better be right,' mocked Toby from the driving seat. 'Don't want yesterday again.' On a long drive over the mountains to Agrigento the day before, Alec had managed to guide them on to a road no better than a sheep track – and barely wide enough to take a hand-painted Sicilian cart, let alone an Alvis. They had finally become wedged in the narrow main street of a mountaintop village before finding a way out.

Alec shrugged, and Toby laughed. The third passenger, Hugo, managed a smile. It had been one of the few worrying moments they had had on the long tour. They were usually a happy threesome. With little difficulty, Toby had won permission from his father to drive all over Europe in the Alvis tourer. Sir Donald Blair did, after all, have eight automobiles of one sort or another in his garages. Indeed, when his industrial commitments allowed, there was nothing he liked more than racing on his own private circuit in Hampshire. He looked upon the Alvis as a runabout. Of course Toby could take it on the Continent during the summer vacation.

Hugo, Lord Wymark, had taken the opportunity to mount a European tour. His rooms at Oxford were directly over Toby's in the Meadows Building at Christ Church – the result of a move, apparently initiated by the Dean, to bring together the aristocracy of class and the aristocracy of trade. Hugo and Toby had plotted the jaunt together. Then Hugo had suggested allowing his brother Alec, two years younger and just down from Eton, to accompany them.

The Hon. Alec Hooke had so far failed to gain a place at either Oxford or Cambridge – which was odd, as he was far more academically inclined than his elder brother. What he would do with his life, he had no idea. For the moment, it was he who dictated where the travellers should go. Toby claimed that he had seen quite enough ruins. 'Why can't they mend 'em?' he asked, only half-jokingly.

'Philistine!' Alec retorted.

As for Hugo, it was not totally clear whether he enjoyed looking at ruins, or even at paintings in churches and galleries. He was, after all, only going through Oxford because it was expected of him. In time, he would proceed to the army as his father, grandfather and great-uncle had done before him. The earldom of Hooke, to which he would eventually succeed, had been created in 1773 following some military service performed by Calley Hooke for the sovereign, George III. When Hugo eventually succeeded his father, he should have been moulded the same way.

In time, the countryside opened up, bordered by rolling mountains. They could see for miles. Closer in, they came to a ravine which contained what they were looking for – or, rather, what young Alec had told them they were looking for.

'That's Segesta,' he announced.

The three fell quiet as the motor stopped on the brow of a hill and they looked down to where a Doric temple stood in lonely seclusion except for a background of dark green trees. Toby switched off the ignition. All that could be heard then was a slight but welcome whistling of wind and the clanking of goat bells.

'It's like a jewel box,' breathed Alec.

'Perfect. No roof, though.' This was Hugo being a touch obvious and matter-of-fact. But even he was not impervious to the grace and beauty of the ancient site.

'430BC,' Alec read from the *Baedeker*. 'Peristyle of thirty-six columns.'

'No naughty pictures, don't suppose?' Toby gurgled. The highlight of their visit to Pompeii had been the greasing of a guide's palm to show them the 'forbidden' wall paintings in the old brothel.

Alec knew the question was not worth answering. 'Lunch first, that right?' he said.

'Indubitably,' replied Toby and opened his door. From the boot, he retrieved a wicker picnic set and a tartan rug which he proceeded to spread on the ground.

Hugo unstoppered a flask of the white Corvo. Toby handed round the bread, cheese, olives, salami and fruit they had acquired from the hotel before setting out. They sat together on the rug. They could see for miles across country but each kept turning to look down to the temple in the ravine.

'This is the furthest south we'll get, I suppose,' said Hugo.

'S'pose your right,' replied Toby, absently, while he crammed another apricot between his thick lips. 'Much further and we'll be in the Mediterranean. Hope the old dear's up to going all the way back.'

'Old dear' was the nickname they had given the Alvis.

3

From the look on his face it did not appear that Hugo had allowed himself a moment's worry on that score. In his view of life, there was a certain assurance that everything would turn out all right. He was born to it. Worrying was for other people.

'I say,' young Alec chirped up again. 'Mr Chamberlain seems a jolly long way away, doesn't he?'

'Mr Chamberlain will see it through,' Toby told him confidently.

'I expect so,' added Hugo, allowing himself one more judicious sip of the wine.

Toby noticed again his friend's wonderful nose, rather burned now by the sun. 'I say, Hugo, what a profile! I've never asked: were you born like that or did you break it?'

'Broke it, you ass. Boxing. A little gadfly called Charlie Pike. Did it when I dropped my guard. I said I'd never forgive him. Mother was heartbroken.'

'It's very distinguished.'

'Fell over when drunk, more like,' Alec suggested with a twinkle, but Hugo did not rise to the bait. It would have been uncharacteristic of him.

'Anyone for pud?' Alec demanded, changing the subject.

'Pudding?' Hugo asked. 'What do you want pudding for? Have an apricot like Toby.'

'It's just I have my little supply of those *biscotti*.'

'Oh, yes, and that sickly wine. It's too hot for that.'

'No, it isn't, Hugo.'

Alec went to the Alvis and extracted a small brown case from which he took a glass tumbler. He poured himself a good measure of *moscato di Siracusa* and sat down once more on the tartan rug. Then he opened a small packet of biscuits which he proceeded to dip one by one into the sticky, sweet wine before sucking and munching them.

'Ummmmm! *Eccellente*! Surely you want some, you two?'

'Oh, all right,' said Toby, leaning over to join him. Toby had no wish to remain slim and underfed-looking like Hugo, though he was puzzled how Alec seemed able to put away sweet things without becoming podgy.

'You're gluttons, both of you, victims of the senses,' Hugo announced drily. 'You'll come to a sticky end, both of you.'

'Sticky, certainly,' laughed Toby, and popped another biscuit in his mouth.

'If you've finished, I think it's time we looked more closely at these little gems.' Hugo stood up, ready to lead off, as always.

They left the car rug and picnic things on the ground and sauntered over to look at a semi-circular theatre built into the hillside. Then they

4

strode through clusters of agaves, prickly pears and cypresses towards the temple.

'It's one of the *mirabilia Siciliae*,' Alec quoted from the guide book. Hugo noted how his little brother's fondness for the sticky pudding was equalled only by his enthusiasm for old monuments. Perhaps his own more reticent attitude had something to do with the fact that he would one day, along with the earldom of Hooke, inherit his own ancient pile. Castle Cansdale in Wiltshire was in vastly better repair than the temple at Segesta, but it was still a monument to an earlier, more expansive age.

Hugo wondered whether Alec's interest in old buildings was compensation for not inheriting Castle Cansdale. Hugo would succeed to the estate simply by virtue of being the first-born male – he who would not have accepted the responsibility if he had not felt obliged to honour the code. Birth was everything. It dictated everything. And even Alec with his 'Hon.' was not entirely without benefit from it.

The three of them rooted round the temple, quietened at last by the awesome site, but also tired from the oppressive heat and the journey. Toby propped his box camera on a large stone and arranged to take yet another group shot with the automatic timing device. They stood before the temple, frozen in time and monochrome. Three young men, with age behind them, their whole lives before them.

At the end of the day, as the sun sank low behind the *Conca d'oro*, the golden conch shell – the fertile plain on which the Sicilian capital lay – they drove into Palermo once more. There were plenty of people in the dark streets here in the early evening. Heads turned as the foreigners in their exotic motor swept along the Corso Vittorio Emanuele towards the harbour and the slopes of Monte Pellegrino where their hotel lay.

The Englishmen passed under large banners slung between trees and lampposts. One proclaimed: MUSSOLINI HA SEMPRE RAGIONE – 'is always right', was how Alec translated it; another, MOLTI NEMICI, MOLTO HONORE – many enemies, lots of glory; and a third, IL GUIDO D'ITALIA E UN GUIDO DI GIUSTIZIA ED UN GUIDO DI VITTORIA – Italy's guide is one of fairness and victory.

But the fascist leader was far away in Rome. He might try to impose himself upon Sicily, even try to suppress its traditional barons, but the Sicilians were too proud and independent to pay anything but lip-service to him.

At the harbour, Toby turned the Alvis up a steep, narrow, twisting street. A gaggle of barefoot children ran along by the car, calling out for money. One even jumped on the running-board and held out his hand inches from Hugo's nose. He stared back impassively, but warned Toby not to go too fast lest the urchin fall and injure himself. Eventually, the boy realized he would receive nothing from this foreigner and jumped off, uttering an obscene Italian phrase which Hugo did not catch.

Hugo looked wanly at Alec, but made no comment.

'Home at last,' said Alec, uncomfortably.

Hugo noticed that his brother did not look well. 'Are you all right? You look a little peaky.'

'I'm all right.'

But he was not. Too much *moscato* at lunchtime, too much exposure to the heat, too much bouncing about on primitive roads had made him feel sick. Back in the room he had to himself at the end of the Hotel La Torre's long corridor, he finally succumbed.

His brother, who was standing by, waited until Alec had finished.

'So you won't be dining this evening?'

'No,' Alec choked sheepishly. 'I rather think I won't, Hugo. But it was a wonderful day we had, wasn't it?'

Hugo touched his shoulder in a rare show of affection. 'Yes, it was. You'd better be all right tomorrow, or we'll have to leave you behind.'

'*No*, Hugo, please!'

'I don't mean it, you fool! Get yourself better. I'll tell them to bring you something on a tray.'

Hugo closed the door to Alec's room and walked up to the tower room he shared with Toby. Again he glanced at the old photographs along the long corridor. They dated from twenty or thirty years before. Edward VII and George V, their consorts and flunkies, all well wrapped against the heat. And one or two more exotic Eastern royals he could not place.

Toby was in the bath already. Hugo followed him. When they had both removed the dust and heat of the day, they decided to go back down to the city to dine.

'Without wishing to be unkind,' Hugo observed a trifle coldly, 'I think that little bro. may have done us a favour. We can have a quiet evening on our own. I've quite an appetite.'

'That's not like you, Hugo. You're always saying it's Alec and me who are the greedy ones.'

'I wasn't talking abut gluttony, Toby. Stuffing your face isn't the only appetite.'

Toby looked thoughtful for the merest of seconds. 'Ah, yes. See what you mean. *Ragazze?*'

'You understand perfectly, Tobers.'

'I suppose we *are* far enough from home.'

'What's that got to do with it? We've waited far too long. This is just the place. Palermo will provide what we want.'

'But how? I don't speak the language.'

6

'And I don't suppose they speak English. But talking isn't what I had in mind . . .'

Toby smiled a touch resentfully. He was aware that Hugo was the 'leader' in their relationship. It came naturally from his birth and position, but Toby still couldn't see why it had to be that way.

They slipped quietly out of the hotel – as unnoticeable as two very English-looking young men in cricket flannels and white shirts with rolled up sleeves could be among so many dark Sicilians. As soon as they were away from the hotel grounds, they saw the gaggle of urchins playing in the street.

'Let's take a ride, shall we?' Hugo said.

'Good idea,' chimed Toby, never one to exercise himself if he could avoid it.

They returned to the hotel entrance and climbed aboard one of the horse-drawn cabs that were waiting. They set off at a trot, down the hill, and into Palermo proper.

'Where's he taking us? What did you say?' asked Toby, apprehensive still.

'The opera house – Piazza Verdi.'

'Is that where . . .?'

'It seems a reasonable place to look.'

It was now quite dark but still agreeably warm. After a temperature in the nineties during their visit to Segesta, it was now in the seventies. Hugo looked as close to happiness as his impassive features were ever likely to admit. Toby anxiously allowed himself to be bounced around by the carriage.

'I say, you don't think we ought to dine first?'

Surprisingly, Hugo agreed. He was not so rigid in his determination to lose his virginity (with a woman, that is) that he could not feel the pangs of hunger. They found a restaurant in the Via Maqueda and soon demolished a vast *pasta con le sarde* which contained not only salted sardines, but onions, pine nuts, sultanas, saffron and fennel, and plenty of tomato sauce. Toby insisted on having a large, delicious *zabaglione* to follow. Hugo joined him and even took a little more wine than he usually did.

They talked, and more to the point than usual, too; Alec was not there to distract them. Toby was nervous, Hugo excited – but too proud to show it. They were odd, these friendships that Oxford engineered for her under-graduates. There was chance involved, like whose rooms you found your-self next to, but beyond that these were not like schoolboy friendships.

Here were two young men who would probably not have formed any sort of link at school. Toby Blair was trade, after all. His father had hundreds of thousands of pounds maybe, but no 'family' or anything like that. Hugo was a lord, the son of an earl. There was possibly an element of altruism in Hugo's taking him up. But it was not charity. Toby had plenty of cash at his disposal – probably more than Hugo, in terms of ready money. Perhaps Hugo liked Toby because he was in a similar position to him, but different. No complications on that score. It was also typical of Oxford friendships in that although Hugo and Toby had been away together now for six weeks almost, they did not really know each other. It was not an intimate relationship.

Toby, for his part, was fascinated by Hugo. The young Lord Wymark seemed so much more of a complete human being than Toby himself. It was almost as if he had been born as he was now – sober, serious, responsible, not overly endowed with a sense of humour. A little unbending, rather too conscious of his position.

'Do you think Alec'll get a place?' Toby asked out of the blue.

'At the House? Rather depends on Father. If he can't get another Hooke in, no one can. Alec deserves to. Darn sight more brains than me.'

'I suppose it must be a bit hard on him. You inherit everything from your father, and he gets nothing. Didn't you have a sister or something?'

'Yes. She died when she was four – Alice. Now there's just Alec and me. And, of course, if I pop off, Alec's next in line. So he's in with a chance.'

'But, chances are, he won't.'

'Who can say? Anything might happen.' Hugo managed to suggest with a look that these were questions he did not like to discuss and that they ever so slightly irritated him.

'I expect he is a wee bit jealous, yes,' he nevertheless went on. 'I know I'd be if I was him. And, of course, it's terribly unjust from the outside, from his position. I follow my father – I inherit Cansdale and all the rest – simply because I was the first pea out of the pod. If you weren't a damn only child, you'd know what it was like. I mean, Alec gets *nothing* by right, and I get everything.'

Toby nodded vigorously. 'Yes, yes, I'd be terribly jealous. But I might be relieved I wasn't being handed a bit of a burden, too – with no choice in the matter. I mean, if you're like you, Hugo, your whole life's plotted from the first breath you take. You can't do what *you* want to do.'

'Well, you can. There've been plenty of people with titles and such who've let things go hang. But, it's true, I've a course laid out for me to follow, if I want to follow it. When I go down, I'll join the Guards. In time, I'll help Father with the estate. And then it's just waiting, if you like, for him to drop off the perch. After all, he's not old.'

'What is he?'

'Nearly forty, I s'pose.'

'Good grief! So you were born . . . before he was twenty?'

'That's right. Started early. Married early. Makes me feel quite tardy. Here I am, twenty, not married, and I'm certainly not a father.'

Toby blushed at Hugo's mention of their common lot.

'And, one way and another,' Hugo went on, 'I'm unlikely to follow my father for years and years. Could be forty or fifty myself by then.'

'I'd hate that,' Toby mused. 'I'm sure I could work for my father if I wanted, but he's such a bugger I never would. I'll do what I want – and that's what you don't have, the power to say that.'

'Hmmm.' Hugo rubbed his nose in the characteristic way he had, not to relieve an itch, more an acknowledgement of the outstanding nose's existence. 'Well, you're born to it. I've never known anything else, have I? Always expected a particular future, if you like, as soon as I was old enough to realize it. But who's to say it *will* happen? You just have to look back through my family's history. It's far from an orderly transition from father to first-born as the generations roll away. I could fall under a tram tomorrow. Then Alec would find himself pitchforked into my place – and he wouldn't have been expecting it. Everything could be different.'

'It does strike one as rather an *odd* way to manage family life, when you think about it,' Toby laughed. 'Like Russian roulette?'

'P'raps.'

Toby was rather enjoying his proximity to the phenomenon that his friend represented. They said that everyone liked a lord, and it wasn't so surprising. A title had a devastating way of entertaining people. Like royalty, there was a magic to it. A lord could walk into a room and instantly change the atmosphere, just by being there, however unexceptional he really was.

But Hugo was exceptional in his way, and Toby continued to enjoy their friendship without ever quite being able to forget that there was something different about the other man.

'Don't you think we ought to make a move?' Hugo briskly inquired of Toby.

They paid for their food and wine and went out into the piazza, thinking they would soon find women of the street who would expertly and quickly relieve them of the intolerable burden of their virginity. But either the women didn't exist or the Englishmen did not know where to look for them. Hugo and Toby drew a blank.

Until, that is, just before they were about to return to their hotel, crestfallen. Hugo spotted a woman who was unmistakably all too keen to surrender her body for lire. He approached her, with Toby somewhat reluctantly in tow.

The woman turned as they approached. The light from a street lamp high up on the old walls half showed her face. Hugo stopped suddenly. Her skin was pockmarked, diseased. Hugo turned away decisively and briskly. Toby hopped about trying to see what it was that had repulsed his companion.

Shamefaced, the two returned to the Hotel La Torre and went straight up to their room. Toby felt both disappointed and relieved. Hugo took it much more to heart, as though he had been thwarted in a great matter. He was used to getting his own way.

He did not sleep, or not very much, so exercised was he on this last night before their homeward journey began. Perhaps he could remedy the failure somewhere along the route home, but he was agitated. Indeed, he was frustrated.

So it was that just before dawn he slipped from beneath the single cotton sheet that covered his form in bed and went quietly, so as not to wake Toby (who slept annoyingly well), on to the tower balcony.

Hugo drew his striped dressing gown about him to fend off the slight chill and watched as the ochre sun rose through the mist in the harbour. It was a moment of great beauty and promise of what the day would bring. Hugo consciously registered the occasion as important.

As the sun rose higher, he felt hungry but thought it would be too early to get any breakfast in the hotel. Knowing it was useless to return to his bed, he dressed and slipped out of the room and on to the long silent landing. Quietly, he glided down three flights of stairs until he came to a glass door which led out into the hotel garden. He opened it and walked down the path bordered by sweetly smelling flowers until he came to a group of five ancient pillars which stood near the edge where the garden fell away to the harbour below. The pillars looked as if they had been forced together into a little circle, their stones held together with iron bands, but they gave an adequate impression of a small temple on a headland by the sea.

Hugo watched as a few fishing boats plied in and out of the harbour, then turned to wander in the deeper recesses of the garden.

He suddenly sensed that he was being watched in his dawn wanderings. He noticed the girl's eyes first, hard but bright in their gaze. They shone from her dark face, from beneath dark hair, so that it was hard for Hugo to discern the face.

He moved towards her. She did not move away.

'*Buon giorno*,' he murmured.

She looked away and tried to hide behind the flower bush from which she had been observing the young foreigner.

'What is your name?'

She did not reply; did not understand the question.

'I am Hugo,' he murmured, sounding very English and touching his chest with the tips of his fingers.

She understood at last. 'Consiglia.' With a gesture, she showed that this was her name.

Hugo moved closer and saw that she was wearing a simple cream coloured dress, as plain as a uniform. A member of the staff, he assumed. Come to make the beds or sweep the corridors.

He knew then that he must have her. She was not beautiful, but she was a woman. She had a curious scent about her which he had never encountered before. Not even among such women as he had been close to.

The scent spoke of a different world to his. It was dangerous and alluring. It rivalled the equally beguiling smells of the flowers that were near them.

He put out his hand and touched her. She flinched, but did not make to run away. He was encouraged to go further. He kissed her forehead. The scent was even stronger now. She was smaller than he was. He took her clumsily in his arms.

The wordless encounter moved forward. She could not have escaped now even if she had wanted to. He held her firmly and guided her deep into the bushes. He lowered her to the dusty earth and opened her clothing.

Quickly he took her, and was done.

Hugo was still enjoying a sense of triumph and relief when the girl Consiglia picked herself up, buttoned her dress, and vanished from his presence as suddenly as she had come into it. Hugo noticed there were tears in her eyes.

'Consiglia!' he called after her – too loudly in the early-morning quietness of the garden.

He felt shame. Then he felt triumph again. At breakfast he was scarcely able to contain himself. Both Toby and Alec saw what a good mood he was in, though neither knew the reason for it.

When they were back at Oxford, the following term, Toby was to learn that Hugo had overcome the hurdle, though not where, or how, or with whom. Toby himself was not to achieve it until he was past his twenty-first birthday the following summer, just before the outbreak of war. His father, Sir Donald Blair, actually paid for him to be relieved of his virginity, to get the matter out of the way. As for Alec, when his father did eventually manage to get him into Christ Church, he went through a period of only being interested in men. His awakening towards women would not happen for several more years.

And the girl Consiglia did not know what role she had played in the life of a future Earl Hooke. She was too deeply ashamed to tell anyone. There came a time, however, when she had to speak about the events that took place in the hotel garden before the Englishman had his breakfast on that summer morning in 1938.

'*Ugo*' was how she remembered his name. Another person, close to her, worked through the records of the hotel's guests until the name 'Hugo Hooke' was found. Alongside it, the reception clerk had scribbled in brackets, 'Lord Wymark'.

This information was copied on to a piece of yellow paper, folded and put away. And then it was forgotten.

# CHAPTER 1

ENGLAND, APRIL 1988. There was nothing to say they had arrived at Castle Cansdale. The South Lodge gate was open and Drew Elliot drove through it past the discreet notice saying PRIVATE. It was simply expected that if you did not know where you were, or had not been invited, you would not proceed any further.

'This is it,' Elliot said to his passenger. 'Brought you this way round so you could get the view. Best bit's just inside.'

Elliot steered the elderly Rover through the gates and along a narrow road by rhododendron bushes for a few hundred yards. Then the road dived between two mounds and out into the open once more.

Elliot stopped the car. 'Let's get out. You must see this, Sidney. There's nothing like it!'

His companion Sidney Templeton loosened the seat belt from over his sizeable corporation and opened the door on his side of the car. Even Templeton, accountant by profession and in outlook, had to agree that the prospect before them was splendid. They had joined the main drive which ran from the ceremonial wrought-iron gates – closed to traffic for many a year – and on for what seemed like a mile right up to the house.

'They call it the Fair Mile,' said Elliot, 'and it really is.' He paused. 'And that's the house.'

Or abbey, or castle, or whatever anyone wished to call it. Castle Cansdale was its name, though it had never been besieged or witnessed a battle. It had no drawbridge, crenellations, machicolations, arrow slits or moat. It was simply a very grand nineteenth-century house which fell just short of being a palace.

'Splendid, eh?' said Elliot, whose firm of solicitors in Craswall had advised its owners, the Earls Hooke, for three generations. 'Best view in the county, I'd say.'

'Must cost a bob or two to run,' the accountant remarked matter-of-factly. It was hard not to be impressed, though. The drive swept majestically towards the great house in the distance. Remote it was, regal, a touch forbidding, but nevertheless human in scale, softened as it was that afternoon by gentle April light.

'That's the problem,' Elliot said softly, as though answering an unspoken question of Templeton's. 'It's not just *property* . . .'

Even the drily practical accountant could sense that Castle Cansdale was more than bricks and mortar.

'It should be open to the public,' Templeton concluded. 'Make a nice day out for people.'

'Now that's anticipating, if I may say so, Sidney,' Elliot told him sharply.

'All I mean is,' Templeton quickly clarified his assertion, 'it's too good to be kept hidden away where no one can see it.'

'That's a point of view, certainly. I'd be careful how you put it to his lordship, though.'

Without further disagreement they climbed back into Elliot's car and began a slow drive up the Fair Mile. The car tyres finally crunched to a halt in front of the house.

'Is this really the way in?' Templeton asked, hesitantly. 'I mean . . .'

'It certainly is. No servants' entrance for us, Sidney.'

Drew Elliot was in his mid-sixties, dapper in his dark morning coat and light grey-striped trousers, quite military in bearing and with an imperceptible but neatly-trimmed dark moustache. Sidney Templeton wore a blue shiny suit that he had bought off the peg in Craswall.

They stepped up to the doorway where no doorbell presented itself to be rung. Elliot, having been to Castle Cansdale many times before, was undaunted. He grasped the burnished doorknob and simply pushed. Once inside the entrance hall, even he was slightly put out that no one was to hand to greet them. It was always a problem when visiting the house. Plenty of mahogany chairs decorated with the Hooke coat of arms to sit on, but no one to welcome visitors.

Sidney Templeton stared almost disapprovingly at the naked statuary amid the church gothic columns and fan vaulting. He went and examined a heraldic beast carved out of dark wood, but quickly gave up having decided he did not like it.

'It's always like this,' Elliot muttered, and ran a weary hand through what remained of his once red hair. 'I don't know why.'

In time there was the sound of footsteps on marble. It turned out to be Compton, the butler.

'Ah, Compton, there you are,' said Elliot, relieved. 'I think his lordship is expecting us.'

'Indeed, he is. If you'll just follow me, he's in the library.'

The three men crossed the great Saloon which was further crammed with paintings and furniture, until Compton paused reverentially before a door. He knocked, paused for a few seconds, and then pushed it open.

Solicitor and accountant were ushered into the magnificent Gold Library, though Templeton sensed immediately that it was not full of books that were read regularly, if at all. Indeed, most of the books were locked away, inaccessible behind gold mesh or glass. Handsome in leather and with gold inscriptions on the bindings, they had no appeal for him. The room was known as the Gold Library because every piece of furniture and every column appeared to gleam with the stuff.

At the far end stood an elegant, tallish, aristocratic figure – exactly what Templeton had imagined he would find, in fact. Indeed, the owner of Castle Cansdale fulfilled his expectations to the smallest detail. Hugo John Stanley, 8th Earl Hooke, stood resplendent in a worn tweed jacket with frayed sleeves. His Viyella shirt had seen better days. A red polka-dot neckerchief and green pullover, scuffed suede shoes and beige corduroys, baggy and unpressed, completed the uniform.

'Lord Hooke,' Drew Elliot snapped into his introductions, 'this is Mr Templeton of whom I spoke to you.'

'Ah, yes,' said Hugo, extending a hand, 'what a pleasant surprise. Good of you to come, Mr Templeton. Not too bad a journey?'

'No, no, not really. Not far to come.'

'You from Craswall, too?'

'That's right.'

'Well, I'm most grateful to you. Mr Elliot kindly suggested, now he pretends he's retired, that you could bring us up to date with all this wretched tax nonsense.'

'I'll do what I can, certainly.' Sidney Templeton's large and wide form, as bottle-shaped as any body was likely to be, swayed with uncertainty. He was displaying the nervousness he had hoped to avoid.

'That's good then. Kind of you to come. Won't you take a seat?'

Hugo ran a finger across the bridge of his nose in that gesture he'd been making all his adult life. Then he indicated two chairs already drawn up on one side of a large desk upon which were a large, clean blotter, a few old copies of *The Field* and *Country Life*, and an impressive collection of fading photographs in silver frames. There were two wedding groups, both featuring Hugo as the groom, several of Hooke children in various stages of development, a signed portrait of the Queen, and a polaroid of the bachelor Prince Charles walking on the Fair Mile.

'I can see you like the desk.' Hugo was about to launch into one of his anecdotes, Elliot could tell. There were times when the Earl seemed able

15

to speak only in stories, as though he considered this the most effective currency of conversation for talking to strangers.

'Er, yes, it's very nice,' Templeton said, allowing himself to settle slowly into one of the chairs, a briefcase balanced on his knees.

'Carved from the timbers of the *Victory*, you know.'

'Really?'

Elliot had heard it all before; he patiently smoothed his hair and made patterns with his fingers and thumbs.

'Oh, yes, indeed. The third earl had it done. Seized his opportunity. Mind you, it's damned uncomfortable if you've got long legs like me. Always biffing them on the edge.'

Sidney Templeton had never actually met an earl before – or anyone with a title, for that matter – and he was struck first of all by the fact that the Earl was, in one sense, a perfectly normal human being. Gauntly handsome, slightly pink about the face; thinning and greying hair, though he had obviously had a good head of it once; a wonderfully broken nose; a slight problem with the teeth – which were nevertheless his own. He also had a way of looking at you intensely and then suddenly turning away his glance when he knew you realized.

'Well,' he said, 'everyone tells me I'm a bloody f., so that's why I asked you to come and help me out. You know I'll be seven-oh in July?'

Elliot was intrigued by the euphemistic turn of phrase. 'Three score and ten, as the Bible would have it,' he volunteered. Hugo did not react.

'As you also know, Mr Elliot, I've done nothing about the . . . well, y'know, *everything* and, if I haven't left it too late, I suppose I jolly well ought to do something.'

Elliot wholeheartedly agreed. He had been the Hooke family's legal adviser for twelve years, following in his father's and grandfather's footsteps. But he had gone into semi-retirement in 1986 when the firm was taken over by a group of young solicitors from Cheltenham. Hugo had refused to contemplate dealing with these and stuck to Elliot, presumably on the grounds that what had been good for the previous two Hooke generations was good enough for him. Drew Elliot would have much preferred to retire completely to the Côte de Beaune where he spent most of his summers anyway. But he felt an obligation to continue handling the Hooke family's legal affairs, even though he had not succeeded till now in getting Hugo to safeguard the handing on of the estate, with minimum benefit to the Inland Revenue. Hugo had refused countless times to do anything about it, or even to discuss the matter.

Then, suddenly, for whatever reason – maybe the approach of the significant seven-oh birthday – the Earl had stirred himself. That was why Elliot had come with Sidney Templeton in tow. Action must be efficient and rapid if the Hooke inheritance was not to be squandered. Even so, it might be too late. Elliot felt a little rusty on death duties, or inheritance tax as they had now become, and he felt that bringing in a good accountant would ensure there were no costly mistakes.

'Yes, yes, these are delicate matters.' Elliot smoothed his hands on the table as though to signal how warily he was treading. 'But you will know, sir, how agonizing these things can be, so I hope you will allow me to speak frankly.'

'To the point, yes, I should hope so,' said Hugo flatly, rubbing the skin on the back of his right hand, as an old man would. 'What's to be done?'

'Sir, you see, I'm sure you know – and Mr Templeton has all the details – there are several courses open to us. Action of some sort there must be, otherwise, in the unfortunate circumstances of your passing on—'

'My *death*, you mean? Say it, man, say it!'

'Yes, well . . . your death . . . your estate could be consumed by inheritance tax, as it now is. It could run into millions and your eldest son – who would, I assume, be the principal benefactor – might well find himself out of house and home. He'd have to sell off large tracts of land to pay the tax. The selling off of works of art and so on is very much dependent on the good will of the government agencies and would only be a very troublesome alternative.'

'Don't blather, man. Tell me the alternatives. Give me your advice. Mr Templeton, perhaps you can be more to the point?'

Thus rebuffed, Drew Elliot shrank back in his chair, thought of fees, and waited for his moment to return.

'Ah, well . . . you see . . .' Templeton, perspiring slightly, mopped at his forehead. The Earl had already noted how the accountant's hair was remarkably free of grey for a man who must be near the fifty mark. The hair on his head was as rich and dark as the large eyebrows that decorated his otherwise white and featureless face. Equally surprising was the pair of silver-rimmed spectacles that Templeton now slipped on. They seemed altogether too delicate for such a large man. The Earl was also interested to see that in Templeton's large white hands he held a sheaf of notes which, if he had written them himself, were wonderfully neat and tidy.

Without delay, Templeton got to the point.

'The present Chancellor, as you know, has cleared up some of the anomalies. The difficult capital transfer tax – CTT, as was – has been absorbed into inheritance tax, but the ground rules have barely changed. To avoid fairly tough penalties you may do one of several things. Firstly, you can make your property over to the National Trust.'

'Give it away? No, no, I'm not having that – public climbing all over you, tea towels on sale in the pantry. No, no, not at all.'

17

'I understand,' Templeton conceded, diplomatically. 'That option is never a straightforward one anyway. The National Trust, even if they accepted your gift – and they're dreadfully choosy these days – would expect an endowment of thousands towards the upkeep.'

'No, no, not worth bothering with. What else is there?'

'Well, you could seek exemption from inheritance tax as heritage property.' Templeton was not only perspiring heavily now, but the notes in his hand were shaking. 'The exemption is capable of extending to the house, major works of art, and to a reasonable amount of supporting adjacent land. However, and I fear this may be a problem, in order to seek exemption you would have to undertake to keep the property in good condition and also permit reasonable public access.'

'No, I'm sorry, that's quite out of the question. I am not having that. This is a family house. There has been a house on this site since 1508 and I'm not going to go the way of all the others and turn it into a zoo or a museum or some such thing. I don't want to appear difficult, Mr Templeton, but that's final.'

Drew Elliot observed that the Earl was getting unusually animated. His body remained still, but his eyes were flashing this way and that.

The Earl tried to be more accommodating. 'What about trusts and such?'

'Well, this is more Mr Elliot's line of country than mine, but if you were simply to pass the estate over to a trust under which you can retain a life tenancy in the castle, there's no tax saving whatever. For IHT purposes, a life tenant is treated as owning the trust property.'

'IHT, that's inheritance tax, I take it?'

'Yes. I have to say it, your lordship,' Templeton swallowed, 'to put it bluntly, there is no way in which you can continue to live in this house unless you wish to create immense difficulties for your heir.'

Templeton came to a sudden stop, noticing the watery look which had replaced the flashing in the Earl's eyes.

'God, the buggers!' Hugo cried. 'Why do they have to go for us like that?'

No one volunteered an answer. It was the lot of hereditary owners of great properties, even in a Britain otherwise so congenial to the accumulation of wealth.

'Why can't I die in my own house?'

Elliot and Templeton could think of nothing to say. Hugo gestured at the walls and the furniture in the Gold Library as if trying to make a point.

'I didn't ask to take all this on. Not that I don't like it, or anything. I just don't feel it's mine. Just looking after it for the family, as it comes after me.'

'I'm very sorry,' Elliot interposed. 'You will appreciate that we sympa-thize with you in your position?'

'So what's to be done, Templeton? You seem a sensible chap. What's all this about PETs? I've seen them mentioned in *Country Life*.'

Templeton promptly stood up, as if this would be a better way of dealing with his tension.

'Potentially exempt transfers, yes. Basically, they work like this. You make an outright gift of your estate to your heir in your own lifetime, but to demonstrate that it's not just a dodge, you have to be seen, very visibly, not to be enjoying any benefit from the gift after it has been made. By which I mean, you cannot continue to live in the house or any part of it. You must live elsewhere. And that is not the end of it. Only if you survive the settlement by the full seven-year term do you avoid IHT. It comes on a sliding scale. Should you die in the first couple of years, the payment is probably in full. The following year, it is a little less, and so on. So rather a lot depends on your remaining alive.'

Hugo rubbed the bridge of his nose. His eyes were still watery. He looked momentarily much frailer than he in fact was.

'So I've got to stick it out till I'm seventy-seven, you're saying? What d'you think? Can I make it?'

'Sir, I don't know your medical history, but just looking at you, I would say there's every chance. Do people in your family live a long time?'

'My mother's still alive, God bless her. She'll be ninety a year next December, if she's spared. My father died at forty-four, but he was killed in action.'

'There's always a risk with a PET but, frankly, as I've explained, there's no real alternative.'

Elliot nodded. The Earl stood up to join Templeton, so Elliot felt obliged to follow him. Hugo drew them to the windows of the library, which was on the north side of the house. A few flowerbeds clustered under the windows, then a lawn extended some distance until it was interrupted by a narrow roadway which ran from the stables by the side of the house to the North Lodge at the edge of the park. The grass continued on the other side of the road until it reached the domed Pantheon, and then the woods began.

It was a restful yet magnificent prospect, but Hugo seemed to derive little comfort from it.

'I have heard stories of strange goings-on by people to avoid paying the tax. Concealing time of death and such like.'

'There are many stories, sir,' Templeton conceded, 'but I've no idea whether they have any substance. It is said that where the donor has died in the seventh year of a PET, dates of death have been fudged by willing doctors, and bodies even been put in the deep freeze to preserve them!'

'Ha! Good Lord!' Hugo brightened, evidently liking the idea of getting his own back on a difficult law.

Elliot cleared his throat. 'I suppose,' he began, 'we have to consider what Lord Wymark's objections might be to any such arrangement?'

Hugo looked like thunder at the mention of his son and heir. With a vitriol that shook both Elliot and Templeton, he barked, 'Objections! Objections? Why the hell should he object?'

It wasn't the first time that Elliot had encountered the Earl being difficult, so he was less apprehensive about going on than Templeton.

'I merely wondered whether he would mind taking on the burden of the house and the estate. It has been known for eldest sons – and their families – to jib at being presented with similar proposals. Not everyone wants the responsibility early – even if they know it'll be theirs eventually.'

'I don't know. I just don't know.' Hugo pressed his forehead against the windowpane and stared down into the flowerbeds. Then he turned to look at the two men – two men who were happily not burdened with such concerns. 'Y'see, I know that Duncan takes the title when I go. And I know he has a kind of moral right to have the house to go with it. That's the way it is, and I understand that. But I must be honest with you, gentlemen, I don't think he's up to it – the running of it, the responsibility. And that, you know, is probably why I've dragged my feet, waited till now to do anything about this bloody business. I won't go into all the ins and outs of it, but he's a shit, quite frankly. I can't abide him. Never have been able to. He's a bounder. Not fit to call himself my son. Treats my wife abominably. She can't help it she's not his mother. Yet the law says, he has to have all this. Frankly, the thought of handing it over to him while I'm still around, which means I'll be here to see what a damn mess he makes of it, is almost too much to bear . . .'

There was silence in the library. Neither Elliot nor Templeton felt he could say anything. It was certainly a predicament for a man to be in, forced to play along with the hereditary system but disliking the principal beneficiary. From his years of looking after the Earl's legal affairs, Drew Elliot had already had a good idea what Hugo felt about his son Duncan, the present Lord Wymark, but he was only now beginning to appreciate how strong the animosity really was. Even Sidney Templeton had been aware from the newspapers that the name 'Lord Wymark' was one never mentioned except in their gossip columns and in a bad light.

Hugo snapped out of his gloom and turned once more to his visitors.

'There's only one thing to do.'

Elliot turned to listen expectantly.

'Have a word with Molly over a cup of tea.'

Templeton wondered who this fount of wisdom could be. From her name perhaps she was the housekeeper or some such homely body.

'Care to join us? She'll be in the Drawing Room.'

Elliot nodded, and as they followed the Earl out of the library he relieved Templeton's curiosity by mouthing at him, 'The wife . . . the second one.'

When Molly was located, dozing over her needlework, and instructions for tea had been passed to Compton by a phone call to his pantry downstairs, Hugo told the Countess what he and his visitors had been discussing.

'Oh, I see,' said his wife (who had always been known as Molly to one and all, though her real name was Lydia), and peered at the visitors over half-moon glasses which she wore attached to a pearl rope round her neck.

Elliot had met her only a couple of times previously. He had drawn up her will. She was ten or fifteen years younger than Hugo – in her late fifties, certainly. She was pleasantly stout, with a rather beautiful soft voice. Her hair was quite grey by now, but elegantly styled. This afternoon she was wearing a yellow silky top, sensible brown skirt, and rather forbidding dark suede boots, which even Elliot registered were remarkably unflattering to her legs.

'Well, y'know, Hugo, I can't speak about Duncan,' she said softly but firmly when her stepson's name came up. 'He's not mine and whatever I say about him only sounds a trifle sour.'

Hugo coughed. 'Yes, dear.' Templeton saw that the Earl behaved considerately and affectionately towards his wife, though she herself did not appear to radiate much warmth. But then, neither did the Earl, as far as Templeton could tell. The truth was that the Earl and the Countess were both forbidding at first acquaintance. The difference was that Molly came over much more warmly as people got to know her.

'I hope you won't mind my asking,' Sidney Templeton ventured, encouraged to be inquisitive by his earlier success at explaining things to the Earl, 'but how many children are there?'

'You tell him, Molly,' Hugo instructed her.

'Well, Duncan's the eldest, of course. Then there's Sophie.'

'They were my first wife's,' Hugo put in, helpfully, thinking that Molly was being hesitant. 'Died in 'fifty-five. Married Molly four years later.'

'And we just have the one son – Rupert. He's much younger than the others, of course.'

'Duncan just had his fortieth—'

'No, that was last year, darling.'

'And Rupert's what?'

'Oh, you're hopeless, Hugo. Rupert was born the year after we married. So he's twenty-eight. Sophie's in between. They're quite well-spaced, if you think about it.'

There was an interruption as Compton arrived with the tea. Lest Templeton encourage further rambling round the family tree, Elliot tried to bring the conversation back to the point where they had left it in the library. Hugo then quickly recounted to his wife what Elliot had recommended.

'I knew it would be that,' the Countess drawled flatly as she poured the tea. 'I've heard about it before. It won't be easy for us, giving up everything and moving. I expect it'll take some getting used to. It's such a dear house, and we've spent so much time on it.'

Elliot might have challenged her choice of the word 'dear', as he found the castle much too forbidding for that adjective, but he knew she was terribly fond of the place. As for having spent so much time on it, that may have been so but it really wasn't in very good repair.

Hugo brought his wife up sharply, as was his way. 'Nothing's been decided yet. You're getting ahead of yourself. I've got to think it over.'

Elliot then again dared to propose that the plan ought to be explained – at least in general terms – to Lord Wymark for his reactions. Hugo's eyelids appeared to snap down cuttingly.

'Don't see why there's any need for that,' he said. 'If it's a gift, it's up to the giver, eh?'

Elliot waited before suggesting anything further.

'I expect Mr Elliot would draw up a draft agreement, if you asked him,' the Countess said to her husband, tapping him on the knee reassuringly.

'Well, I don't suppose there'd be any harm in that.'

'I – we – we'd be glad to,' Elliot said, glancing at Templeton. 'Just so you know what it would entail.'

'And I shall talk to Duncan, if I must,' Hugo announced with sudden resolve.

'Good, darling. It's only right you should.' The Countess handed round a plate of biscuits.

'I can think of things I'd rather do.'

'I think it would be for the best, in the long run,' said Templeton. 'Then we could draw up the necessary—'

'Don't rush me, man. I've not said I'm doing anything yet.'

The Countess gave Templeton and Elliot reassuring looks to suggest they ignore this show of irritation.

'I'll let you know my decision just as soon as I've made it. I won't be rushed.'

'We quite understand,' said Elliot primly.

'I might decide to do nothing, and let the bugger go hang. Don't put it past me.'

Templeton, who had begun to warm to the old man because he had apparently warmed to him, had a change of heart at this point. The Earl was a difficult old sod. No wonder a permanent state of hostility existed with the eldest son. Perhaps it wasn't only the son who was to blame.

The Countess offered Templeton another shortbread biscuit as though she knew what was going through his mind. He wolfed it down rather more quickly than was polite in that setting.

'Now I expect you'd like a tour of the house?' Hugo stood up, letting the crumbs fall from his lap on to the red carpet.

Elliot looked at Templeton. 'Well, if you have the time, sir,' he told the Earl. 'I have, of course, seen most of the house before.'

'I haven't,' said Templeton. 'I'd love a tour.'

'Just a short one, Hugo,' Molly put in, and went back to her needlework.

# CHAPTER 2

The Earl led the solicitor and the accountant out of the Drawing Room and down a few doors to the Dining Room. This was in a style of Victorian interior design called Stuart Revival. Family portraits stared down from the walls on to a large circular table upon which a silver dinner service was laid out as though ready for a banquet. But the cutlery didn't look as though it was used much. A vast solid silver wine cooler dominated the centre of the table.

'Cost six hundred in 1782,' Hugo pointed out. 'I've got the receipt somewhere. Biggest in the country.' Sidney Templeton murmured amazement.

The Earl continued the tour. 'Now this is what you should see, even if you don't manage anything else. Each earl back to 1773 – oils mostly.' The line of portraits filled one whole wall. It began with a Reynolds of a smug-looking man in military attire – Calley Hooke, the first earl – and continued through the Victorians (mostly shown in the company of animals they loved or had shot). And so to the turn of this century. 'That's my grandfather, the sixth earl, nephew of the fifth. He died just in time to miss the First War, lucky fellow. Never knew him. Died before I was born.'

Templeton went close to the Edwardian-looking figure who was portrayed wearing a pair of enormous shiny cavalry boots which threatened to overwhelm him. He had the Hooke nose all right but without Hugo's distinguishing break. Drew Elliot held back, a half-smile on his face. He had seen all this before.

'Then that's my father. Killed in the war, y'know. Had to be done from a photo, but it's quite fair.'

Templeton did not like to linger too long over the dead earl's picture and moved on to look at the next, of a young man in tweeds, done in pastel colours.

24

'Ah, that's me.'

'Who painted it?'

'Chap called Halliday. Quite good, but that was forty years ago, goodness gracious. You're supposed to have the picture done as soon as you succeed, in case of accident.'

'You're not wearing uniform.'

'No, I'd had enough of the army by then. The war was over. I began to see myself as just a landowner – and farmer, if you like. That's why I had him paint me out of doors, in the park. Wanted to do me in the library, but I put my foot down. I told him no – that wasn't the man.'

Sidney Templeton risked remarking how the eight portraits completely filled the wall along one side of the Dining Room with no space for any more. Where would the Earl's descendants be hung?

Hugo gave a sudden smile. 'That's not a problem I need worry about. Besides, I doubt if they'll have paintings next time round. Photographs, I expect. Videos even.'

Nevertheless, Templeton and Elliot both had the same thought – no portrait, no next earl. It might be Hugo's way of indicating that when he went, that would be the end of everything. Yet Hugo's blunt, spare, military manner disguised a certain strength of feeling for the Hooke inheritance, both the property and the family's history. There was no denying it was a long and fascinating tale and Hugo, like any military man, warmed to anything that was wrapped in tradition, and to anything that was colourful and old.

Sidney Templeton wandered back over the thickly-carpeted floor to the beginning of the line of portraits and stood staring at the second earl (who succeeded his father in 1776 and died in 1798, according to the small caption).

'Is that a dagger I see before me?' This was quite a good joke for Templeton, but the Earl took the question at face value and ignored the literary reference.

'Ah, you've spotted it. Good.' He strode down the carpet to Templeton, and Elliot followed a trifle dog-like behind. 'Yes, it is a dagger he's holding. The story has it that Sam Hooke – that's him – met a Scotsman playing the bagpipes. Like me, he didn't exactly swoon at the noise they make and, having taken a few drinks, stuck his knife through the chanter to put a stop to the racket. Unfortunately, it went straight on through and stabbed the fellow, who died.'

'Did he get away with it?'

' 'Course, he did.' Hugo did not elaborate. As an afterthought, he added: 'My first wife hated that picture. Mind you, she was a Scot, you see. That's why my first boy's called Duncan.'

25

Templeton did not quite follow the logic of this information, but nodded vigorously.

'Well, I think we really ought to be going, sir,' Elliot suddenly said. 'I've got to drive Mr Templeton back to Craswall. So, if you'll excuse us. Perhaps we could finish the tour another time.'

Hugo looked for a moment as though he was rather taken aback by this abrupt announcement, but then mildly said, 'Oh, gosh, I'm so terribly sorry. So rude of me to go on like that. Delightful to see you, gentlemen. Next time you must come for luncheon. Forgive me for boring you like this. I always get carried away.'

'Not a bit. Most enjoyable, as always.'

Hugo walked them to the entrance and then out on to the gravel where Elliot's Rover waited.

'So you'll let me have a few details on a piece of paper?' Hugo asked, tentative again now. 'Haven't made up my mind, you know.'

'Very quickly,' Elliot replied. 'Just as soon as Mr Templeton and I manage to work out the details. And you'll have a word with Lord Wymark?'

The frost descended on Hugo's face once more, but he had no time to say anything because, at that moment, there was a frightful commotion. Two magnificent but fierce-looking Irish wolfhounds bounded down the steps and made for Sidney Templeton, having identified him instinctively as the one who didn't like dogs. He twisted and turned to avoid having his private parts nuzzled by the grey-bearded creatures.

'Forager, down!' Hugo ordered. The hound in question pulled off the cringing accountant and went and rested its front paws instead on the boot of the Rover.

Elliot and Templeton scuttled into the car clutching their briefcases and quickly closed the doors. Hugo stood with the dogs and gave the visitors a cheery wave as the car crunched off down the Fair Mile. The dogs galloped after it for a couple of hundred yards and then gave up the chase.

Hugo watched the car until it disappeared from view into the trees by the South Lodge. He gave a deep sigh, felt the rim of his nose, and went indoors to find Molly. He was unsettled – as he'd known in advance he would be – by the digging about that his visitors had done, however necessary it might have been. But at least he had made a start in sorting out the bloody business.

'Molly,' he called out, coming into the Drawing Room.

He saw she had fallen asleep again over her needlework, but he decided to continue with what he had been planning to say, even if she wasn't listening.

'We'll have to leave, y'know. Better start thinking where to go. Get it over with before I'm too decrepit. Have to talk to Duncan about it. No, I won't, I'll write . . .'

Molly did not stir, and he suddenly felt very lonely and vulnerable, as though she were dead. God forbid! He'd never be able to manage then. She was a wonderful old thing, kept him going. If only Duncan would realize that, instead of treating her still like an interloper! Hugo tried to leave the room more quietly than he had entered, went to the Gold Library, sat down at the desk made from timbers of the *Victory*, and took a sheet of notepaper from the rack.

It was headed simply 'Castle Cansdale, Wiltshire' and, being very old stock, bore the original telephone number, 'Bourton Cansdale 1'. Hugo took his fountain pen and wrote: 'Duncan, you are to have the house and the estate forthwith. Elliot will give you the details. Your father, Hugo.'

The village of Bourton Cansdale clustered round the North Lodge of Castle Cansdale park. It was partially hidden from view by an artificial hill (created by Capability Brown) which had been further heightened for many years by a clump of thick elm trees. As a result of the depredations of Dutch elm disease in the mid-1970s, Bourton Cansdale had jumped alarmingly back into view to anyone looking from the castle.

St Michael and All Angels, the sixteenth-century church with its tall spire, was no hardship for anyone to look at and was all that remained of the 1508 development which had included the first house on the Castle Cansdale site. But some of the modern property – the 'council houses' as Hugo called them, though they were not in fact – would have saddened Capability Brown. And so, new trees had once more been planted, but it would take several years before the village was once more rendered discreetly invisible.

Relations between castle and village had always been at arm's length, though the two were mutually dependent. The Hooke family had for generations relied on the village to provide household servants and estate workers, together with all the supplies that were not imported from further afield. The village, in turn, looked on the Hookes as the source of all work. Without the great house, the village would not have been able to exist. Consequently, there had always been a good deal of to-ing and fro-ing on a practical, commercial basis. Sometimes, too, there had been more personal contact. The Rector of St Michael and All Angels, whose living had long been in the gift of the Earls Hooke, had customarily been a visitor to the family, though the frequency of his visits had necessarily depended on the degree of interest in spiritual matters of the current earl.

Hugo, though not a conventionally religious person, quite enjoyed the company of the Reverend David Dutson, the present incumbent. The name of God was seldom mentioned in their conversations. Hugo took the brisk, matter-of-fact view of the deity that one might expect of a military man, even one educated at Oxford, and he was encouraged in this approach by Dutson who had been a chaplain with Montgomery in the Western Desert and was therefore himself completely at ease with a frank, no-nonsense view of religion.

Other contact between castle and village over the years had been at a less elevated level. Hooke sons had climbed over the park fence, both literally and figuratively, to sow their wild oats among the women of the yeomanry. Again, such activities occasionally skipped a generation. Insofar as Hugo himself had sowed any wild oats during his youth in the 1930s, he had sown them elsewhere. His younger brother, Alec, had declined to spend his seed among this particular peasantry.

Perhaps it was a thing of the past. Hugo's sons, Duncan and Rupert, had also avoided the buxom delights of the village and found their pleasures elsewhere. In fact, Rupert had rarely ever been seen in the area. Since leaving Harrow, he had preferred the urban delights of London to the bucolic pleasures of Wiltshire. He had a reluctance to come home to Castle Cansdale even for great family festivals. The reason was a simple one: the house held nothing for him. It belonged to his father and his elder brother would inherit it. To visit the house would only bring home to him impractical dreams, and jealousies that were unworthy. And so he stayed away – to the distress of his father and mother.

Duncan, on the other hand, as the heir apparent, was never far away. Both his stepmother and his father had reason to wish, on occasion, that he was. He occupied a Georgian manor farm at Maidens Constable, about eight miles' distance from the family seat. From his point of view, it was just near enough but not too near. Since leaving the army, he had run the Hooke estate – or, rather, he had worked to do so with Colin Blakiston, the land agent, who really knew about such matters. And he enjoyed himself. He did not hunt with the Bourton (displaying on this point an unusual unanimity with Hugo, who disapproved of blood sports); his quarry was two-legged.

It was from the quaintly-named Maidens Constable that Duncan, though now a married man and father of three young daughters, appeared to be reviving the tradition of informal goings-on between the Hooke family and the lowlier folk of Bourton Cansdale.

Not that Merrilee Bridgewater could be called a member of the peasantry exactly. She was the wife of an architect who operated out of Craswall, the largest town in the immediate area of Castle Cansdale. The Bridgewater children were away at school and university and Merrilee, apart from doing what passed for good works around the village, was left at home with not a great deal to occupy her.

Lord Wymark's eye had first fallen on her at a meeting of the Craswall Show committee. He was there by tradition as the representative of the Hooke estate. She was there as a committee lady, of the type with time on their hands who can be relied on to do the dogsbodying without complaint. The secretary of the committee was being his usual pernickety self whilst pretending to cater to Duncan's whims and being insufferably ingratiating. Duncan simply switched off and started imagining what the women on the committee would look like with their clothes off. With some it was too horrible to contemplate, but Merrilee looked promising, if her cleavage was anything to go by. She suddenly looked up from the pad on which she had been doodling with a biro and caught his eye. She looked down again, fetchingly.

Right, Duncan had thought, I'll have her.

Merrilee, like a lot of women in the area, found Duncan fascinating. It was hard to tell how much of the attraction was natural and how much resulted from his title. Never mind what it was, it existed. When the meeting ground with agonizing slowness to a conclusion, Duncan found a way of offering to run Merrilee home. This was difficult as she had her own car, but she accepted a ride. He took her to Sniggs Wood and they indulged in a little heavy petting in the front of his Volvo.

Craswall Show took place several months later on a wet Saturday in July. By that time, Duncan's Volvo had become a familiar sight parked on the short drive outside 'Steeples', the Bridgewaters' chalet-like house upon which Roger, Merrilee's architect husband, had worked out all the curious design features he had been unable to persuade his clients to adopt. Duncan thought the house a disgrace, an eyesore that should never have been given planning permission, but he found it no great hardship to close his eyes to the folly of the building when he was occupied with its mistress within.

By now, Duncan had given up finding excuses for his visits to Merrilee. He had stopped calling in for elevenses, even for prelunch drinks. He now went almost daily for his 'lunch' which, more often than not, was skipped, uneaten, as he chased his lover up the pine stairs with the open risers to the bedroom.

It was fortunate that the bed was a strong one. Duncan was a substantial bull of a man without being much overweight for one in his early forties. His hair was thinning and greying, and his large dome-like head was usually tanned and freckled from the large amount of time he spent out of doors. Merrilee was similarly buxom. The word 'strapping' was one that Duncan liked to use about any woman he fancied, and it suited Merrilee well enough. She looked the countrywoman she was, although in point of fact she did not actually climb on any of the horses she professed to be interested in, or ride to hounds, or any of that.

'God, woman, I fancy you today,' Duncan said in a way that sounded if he might burst if his urge wasn't satisfied quickly.

'Come on then,' was Merrilee's response, kicking off her white high-heeled shoes and reclining backwards on the fluffy white counterpane so that the bottom of her housecoat fell open, revealing stockinged legs.

Duncan knelt over her, then lay to one side. He attempted to expose the breasts with which by now he had become obsessed, but finding himself baffled by the technology of her underwear he abandoned the attempt. Merrilee put her own hand round the back and undid the bra hook. Then she reached down and began to loosen the leather belt that held up Duncan's battered old green corduroys. She slipped her hand inside.

Duncan had been intrigued to find that, if he wanted to, he could add to his pleasure by looking at the physical activity reflected in the mirror on the bedroom unit. So now he told Merrilee to roll over, sideways on, so that her wonderful breasts were exposed to the mirror. Duncan then nestled against her back and, breathing hotly against her neck, fondled both nipples with his one free hand.

It wasn't long before Merrilee was heaving and sighing, and for a moment Duncan feared that he was being left behind – indeed, might even be cheated of his climax if he didn't act quickly.

Accordingly he decided that they would finish the tumble in their clothes. He opened Merrilee's housecoat, unbuttoned himself and pushed hard inside her. It was a delicious sensation even after so short a wait.

'Oh, Duncan,' Merrilee gasped, 'come to me . . . give it, give it . . .!'

Duncan plunged on, enjoying the ride, and not in any way disconcerted by the clattering of bed-slats beneath the mattress and the banging of the headboard against the wall. But to his surprise he found that he wasn't coming. His erection was firm and hard, he had this strapping woman beneath him, and yet he felt no sensation of his own juice rising. With his wife Joanna, 'rutting', as he always called it, was a fairly perfunctory matter. There had never been much pleasure in it. She was a tough old boot, and about as sensuous as a stick-insect, but even with her the mechanics were capable of working all right and they had produced three children. He continued his rhythmic thrusting.

Then Merrilee cried out, 'Oh, darling, give me your seed!'

This completely threw Duncan. He missed a stroke but then managed to return to the rhythm, feeling himself shrinking as he did so.

Why the devil had she said that? Was it something she said to the dreaded Roger when they were doing it? Whatever the case, Duncan very much wished she hadn't said it. He now had a considerable salvage operation on his hands.

Merrilee continued to groan and heave as though rushing towards her orgasm. Duncan was in severe danger of achieving nothing at all. He had grown even smaller. He felt he was being ground between the wheels of some immense piece of machinery, and he was beginning to puff. He was not as fit as he had once been. It was going to take all his reserves of energy if he was not to be humiliated.

He shifted so that he was moving at an angle and, as he did so, quite by chance, he caught sight of himself in the mirror. He experienced a sudden charge, felt himself regain a certain amount of lost ground. He enjoyed the sight of himself, could imagine from what he could see that he was a rather special lover.

Merrilee apparently noticed the change and now began to groan so deeply that Duncan knew that she was genuinely coming. And oh, thank God, so was he! He felt the numbing sensation and moved on irresistibly now; looking at his own reflection was no longer important.

They came together, noisily and triumphantly.

And then they both lay in a sweaty, exhausted heap – all the more exhilarated, perhaps, because of the uncertainty involved. Duncan dozed for a couple of minutes, somewhat painfully on top of Merrilee's arm. Then he awoke and wanted to talk – and not of romantic matters.

' 'Spect you'll be getting an invitation shortly,' he said.

'What to, dear?'

'The castle.'

'Why?'

'Father's seventieth.'

'God, is he really that old? Hardly looks sixty. Always rather fancied him until you came along.'

'Oh, did you? Hate to tell you, but there's not much going on there. Father's a bit funny like that. He marries them, and keeps the faith. Not the sort of thing he's ever talked to me about, but I 'spect the only women he's ever bedded are my mother and that dreadful old bag he's got at the moment.'

'How can you be sure?' was the question from the other pillow.

'I just feel it, that's all. He's just not interested in that kind of thing. You can tell.'

'How can you tell? It's one of those things, you can never imagine your daddy doing it.'

Duncan didn't know what to reply, but he felt sure he was right.

'What's it to be then?' asked Merrilee after a pause.

'What's what going to be?'

'This party.'

'Just drinks. Then there'll be a family dinner for the old fart.'

'And we're invited? That's lovely, darling, but we hardly know—'

'What d'you mean *we*?'

'You'll invite Roger, won't you? I can't go as your . . . well, you know.'

'Ah . . . s'pose not. I'll see to it. The booming Rector'll be there, and a few other worthies, so I s'pose your architectural genius'll fit in.'

Merrilee made no comment on this gibe. 'When is it?'

'Week on Sunday. Actual birthday's the seventeenth.'

'What time?'

'Sixish.'

'Won't go down well with the Rector.'

'Why not? No one ever goes to his five thirty at Stoke, so he can skate through that and be over in a flash to sink a few bottles of the Old Oloroso – as no doubt he will.'

'Not champers?'

'Well, yes, I suppose so. Yes, yes. So you'll come then?'

'Yes, darling, if that's what you want. But I'll have to see what Roger feels. Who's doing the invites?'

'The stepmother, I suppose. She's organizing. As always.'

'Hmmm.'

'Why don't we find out?'

'What?'

'Whether your beloved husband'll come.'

'Is it so important?'

'Go on, give him a ring. Is he at the office? Put it to him.'

Merrilee sighed, detecting something mischievous in Duncan's demand. 'Oh, all right . . .'

She wrapped the housecoat once more round her – as though it would be somehow improper to talk on the phone to her husband in a state of undress – and quickly dialled his Craswall number.

Roger Bridgewater was only mildly surprised to receive a call from his wife while he was at work. But before she had begun to tell him her reason for ringing, Duncan snatched the phone, coughed loudly into it, and shouted, 'That Bridgewater? Wymark here. Just been telling Merrilee, the old man's having birthday drinkies a week on Sunday. I want you both to be there. Mm?'

Roger Bridgewater was less surprised at the invitation – though it was the first time he had ever been asked to Castle Cansdale – than at the method of delivery. Why was Lord Wymark on the phone, and what was he doing with Merrilee?

'Yes, I'm sure that would be very nice,' the architect answered meekly. 'Merrilee knows about it, does she?'

' 'Course she knows about it!' Duncan snapped. 'I mean, we are *in bed* together, Roger, so she picks up quite a lot!'

Merrilee went bright red and gasped with horror. The phone conveyed no whisper of reaction from the husband.

Duncan reached over and popped the phone back on the hook. 'Odd feller, your Roger. Hung up without saying anything!'

'Duncan, how *could* you?' The colour had now drained from her face.

The heir to the earldom of Hooke gave a hearty laugh and climbed off the bed.

'Oh, by the way,' he said, as Merrilee followed him, pale and preoccupied, down the pine stairs, 'you know that tax thing my father's up to over the house? Well, it's going ahead. So I'll be moving in with Joanna and the girls. It'll be all mine. How about that?'

Merrilee did not find it in her to utter lines like 'But where does that leave *us*?' or 'What difference will it make to you and me?' She was still contemplating the possible consequences of Duncan's appalling mischief. She just stood by the front door, none too keen to be observed from the road, and said nothing.

'How's that strike you?' Duncan taunted, trying to elicit some sort of a response.

'If that's what you want . . .' she managed at last.

' 'Course it's what I want! It's so bloody boring waiting for the old bugger to pop off. Best thing that could happen.'

'I'm pleased for you, then.'

'Good,' said Duncan, jumping into the Volvo. 'Thanks for having me!' Then he gave her a cheery wave and drove off.

# CHAPTER 3

Hugo's seventieth birthday was duly celebrated by the select band of estate workers and villagers who had been bidden to join the family for drinks at Castle Cansdale on the appropriate Sunday. There was champagne, and also Maidens Constable Special Brew for those who preferred it, and orange juice for the three young daughters of Hugo's heir.

The party was held in the Salon, the Music Room and the Gold Library. There was a certain benefit to be had from holding a social occasion in more than one room, and in rooms where there were lots of nooks and crannies. It was easier to avoid those whose eyes one did not wish to meet.

Roger Bridgewater had borne himself magnificently in the face of Duncan's revelation. He had thought about it for the rest of the day and, when he eventually laid down his T-square, he drove home to Bourton Constable to find his wife cowering, almost literally, in anticipation of his wrath.

He told her he had known about her affair with Duncan all along – in fact he hadn't – and that he wasn't at all surprised. He wasn't going to make any fuss because – and this was a complete fabrication, too – he had been unfaithful and was having an affair with Marigold Baker at the office. Had been for the past six months.

This stoic mendacity at least enabled the Bridgewaters to present a united front at Castle Cansdale, whatever long-term difficulties it held in store for their marriage.

As it turned out, Duncan managed to avoid both Roger and Merrilee for the duration of the party. He spent it instead putting away as much of the celebratory champagne as he could, while speaking volubly to all and sundry about the great news that he would be taking over the running of the house and the estate very shortly. The imminent change of ownership had only just been announced officially in the neighbourhood.

Hugo looked almost all of his three score years and ten on this occasion. It was probably the knowledge that this day not only marked a milestone in his life but also the end of an era in Castle Cansdale's history. During the three months since Elliot and Templeton's visit, he had gradually allowed himself to come round to the wisdom of the move. But the fact of the move itself had not become any easier to bear. It felt like an abdication, not the death of a king, and just as wrong. It was especially hard to stomach because Duncan was so enthusiastic about it.

'So, are you looking forward to it?' Hugo was talking now to his daughter-in-law, the much put-upon Joanna.

'Oh, I don't know,' she said, her eyes avoiding his. 'Don't do that, Josie!' She turned sharply to reprimand her eight-year-old daughter. 'Grandpa doesn't want you spoiling his books.'

Hugo tried to smile as though it didn't matter, but only came out with a frown.

'I'll not let it worry me,' Joanna eventually replied to Hugo's question. 'I mean, you and Molly never had any trouble, did you?'

Not for the first time, Hugo wondered what Duncan saw in this weather-beaten beanpole of a wife. She was as thin as a rake, had jumbled teeth, and her hair was a mess. She looked more like a countrywoman you'd find living under a hedge than Reggie Sulgrave's daughter. Lady Joanna Sulgrave she'd been when Duncan first brought her home. All that messing about with horses and dogs and, well, anything on four legs, hadn't helped Joanna's complexion. Her colour was high. Perhaps she was into the port as well, Hugo thought. It had been known for her even to smoke cigars at Christmas luncheon. All in all, she was hardly more to Hugo's taste than her husband.

Molly came to Hugo's rescue. 'You mustn't let it overwhelm you, Joanna. That's the important thing. When all's said and done, it's only a home in the end, and you must make it one to suit you.'

Hugo still frowned, as though this was not quite how he saw it, but said nothing.

'Well, we'll see.' Joanna glanced over to where Duncan was chatting to Colin Blakiston, the land agent, and his wife. He seemed to be behaving himself, thank goodness. She turned back to Hugo and Molly. As in-laws went, she quite liked them. Indeed, given her husband's behaviour to both of them, she felt under a certain obligation to compensate. But it was difficult. Hugo could be so infuriatingly crusty, and Molly was so terribly homely. There was very little common ground. Joanna rode with the Bourton and that didn't go down with Hugo any better than it did with Duncan. Worst of all, though, Hugo didn't seem to like her daughters. Molly went through the motions, but her distaste was obvious. Joanna

35

looked round rather desperately. Wasn't there anyone here she could talk to?

The Rector arrived late, as expected, having got through evensong at Stoke Cansdale in record time. He was now proudly downing a glass of Maidens Constable Special Brew and not the bottle of Old Oloroso that Duncan had predicted.

'Your very good health, Hugo,' he said to the Earl with slightly unwelcome familiarity, 'and may God give you many, many happy returns.' He jingled the coins in his pocket against the tobacco tin that also resided there and sipped deeply on his beer.

'Thank you, Padre,' Hugo answered. 'What a most pleasant surprise to have you here. I wasn't told a thing about all this. Molly did it all without telling me.'

'Well, you're blessed to have such a wife.'

Molly gave her little trill of a laugh and turned away to seek new company.

'A turning point in more than one way, I suppose?' Dutson boomed on.

'Meaning?'

'Your leaving this wonderful house. You must be very sad, after all these years.'

'P'raps.'

'Do you know when Duncan'll move in?'

'Mmmm.' The Earl wondered how much to tell the Rector. But Dutson was a convivial sort and not to be dealt with dismissively. 'Not too sure. I tell you, though,' Hugo said, taking a certain amount of care that others were not listening, 'Molly and I are going to Huddleston.'

'Huddleston? I thought it'd been demolished?'

'Not quite, no. It's not been lived in for a year or two, but we're going to do it up. I had to remove it from the estate before I made the gift to Duncan. It's on a rent-free lease, thank God! The leasehold reverts to him eventually. You know Drew Elliot, don't you? He's been our legal adviser for years. Had to work overtime on this one, but I think he's got it right this time.'

'A little bird told me that Sidney Templeton has also been helping you.'

'Oh, you heard that, did you? Well, you're right. Chief thing about Huddleston is, it's not too big and it's not too close to here. I don't want to be breathing down Duncan's neck. And,' the Earl gave the Rector a dry look, 'I don't suppose he'd want that either.'

'We'll see a change or two hereabouts, I'll be bound,' the clergyman said loudly, impervious to Hugo's likely apprehensions on the matter.

'Oh, I don't think so. Much as it's always been, I should think.'

The Rector gave a narrow smile and took another quaff of his Special Brew.

At that moment, there was a minor commotion caused by the entrance of the two Irish wolfhounds, Forager and Admiral. They preceded the arrival of Lady Sophie Hooke, the Earl's only and much-adored daughter. She was in her late thirties, brisk in manner and striking in her overall appearance. Close up she had a pleasant face with a pretty version of the family nose over a happy smile. But from a distance the effect was slightly forbidding. She was dressed entirely in black. Very handsome. Yet her stepmother wondered whether black was quite the colour for one's father's seventieth birthday, especially when it was in the middle of July.

But that was Sophie's style. She was nothing if not independent, her own woman, and – indeed – a woman on her own. She had resisted matrimony for many a year, not for want of lovers, it was said, but because no man she had met among the chinless wonders of the shires could possibly supplant the love and admiration she had for her father.

Sophie went straight up to Hugo and planted a kiss on his cheek.

'Happy birthday, Papa,' she said boldly and dangled a small parcel before him. 'Prezzy for you, but you mustn't open it till you're on your own.'

'I shall obey,' said Hugo, his eyes unusually bright with pleasure, as always at the sight of his daughter. He popped the parcel in the pocket of his old grey suit which only added to his rumpled appearance.

'Evening, Rector,' Sophie said with equal boldness to the Reverend Dutson.

'Oh, hello, my dear,' said the clergyman – he seldom had an opportunity to greet her in church. 'You look as if you've just got back from somewhere.'

'London. The M4's hellish – as always.'

She swept up the glass of champagne that was brought to her and kissed her father again with the bubbles still on her lips.

'Many, many of them, Papa! Where's Molly?'

Molly was found and Sophie greeted her with kisses on both cheeks. It was almost as though she had to compensate her stepmother for Duncan's lack of attention. But Sophie appreciated Molly and all she did and had done for Hugo. As the years went by, there was an ever-present possibility that Kay, Hugo's beautiful first wife and mother of Duncan and Sophie, would one day be elevated to the sainthood, largely on the basis that she had died young. But Sophie had been only five when that had happened, and to go on about her mother's beauty and wit (as Duncan did) was deeply insulting to Molly, who was a completely different kind of woman.

Molly appreciated Sophie's kindness, but found it a little hard to be close to her.

'Will you be staying on here, when your father goes?' the Rector asked rather pointedly.

Sophie answered him directly. 'No. Decided not to, though I could. Papa's given me Bethany Cottage.'

'Oh, I know. Just over from the Bridgewaters?'

'P'raps it is.'

'I saw them here somewhere. He's an architect, you know.'

'No, can't say I do. Bit of a problem what to do with the horse, of course. Could leave her here, but I don't want to get in Duncan's way. May have to put her in Hagger Farm.'

'My, what a time of change!'

'It's only because I'm a dried-up old spinster, really,' Sophie laughed. 'Papa thinks I'll spend the rest of my life knitting in a cottage!'

'Some *very* nice people live in cottages, Sophie. I hope you'll be very happy. Maybe we'll see rather more of you in the village?'

'Maybe.' Sophie took another sip of champagne.

With his daughter safely arrived, Hugo could begin to enjoy the little gathering and began to circulate among the locals. He had made it very clear in advance that he would not be making any speeches, nor would he accept any kind of birthday present from those who had been prevailed upon to attend. The family was a different matter. They could give him whatever they liked, over dinner, if they could be bothered.

He took the little parcel Sophie had given him from his pocket and, never one to obey an unnecessary order, he slipped off the wrapping paper and stared at the small framed print before him. It was an Ackermann print dated 1814 showing the previous Castle Cansdale – the one that was demolished to make way for the present one. He had seen it before, needless to say, but this was special because Sophie had bought it. It was also a token of Hooke family history that he could take with him to Huddleston. It was a delightful gift and absolutely right for the occasion.

Hugo noticed Duncan talking rather volubly to an admiring group of tenant farmers and steered Molly and himself in the opposite direction. There would, unfortunately, be plenty of time to hear what Duncan had to say over dinner – provided he was not so drunk as to be incomprehensible, as had happened several times before.

'There's just one thing missing, and I'd be happy,' he murmured at, rather than to, Molly.

'Rupert, you mean?'

'Yes, where's he got to? He's coming, isn't he?'

'Said he'd try. But you know Rupert, there's no predicting.'

Hugo brooded. With Duncan around, he really did need Molly and Sophie and Rupert to give him support, to make a family occasion like this bearable. His brother, Alec, had turned up, of course, but he was downright peculiar these days, with his funny bachelor ways, his hypochondria, and all that. Alec had come up for the whole weekend, by train and taxi, as he always did, which Hugo saw as an imposition. But he is my brother, he would tell himself, so I have to oblige.

'I do wish he'd hurry up,' Hugo said, returning to the subject of Rupert. He thought he loved the boy. Rupert made up for so much that was unpalatable about the son and heir, but he was what he was, and his behaviour could be infuriating.

Eventually, Compton deftly signalled to the outsiders that the party was over and Hugo stood in the entrance hall as people departed. He shook everyone by hand and managed to be pleasant to everybody, even those he didn't really recognize.

Then, with just the family, and without Rupert who was clearly not going to show up, he went through to the Dining Room which was to be used, unusually, for what it had been built for. Duncan was suspiciously restrained in his behaviour and barely exchanged a word with his father, though he did run to a toast at the end of the meal and made Hugo a present of several bottles of port that were even older than the Earl.

In spite of all, Hugo continued to brood for the rest of the evening on the absence of his favourite son.

# CHAPTER 4

The Hon. Rupert Hooke was very good at letters of apology. He would miss some social event with the most maddening casualness, and then would come the little note, handwritten in a delightful, rather schoolboyish way, which totally removed any annoyance and left him forgiven and loved all the more. It infuriated Hugo.

The excuses, or reasons, Rupert gave for his missed engagements would have filled a book. Sometimes they had the ring of truth. There was the occasion he explained to one hostess that her invitation had got stuck behind the clock on his mantelpiece and he had only found it by chance two days after the dinner had been missed. 'Horrors!!' he wrote:

> Infuriating and rude. Infuriating also for me because I spent the time I should have been dining with you having the most frightful row with Amanda [or Harriet, or Caroline, or whoever it was]. I *am* sorry.
> Oh God.
> Oh dear.
> Oh.
> Love, Rupert.

On another occasion, he explained to someone he knew less well – and whose credulity would thus be less strained – that a favourite aunt had just died and the invitation, being a formal card, had got mixed up with all the letters of condolence . . . But he really was very sorry and he hoped that the person would not be offended because he really *did* not deserve to be invited when he did such things, and so on and so on.

Such was the Hon. Rupert Hooke, adored by as many as he maddened. It was not that he was wantonly disorganized or that he was unintelligent. Quite the reverse on the last point. But he had a streak of laziness and, unfortunately, was only too well aware that his charm and good luck would carry him through, even if exercising his little grey cells might not. Besides, he was a younger son, he had no hereditary responsibilities and he was glad of it. This shaded almost dangerously into having no sense of responsibility at all.

To say that he was lazy was not to mean he was particularly dissolute or reprehensible in any way, merely to reflect that he could have achieved so much more had he set his mind to it. But he always seemed to take the soft option and to date it did not seem to have done him any great harm.

That Sunday night when he should have been dutifully celebrating his father's seventieth birthday, the 28-year-old Rupert was recovering from breaking up with his latest girl friend. The affair had run longer than most, a good six weeks in fact, but like all the others it had to end.

Georgina Bentley-Ross, a Sloane blonde, did something at a publishers. Rupert had never managed to extract from her precisely what. He suspected it was secretarial, but Georgina always gave the impression that she hobnobbed with all the top authors, indeed directed their successful careers. Whatever she did, she didn't get paid much for it, but she had all the kit, right down to the sit-up-and-beg bicycle with a basket on the front in which she carried a batch of important-looking files.

Rupert first met Georgina at a bar called Slates, in the City. Quite why she had strayed there he had never bothered to find out, but he was there with his best chum, Henry Rowlandson. The two had met at Harrow when Henry had forcibly buggered Rupert during an initiation ceremony. After that they became very good friends and managed to establish their sexual tastes on more orthodox lines.

Henry now ran an entertainment organization called Spoofs which supplied many of the most fashionable balls, dances and parties with bands, DJs, tents, discos, and all the bits and pieces. Spoofs was thriving in its way, not that Henry seemed to need the money; he had always given the appearance of rolling in it, even at school. Currently, he was angling for Rupert to do a spot of disc-jockeying. Henry knew all about Rupert's good looks and charm. He could quite easily pick up the patter with a little instruction. 'Why, it could open up a whole new career for you, dear boy!' Henry told him.

As for his present career, Rupert worked for a venture capital company based in the City. He did not have a great deal to do except be charming and allow his name to go on the letterheads of companies the firm he worked for managed. Wearing a suit was rather a chore but he went along with it. He had, however, managed to fight off the Filofax and the car phone. At his age he was not earning anything like what high-rollers elsewhere in the City were making, but at least he had a job, and one that was reasonably interesting and enjoyable.

While Henry Rowlandson dangled the prospect of rather more glamour

41

and excitement before his old friend, Rupert's attention kept wandering off to examine the firmly-enunciating young ladies who were also drinking at Slates. And that was how his eye fell upon Georgina Bentley-Ross. He imagined what her face would look like on the point of orgasm, and decided he would do what was necessary to enable him to compare fancy with reality.

'Okay then, I'll do it – just the once,' he told Henry, languorously, to make him shut up. 'Should be fun. 'Nother drink?'

'Don't mind if I do,' said Henry, emptying his glass of g-and-t. 'Same again, please.'

Rupert pushed his way to the bar and managed to get himself served well before any of those who had been waiting for ages to catch the barman's eye. He was standing next to Georgina who was waving a fiver in the hopes of getting service.

'Oh, sorry, were you first?' Rupert, in a reflex action, pushed a hand through his hair, lowered his unusually long eyelashes and looked at the girl steadily with little-boy eyes.

'Yes, I jolly well was,' she shot back.

'Put that money away and let me buy you one.'

The barman's eyes moved heavenwards, having seen it all before.

'Dry white wine, then – I'm Georgie, by the way – and the same for my friend. She's Diana.'

'Of course – two dry whites. My name's Rupert.'

'You surprise me . . .'

And so they began. Diana was palmed off on Henry for the duration, and Rupert began the mental undressing of Georgina as a prelude to the physical and much more which occurred a few nights later in his small mews flat, crowded with masculine armchairs and old school photos, just off Lowndes Square.

It was quite an aphrodisiac, the way Rupert casually let slip his 'Hon.' to Georgina. Then there were the equally casual mentions of 'our house in Wilts'. Finally, he tossed at her the information that he was the youngest son of an earl.

By this stage, Georgina was quite pink with anticipation and had absolutely no hesitation in tearing off her skirt and top at Rupert's cleverly delayed invitation. In fact, if anything she was a little too eager for him. He was lazy when it came to seduction but he did like a girl to put up a *bit* of a struggle. He found it faintly embarrassing when Georgina simply lay there on the sheepskin rug in front of the unlit gas fire with nothing on but her pants and a pair of little white socks.

He turned out the lights to lessen her curious isolation, slipped off his jeans and lay down beside her. She was slightly surprised that he wanted her to take him in her mouth, but she chomped away until the deed was done. She was disappointed that he did not immediately climb on top of her and take her properly, but this he seemed reluctant to do just yet. Perhaps next time.

'You're not really going to do that disco thing, are you?' Georgina asked, when her clothing was restored. 'I mean, is that *really* what you want to do?'

'Don't see why not,' Rupert laughed. 'It sounds fun, don't you think? Would you like to come along?'

'Yeh, great. Whose do is it? I mean, it would be totally embarrassing if one found one *knew* any of the people.'

'Don't see why. It's just for fun, isn't it, even if I do get paid. Anyway, I need the money, so what the hell.'

'Of course, I'd *love* to come,' Georgina said quickly, keen not to let him slip away. He was smashing. Such a brill body. And those *eyes*!

So it was that Rupert Hooke, bereft of his 'Hon.', in the billing at least, did his first stint as a DJ in a marquee erected by Spoofs at a coming-of-age party in Alresford.

'You were brill,' Georgina reassured him afterwards, giving little thought to which of her adjectives she would apply this time.

'I said you could do it,' Henry Rowlandson chimed in, and booked him up on the spot for another three dates.

Rupert was modestly pleased with his success, but he and Henry and Georgina were each in their separate ways quite aware that it was an interest that would fade very quickly.

Rupert never stuck at anything, or with anyone, for very long. There had been his 'working class' phase when he was down from Harrow and had just flunked his chance to go to university. He had decided to turn his back on his family, name and upbringing – in the customary way – and rushed about on a motorbike wearing jeans and leathers. That craze had given way to sports cars, even to a touch of motor-racing. But nothing lasted with Rupert. Everything faded in the end, and sooner, usually, rather than later.

Georgina was torn in another way by Rupert's disc-jockeying. If she went to one of the parties at which he was performing she had to stand around on her own with no one to dance with while Rupert looked so bloody handsome and oozed his brand of English aristocratic sexiness all over the admiring customers.

So she stopped going along. Then she found it difficult getting him to see her. She ran through the whole work-book of how to ring him up on any old excuse, just so he would invite her out. But by that Sunday in July she had reached her limit. Love Rupert she thought she did, and yet it was almost cruel the way he played the vague card so often. Tired of his unfailingly polite and ever so charming evasions, Georgina thought she would bring their 'affair' to a climax, of one kind or another.

Rupert had said he was down to do another disco on the Saturday night – in Suffolk somewhere. Georgina supposed she believed him, but it was difficult to be sure. She had better not ring him up until he'd had time for a lie-in. Question was, was he lying in with another girl?

He was always so wonderfully evasive when Georgina taxed him about other girls in his life. He would tell her she was the only one with such a sincere expression on his face that there really could be no doubting him at the time. Doubts set in, however, just as soon as she was away from him.

It stands to reason, doesn't it, Georgina mused, that he's not going to go to bed alone of a Saturday night if he can help it? Knowing Rupert, he's bound to have picked somebody up on the disco job and either spent the night in Suffolk or dragged her back to London.

Georgina waited until eleven o'clock on the Sunday morning and then rang his flat. The number was engaged. He must have taken the phone off the hook, as he often did for sleep or sex. Her worst suspicions began to be confirmed. What made it worse was that it was partly her own fault for not going along with him on the disco jobs. At twelve fifteen she rang his number again. The phone was still off the hook.

Georgina decided to take matters into her own hands. She would go round, on her faithful velocipede, and knock on the door and lean on the bell until Rupert was forced to come out and be civil to her. The bike was duly unleashed from the porch of the little house in Fulham which she shared with three other girls and pedalled hard over to Knightsbridge.

When she reached Rupert's flat, some of her temper had evaporated; and her courage almost failed her when she confronted the small white door. There was a *Sunday Times* sticking out of the letter box, so he must still be in bed – if, indeed, he was at home.

She tapped meekly on the knocker as a first measure. There was no response. But was that someone stirring within? The sound of bedclothes being hurriedly draped over naked forms? She rang the bell.

A few seconds more and she heard the languid plip-plop of Rupert's slippers as he came to the door.

'Oh, hello,' he smiled, all innocent, as he opened up.

Apart from his slippers, he only had a towel between himself and the outside world. Georgina again suspected the worst.

'Come in,' he said, to her surprise making no attempt to send her away. 'I was asleep.'

In the hall, Georgina noticed that the phone wasn't off the hook. 'I tried to ring you, but you were engaged,' she said as unaccusingly as she could manage.

'Funny.' Rupert lifted the receiver and listened dozily for a second or two. 'On the blink. Never mind.'

'I thought you'd taken it off the hook.'

'No. I don't think so. Coffee?'

'Let me get it.' Georgina seized the opportunity to glance into the bedroom. There was no one there. No one in the kitchen either. Her suspicions had been ill-founded.

'Oh, Roo,' she cried and flung her arms round him, with no explanation. 'You must have had a very late night. And I woke you up!'

'Yes, you did. It's a bit of a blur actually.'

'Did you drink a lot?'

'No, the other. Someone had some coke and, well, you know it has a funny effect on me.'

'I wish you wouldn't, darling.'

Georgina fixed the coffee, while Rupert made absolutely no move to put any more clothes on. His lethargy coupled with the drug-induced hangover left him even more sleepily languorous than usual.

'I thought you were trying to avoid me,' Georgina persisted.

'You know how it is,' Rupert smiled, with a small wave of his hand. 'Busy, busy. But now you're here, so everything's all right.'

'It's not *totally* all right, Roo. You don't make it easy for us to have . . . a relationship.'

'Ah, "relationship".' Rupert spoke the word slowly as if he were exhaling a cigarette, but made no deeper comment.

Georgina tried a different tack. 'So what are you doing for the rest of the day?'

'I don't know, really. I ought to go down to father's. Having a birthday or something.'

'Oh, you should, surely,' Georgina enthused, thinking this might be her chance to tag along. Rupert was very sparing in references to his family. They might just as well not exist. Which was odd, thought Georgina, what with their being such a *special* family. But that was Rupert's way. He hardly ever mentioned his family name, never mind *used* it.

'But I don't know . . .' Rupert stretched out on the sofa, allowing the towel to reveal more of his legs, but not calculatedly.

'Have you said you'll go?' Georgina pressed him on the subject of the birthday.

'Georgie, you're sounding just like my mother!'

Georgina hated his saying that, and frowned.

'Ah, sorry,' Rupert quickly said. 'Let me kiss it better.'

She went over, kicked off her shoes and snuggled up to him. He was unshaven, tousled, and his eyelids were heavy with exhaustion. And she thought he was ravishing. There wasn't a surplus ounce of flesh on him; if this was what living a dissolute life led to, she was all in favour.

45

'Don't you ever find your family just a little bit heavy?' Rupert asked her, uncharacteristically opening up rather than closing down an area of inquiry.

'Not really,' replied Georgina honestly. ' 'Spect I'm a little unusual. I've got a super daddy and a super mummy. We don't seem to have rows. They never interfere with me or my sister. So I don't really know about family strife.'

'Well, you're bloody lucky then. You see, I come from a very *family* family. The family's everything. I suppose it's inevitable, what with the title and the house and everything. It can't be any other way. Trouble is, everything seems to depend on it. People only seem to have kids in order to prop up the family tree – not because they want them for their own sake or anything like that. It's the same at Buck House. The important thing's to produce an heir and that's that. It's all a matter of screwing, and not even screwing for pleasure. Screwing as though the family depended on it. As I'm the younger son, it's all rather remote for me.'

Georgina felt uncomfortable that Rupert was somehow portraying himself as unimportant. 'It only looks that way if you look at it that way,' she said, trying to be helpful.

'Well, that's why I keep away from them. I mean, they're down in Wilts and I'm here. They never come to town – except my stepsister, and we're not terribly close. I leave them to get on with worrying about wills and heirlooms and all that without me. I have my own life.'

Georgina put her hand beneath the towel and gently began to play with Rupert's body. 'I suppose it's a bit odd – so much depending on *this*.' She squeezed him playfully and Rupert started to stir.

'Stop it, Georgie! Not now.' He laughed, so she knew he didn't mean it, and she didn't take away her hand.

'Isn't it rather exciting?' she asked. 'I mean, you know, being part of a long family tradition, and all that? Knowing who your ancestors are is more than most people can claim. I'd find it exciting.'

'Unfortunately, Georgie, people born into family situations like ours are not usually the ones who enjoy it. And if people do enjoy it, there's not much they can do to be born into it! Catch-22.'

'But your brother, doesn't he enjoy the prospect of taking over from your father?'

'I don't really know. If he does, knowing him, it'd only be out of spite. You have to realize, Georgie, that my brother is a number one shit. Frankly, he could do anything, once my father goes. He could even give up the title. He might sell the house. He might turn it into a funfair. He's really wild. I don't know where he gets it from. I mean, the old man's a pretty dry old stick. But he's certainly not mad. Must have got it from his mum.'

'But you're not mad.'

'Different mother. Duncan and my sister Sophie were from father's first marriage. A woman called Kay.'

'Was there a divorce?'

'No. You might expect that, but she did in fact just die. She was an Allan. She looks very beautiful in all the photos. Father was terribly cut up about it. Sophie says he's never been the same.'

'What did she die of?'

'I think it was leukaemia. They couldn't do much about it then. That was in 1955. There'd been a touch of mental trouble, too. You can never find out about things like that, though, can you? Not what families like to talk about.'

'But you don't really think she's responsible for your brother?'

'How should I know? I say he's mad, but I don't mean he's *mad*. He just behaves unpleasantly. Wildly. That's not madness. And there's nothing wrong with Sophie. A touch outspoken, maybe, very *direct*, but nothing out of the ordinary. I quite like her. She's okay.'

'How old is she?'

'Thirty-seven, round about that. No, thirty-eight – she's ten years older than me.'

'And not married?'

'No. She's very much her own woman. Quite likely not to get hitched at all, I'd say. Which'd be a pity, 'cos she's a super person. Trouble is, the guys around Cansdale think she'd bite their balls off, and they're probably right!'

'Does she have a job?'

'She says she works for a design outfit. You know, doing up people's houses with tasteful wallpapers and charging them a fortune.'

'What's it called, the design firm?'

'Waterwheel, or something. Don't ask me why. I suppose it helps that she's Lady Sophie. People like that, you know. Snob appeal. She spends a lot of time fiddling about with her horse, too. Hunts with the Bourton.'

'Oh, how awful! Is she one of those?'

'Doesn't bother me. No one else in the family does, except Joanna.'

'Who's that?'

'My brother's wife. Mind you, she's barmy anyway. Must be to have married Duncan. Father's quite outspoken against it. He doesn't say much in public. He's not one for sounding off. But what he has said didn't go down at all well with the hunting lot. The old Duke of Beaufort threatened to ride over and horsewhip him!'

Aware that she wasn't making much progress, Georgina left Rupert's parts alone and simply hugged him. Then another inquisitive thought struck her.

'Why's your sister Lady Sophie and you only an "Hon."?'

Rupert looked at her – tolerantly, but slightly bored. 'Sweetheart, the ins

47

and outs of the peerage keep some people occupied twenty-four hours a day, three hundred and sixty-five days a year. There's no rhyme or reason.'

'But younger sons of earls are sometimes lords?'

'I know, I know, but I'm not. It's all to do with courtesy titles. Some first sons of earls are viscounts, but Duncan isn't, he's just a lord – because there's no viscountcy for him to have. And there's no spare barony lying around for me to have. So I'm an Hon.'

'Wouldn't you like to be Lord Rupert Hooke? It'd sound terribly grand.'

'I couldn't give a fuck, frankly.'

'I don't believe you. You're just saying it's a bore because you're not the heir.'

At this taunt, which was much too near the truth, Rupert suddenly pushed Georgina off the sofa and landed on top of her. He wrestled with her until they both got the giggles.

Georgina wasn't giving up, however. 'What would happen if something happened to your brother? Don't you ever think about that?'

'Oh, shut up! I don't. Honestly. It's most unlikely. Mind you, he's only got three daughters, no son. So he's blotted his copybook there. No little male heir. It's all such a bore. Such a bore that the future of the family firm *depends* on such matters. But there it is.'

'I think it's fascinating . . .'

'Do you? Well, lucky old you.'

'You're obviously beastly to your father. Fancy not going to his birthday. How old is he?'

'Seventy, or something.'

'Seventy! You've got to go. You can't miss out on that.'

'It's nothing to do with you. Like I said, I keep out of the way.'

'But he'll miss you.'

'Too right he will. In fact, he dotes on me. But that's only because he can't stand Duncan. And he can't stand Duncan because he's so beastly to Mother. But he'll have to leave everything to Duncan, 'cos he's the one with the title. And so it goes, round and round. Let's not talk any more about it. What about lunch?'

Georgina was absorbed by Rupert's revelations about his awful family and didn't really want him to stop. 'Want me to make some?' she offered.

'No, let's go round the corner.'

'Promise me you'll go and see your father?'

'No. Talking about them has reminded me how tedious it'll all be. They can get lost.'

'I'd love to go with you.'

'Now that,' said Rupert standing up, clutching the towel to himself and looking more directly at Georgina than was usually his way with anybody, 'is another matter. I never take anyone home. Never.'

'Why not?'

'Because they'd start sizing you up. Would you be right for me? Are you "of good family"? Have you got good hips for child-bearing? I'm not kidding. They'd give you a good going over. They'd look at your teeth, as if you were a horse.'

'Oh. Well, I don't mind . . .'

'Last time I took anybody home was five years ago. Disaster. Father wouldn't let us sleep in the same room. He's odd like that. Real old prude. Mind you, it wasn't too difficult to get over it. I know my way around in the dark! But then Duncan came along and was supremely rude to the girl, and that was it. I vowed I'd never put anyone through it again – or myself, for that matter.'

Rupert slipped into some clothes and they went round to the pub for a glass or two of wine and a salad each. Then they returned to the flat in order to go to bed.

Georgina tore off her clothes and lay waiting in bed for Rupert to join her. She felt wonderfully happy. Rupert took off his jeans and striped shirt and slipped beneath the sheets beside her. She felt this had to be the best-est time of the whole week. No work to go to, no one calling, nothing to worry about. Perfect peace.

And yet she was anxious. She hadn't entirely forgotten how they had come to be where they were now. She had had to make all the running. Her suspicions had not been borne out by the facts, and yet he was a great one for convenience was Rupert. He never exerted himself. She had plopped into his bed. He hadn't even suggested it. There was something not quite right about that.

These worries were soon lessened by their lovemaking. For someone who, out of bed, occasionally had the air of a little boy lost, needing a reassuring pat on the head or his hand held, Rupert was rather more positive when making love. It was almost a different person who was now attentively stroking and licking and sucking every square inch of her body. He began to treat her skin more roughly – lightly scratching, then manipulating, then slapping her.

'When are you going to . . .?' she muttered very quietly.

Rupert guided himself inside her. It was hard, so very hard, and Georgina started to come almost immediately. She came quickly but Rupert went on and on for many minutes. Images flashed through Georgina's mind of horses and hunting, of country scenes, of great houses and coronets, of an earl's eight silver balls and eight strawberry leaves . . .

She came again at the same time as Rupert. It was achingly, satisfyingly marvellous.

49

It was only when Rupert woke from a short sleep that Georgina realized that it was all over between them. They didn't need to talk about it, she just knew. There were no recriminations to be made either. It wasn't his fault. He hadn't taken advantage of her – there was no advantage to be taken, she was so willing. He hadn't deceived her in any way in order to make love to her.

Simply, out of the lovemaking and the long talk they had had beforehand had come a realization that they were not for each other. She would never be able to get through to Rupert. He would always be unobtainable. He was a different breed, if not a different class. He would never be able to give himself to her.

Which was odd. Wasn't he what people called God's gift to women? What sort of woman would be able to get through to him?

Well, that was of no concern to Georgina now. She extracted herself from Rupert's bed, only just keeping back the tears, made an excuse and bicycled home feeling pretty mizzy, as she would no doubt put it to her flat-mates on her return.

Rupert did not give much thought to Georgina's sudden departure. They had not talked it out. Rupert had no time for that kind of heart-searching and self-analysis. 'Digging over old turnips' was how he described the endless evaluating of relationships that women always seemed to go in for. No, his chief feeling was simply one of relief. That it followed quite soon after an orgasm was not entirely coincidental. Although he was not the kind to kick a woman out of bed on achieving his end, he nevertheless felt a wonderfully rich sensation of release – from obligation to her, from the pressure of another human being's personality – when Georgina upped and went of her own accord.

He had a shower and washed his hair, left his stubble as it was, and actually found himself singing while he did all this. He did not boast about it to himself – this apparent good fortune in landing so many girls with the minimum of rejection or effort – but he was dimly aware that he had something which other men lacked. He had been born with it, had never known anything else, so getting his own way, and not only with regard to the opposite sex, seemed a perfectly normal matter to him.

No sooner was he out of the shower, and confirming with his watch that it really was now completely out of the question for him to scoot down to Castle Cansdale for his father's do, than the phone rang.

It was his friend Henry Rowlandson. 'Fancy losing some money, Rupert?'

'Henners, you know I don't *do* that.'

'Oh, come on. I'm going to the Carillon. Even just for a snort and sniff you ought to come. I'll lose the cash on your behalf.'

'As long as it's yours in the first place.'

'Of course. And I've got a couple of bimbettes to cheer you up.'

'Oh, okay. Fancy dress?'

'Of course.'

Two hours later, Rupert was driving over in his MG to the Carillon in Curzon Street and parking on a double yellow line. Well, it was Sunday; he'd probably be all right.

He rather dreaded getting pissed on Henry's terms. There had been a time in their friendship when Henry's idea of a merry evening was to sit down with Rupert at a small table with a pack of cards and a newly-acquired bottle of Gordons. They would solemnly play, not even for money, while passing the bottle between them. They were a touch younger then, and the neatness of the gin was neither here nor there. After a while, Rupert would lay down his cards and scuttle off to the loo to be sick. If they happened to be playing at Henry's parents' home in one of the Regent's Park terraces, Rupert would have the pleasure of vomiting beneath a Picasso drawing which the Rowlandsons had thought to place in that location. He would then return to the table and the gin before staggering home. In bed he saw the room revolve round him, even though the light was out. The following morning he would have a floor-clutcher of a hangover from which it was impossible to get up even to take one of the suggested cures.

After a few such occasions – which also necessitated a morning off work – Rupert had managed to exert some control over his destiny by cutting out the neat gin, or diluting it at least, without losing his friendship with Henry.

At the Carillon now, he settled on the Pouilly Fumé at God knew what a bottle, in the fond hope that Henry would do something with the bill when it was finally presented. Henry had found himself a floozy for the evening, a perky thing called Gloria who announced she was in advertising, which figured. He had also laid on a blonde for Rupert.

At first Rupert did not like her. She was good-looking but much too self-assured, gift-wrapped, almost mouthing 'Keep your distance'. He shook her hand and, without thinking, came out with a lame chat-up line: 'Haven't we met before?'

She froze him out, and let go of his hand. It was like a sobering glass of water in the face.

Rupert became unusually attentive. She was a hard case, a difficult nut to crack which made him want to succeed with her all the more. He wasn't used to being kept at arm's length.

He paid no attention to what he was doing at the tables for the rest of the evening, his concentration was focused on the blonde, with the result that he won more than enough to cover their entire expenses for the evening. But the girl . . . Where had Henry found her? She was stunning, now that he came to take a good look at her. A wonderfully clear complexion, high cheekbones, a neat nose, laughing eyes, perfect teeth, and the broadest of broad smiles. Very, very beautiful. Who was she? 'This is Jacky,' was how Henry had introduced her at the start of the evening. 'She's a poppet.' It wasn't the right word for her.

'You're . . . er . . . very nice,' Rupert managed to say at one point. He was so unlike his usual self that Henry wondered for a moment if his friend was all right.

This was not the witty, charming bloke she had been promised, Jacky thought. Yes, he was good-looking – wonderful dark hair, amazing eyelashes, sexy nose – but what was all this bashfulness?

In due course, Rupert regained some of his composure and tried to find out who this Jacky was.

'What do you do?'

'I'm a top model. You're supposed to know!'

'Oh . . . really?' Rupert swallowed. 'Well, where would I have seen you?'

'*Vogue, Harpers*, that sort of thing.'

'Sounds all right.'

'And what do you do, Rupert? Henry thinks you're wonderful.'

'Well, I think he's pretty wonderful, too, so we're quits. In fact, we're deeply in love with each other!'

Jacky didn't laugh, just thought it rather strange.

Rupert tried to reclaim the lost ground by asking another question: 'What's your name?'

'Jacky – you *know* that.' Then she softened a fraction. 'Family name, you mean?'

Henry interrupted, leant across his Gloria and brayed, 'Moore, Rupert. M-O-O-R-E. You know, "Don't have any more, Mrs Moore . . ."!'

Jacky gave Henry a funny look. Everyone else was a good deal more drunk than she was. In fact, she wasn't drunk at all. When your body was your fortune you simply couldn't risk it.

Rupert smiled and asked her somewhat seriously, 'Miss, Mrs or Ms Moore?'

'Mizzzz,' said Jacky, smiling.

'Not married then?'

'You're a sharp one.'

'Jacky Moore, eh? I'll remember that name.'

'Good.'

She was hard work this woman, Rupert thought. She certainly wasn't throwing herself at him. Nor was she allowing him to throw himself at her. It was a new experience, and he felt compelled to go along with it.

# CHAPTER 5

The village of Stoke Cansdale lies only four miles as the crow flies from Castle Cansdale but, to Hugo Hooke's slight shame, it was not a journey he made as often as he should. There was no excusing the fact on grounds of age, or that he didn't like motoring these days, when the object of his visits was so much older and frailer than himself.

Marjorie Hooke, the Dowager Countess, had been a widow now for forty-five years. Married to Richard Hooke in 1917, she produced Hugo and Alec one year and three years later respectively. A daughter, Lady Alice, died as a child in 1929. Marjorie had then lived in reasonable content as the wife of the 7th Earl until he was killed in action in 1943. She had not married again – anxious to retain her title, so it was said – and for the past fifteen years she had been living alone in Saffron Lodge, a delightful old building next door to Stoke Cansdale church. She was in her eighty-ninth year.

Hugo felt obliged to put on an air of sprightly youth when he went to see his mother because she was a vivacious, brittle thing who, despite her various ailments, still had a lively mind and an interest in the world around her. Hugo was rather fond of calling her his 'old whale', but that gave a totally misleading impression. She certainly had no blubber on her, nor was she 'old' in any sense except age. She was as slender as a birch tree, slightly stooped now, where once she had been ramrod straight, and a touch beaky in the face. She wore no make-up and was rather red or white depending on which patch of skin you were looking at. Her hair was thinning but she always kept it stylishly permed in a way she had probably first adopted in the 1940s.

Her son's 'motoring car', as he called it, a two-door 1964 Silver Cloud III with burgundy coachwork by Mulliner Park Ward, drew up outside Saffron Lodge a day or two after the seventieth birthday party. Hugo knew to walk straight in without knocking so that his mother did not have to stagger to the door; as usual he banged his head against a beam on the way in.

'Hello, Mummy,' he called out.

He navigated his way through the sitting room littered with stools and small tables piled with books, papers and sundry devices, all disposed so that they were in easy reach of the 'old whale'.

'And how are we today?' Hugo said, a touch patronizingly, as he bent down to kiss his mother.

'Quite well enough, thank you, Hugo. You don't have to ask if you don't want to.'

It was a strong but reedy voice that swooped up and down. It had all the confidence derived from centuries of English breeding. Marjorie believed there was no excuse for mumbling, as she thought Hugo often did. Indeed, she had noticed his speech becoming rather affectedly doddery over the last few years. She thought he was doing it because that was what was expected of an aristocrat, but she wasn't going to go that way herself despite a little difficulty with her hearing.

'I would have come to your party, dear boy, but you know how it is . . .' This was the nearest Marjorie would get to admitting she had her limitations. 'Did you have a good time? Fancy me having a seventy-year-old son! Who was there?'

'Passable time,' replied Hugo. 'Little drinks for the people. Village, you know. Then the family to dinner. Or some of them. Thank you for the flowers. Made it seem like a funeral.'

'Oh, Hugo, don't be such an old misery! Funeral, indeed. If you take after me, you've got a long haul ahead yet. If your father hadn't been killed, he'd have still been here with me. You know that. You're from long-lived stock.'

This was reasonably true of the Hookes, but very much so of the Pinningtons. Marjorie's father, Lord Pinnington, had in fact made it to ninety-nine. All her sisters and brothers were still alive in their seventies and eighties.

'Reminds me of the old woman of a hundred,' Hugo said, venturing an anecdote. 'She was asked if she had any worries and she replied, "No, not since my son went into a home . . ." '

Marjorie chortled. 'Very good, Hugo! And who was at the dinner?'

'Well, there was Molly and me, and Alec; Duncan and Joanna and the girls; and Sophie. That's all.'

'Not Rupert?'

Hugo coughed and then paused. 'No.' He did not elaborate.

'Why ever not?' the Dowager Countess asked peremptorily.

'Rupert is Rupert, and I'll be damned if I know.'

54

'Didn't he write, or send a message?'

'Of course he wrote – to apologize. He's always writing and it's usually to apologize for something. Another of his damned short, *sweet* little notes. How something he *had* to attend to came up, how he loved his old father, absolutely unforgivable, and all that sort of thing. Probably wasn't telling the truth on either count, but that's Rupert.'

'I'm sure he loves you, Hugo. He's a lovely boy. He can do no wrong, in my book.'

'Glad to hear it, Mummy. He's a good boy. Just that he doesn't like coming home, it seems. I don't think it's because he's ashamed of us, or anything. He just wants to live his own life, make his own way. He may like to keep out of Duncan's way as well. I think there's a little resentment there. Both ways. I've a feeling Rupert would rather like to have the house, and feels badly about Duncan getting it. I s'pose he's entitled to do things his own way.'

Marjorie nodded vigorously, her hands resting tidily on her lap when they weren't rubbing the tight old skin on her wrists.

'I've been hearing things about Duncan,' she said, abruptly changing the subject.

'On that telephone of yours?'

'Yes.'

The telephone had been a particular object of love and hate at Castle Cansdale ever since the 6th Earl, Marjorie's father-in-law, had one of the first installed in the early 1900s. Hence the number: Bourton Cansdale 1. The 6th Earl's wife – Countess Kitty she was called – objected strongly to the device and at first only permitted it to be kept in the butler's pantry, to which the Earl had to repair whenever he wanted to make or receive a call.

When the telephone was eventually let out and installed in the Gold Library, Countess Kitty had been adamant that the new-fangled device should not be visible. A special ornate wooden box, rather like a commode, had been made for it. Holes were carved in the sides to let out the tinny sound when the bell rang.

Marjorie still had that box with her, but used it as a stand for her 1940s vintage telephone to sit on; it was too much trouble fishing the thing in and out every time she wanted to make one of her many calls.

It was said of some huntswoman when her days in the field came to an end through injury that she used to ride to hounds by telephone – phoning up for detailed reports on several meets every day and enjoying the chase at one remove. Marjorie used the telephone in a similar way to keep track of social life in Hooke country. It enabled her to hear about what she was no longer able to experience herself.

But Hugo was reluctant to play along with her. 'Are you sure I want to hear anything about Duncan you've picked up on the grapevine?'

'You may not want to, you may not like it, but you're going to,' his mother told him flatly.

'Oh, all right.'

'Well, there's no doubt about it. He's been carrying on again. This time it's a woman in Bourton. Wife of an architect. He goes round to see her every day. Usually at lunchtime.'

Marjorie thought this last point particularly damning and did her best to thump the telephone pad with her right thumb and forefinger.

Hugo looked as though he was trying to think who the architect was, and whether he had ever met him, but came to no very firm conclusion.

'What's the name?' he asked.

'She's called Merrilee Bridgewater. I don't know what the husband's called.'

'Ah . . .' Hugo sighed. Perhaps he had heard of some people with the name Bridgewater, but he wasn't terribly sure. He was more concerned about Duncan. 'He's a beast', was all there was to be said about him, and Hugo applied the description to his eldest son generally, not specifically to this most recent example of his behaviour. Yet sexual misdemeanour was especially offensive to Hugo. He had brought up all his children as strictly as he could, especially in matters of sexual morality. He himself had always acted impeccably in that field, so he believed.

Marjorie seemed to be not so disapproving; delighted rather at the excellence of her gossip.

'There's nothing I can do, anyway,' said Hugo, sticking his hands deep in his pockets and stretching his legs out as far as they would go across the hearth rug.

'You could try talking to him, I suppose.'

'No point. Whenever Duncan and I talk about anything we end up having a row. I have to send him notes now if there is anything important I want to tell him.'

'I don't know where you got him from,' Marjorie said, opening up an old, old family topic. 'Never saw the likeness to you or poor Kay. In times past, one might have thought there'd been a warming pan trick, or some stupid midwife had got hold of the wrong baby.'

'Oh, he's ours all right. I think he got that burly, hairy look about him from the Allans. Born to wear a kilt, though I'm glad to see he doesn't.'

Hugo took out his wallet, as he was prone to do when he was bored, and started looking through it.

'Hugo, don't do that!' his mother swooped.

He made no apology. 'These things happen,' Hugo drawled, not terribly to the point. 'Been writing to him quite a lot lately, in fact.' He was off on another track.

'What about?'

'All this business of the gift. The "potentially exempt transfer" as Drew Elliot and his chum Templeton call it.'

'Ah, yes. Frightful business.'

'It's dashed tricky, but I had to do something about the future.'

'Good, good, Hugo. It was about time.'

'My seventieth brought it on, I s'pose. Been putting it off and putting it off, chiefly because of Duncan. Couldn't bear to think of it. Anyway, I had Elliot over for a chat a little while ago and he presented me with Hobson's choice. We've got to get out, that's the long and the short of it. I've made over everything to Duncan, as a gift, and if I'm spared for seven years he won't have to pay any tax.'

'Well,' commented Marjorie wisely, 'at least it means he'll have a reason for looking after you, making sure you don't come to harm.'

'Maybe, but I doubt I'll notice any difference in his attitude.'

'Oh, my darling Hugo, but it's so *sad*! Fancy having to leave that wonderful place! I know it's a headache, but it's so gorgeous. Why do they have to make it so frightfully difficult for a person? I think the present lot are doing a good job' – here the Dowager Countess kicked with her toe towards a pile of back copies of the *Telegraph*, *Sunday Express* and *Times*, as though they represented the Government – 'but even they have hardly let up on people like us. It's a disgrace, dear. Is there really no other way?'

'I could try to get the National Trust to take it, but they're very choosy these days, and they demand a heck of an endowment which, frankly, I don't have. Anyway, as you know, I've always loathed the idea of throwing it open to public. People scrambling all over you while you hide yourself away in some blasted little flat. Ropes everywhere to keep the hordes at bay. Sticky fingers on the paintings. Loathe all that. It's all right for Bath and Montagu, they actually like that kind of thing. But I've never had any wish to be a circus proprietor! And Cansdale has *never* been open to the public. I won't enter into any scheme which gives them access.'

'Mmmm. I suppose that's why the Government are so mean. They think you're being dog-in-the-mangerish. So they penalize you.'

'Damn 'em, then! I think what I think. Anyway, the upshot is that Molly and I are moving out. Have to. Terms of the agreement. We're going to do up Huddleston and live there, so we'll be nearer you, even if it does mean Duncan has the freehold!'

'Perhaps he'll learn to behave himself when he has responsibility for the house and the estate.'

'Wouldn't bank on it, Mummy. It'd be a start if he gave up this woman.

There's no excuse for that sort of carry-on. I know everything hasn't been right with Joanna for a while now, but they have the girls and he ought to behave himself.'

'I suppose he feels guilty because they haven't got a boy. Perhaps that's why he does it. As a substitute.'

'Oh, that's all psychological stuff,' was Hugo's comment.

Marjorie saw that it was pointless to discuss the matter any further. She was feeling peckish.

'Would you like some tea?' she asked, and Hugo ritually went and made it for her. He wasn't very good at boiling a kettle, any more than he was at opening a tin, but he had just about managed to get tea-making right. Marjorie lived without servants, so there was no one else to do it.

As Hugo pottered about in the kitchen, waiting for the kettle to boil, Marjorie kept up her running inquiry into everybody's affairs from the command post in the sitting room.

'What of darling Sophie? A little bird tells me she's been seeing a lot of Billy Wiltshire's boy.'

'Eh?' Hugo half-answered from the kettle position.

'Edmund, I think he is. Quite a good show-jumper, they say.'

'Edmund the Bastard,' Hugo muttered quietly to himself.

'What did you say, dear?'

'Nothing, Mother.'

'She must find someone, someday. What d'you think, Hugo?'

'I'm sure you're right,' he called out louder, so she could hear. It was Hugo's way of settling any question. 'I'm sure you're right', 'That's certainly a point of view' – phrases to put a stop to more of the same, and convey neither agreement nor disagreement.

He bore the tea tray to one of the little tables near his mother, balancing it in one hand while with the other he cleared away a stack of jigsaw puzzles, to make room.

'You'd make a good butler, Hugo,' she teased him. 'It's so hard getting them these days, perhaps you should take it up!'

'Yes, Mother,' said Hugo, drily. A sense of humour had never been among his most obvious qualities and he hated being teased.

He sat not saying anything while the Earl Grey cooled in his cup. Then he realized he had been staring at the picture over the fireplace for most of the time he had been with his mother. It was a Franz Snyders of the goddess Ceres surrounded by the fruits of the earth. I forgot we lent her that, he thought, and took a sip of tea. It should have been on the inventory Elliot and Templeton drew up for the handover to Duncan. He made no note to rectify the omission.

'I can see the problem,' he said, somewhat surprisingly re-opening the subject of Sophie's marriage prospects. 'It was difficult enough in the old days, finding a suitable match, with all the hassle over suitability, marriage portions, and so on. But now there's new difficulties. She dashes about so. She's sometimes here, sometimes in London. I don't know what she gets up to. She's not coming with us to Huddleston – she's taking Bethany Cottage – so I'll have even less idea what she does. But if she doesn't get a move on, she'll get left on the shelf. Too old to have children.'

'She's got a year or two yet,' Marjorie observed safely, not quite counting them up on her stiff old fingers. 'So she's chosen not to stay on when Duncan moves in?'

'She could have done, but I doubt if she'd have enjoyed it much. You know, it's odd she's not got herself fixed up,' Hugo ruminated. 'I mean she seems pretty all right, don't you think? Not too bad to look at. Not stupid. Can't understand it.'

Marjorie wasn't sure whether she should say it, but that had never stopped her before: 'You know, dear, I think it's sometimes a little *difficult* in these modern times for young people who have a title. I mean, I think it frightens people off – people who don't have titles and family. They think they're forming an alliance with an institution. It's quite understandable.'

'And so they are, so they are, damn it,' cried Hugo with unaccustomed animation. 'In the hot flush, people think they're marrying the person they're in love with. But they're not, they're marrying the whole dratted family! You don't just get a wife, with all her problems, you get all the blinkin' family's problems into the bargain!'

'And *vice versa*, Hugo. *She* gets *his* family's problems. I should know! Your father was a saintly man, but some of the riff-raff on the fringes, well . . . !' Marjorie raised her hands in horror at the memory.

'I s'pose it's true of all families,' replied Hugo, 'whatever their station. When people marry, they take on a hell of a lot.'

'But I think it's more acute,' Marjorie emphasized, 'when you belong to our sort of family. D'you understand what I mean, dear? I mean a family where everything depends on primogeniture, on wills and settlements, where everything depends on family structure. I think that puts a lot of strain on everyone.'

'And we're told the family is the salvation of the country, the answer to everything!'

'I hear that, too. And I read it in the paper. But it's not said by people from families like ours. I have to say, it doesn't make my heart lift when I hear it! I've lived too long not to know that families are a mixed blessing, even if they're the only real way of doing things that we know.'

'Have another biscuit,' her son suggested.

'I shouldn't really, dear. My teeth can't cope, but still . . .'

She seized a tough oatmeal biscuit from the proffered plate and ingeniously contrived to snap it using the real teeth at the back of her mouth.

'And what of Rupert?' she went on, having barely swallowed the biscuit.

Hugo was even less well-informed about his younger son's doings than those of Sophie. He rather envied Rupert his position: no family responsibilities, such as he had always had; blessed with good looks and an appealing manner, and able to enjoy them. Drat him. It had never been thus with Hugo. There had always been the responsibility of being the big brother, the heir. Never had any real opportunity to let his hair down, not even before he succeeded to the title. He had been much too well-behaved at school and at Oxford. Then the war broke out and he was into uniform. And when his father was killed, he was head of the family at the age of twenty-five. His youth had passed him by. Partly his own fault. He had never found it easy to unbend. Partly it was the responsibility he had thought necessary to show in his position. It was odd how Duncan hadn't inherited any of the same responsibility from him.

But, Rupert! Hugo didn't really know what Rupert was up to in London. He assumed the boy had lots of girl friends and had a right old time. It was odd thinking of your own flesh and blood carrying on as you yourself had never known or dreamed of, but there it was. He picked up odds and ends of tittle-tattle. Marjorie heard things on the grapevine. Rupert even made the occasional appearance in the gossip columns. This 'disc-jockeying', or whatever it was, had been the latest manifestation.

Marjorie repeated her question in different words, as though she saw that Hugo had let his mind wander. 'What'll happen to Rupert, d'you think?'

'Ah,' muttered Hugo, returning from where he'd been. 'More tea?'

'Please.'

'If you ask me, he'll try and marry out. I just feel it. He's so *independent* of us. Always has been. Always gone his own way. I think that's what'll happen. He won't want to form any useful alliance. I expect he'll marry for love.'

'Good for him,' trilled Marjorie. 'That's his prerogative. The youngest can always do what they like.'

'Alec would certainly agree with you there.'

'Ah, yes.' Marjorie frowned almost as much as she had when mentioning Duncan's terrible exploits. 'Your brother's always been a *complete* mystery to me. Frittered his talents away. No wife – that lasted, anyway – no children, nothing useful done. I've often wondered if he hasn't a bit missing, you know.'

'Harmless enough. But rather a waste, I agree.'

'Well, Rupert won't go that way, I feel sure. He seems to look after himself. Has a job. Good for him. I hope he marries *money*, though.'

' 'Spect he will. He's not a fool. Might be *new* money, of course.'

'Never mind, Hugo. Old money, new money – any money'll do, whatever sort it is!'

'Probably want to marry someone entirely unsuitable – just to upset Molly and me.'

'Well, we've had plenty of oddities in the family. I mean, remember your great-uncle Charlie, dear. That chorus girl he was infatuated with! They let him marry her, but of course it didn't last. Just one of those things.'

'I wish I could take your easy attitude, Mother. Trouble is, I can't. I worry about what's right for the family.'

'That's your job, dear boy! Anyway, I'm too old to let that sort of thing bother me any more. But I do like to be kept informed!'

Hugo managed a half-smile. His mother was a phenomenon. Slept soundly, took no medicines of any description – though she was rather too keen on vitamin pills from the health food shop. She had so many of the damn things inside her, by rights she ought to rattle.

He stayed talking to his mother for another half-hour. In a way he quite enjoyed it. Molly came to see Marjorie most weeks, on the basis that it's always easier to talk to your husband's parents than your own. But Hugo had owed his mother a visit after his important birthday.

As he bowed low out of Saffron Lodge, having kissed Marjorie goodbye, he wondered as always whether he would ever see her alive again. But that was a morose thought. She would go on for ever. What did she think when she woke up each morning? he wondered. What did she have to look forward to? He knew after a fashion that that was probably not a question ever to bother her. Watching the family grow, watching the family behave was sufficient occupation.

A more relevant question was, what did Hugo have to look forward to each day? He did not have a satisfactory answer.

# CHAPTER 6

Hugo adjusted his cap and climbed into the Rolls. He set off back to Bourton Cansdale at a stately pace. Along the way he did not acknowledge the hesitant waves received from the one or two pedestrians and drivers he encountered. He didn't intend to be aloof, he wasn't wishing to cut them, he just considered it his duty to concentrate on driving.

When he reached Bourton, Hugo drove round the green and pulled up outside the church of St Michael and All Angels. He alighted from the vehicle and strode as briskly as he was able through the lych-gate, up the hedged path, and into the old church.

He eased open the door, taking care not to let the latch clank down in case there was a service in progress or someone at prayer in the church, but there was not. He respectfully took off his cap and smoothed his hair.

Hugo loved the church deeply. Even more than Castle Cansdale itself, it seemed to speak of the generations, of the seasons, of the continuity of human life. The musty smell was powerfully nostalgic; the peace and quiet mournful and touching.

As he felt increasingly drawn to do, he went and stood in the Hooke family chapel. Here, each Earl Hooke since the creation lay buried with his wife. There was, of course, the Bachelor Earl who was on his own. And there was one Earl missing: his father. Richard Hooke had been killed in a commando raid during the Sicily landings of 1943. The body had never been brought back to England. There was said to be a grave somewhere on the south coast of Sicily, but no one was very sure what it contained. Hugo had never been back to the island since his own visit as an undergraduate just before the war. It was not something he would probably ever do now. If he wanted to feel close to his father, Hugo had only to look up at the marble plaque he had had placed on the wall shortly after the war was over. Beneath the family crest were the words:

*A Family Matter*

In Memory of
Richard Giles Cansdale, 7th Earl Hooke
1899–1943
He was a devoted father and husband
and earned the approbation
of the entire community in which he lived.
His mortal remains lie in a foreign field.
PRO PATRIA MORI

Hugo read the words and, as always, felt a slight lump in his throat. He pulled up a chair, which made a scraping sound in the empty church, and sat staring at the plaque while sunlight came through the stained glass, casting kaleidoscopic shades of amber, green and red across the chapel. Then the sun went behind a cloud and the chapel was cast into gloom and further chill.

Hugo heard quiet footsteps approaching and turned towards the dark-suited person, smelling faintly of tobacco, who now stood by him.

'Ah, Padre,' he said, 'you've caught me at it again.'

'Never mind,' said Dutson, the Rector, 'that's what it's here for.' He pulled up another chair and sat down next to the Earl.

'You see, I was thinking about my father,' Hugo tentatively admitted.

'Of course.'

'I feel I'm letting him down.'

'In what way?'

'Because I'm leaving the house. It's got to be done, you see. Other-wise . . .'

'The death duties, or whatever it is?'

'Quite. The only way I can save Duncan from – well, from having to carve up the estate when I go is to give it to him now, and trust that I'm spared for another seven years. I've looked into it with the legal boys, and it's the only way.'

'I had heard, in a roundabout way,' the Rector admitted.

'It's got round then?'

'No, I wouldn't say that, but people put two and two together.'

'How?'

'When the surveyor went to look at Huddleston.'

'Ah.' Hugo frowned. He looked up again at his father's name. 'I feel my father wouldn't have approved of my quitting before my time was up. It's so against tradition. I'm the first Hooke that's ever chosen to do it.'

'I don't expect you've exactly *chosen* to do it,' the Rector said soothingly. 'In the world in which we live, many things are forced upon us. Tradition can't be respected with the governments we have today. No one will blame you. In fact, you could try seeing it in another light. You are doing a good deed, by sparing those who follow you a lot of anxiety and expense.' It was not exactly the sort of problem he, as a clergyman, would ever have to face, but he could sympathize, and it was his job to do so.

'Hmmm,' said Hugo, not entirely convinced, but grateful to the Rector for trying to put his action in a better light.

The two men ambled slowly out of the church and into the churchyard. They stood beneath the lych-gate, chatting. Hugo told the Rector of his visit to the Dowager Countess. 'She'd be glad of a call from you, you know,' he said. 'Nothing religious, just the gossip. She likes that kind of thing.'

The Rector laughed and took out his pipe to begin the long business of lighting it. He liked gossip, too. He could hardly believe some of the titbits he picked up as he went about on his visits, and he enjoyed them hugely.

'I'll go and see her, most certainly.'

At that moment, Hugo's attention was drawn by the hooting from a Volvo which was about to run down some stray hens that were pecking about in the middle of the road on the other side of the green. The hens flew and flapped out of the car's way just in time to save their necks. The car drove on at speed and disappeared from view.

'Your son, I think,' said the Rector, puffing his pipe, now lit, and jangling the coins in his pocket.

'Yes,' answered Hugo non-committally.

There was a pause. Hugo was reminded of what his mother had told him.

'Frankly,' he said, 'one of the chief reasons I'm sad at leaving the house is him. It may not be a very Christian thing to say, but I don't trust Duncan. I'm not sure he'll look after the place properly – yet I've got to give it to him.'

'Is there nothing you can do on the legal side? To make sure?'

'I've tried. But what do I do if he doesn't stick to the agreement? I can't turf him out on his ear, or impose any sort of sanctions. It's his affair now, he'll do what he wants with it, and that's that.'

The Rector puffed on his pipe and played rather more nervously with the coins in the pocket of his black trousers.

'You know, I may be speaking out of turn,' he said, after some hesitation, 'but there's talk in the village that Duncan is seeing a lot of Mrs Bridgewater, wife of Roger the architect.'

Hugo didn't bat an eyelid, and merely said, 'I thought there was an architect involved somewhere.'

'So you've heard?'

'Only what Mother told me. She knows everything that's going on.'

64

'I was rather surprised to see them at your party.'

'Who?'

'Roger and Merrilee – the Bridgewaters. Though I didn't see Duncan talk to either of them.'

'He's a bounder. Don't know how they got invited. Don't know them. S'pose he must have fixed it with Molly. How disgusting!'

'I presume the husband knows what's going on.

'Makes it worse, then, don't you think? Rubbing everyone's nose in it.'

'Would you like me to have a word?'

'With whom, Padre? With whom? If you speak to Duncan, he'll spit in your face. I don't know about these Bridgewaters. Sound a rum couple.'

'I'll think about it. But I do sympathize. It must be very vexatious for you to have a problem like that in the family – and at such a moment. Whenever you need a chat, you know where to find me.'

'Thank you. I do, indeed.' Hugo sensed the Rector was itching to be away – probably to spread what they had discussed around the countryside.

'See you Sunday morning. I'll be on church parade.'

'You've got a note of the lesson?'

'I have, if I haven't lost it.'

'I'll see you on Sunday, then.'

'Yes – thank you, Padre.'

The Rector watched as Hugo entered the 'motoring car' and then went over and said one more thing through the window to him before he drove off.

'There's talk in the village,' he said, 'of what Duncan will do now the castle's his.'

'And what's that?' Hugo asked wearily.

'They say he'll throw it open to the public. People are quite excited. They think there'll be lots of work coming their way, running the tea rooms, acting as guides. I think they'd rather welcome it. In fact, I'm sure they would.'

Hugo looked genuinely angry at this. 'Well, you can tell them from me, it won't happen. Not while I'm alive. The house is a house. It's a family home, not a museum or a circus. I'm not having it go the way of Woburn or Longleat or any of those other places.'

'Well, let's hope it all turns out for the best,' said the Rector, equivocally. He was quite well aware that Hugo wouldn't last for ever. One day, maybe very soon, he'd have to deal with Duncan as lord of the manor, so to speak.

Poor Hugo, the Rector concluded as he waved him off – not a happy man, not a happy man.

As Hugo gazed out from the high cockpit of the Silver Cloud and turned the vehicle towards the North Lodge of Castle Cansdale, he sensed that Dutson was buttering his bread on both sides. Vicar of Bray, he snorted.

As summer moved into autumn, profound and far-reaching changes were made, or at least initiated, in the life of the Hooke family. The reluctant gift of Castle Cansdale and the estate from Hugo to his eldest son was concluded. Hugo did not talk to Duncan directly about any aspect of the matter. Everything was carried out by the ever-willing and discreet Elliot and Templeton.

Then, in October, with great sadness and emotion, Hugo finally bade farewell to the house of his ancestors. It would not be true to say that it broke his heart, but the move was a terrible lingering hurt, made all the worse by the fact that his successor was someone he thought unfit to occupy the house.

There was very little for Hugo and Molly to take with them, just a few sticks of furniture and one or two favourite pictures and drawings, the removal of which had to be agreed like everything else through Elliot and Templeton.

On the actual day of the move – to temporary quarters in the Craswall Arms at Stoke Cansdale, for Huddleston wouldn't be ready for another six weeks – Hugo resolved to get it all over with as quickly as possible. He rose early, hustled Molly through breakfast, and then told Compton to arrange for the Silver Cloud to be brought round to the front entrance. The Earl and Countess's cases were loaded into the Rolls. There was no appearance by Duncan to signal the handing-over.

'Thank you, Compton,' Hugo said, almost inaudibly. 'We shall miss you.'

'And you, too, my lord. We all shall.'

'I hope that . . . everything will be all right.'

With that oblique reference to what would come after, Hugo stepped into the Silver Cloud and drove off down the Fair Mile to the South Lodge, rather than take the short route to Bourton. Hugo did not turn to look at the old house as it receded into the distance.

Rupert did not know it at first, but he too was reaching a significant turning point in his life which was to have a far-reaching effect on the family fortunes.

It was unusual for him to be so struck with a girl at first sight and he spent a little time puzzling over why this should be. Of course, Jacky was immensely impressive to look at. That was her job, after all. But that in itself was insufficient reason for him to be so hooked by her. She had other

66

ingredients that Rupert could not at first define, or, if he could, was reluctant to concede. It was when she spoke that Rupert was principally fascinated. From the look of her – and the day after they met Rupert confirmed that she was indeed appearing all over the more upmarket fashion magazines – she would have been hard to place in the class spectrum which Rupert affected to ignore but which nothing could really destroy. She had classless good looks, which is to say that she was certainly not aristocratic, but not common either. She could have emerged anywhere on the social scale, timeless, of her own kind. Rupert liked that. But when she spoke, she gave away a little more of her origins. She had a London voice – not Cockney – just slightly 'off' in accent. She might be from standard middle-class stock, he thought. Home Counties, but not in the superior sense of the term. This was a considerable turn-on for Rupert. It stemmed from an inbred conviction that the classes lower than his own had earthier, more straightforward and thus more enviable sex lives. Rupert had never derived all that much excitement from sex with his own kind. He had always imagined he would enjoy it more with these different folk.

Not that he was going to find out whether this was true from Jacky straightaway. And that was another turn-on. He was not used to girls putting up any kind or resistance. Yet she had managed to keep him at arm's length from the night they first met at the Carillon. She had declined to let him drive her home. She had kept her address and phone number from him. She politely but confidently deflected the initial passes he made at her when he did track her down with Henry Rowlandson's help.

He tried again when, after many postponements, they managed to arrange a date. He took her out for a meal at a brasserie in the Fulham Road. But she refused all his overtures – right up to the time she arranged for the taxi that took her home.

'I know you expect it, darling,' she said, giving him a flash of her gorgeous smile, 'but some of us have to work tomorrow.'

'I know, but what's that got to do with it?'

'Really! You'll just have to wait.'

Rupert put on his disappointed little boy look. But, Jacky wasn't going to give way just yet. She would bide her time. Besides, she did not know the man. He seemed like any other ex-public schoolboy in a suit who did something incomprehensible in the City. True, he was handsome in a certain way and had an appealingly shy manner, but so had plenty of others.

Rising to the challenge, Rupert did not let up. The more frequently Jacky resisted, the more persistent he became. What would people think if they found that he had been out with Jacky three or four times and nothing had happened? He did all the things he was supposed to do, like taking her out for meals, taking her to the theatre, buying her flowers. But still nothing.

With another type of girl, this holding out would have been known as winding him round her little finger, but Jacky was testing him, making sure that he was really interested in her and not in the fake glamour she derived from being a model.

He kept on asking her questions. Like how much she earned.

'The most I've had for a job is a grand, but the agency takes a lot of that, and it costs a fortune looking after myself. Most jobs pay much, much less.'

'But you just have to *stand* there!'

'It's all the hassle. Going to see clients – it's a real meat market, that is – and having to look good all time. It takes *hours* every day, doing my hair, my nails, everything.'

'Ever take your clothes off?'

'No, I don't. Different type of modelling. Anyway, it's not a pretty sight, I can tell you.'

'Never been in a position to judge . . .'

Jacky made no reply. It was the old portcullis coming down, as always.

'Sorry . . . but it's a living then?'

'Can't complain. Maddie Shapiro keeps me busy – she's my agent.'

'You get any foreign trips?'

'Not as often as I'd like. Have you seen my show card? Hand me my bag.'

Jacky fished out her show card which was a small catalogue of various poses in a variety of clothes and hair-dos. Her name was printed in bold at the top, and on the back was the number of the Maddie Shapiro Agency.

'There – that one was taken in Algiers, and that one was Mustique.'

'Quite a lot of you showing there. Looks all right to me.'

Jacky thanked him for his compliment and took the show card back.

'I suppose you have greasy photographers wanting to get their paws on you all the time?'

'Not at all. They're mostly very sweet. You do get the odd one who tries it on. But they're only doing a job. It's the fellers from the agencies who are worst.'

'I can imagine,' said Rupert with a smile. 'Well, this is all very good. How long have you been doing it?'

'Since I left school, on and off.'

'Really?'

'Well, when I left school, I didn't have qualifications, so I went to secretarial college, and then I worked for my dad.'

'What's he do?'

Unaccountably, Jacky laughed at this inquiry.

'What's so funny about that?' asked Rupert.

'Nothing. It's just blokes like you are interested in all that, aren't you?'

'Blokes like me?'

'Yes. "What's your daddy do, lah-di-dah?" I tell you, he's not the bleeding Archbishop of Canterbury!'

Rupert was captivated by Jacky's lurch into full-blooded Cockney.

'No, but what is he? I'm interested.'

'He's a businessman.' Jacky was back using her normal voice. "Company director" – that's what they always say in court, isn't it?'

'Ah, yes. What sort of business is it?'

'You name it, he does it. Travel, insurance, property, he's into everything.'

'So he does all right then?'

'I should think so. D'you know what your dad earns?'

'No. Haven't a clue.'

'Well, there you are then.'

'Where do you come from?'

'Brentwood. Beautiful Brentwood, that's me.'

'I've never been to Brentwood,' Rupert added, but without a trace of irony. Merely as a statement of fact. 'In fact, I'm not totally sure where it is.'

'Well, you know the East End? You just keep going, and there it is.'

Rupert ventured an arm round Jacky's shoulders to reassure her that he was only asking out of curiosity and not because he wished to pry. She returned the compliment by quizzing him.

'What's the "Hon." then?'

'Who told you about that?'

'Henry Rowlandson. Time we first met. He said, "How'd you like to meet my very old chum the Hon. Rupert Hooke?" '

'Oh, did he?'

'Well?'

'It's just something some people have. I don't use it, but some people never let up; they're always putting it on things.'

'I thought you must be a judge!'

'Goodness, no. Why did you think that?'

'They get called "your honour", don't they?'

'Not the same thing.'

'So what d'you really do? Old Hen says you make a packet.'

'Oh, does he? Well, Hen's into entertainment, so he likes to build everyone up. I work in the City. I make money for other people – well, that's the general idea – but I don't make a great deal for myself.'

'Your dad loaded?'

'Now who's asking that sort of question! No, he's not. Not particularly.'

The fact that the 8th Earl Hooke's house and land had recently been valued at seventeen million pounds would only have confused the girl and been impossible to explain. So Rupert chose not to. In a sense he was right in what he said. The estate comprised 1,876 acres, two houses, two farmhouses, nine cottages, not forgetting the village of Bourton Cansdale with its eighteen houses and two cottages. It was just that the millions were not easily realizable. This accounted for the poor condition of the castle and the parsimonious life-style of the Hookes despite the Rolls and the servants.

'Where do your folks live?' Jacky asked.

'Near Craswall.'

'Where's that?'

'Swindon way. Down the M4. In fact, they're moving shortly.'

'Is it in the country? I'd just *love* to live in the country.'

'Yes, it is. Right in the country.'

'Is it a nice house?'

'They did have a nice house, but I haven't really seen the new one. It's smaller, more convenient, so I'm told.'

'Your mum still alive?'

'You bet.'

'What's she called?'

'Her real name's Lydia, but she's always known as Molly.'

'That's nice. Friendly sort of name.'

'Well, she's very nice. But I don't go home much. Hardly ever. Christmas and Easter – if then.'

'Oh, I'm always going home. Lived there till two years ago when Dad bought my flat.'

'Ah, the secret hideaway! Aren't you ever going to tell me where it is?'

'Westbourne Terrace.'

'Mmm. Now all I need to know's the number! Nice of him to do that – buy you a flat in town.'

'Like I said, he's in property, so why not?'

And so in the small change of their conversation, the facts were established up to a point. They learned a little about each other, but not everything. The cautious friendship developed as it would have done even without the glazing of background details that they extracted from each other.

They first made love on one of the rare warm days in August, when Rupert managed to persuade Jacky that he should pick her up direct from her flat. He said he was curious to see it, and she gave way.

It was on a Saturday afternoon. He drove over to Paddington in his MG and discovered Jacky's fourth-floor flat in a terraced row which had been converted to a myriad of little box-like dwellings, like a dovecote.

'Interesting neighbours you have.' Rupert gave a twisted little smile as he arrived a touch breathless from climbing the stairs.

'You can say that again.' Jacky waved him in, quickly shutting the door. She was wearing a swimsuit top and a miniskirt, leaving plenty of skin exposed. 'On the game, most of them.'

'Hope you're safe . . .'

'Safer here than most places. The only ones you bump into are either on their way in, or on their way out. They don't bother me.'

'But what about the . . . you know . . . the men who . . .?'

'Ponces? Don't get any trouble from them,' Jacky said flatly.

'Well, that's all right then.'

Rupert looked round the tiny room. A single bed was pushed up against the wall covered with pop posters, slightly out of date. Every surface and a good deal of the floor was taken up with Jacky's 'equipment' – hair-drier, curlers, make-up boxes, and clothes, lots and lots of clothes.

Rupert poked his nose into the bathroom, which was even tinier and full of bottles, jars and soaps. And then into the minute kitchen which contained a tiny fridge and a small electric cooker. From the windows was a grim view of acres of pipes covering an adjacent wall.

'I don't eat much,' Jacky said, as though by way of explanation.

'I suppose not,' said Rupert, in his funny, half-distracted way. He went and sat on the edge of the bed.

'I like your shirt,' she told him. 'You wear nice shirts.'

'Very boring, I'm afraid. Jermyn Street sort of thing.'

'I like the stripes. I like the material. Always like a nice shirt. Well made.'

'You'd look good in it . . .'

Jacky didn't take up the offer. 'Nice shoes, too,' she said. 'Where are they from?'

'I don't know really. Mr Boot, I expect.'

'Expensive?'

'Not really.'

'You know, there's something I've noticed about nobs like you,' Jacky announced. 'You always say you've got no money, you're "strapped for cash", yet you don't half know where to pay through the nose for things.'

Rupert heard himself about to say something like, 'Well, one has to keep up standards,' but stopped before he did so. He contented himself with a 'maybe' and another of his self-deprecating laughs.

Jacky let him put his arms round her. Then she put her arms round him, to feel his shoulders under the fresh, new quality of his shirt. Being slightly taller, Rupert bent his head down to nestle against hers and found how warm hers was.

'You're a hot one,' he said. 'How did you get like that?'

'Washed my hair before you came.'

'That must be it.'

She smelt lovely, whatever it was, and he had no hesitation now in cradling her head in his hands and kissing her lips.

Jacky made the important move. After all these weeks, she had obviously decided she was ready. She slid down the zip on Rupert's jeans and unbuckled the belt.

They stepped wordlessly out of their clothes, then cuddled together naked on the narrow bed under the sloping ceiling. Jacky stroked Rupert's legs with their light covering of dark hair. Then he did the same to hers, finding as he did so a small gold chain on the ankle of her left leg. He was curiously excited by this. It wasn't the sort of thing Georgina or any of her sort would wear.

Jacky pulled herself up and bent over him and took him in her small hands. Then she bent over further and put him between her lips. Rupert lay, pleasantly gratified by her taking the lead. He felt himself coming already and had to stop her. Jacky guided him inside, put her hands on either side of his body, arched her back and very slowly drew the love out of him.

They lay for a long time afterwards without saying anything. Rupert was enjoying being away from his own bed, in a strange place, especially in such a seedy place.

'There you are, you see,' he said. 'I'm not such a pushy one after all, am I?'

'Shhh . . .' Jacky pressed a finger to his lips.

He pushed the fingers away by shaking his head.

'I may be mad,' he went on, 'but I think I love you.'

Jacky had never heard anyone say that to her with anything like conviction, and she wasn't going to stop him from saying the words, even if it was a silly thing to say and much too early.

In the late afternoon, they got up. They wandered about the West End aimlessly for the rest of the day. They both felt heady over what they had done. That night, Jacky agreed to go to Rupert's flat for the first time. It was to be the first of many times.

# CHAPTER 7

The leaves had finally turned to gold and winter was waiting in the wings. But still autumn smiled. A peach-coloured sun could be glimpsed through the mist that clung around the woods and water meadows until well into the morning. Being November, the hunting season was under way and the Bourton was due to meet at ten o'clock on the Tuesday outside the Craswall Arms in Stoke Cansdale.

Inside, Hugo and Molly were having a late breakfast. The decorators were still working on Huddleston. The Earl and Countess could hardly miss hearing the sounds of the hunt gathering outside. First, the horseboxes arriving from all around, and finally the yapping of the hounds when they were brought over from the kennels at Stoke.

Hugo would not be showing his face at this picturesque scene. His disapproval of hunting was widely known. Not even the fact that his daughter and daughter-in-law were mounted and dressed for the field would bring him out of the hotel.

Lady Sophie Hooke cut her customary dashing figure in her hunting clothes and shiny boots. So tight were her breeches and so curvaceous a pair of thighs clasped her horse that a number of men risked injury as they jostled forward for an ogle. Even the hunt saboteurs couldn't take their eyes off her.

Lady Wymark – Duncan's Joanna – cut rather less of a figure. She had done nothing to lessen her already weatherbeaten look. Her greying hair was shoved untidily under hairnet and bowler. She was riding side-saddle; she was an expert horsewoman and possibly felt that this style of transportation accorded more with her new dignity as lady of the manor. Having to move from Maidens Constable, the farm where she had been perfectly happy with what Duncan always called her 'four-legged friends', into the 'dreadful dump' of Castle Cansdale had not been to her liking. But she was already aware that people regarded her slightly differently now that she was chatelaine.

Her presence on the field that morning was a signal to everyone, and not least to her husband, that she was sacrificing nothing by the move. She would continue to hunt; she would continue to live life exactly as before.

'Bright morning,' she greeted Sophie huskily, steering her mount, a grey mare called Lusty, nearer to her sister-in-law's chestnut mare, Karberry.

'Great, isn't it? Good to see you.'

It was the first time they had met since Sophie moved out of the castle. Hunting was the only activity they had in common. Sophie thought that Joanna was mad as a hatter, didn't like her much, but considered she couldn't be all bad if she liked horses. For her part, Joanna thought Sophie something of an amateur. She felt Sophie was probably more interested in dressing up and seeing who she could pick up on the field, whereas she, Joanna, took it all very seriously. Sophie never seemed to be in at the kill; Joanna invariably returned with specks of blood and mud all over her clothes.

Both women swallowed the sherry they were offered from a silver tray by the landlord of the Craswall Arms.

'How's Lusty?' asked Sophie. 'Settling into the big stable?'

How else was she to find out what was going on in her old home? None of the family had been invited back to Castle Cansdale since the move.

'Oh, the horses are all right,' Joanna answered, shrilly. 'It's *us* I'm bothered about. Like a bloody morgue, that place. Bloody uncomfortable, and bloody cold. And all the time Compton runs round after me wiping mud off the carpets!'

'I expect the girls like it.'

Joanna laughed humourlessly. 'They're the only ones who do. Anyway, Josie and Serena are away at school most of the time, thank God.'

It was not the most motherly of things to say, thought Sophie.

'We're off!' she said.

'Thank God for that,' cried Joanna, pushing Lusty forward. 'Too much bloody hanging around.'

Already, Sophie could see she would get left behind. Joanna was thrusting her way to the front. As usual, Sophie herself would bring up the rear with some of the men who were new to the field. One of them was Edmund Wiltshire – 'Billy Wiltshire's boy'. She knew he was only there because of her. Just because she had once pressed him between her thighs for a night he was convinced she doted on him. He buzzed around her like a fly, a real pest – always ringing her up and sending flowers. She had no idea how she was ever going to throw him off. Perhaps today he would fall off his horse and break something. All things were possible on the hunting field. For the moment, she bid him a polite good morning and made sure he couldn't manoeuvre his horse alongside hers.

The Bourton moved away from the village, but before it took to the fields it had to follow a narrow, winding 'B' road which, after a quarter of a mile or so, crossed an 'A' road. With the arrogance of the hunt fraternity, traffic on the 'A' road was held up as the twenty or thirty horses, the forty or fifty hounds, and several following 'car hunters' crossed their path. A jumble of vehicles was held up by this procession – a cement mixer, a juggernaut, a bus, a milk tanker, and a handful of private cars. The very first car in the queue – to the intense fury of the driver who had thought he could nip across ahead of the hunt but had been flagged down by the policeman in charge of the crossing – was the Volvo belonging to Duncan, Lord Wymark.

Duncan sat fuming while the hunt passed before him. He half hid behind the sun visor, but knew his car could easily be recognized. And so it was that his wife, Joanna, at the head of the hunt, looked down from the height of her mare and saw not only her husband lurking in the Volvo but also, seated in the front seat, Merrilee Bridgewater, the architect's wife, fixing her make-up in the rear-view mirror.

The penny dropped. Joanna learned what she simply had not known, whatever she might have suspected in general terms. For a second or two, her eyes met her husband's. Then she rode on, rather as the Queen had once done after surviving a nasty incident in the Mall on the way to Trooping the Colour.

'That's torn it,' Duncan muttered, not too seriously, to Merrilee.

'Had to know sooner or later,' the woman said complacently. 'Probably knew already. Everyone else does.'

Duncan snorted.

Indeed, almost everyone in the hunt did register the couple in the front of the Volvo. Duncan couldn't have broadcast the liaison better if he'd put an ad. in the *Craswall Echo*. Last but one to cross the road was Sophie on Karberry. She, too, saw her brother and another woman. She had vaguely heard, but this was confirmation. She realized that Joanna would have seen the display as well.

What followed was a good morning's hunt. They had a brisk ride, a female fox was torn to shreds, and Joanna Wymark was in at the kill. At the end of the meet, still seeking to avoid Edmund Wiltshire, Sophie cantered up to Joanna and exchanged the customary small talk of hunting folk.

It was clear that Joanna was not quite her usual self.

'Join me for lunch, at the house?' she almost barked at Sophie.

'All right,' her sister-in-law answered, surprised at the invitation. 'I'll take Karberry home and come over by car.'

'Yes, you do that. I'll expect you.'

In forty-five minutes, Sophie had stabled the horse at Hagger Farm and, still wearing hunting gear, had transferred to her Golf and driven over to Castle Cansdale. She parked outside the front entrance, but the door was locked and she quite clearly wasn't going to get any response. She had never really liked the gloomy church-Gothic entrance anyway. So she nipped round to the kitchen entrance by the Spring Lodge and soon found herself in the warren of 'downstairs' rooms beneath the house.

Sophie knew her way around down there pretty well, but found it rather strange there was no one about. She went up the servants' stairs to the ground floor and, from habit, made for the Drawing Room – where the family had always gathered when she lived there with Hugo and Molly. She opened the door, went in, and was shocked to see that the room had been transformed.

There was a large television set – something Hugo would never have countenanced – and two new chairs made of chrome and leather, very hi-tech and with only the slightest chance of being comfortable to sit in. They would have suited the offices of an advertising agency but were singularly out of place here. Sophie also noticed that the Stubbs had been taken down and left standing on the floor, face to the wall, while a rather amateurish painting of a horse, presumably by one of Duncan's daughters, had been put in its place.

Sophie gulped. She hesitated about peeping into the Gold Library for fear of what Duncan might have done there. Installed a sauna perhaps?

Perhaps Joanna was upstairs in one of the bedrooms, changing out of her hunting gear. Sophie went through the Saloon and made for the stairs. As she did so, she came upon Compton, the butler, lurking somewhat and looking but a shadow of his former smooth and confident self.

'Good afternoon, my lady,' he said.

'Hello, Compton,' she replied. 'I was looking for Lady Wymark.'

'She came in fifteen minutes ago. I do believe she may be upstairs.'

'Oh, good,' said Sophie briskly, and turned to mount the staircase. As an afterthought, she asked, 'Everything all right, Compton?'

'Yes, thank you, my lady,' he answered, but it was perfectly apparent to Sophie that it was not.

'Good,' she said. 'Hope so.'

She found her sister-in-law in the Green Bedroom. Joanna was lying in her hunting gear on the bed, her boots muddying the green coverlet. And she was sobbing. She had put on a brave face out in the field, but now the pent-up rage against her husband had broken out.

76

Sophie went closer, sat on the edge of the bed and put a hand on Joanna's shoulder. 'I know, Joanna.' she said. 'I know what is.'

'God, he's such a shit,' Joanna cried, turning to look at her. She had taken her long, greying hair out of the hairnet and wisps of it were now getting stuck amid the tears on her ruddy face. 'You saw him?'

'I think everyone did. Was it that Bridgewater woman? They live near me.'

'Yes, it bloody well was! To think he got her invited to Hugo's party – and her husband! Talk about rubbing it in.'

Sophie didn't know quite what to say. The trouble was, whatever her brother got up to, she always felt an obligation to side with him.

'I didn't know till today, I promise you,' said Sophie, still not sure whether to take sides.

'Of course, I knew he was up to something. It's been separate beds for a year now. And he's such a rotter, he's always got to be doing it.'

'What'll you do, d'you think?' Sophie asked.

'Certainly not going off in a huff. I live here now and I'm bloody well going to stay.'

Sophie sought to change the subject. 'I saw Compton on the stairs. Didn't look very happy.'

'Not surprised, the way Duncan shouts at him and makes him run around all hours. He's leaving anyway.'

'No! Surely not?'

'Yes. Gave in his notice three weeks ago. Of course, Duncan is making him work it out. We'll have to get a new one. God knows how we'll do that. I don't know . . . it's awful! And then he's talking about opening to the public. That's all I need – smelly oiks sniffing around while we have to hide away in a family flat. He's only doing it to spite his father.'

Now that Joanna was sitting up, Sophie noticed there was a cigarette burn at the top of the green counterpane. That was new. Molly would have a heart attack if she found out.

'I tell you what, Sofa,' Joanna was looking at her meaningfully, 'you're bloody clever not to have married. Men are shits. Stick to horses.'

Sophie recalled Duncan joking once that Joanna was only happy going to bed with a horse. Now she thought she saw the point of the joke, stripped of Duncan's self-serving implication that he was hung like one.

'Let's have lunch,' she said, looking at her wristwatch.

'God, yes. Sorry, darling. Let's go down and see what's in the fridge. I fancy a whisky, how about you?'

'Oh, all right. But some of us have to work this afternoon.'

'Work? That Waterwheel lot? You go dressed like that?'

'Why not? Gives the men a hard-on. I don't care.'

'Are they any good? I'll have to talk to you about that. I'm hopeless at that sort of thing, and Duncan says we need to do up the whole ground floor if we're "going public", as he puts it.'

'Ah,' croaked Sophie, appalled in anticipation of the havoc that would be wrought if Joanna did any decorating or restoration on her own. If that was to be the case, Sophie would have to give a hand, feeling the embrace of the family drawing her into trouble on the score of obligation.

Downstairs, in the old kitchen – which hadn't been decorated, it seemed, since the turn of the century – the two women duly had their whiskies and then found some ailing tomatoes in the fridge.

'Cook's day off?' Sophie inquired gently.

'God, no! She was the first to go. First week. Floods of tears. Wherever Duncan is, there's always tears! You must know that by now.'

Sophie gave an embarrassed smile.

'Now then,' she said, firmly changing the subject, 'tell me what needs to be done – decoration-wise – and I'll mention it when I get back to the Mill.'

Every family has a black sheep, or at least a figure of fun, and with the Hookes, Uncle Alec was it. Being Hugo's younger brother and thus without a clearly-defined role in life, the Hon. Alec Hooke was happy to play the part.

Hugo, though occasionally embarrassed by Alec's peculiar behaviour, had a certain affectionate regard for his 'little bro.' as he still often referred to him. Molly thought him plain silly and a touch menacing, but she wasn't a blood relation after all. Rupert, who was his godson, as well as nephew, didn't mind at all the way his Uncle Alec carried on – as long as invitations to excellent dinners continued to be issued on birthdays and other important occasions. These treats were always preceded by a phone call, never by letter.

'Is that young Rupert?' Alec would demand in his slightly mannered voice. 'It's your Uncle Alec. I was wondering if you'd care to dine with me at my club some evening soon? I've some interesting tales to tell.'

The invitation was always to Alec's club, and though Rupert knew his uncle was a member of White's, he also knew they would never actually eat there. And as for having interesting tales to tell, that was an exaggeration, too. It was Rupert's interesting tales that Alec wanted to hear. The most remarkable thing about Alec's invitations, however, was that Rupert always accepted them, never pulled out at the last moment, and never had to send one of his sweet little notes of apology. The invitation Alec issued in early November was no exception.

Dinner, said Rupert, would be preferable to lunch. No, he didn't have a 'pretty lady' he had to see every evening (in fact, Jacky was away abroad on a shoot for a couple of weeks). Yes, he'd be delighted.

When the evening came, Rupert was not at all surprised to receive a call at about seven fifteen from Uncle Alec telling him the location had been shifted to Scott's in Mount Street. When he got there, the Hon. Alec Hooke was already well into a bottle of Pol Roger and popping handfuls of nuts and nibbles into his mouth at regular intervals.

'Dear boy, you *are* looking well!' Uncle Alec clasped him by the arm and shoulder, and drew Rupert down to the chair next to his. 'You are looking *particularly* well, if I may say so. I even detect a look of happiness in your eye. How do you account for this? You'd better have some Polly Rodge to celebrate whatever it is. We're having snails to start.'

Uncle Alec was dressed as always in the kind of clothes Rupert wouldn't have known where to buy even if he'd wanted to. His suit was of a dark brown, velvety appearance, with a particular velvety look to the collar, which was rather like a smoking jacket's. He wore a luxuriant yellow silk tie with a not very successful knot. A green and purple paisleyish handkerchief tumbled out of his breast pocket.

The front half of Uncle Alec's head was almost completely hairless, the back very thinly covered. The skin was thus clearly displayed, tanned, blotchy and mottled. He had a pointed face, but the principal feature was the pair of tinted glasses that rested on Alec's version of the family nose.

He was small in build, stooped now, and had a particular way of gesturing with his hands. He held the knuckles down, fingers up, before him, and drew the fists somewhat jerkily together as though scooping up something between them. He had a twinkle in his eyes – insofar as the eyes could be seen beneath the tinted glasses. And he radiated an enjoyment of the good things in life. If Rupert had not known who his uncle was, he might have thought he was engaged – or retired from – some rather *louche* profession. An art dealer, perhaps, with overseas connections.

But that was not the case. After Eton and Christ Church (where he eventually followed Hugo after a good deal of pressure had been applied by the 7th Earl), he had entered the diplomatic service after the Second World War. He held a number of minor postings in eastern capitals – Cairo, Baghdad and Khartoum – during which time his elder brother had always assumed he had been engaged in intelligence work. Hugo had no grounds for supposing this except that perhaps he *wanted* to believe his 'little bro.' was capable of doing useful work. It would also help to explain the slight air of mystery and eccentricity that clung to the fellow.

Alec did nothing to deny these assumptions. The fact was, however, he was never a spy. Indeed, privately he mocked the whole ridiculous business and in particular the 'Cambridge queers' who seemed to be in on it and who, in the fullness of time, turned out to be the biggest bunch of traitors and misfits anyone could have recruited to the service if they'd tried.

Alec – insofar as any importance attached to him at all in the diplomatic service – was a risk of another sort. He was diligent in his work, but he had a tendency to get much too familiar with the people he was supposed to be being diplomatic to. This is not to say he liked consorting with little boys or taxi drivers in the bazaars of the east. He liked consorting with their sisters.

Alec Hooke had acquired the brothel habit during one of his vacation trips abroad from Oxford (a couple of years after the one he made to Palermo with brother Hugo and Toby Blair) and it remained with him for the rest of his life. It suited him to know what he was getting. He also became a considerable collector of pornographic art in photographs and books.

To those who knew of Alec's secret side (and, of course, there were such people – how else to explain his lack of significant promotion in the diplomatic service?), it came as a slight shock when he suddenly announced his intention to marry. That was in 1958, when he was thirty-eight and after he had been posted to Warsaw in an apparent attempt to lure him away from the fleshpots of the east to the chillier pleasures of the Eastern Bloc, a posting which only increased Hugo's speculation about his connections with the intelligence service. In Warsaw Alec soon met and fell in love with an extremely – his brother would say excessively – glamorous woman, the Countess Farbiszewski. She was about a foot taller than him, very loud, and with barely two words of English to rub together. Alec had acquired passable Polish, certainly enough to understand that, according to the Countess, they just *had* to marry in order to cement the great bond of friendship between their two great peoples. The match was frowned on by the Foreign Office. 'Not quite the d.t., old fellow,' his superior told him. But he was advised that if he returned to Britain, he could take the Countess with him.

They were married in London, at Caxton Hall, and they were divorced after the statutory procedures then in force had been followed (including Alec's alleged adultery, duly witnessed by a chambermaid at a Brighton hotel). The Polish Countess continued not to speak English and, as far as Alec was aware, still lived among the Polish community in West London. Quite what had gone wrong with the marriage Alec never confided to anyone in his family.

Finding himself made to look ever so slightly foolish, he decided to withdraw from the foreign service and attempt to earn his living as a sort of professional dilettante. At first he worked as a language tutor to a number of eminent clients. The wife of the Governor of the Bank of England required Italian lessons. He gave them to her. He embarked upon an edition of the works of the eighteenth-century politician and writer, Henry St John, 1st Viscount Bolingbroke, which he was never to finish. Gradually, though, he acquired a kind of reputation as someone who could hold forth and enthuse, reasonably authoritatively, on artistic matters. He wrote the odd article and gave the occasional broadcast talk. True scholars looked upon him as suspect and pooh-poohed his 'dubious knowledge', but no one could doubt the enthusiasm and wit with which he expressed it.

Naturally enough, given his background, Alec was drawn to the study of his own family's history. He appointed himself the unofficial archivist of Castle Cansdale. Hugo was more than happy to let him loose among the ancestral books and papers as he was less than moderately interested in them himself. Hugo had a feeling for family history and for tradition, perhaps because he felt it was his duty to honour the past, but he derived none of the thrill Alec did from handling dusty documents and reading the minutiae of everyday life in times gone by.

The waiter brought the snails, delicately mounted within nests of pastry, and Alec was the first to plunge his knife, albeit elegantly, into the food. Rupert grinned, and did likewise.

'Been home recently?' Alec asked with an impish grin. He knew that Rupert had not been at Castle Cansdale for Hugo's seventieth birthday.

'No, actually,' replied Rupert, pleasantly contrite.

'Don't you like it?'

'Yes and no, Uncle. I just feel – well, it's got nothing much to do with me. Especially now Duncan's moved in.'

'Ah, yes.' There was a lessening in Alec's little smile. 'That's quite a change. Such a pity your father did that.'

'Says he had to. Should have done it years ago. That or some other measure. Inheritance tax is a minefield. I just hope he's made the right decision.'

'It's a great shame, in my opinion. The house is Hugo's, and he should have it till he shuffles off.'

'I know,' said Rupert, quietly. 'He must be taking it badly.'

'Well, dear boy, you know your father. Doesn't give much away. Wouldn't do, would it? Not like me – always blubbing at the slightest thing!'

Rupert finished the snails, and was already fearing what effect the garlic would have on him during the night to come. He looked at his uncle. 'I expect it's not so much leaving the house as letting Duncan have it.'

'Exactly! Far be it for me to say it, but your brother strikes me not only as a bore with very little brain, he seems all set to ruin his inheritance. The day-trippers are already at the gates!'

'Well, that side of it doesn't bother me, Uncle. I mean, if you've got a place like that, why not share it around and make a bob or two out of it? Makes good financial sense – if you can make a go of it. Anyway, it's not a problem you or I will ever have to face, is it? Both in the same boat.'

'And, like me, would you like to have come into it one day?'

Rupert paused before replying. 'I never like to admit it – and that's why I don't go home that much – but, yes, yes, of course I'd like to have it. Only fate has ordained otherwise.'

'Mmm.' Alec Hooke smiled. 'I understand you perfectly, dear boy. But as to throwing open the gates, it depends how it's done. I'm an old fuddy-duddy when it comes to that. These days it's all so much show business.'

'Well, I agree, we can probably rely on Duncan to get things wrong whatever he does. That goes without saying. The funny thing is, though, if he does get it wrong, Daddy'll die of a broken heart before the seven-year time limit's up on the gift. So Duncan'll be revealed as having pulled the roof down on his *own* head!'

'Ah, you see that, do you? That's good, that's very good.'

The duck arrived wrapped in bacon and Alec demanded that the Morey St Denis be served instantly.

'I have a little confession to make,' he went on. 'I have to be a bit careful what I say about your brother just now.'

Rupert looked startled, as though he, too, had better watch his words.

'Why's that, Uncle?'

'Oh, well, it's very tedious and embarrassing, but it all boils down to money – like most things, eh?'

'Do tell.'

'You see, I've been a little worried about something else, with all this upheaval at the house.'

'And what's that, uncle?'

Alec Hooke laid down his knife and fork and cradled the wine glass in his hands. 'I feel I can tell you this, Rupert – and anyway you ought to know . . .' He sniffed and sipped the Morey St Denis. Then he put down his glass and started fiddling with his tinted spectacles. Whatever he had to say, it was taking him a lot of effort to spill the beans.

Rupert quietly got on with devouring his own portion of duck.

His uncle took a mouthful of the bird, chewed it, and then once more laid down his knife and fork.

'You see, when I stopped playing at being a diplomat – before you were born, of course – and started doing the odds and bobs I do now, your father very kindly, and completely unprompted by me, chose to provide me with a small annual income from the estate. Nothing very much, but it helped me enjoy the, er, the enjoyable things of life.' Alec vaguely gestured about his plate. 'Didn't have to do it . . . most grateful.'

'You're worried Duncan'll stop it?'

'That's the point, dear boy. Precisely!'

Rupert could see that this was indeed a tricky position for Uncle Alec to be in. Clearly, this was the real reason for the dinner. How could he help the poor old chap? His uncle, consciously or not, saw Rupert as an ally in the family wars. It wasn't so stupid really. After all, he seemed a lonely old soul – who else was he to turn to?

'Perhaps the best thing you could do,' said Rupert, finding it refreshingly easy to be sensible about another's affairs rather than his own, 'would be to speak to Duncan direct. Come out with it, say you're worried and what's he going to do about it? That's what I'd do. Mind you, I hope I'll never be in your position.'

'You don't get on with Duncan?'

'Well, I've never really had to. By the time Dad had remarried and I was born, Duncan was in the Guards. I certainly didn't look upon him as a brother of any sort. But I'm aware he treats Mummy very badly, and always has done. It's not exactly fair on her if she can't match his own mother, is it?'

'Well, there's certainly a difference between Molly and Kay – but, I agree, that's no excuse.'

'And the other thing about Duncan is,' Rupert went on, 'I just have a suspicion he sees me as a bit of a threat. He's not managed to produce an heir to the title and I expect at the back of his mind he thinks I might come along and snatch it all away one day.'

Uncle Alec was now once more busy eating his food and sipping his wine, as though filling in time while Rupert gave an airing to his own family concerns. Rupert soon noticed, apologized, and restated his view that the best way of dealing with the problem was for his uncle to tackle Duncan direct.

'Yes, of course, you're right, dear boy. Thank you, thank you. But I'd be frightened he'd turn round and say, nothing doing!'

'It's no skin off his nose. He's not exactly starving, now he's got the estate. A few grand a year for you shouldn't bother him. I'm surprised it wasn't sorted out when the settlement was made.'

'You know how it is. It was a nice gesture by your father, and nice gestures aren't always carved in stone.'

'Would it be any use my saying anything?'

'That's impossibly kind of you, Rupert, but I think you've made me realize I've got to seize the bull by the horns and speak to Duncan about it myself. P'raps I'll pay him a visit.'

'Good idea. Get him on his home ground. I'm sure it'll be all right.'

It was time to order the pudding and both uncle and nephew chose chocolate sponge.

'Now, Rupert, enough of me. You've been so inexpressibly kind to listen to my woes. How about you? Are you keeping busy?'

'I suppose I am,' he replied, trying to sound unconcerned about his level of busy-ness. Relations always asked him the same question, as though keeping busy was more important than being happy or keeping in health or any other state. 'I'm still with the venture capital outfit I joined last year,' he said, obligingly. 'It's quite fun. I've also been doing some other work, after hours. Would you know what a disc jockey was, Uncle?'

'Goodness me! I suppose so.'

'At balls and parties and things they have discos and I get dragged into doing a bit of it. Pays quite well.'

'Fancy! I expect it gives you plenty of scope to chase the girls. I think I've heard that's what disc jockeys do, isn't it?'

'Up to a point.' Rupert had noticed before how his 'bachelor' uncle always liked to talk about such matters and seemed to derive a curious satisfaction from it.

'Is there someone special in your life at the moment?' Alec asked.

Rupert swallowed. This was a line of questioning he would soon have cut off if one of his parents had started it, but with Uncle Alec it didn't really matter. He could be responsive and frank.

'Yes,' he smiled, disarmingly. 'I'm afraid there is rather.'

'Oh, good. I'm so glad! And who is she?'

'She's not someone you'd ever have heard of, Uncle. She's a model.'

'Goodness! Never mind. Is there any other type of girl these days? But would your father approve?'

'Shouldn't think so. I mean, she's not the daughter of anyone he knows. And I don't see her picture ever appearing in *Country Life* – thank God! – though it's all over *Vogue* and *Elle* and *Harpers*.'

'Oh, really? Then she's very successful.'

'Yes, she is. She's in Moscow at the moment. Fur coats in Red Square!'

'Wonderful! And how old is she – a nineteen-year-old nymphet?'

Rupert smiled. His uncle was obviously delighted by the news and seemed eager to set eyes on the girl. 'No, she's twenty-three and ageing rapidly!'

'I suppose part of the attraction,' Alec wondered aloud, 'is because you *know* your father wouldn't approve?'

'Oh, sure. But I don't intend to put it to the test. He'd only rattle on about it being a mistake to "marry out of one's station". Fact is, I don't know a great deal about her or her family. With her, all that doesn't seem terribly relevant. Her father's in business, lots of companies – so she says.'

'And what's she called, this paragon?'

'Jacky. Jacky Moore.'

Uncle Alec appeared not to register this. It wasn't quite his sort of name. Instead, he asked: 'And do I hear the faintest of wedding bells?'

Rupert hesitated. 'I've really no idea, Uncle. I can imagine Jacky and me settling down, you know, like they say. But I just can't imagine our two families coming together.'

'I don't expect that'd matter. As long as you're sure and you're happy.' It was more than obvious to his uncle that the boy was in love, and had found his special person. Uncle Alec felt no envy, merely happiness for the young man's sake.

It was a pleasant dinner between relatives, with no hint of 'family' obtruding although there had been lots of talk about it. The easy familiarity came, it was true, because Alec and Rupert were related, but the relationship was not one like that of father and son in which tensions and obligations were never far from the surface.

Uncle Alec called for the bill. When it arrived, it was covered up. He lifted the cover. Rupert glanced and was able to read, upside down, the total of £186.

Alec didn't bat an eyelid, though he did remark, 'I wonder how they make it add up to that?' But he paid without demur. No wonder he needed income from the estate when his pleasures cost him so much. What Rupert could not know was the extent to which Alec paid for pleasures very different to the occasional meals he bought for his nephew.

They adjourned to Alec's flat in South Audley Street for coffee and brandy. Towards midnight, Rupert departed amid mutual thanks and expressions of admiration and regard.

As he walked the short distance home to Lowndes Square, he looked up at the moon and, so far was he in love, wondered if Jacky was looking up at it from Red Square and thinking the same thoughts.

# CHAPTER 8

Ten days later, Uncle Alec entrained for Craswall to follow his nephew's advice. From there he took a minicab direct to Castle Cansdale. It was a distance of some fifteen miles. He told the cab driver to pull up at the front of the house, as he had always done in the past, and paid off the driver with a reasonably handsome tip.

He had a twinge of doubt about having done so when, after pulling the front door bell, nothing happened. When he tried to open the door he found it bolted. Alec looked at his watch, as if that would help. He had signalled his intended arrival time in advance, but the person who had answered the phone had not been the excellent Compton but someone new. Alec had not actually spoken to Duncan, but the voice had assured him that 'Of course, his lordship's always here – except when he isn't.'

Well, there was no hurry. Alec stepped away from the porch and stood staring up at the honey-coloured stonework. It was in surprisingly good repair, the exterior at least. Alec had always so adored the way the Hooke motto *In Hac Spe Vivo* ('In this hope I live') was picked out in large stone letters that ran right across the centre of the south face of the house. He liked to be given one of the bedrooms on that side. Not only did they have fabulous views down the Fair Mile but you had to peep over the top of the stone letters to see. It appealed to the little boy in him. Even at sixty-eight, there was still a lot of that.

Just now he was starting to twitch. Had he made a mistake in arriving like this, without having spoken to Duncan in person and telling him why he was coming?

No sooner had he resolved to go round to the Spring Lodge entrance than he saw a little girl cautiously but somehow casually coming towards him.

'Hello, my dear,' he called out in greeting. It was obviously the youngest of Duncan's three daughters, the one who wasn't away at school yet. But he was blowed if he could remember what her name was. It was either Serena or Christabel.

'Who are you?' the girl – who was a mere five – demanded. Alec noticed her slightly prominent gap teeth and saw the resemblance to her mother, Joanna. It was not the most flattering feature for a mother to give her daughter. He didn't much like her sandy red hair either.

'I am your father's Uncle Alec,' he said as kindly as he could, given her surliness. 'And you must be . . .?'

'Christabel. My father is Lord Wymark of Wymark in the County of Wiltshire.'

'That's lovely, dear,' Alec said simply. Then he asked if her father or mother was at home.

'Shouldn't think so,' said the girl. It was rather as though the position of Alice and all the unfriendly people she encountered in Wonderland had been reversed, Alec thought to himself, and Alice had become the unpleasant one.

'Perhaps I could step in and wait for them?'

'I don't see why not,' said Christabel matter-of-factly. 'You'd better come in round the back.'

Once inside the house, through the kitchen entrance, Christabel, to Alec's great relief, wandered off. He put down his overnight bag and his coat and went into the kitchen itself. There, a woman whom he did not recognize was listening to some terrible music on a transistor.

Alec had to raise his voice. 'I am Lord Wymark's uncle,' he told the woman. 'He doesn't seem to be here. P'raps I could have a cup of tea?'

'Suit yourself,' said the woman who was attending to a broken finger-nail, but did eventually find the time to throw a tea bag into a mug.

Alec stood, smiling wanly, while the kettle boiled.

'I'll take it to the Gold Library and wait there,' he told the woman, clear in his own mind that one thing he would *not* be doing was sipping his tea with that inane noise coming out of the radio.

He set off, carefully clasping his mug of tea as he opened and closed about eight doors and walked what seemed like a quarter of a mile before reaching the Gold Library. How he adored that room! It represented the acme of eighteenth-century civilization. An age of rest and refreshment was how an earlier man of letters had described it and Alec was deeply grateful that this part of the original house had been preserved when the less distinguished nineteenth-century castle had been thrown up around it.

To his dismay, however, the current occupant's idea of rest and refreshment in the late 1980s was rather different to his own. In the middle of the carpet was what looked like a rowing machine; beside it was a chrome device festooned with bars and levers, from which hung black weights. On the Aubusson carpet was a black rubber mat. Alec shuddered. Surely, if Duncan had to have this ghastly gymnasium, there must be a spare room among the hundred or so in the house where he could more fittingly have put it?

But perhaps it was a statement. Duncan had probably never opened any of the books in the library in his life, so it was just like him to establish a different use for the room. Alec sipped his mug of tea, tepid now after its long journey, while sitting at the desk made from the timbers of the *Victory*.

Then he turned, as he always did, to a corner of the library where he knew there were some delightful French books dating from the late 1730s – limited editions, privately published, which no one else at Cansdale had ever spotted, or admitted to spotting. Certainly not Hugo. They were slightly risqué accounts of the love lives of milkmaids and swains in the Auvergne. They were illustrated in a particularly fetching way with semi-pornographic woodcuts. They had always been a great delight to Alec. He rummaged about, looking for the key to the glass-fronted bookcase in which they resided. He couldn't find it. Disappointed, he had to content himself with old copies of *Horse and Hound* dating from Hugo's time.

About an hour after he got there, the door to the library burst open and Joanna strode in looking as though her horse wasn't very far behind. She wore a threadbare hacking jacket, mudstained jodhpurs, and green Wellington boots.

'Oh, hello,' she barked. 'Fancy you being here.'

Alec, busy coming to terms with the fact that anyone could walk on that carpet in Wellington boots, failed to notice any kind of snub in Joanna's greeting, if snub was intended.

'Yes, Joanna. I've made myself at home. I've had a cup of tea. Well, mug of tea – I hope you don't mind?'

'It's everyone for themselves around here these days. Did we know you were coming?'

'I think you did, my dear. I telephoned a message, though it's possible the person I spoke to didn't take it all in.'

'Duncan's out,' Joanna announced flatly. 'I expect it's him you really want to see, isn't it?'

'I'm always delighted to see you, my dear, but, yes, there was a tiny matter I did want to talk to Duncan about, yes.'

'I expect I could find him, if you really wanted.'

'Yes, well – but there's no hurry. You see, I had rather thought I might stop over. You know, as I used to when . . . Hugo was here.'

At least Joanna gave no hint of exasperation or annoyance at this statement. 'Of course. Whatever you like. I'll give Duncan a ring, though.'

'Very well.'

She clumped purposefully over to the British Telecom Viscount phone which sat, incongruously modern, on the club fender in front of the empty grate. She dialled a number from memory. In a second or two her call was answered.

'Is that Merrilee?' she trumpeted. 'Is he there?'

There was another pause while Alec wondered where on earth Duncan could be that was presided over by a person called Merrilee.

'Yes, it's me,' Joanna continued eventually. 'Your Uncle Alec's here. What shall I do with him?'

Alec listened impassively.

It was possible that Duncan made some suggestion involving an expletive, but Joanna's expression did not give him away.

There was a further pause while Duncan, apparently, continued to speak. When he had finished Joanna did not say goodbye to him but simply slapped down the receiver.

'He'll be over in half an hour,' she told Alec, putting on as friendly a tone as she was able.

'He's not far away then?' Alec gently inquired.

'He's with his girl friend, if you must know.' Joanna stared at him for a second or two. 'Mistress, if you like. That's how I knew where to find him.'

There was no comment that Alec could usefully make.

'He says you can stay – but why don't you go to Hugo's? That's my suggestion. I think you'd be happier there.'

'At Huddleston? Well, I'd certainly intended looking up Hugo and Molly, but I thought they'd only just moved in, so I hadn't made any . . . arrangements.'

'Would you like to give them a ring?'

'All right, my dear, p'raps I'd better do that.'

The matter was soon sorted out. Alec would spend the night with Hugo and Molly. Next day one of them would take him to visit his mother, the Dowager Countess, in Stoke Cansdale. Alec felt happier now that this had been sorted out, but waited with some apprehension for Duncan to come back from his mistress's. Alec didn't know what to make of Joanna's stoic forbearance, whether to admire or pity her for it.

At about six, Alec was aware of doors banging in the distance and sensed the whirlwind that was Duncan approaching. He clutched the arms of the Napoleonic leather chair and hoped the confrontation wasn't going to be too painful.

The library door shot open, and Alec shrank ever so slightly away from the blast. It was quite a shock for him to discover Duncan approaching with a beaming smile on his face and his hand outstretched.

'Hello, Uncle, how goes it?' Alec's thin hand was pumped up and down. 'Had a go, have you?' Duncan gestured at the shining chrome. 'I have to use it. So much flab these days. It's not here permanently, don't worry. Just waiting for a new home. So many changes to be made.'

Alec said he was glad, and wondered quite what the 'changes' would be. 'Fancy a drink? What'll it be?'

Alec noticed that Duncan made for the cabinet where the books he had been looking for used to be kept, fished a key-ring out of his pocket and opened the doors to reveal various bottles and mixers, and a few not very clean glasses.

'I think it's time for a sherry,' Alec said, conscious that he was not being as heroic in his choice of alcohol as Duncan was sure to be.

'We've got some here, I think,' Duncan replied, reaching deep into the recesses. 'Tio Pepe do you?'

'By all means,' Alec said. A moment later his nephew handed him a tumbler-full. Duncan poured himself a Famous Grouse and raised his glass. 'Your health, Uncle!'

Alec was still shaken by Duncan's affability. 'Your health, too, Duncan – and to your stewardship of this old house!'

'Ah, yes,' Duncan said, swallowing deep, almost audibly enjoying the sensation in his throat. He slumped into an armchair not far from his uncle.

'Now, is there something I can do for you?' Duncan shot the question so that for a second or two Alec almost visibly recoiled.

'Well . . . oh, dear . . . you rather put me on the spot, dear boy!' Alec did a little paddling gesture with his hands, almost spilling some of his sherry in the process. 'You see, I have this little worry and . . . and, well, when I told your brother Rupert about it he said to come and see you and spread it out before you.'

'Quite right, quite right,' Duncan said encouragingly, apparently unperturbed by the suggestion that his stepbrother and uncle had been in cahoots. 'What is it then?'

Alec hesitantly told him about Hugo's payments over the years and how he wondered whether they would continue now that Duncan had taken over the Cansdale estate. Duncan could surely appreciate what it meant to Alec, and could he give him any reassurance on this point?

Duncan looked serious, but – for once – not as though he was about to explode with anger. He was thinking, or so Alec took the deepening ruddiness of his complexion to mean.

Then he spoke: 'No, nothing doing.'

Alec felt a sudden stab to his heart. It was true then. Duncan was still the callous lout he'd always been painted. So thrown was Alec by this initial sentence that he barely heard what Duncan went on to say until he was halfway through it.

'That's Father's affair. He should've mentioned it when the legal johnnies were round. Besides, I know you're family and all that, but I don't believe in something for nothing. Never have done. So, I tell you what, Uncle, I've got an idea. I need your help, you see. That way you can continue to receive an income, just as you have in the past.'

'Help you?' Alec inquired tentatively, not sure how he could possibly be of any assistance to a creature like Duncan.

'It's like this, you see. I don't know whether you've heard – I've made no secret of it round here – the house has got to pay its way from now on. We're going public. Making a business out of it. Everybody does these days. Make it a big day out for people.'

'But your father always—'

'I know what Father thinks, and I don't care. And now I have the house I'll bloody well do what I like with it. And that is where you could come in – if you wanted to.'

'I've always supported Hugo, perhaps selfishly,' Alec spoke up, pluckily. 'I've always felt the house belonged to the family and not to the world at large. You say everybody's doing it now, but, you know, less than one in twelve of the great houses in Britain is open to the public, even now.'

'How the others manage to pay their way, then, I just don't know. I'm going to do this, Uncle, and everyone in the family will have to adjust their views accordingly.'

'What precisely would you want me to do?'

'Well, I don't really understand the history of this place, or the family. I need someone to set it all down, write the guide book, and all that. You'd be a sort of official archive-wallah.'

Alec could hardly believe his ears. Duncan was making a brilliant suggestion. There could be nothing nicer! He would be able to have the run of the archives. It would be a rum do having to work for Duncan, but it would be worth it. His objections evaporated.

He smiled eagerly. 'All right, I accept.'

'Bravo,' said Duncan. 'Have another drink!'

Alec accepted another tumbler-full of sherry. Shortly afterwards, Duncan summoned the local minicab service and Alec departed to stay with Hugo and Molly at Huddleston.

He was eager to break the news to them – news not only of great personal satisfaction to him but also, surely, to them.

# CHAPTER 9

Rupert proposed to Jacky and she accepted. No one ever took that step with a clear head and no emotion, so it was not unusual that the move had been made as though the decision had taken them, rather than the other way round.

Rupert saw in Jacky not only an extremely beautiful woman but also a certain innocence. She was not afflicted with his kind of family background – all tradition, complicated loyalties and squabbles. With her, he could forget all that heavy baggage of breeding and heritage. He and she could just be their simple selves together.

Couldn't they?

Jacky saw in Rupert a handsome man – there was no doubt about that – dark, elegant and dashing. But there was much more to him than that. Although she didn't quite understand what he did for a living, she sensed he must be good at it, however diffident he might pretend to be on the subject. Above all, she felt safe with him. He would be kind to her. Rock-like, reassuring, reasonable. She also had to admit she was in love with him. At least, she had experienced all those pangs you were supposed to feel. She thought about him obsessively. Her preoccupation with him had not gone unnoticed. The men who photographed her had remarked on a particular bloom she had had about her in recent weeks. Jokingly they inquired what sort of sex she was enjoying that affected their exposure meters so.

But it was true. She had felt a different person since meeting Rupert. There had not been a great number of lovers in her past, she had kept herself to herself, but his effect on her whole personality was palpable. For one thing, she felt less ambitious. What was a trip to the sun worth if it took her away from him? Fortunately, looking after her body, which was the biggest chore of her working life, became a pleasure if it meant she was made more attractive for him.

Jacky had only one reservation as the inevitability of their getting engaged beckoned her on. She didn't yet feel she knew Rupert very well. It wasn't that there were corners of his heart or personality closed to her. She didn't feel that. It was just that there was a part of his life she felt excluded from. And she had connived at this exclusion. They had both pretended that their families did not matter to them. But Jacky's family in fact mattered a great deal to her; it was Rupert who had really been responsible for the pretence. He clammed up when she inquired, ever so gently, about the Hookes. She could tell he was a bit of a toff, from somewhere higher up the social scale, but she had no idea of the true picture.

'The only trouble is,' Rupert admitted as soon as Jacky had agreed to marry him, 'I'll have to tell you about my people now. I've not been exactly forthcoming.'

'Skeletons in the cupboard?' She laughed, leant over and pressed an elegant finger against his nose.

'P'raps. Literally, even.'

'What *are* you talking about? No, don't tell me. Not until you've given me another kiss.'

Rupert lowered his face to hers and brushed the proffered lips softly. Jacky reached up and ran her fingers through his hair as she seemed compulsively drawn to do.

'I've tried to keep it from you, but I come from a rather complicated family.'

Jacky slid off the sofa and on to the sheepskin rug.

'Don't worry,' she said, soothingly. 'You wait till you meet *my* lot!'

The most immediate questions, however, were how they should marry, and where, and when. Rupert was dead against a white wedding, though Jacky was sure her father wouldn't mind forking out for one. In fact, he would insist on it, given half the chance. Aware of the likely clash of worlds if the two families met, Rupert thought it would be best to make a quick dash for a registry office, and announce the accomplished fact to the waiting world in due course. They would make it known to both families that they were going to get married, and that they were unofficially engaged, if people wanted to think in those terms. It was then that Jacky said, 'You'd better meet my people – just so you know what you're letting yourself in for.' Rupert hadn't begun to think how he would reciprocate.

And so, on a cold, late November Sunday after their minds had made themselves up, Rupert steered his MG in the direction of the City and then on further eastward towards Essex. It was unknown land, a rather disturbing suburbia in a bleak landscape. When they reached Brentwood, with Jacky giving him directions, Rupert began to feel apprehensive. The affair had just been theirs till now, known to none except for a few mates like Henry Rowlandson. It was about to become official, a family matter, and he did not relish the prospect.

Jacky told him to turn left down a tree-lined road – Dorset Avenue, it was called – which had one or two large detached houses sprinkled among the semis.

'Here we are, on the right.'

Rupert found himself parking behind an old but very large Mercedes. There was another on the drive outside the double garage. Inside was a souped up Mini and some sort of Ford.

'Come on, let's get it over with.' Jacky smiled at him sweetly, and gave him a peck on his slightly pink cheek. She unfolded her legs carefully out of the car. They were lagged against the cold in tights. She drew her short woollen coat round her and shook her hair, glad to be out of the confined space. Rupert casually pushed the car door shut and didn't bother to lock it. He was wearing his usual Sunday denim, but with an expensive black leather jacket over it, and a decorative pale blue silk scarf.

They walked up the path which split the small front garden exactly into two. The garden was not cared for. It looked as though it was weeded and mowed and kept tidy, but no attention was ever paid to the plants. Nothing new had been put in for a very long time. The front door was enshrouded in a glass porch, more modern than the rest of the house. Rupert noticed an unsightly security alarm hanging over the door which opened before they reached it.

'This is Rupert,' Jacky said without preamble, tugging him forward.

Rupert assumed the woman smiling in the doorway was Jacky's mother. 'Hello, Mrs Moore,' he said and gave her a kiss. He was rather taken aback to see how young she was. Even though she had to be in her forties, she seemed ten years younger, and certainly dressed like it. She wore quite stylish clothes, her hair was bleached blond, her make-up was a little studied – why did women put so much blue round their eyes? thought Rupert – and she was tanned. All in all, quite a contrast to Jacky who rarely wore make-up when she wasn't working and who chose clothes of the utmost simplicity. Still, Cynthia Moore patently *was* Jacky's mother, even if the gloss of sophistication that Jacky had acquired was lacking. Most curious of all, Rupert observed, on the long false nail of the smallest finger on her left hand, Jacky's mother wore a diamond stud.

'He's very nice, isn't he?' said Mrs Moore, sizing him up. 'If you don't mind my saying, you make a lovely couple. You've found a nice one there, Jacks. And no mistake.'

Rupert bowed modestly, and couldn't help laughing.

'I hope you're right,' said Jacky. 'Before Dad comes, I think you ought to know. We're getting engaged.'

'Oh, lovee!'

'Or we've got engaged – I'm not sure which. It's a bit vague.'

Cynthia Moore hugged her. 'You've done well for yourself, my girl. So glad!' Then she gave Rupert a hug. He was quite amazed by all this warmth. 'My . . .' And she looked at him again. 'You're a real Rupert, aren't you?'

The man so named didn't want to know what she meant by that.

'Come into the lounge. We'd better open a bottle to start with, hadn't we?'

Cynthia Moore beckoned them into a room which had been done up to resemble a lounge in a Spanish hotel. There were long, dark brown, reproduction leather sofas, old-fashioned oil lamps, rather Spanish-looking paintings, and over in the corner a small bar with white stools in front of it.

'Do you go to Spain a lot?' Rupert asked politely.

'Didn't she tell you? We've got a flat in Marbella. Well, not exactly *in* Marbella. It's at a place called Puerto Banus. You know round there?'

'No. I've never been.' Rupert thought he'd heard something about Puerto Banus, but couldn't think what it was for the moment.

'Well, I'm always going there. Where do you think I got this?' She indicated her tan. 'Not in Brentwood. I'd live there all the time given half a chance.' She went back to the door and called upstairs: 'Freddie – they're here. Hurry up.'

She turned back to Rupert. 'Always the same on Sundays. We went to the Alhambra last night. He never gets up before noon if he can help it on a Sunday. Always has to read the papers. Not the posh ones, you follow. More your *News of the World* and that.'

Rupert smiled and made a gesture with his hands to show that Mr Moore's Sunday morning preoccupation was both normal and under-standable. It was hard to get a word in edgeways with Jacky's mother. He'd heard of garrulous mothers-in-law and now he realized he'd found one for himself.

'You any good at opening bottles, Rupert?'

'By all means.'

' 'Course he is,' teased Jacky, lapsing towards her mother's tone of voice. 'He's always opening bottles – aren't you? Bites off the corks with his teeth!'

Cynthia laughed and handed him a bottle of Sainsbury's champagne, pointing at the tall coloured glasses on the edge of the bar. 'Pour four, dear. Mark'll be along shortly, I imagine.'

Rupert had heard talk of Jacky's brother who was a year or two older than her. It looked as if he was going to meet the whole family.

No sooner had he eased the cork out of the champagne bottle than Freddie Moore bounded into the room. He was dressed from top to toe in golfing casuals, a small bullet of a man, stocky, restless, never still for a moment, and curiously pallid for a golfer, if indeed he ever played the game.

He immediately fell upon his daughter and hugged her with great affection.

'How are you, darlin'? There . . .!'

As an afterthought, he shook Rupert by the hand without quite looking him in the face.

'I told you, didn't I?' Cynthia said to her husband. 'They're getting engaged. So I opened the champagne.'

'Fantastic!' said Freddie and hugged his daughter again. 'Is he a good 'un?' She made no reply, but searched for her boy friend's eyes and reassurance.

Rupert lightly suggested that they wouldn't, of course, dream of claiming to be engaged until he'd formally asked Mr Moore's permission.

'Nah, nah,' Freddie rattled back. 'No need for any of that. Honest! I know my Jacks'll do whatever she wants to do – won't you, love? – never mind your mum and me.'

Jacky laughed, knowing her father would say that, as he always did.

'Here's to you both,' said Freddie, raising his glass. 'And about bloody time, if I may say so. I was beginning to think there was something wrong with you.' He squeezed his daughter, then half-turning to Rupert said, 'You've done well here, my son. She'll keep you in the style to which you are accustomed, I expect!'

'Seems like it,' Rupert replied, attempting to remove the sting from the slightly barbed joke. 'She does very well with her work.'

'Yeh. We're very proud of her, aren't we, Cyn?'

Jacky blushed and told them both to shut up.

'You do something useful, do you?' Freddie asked Rupert, swaggering a touch.

Rupert smiled. 'Depends what you mean by useful. I help people run their businesses. Does that count?'

'Strewth! Better help *me*!' Here Freddie laughed a little too mirthlessly and loud. 'Surrounded by dick-heads these days. You're a money man, then?'

'Yes, 'fraid so.'

'Nah, nah, no need to apologize – it's all the go, isn't it? I suppose you're a bleeding yuppie into the bargain?'

'It's very hard not to be called that when you do what I do and when you're my age.'

'Leave him alone, Freddie. He's lovely as he is.'

'Well . . .' Freddie cast around for some other topic. 'Like our lounge do you, Rupert?'

'Yes, it's smashing,' the potential son-in-law replied.

'It's an exact copy of the one we've got in Puerto Banus.'

'I told him about that,' Cynthia put in. 'He's never been there.'

'Never been to the old Puerto? We really, really love it there – don't we, Jacks? Lots of friends live there. Mind you, we have to go to them, 'cos not all of them can come to see us.'

Rupert suddenly understood. Costa del Sol, Costa del Crime.

Jacky pushed a playful fist into her father's shoulder and told him to shut up.

Mrs Moore stood up. 'Time for lunch,' she announced. 'Why don't you come through to the kitchen now? Bring your glass with you, Rupert. If Mark's not here, we'll start without him.'

They adjourned to the kitchen/diner for the traditional Sunday lunch – or dinner as the Moores called it – such as Jacky and Rupert had not had for some time. There was roast beef and potatoes, two veg and a non-stop supply of what Freddie called 'bow-jolly noov'. It had just come in and he had brought home a whole case.

During the meal, Freddie fired a continuous stream of questions at Rupert designed to elucidate who precisely his darling daughter was proposing to align herself with.

'Where are you from – your people, I mean?' he asked, while happily putting away enough food for two.

'Wiltshire, basically.' Rupert knew this sounded unrevealing and added, 'Near Swindon, really.'

'Where precisely?'

'You know Wiltshire?'

'Been through it,' Freddie replied.

'My parents have a house in a little village called Stoke Cansdale – not far from Craswall. Do you know it?'

Freddie chewed on, busily working out whether he did or not.

'Heard of Castle Cansdale,' Freddie announced.

'Ah, well,' Rupert sighed, 'that's very near . . .' Then, trying to get the matter out of the way, he added, 'That's where they used to live, in fact, until last month.'

Freddie swallowed what he was chewing and looked at Rupert properly for the first time. 'In a bleedin' castle, eh?'

'Well, it's not actually a castle. It's a big house. It's just called that.'

'And your name's Hook, or something?'

'That's right. With an "e".'

'Isn't there an Earl Hooke? Or is that the name of a pub?'

Rupert joined in his future father-in law's laughter.

'Yes,' he said, as evenly as he could, 'he's my father in fact.'

'Gosh! Jacky – what have you brought home with you?'

His daughter had stopped eating too, and was staring at Rupert, open-mouthed. How had he managed to keep this from her?

There was a moment's stunned silence round the table as Cynthia looked at Freddie, then at Jacky, while Jacky continued to stare at Rupert.

Finally, Jacky exclaimed, 'You didn't tell me *that*, Rupert! You said—'

'I know, I know what I said. But it's true. He doesn't live in the big house any more, that's what I meant. My stepbrother does.'

'Let's get this straight,' demanded Freddie bossily, extracting a piece of gristle from his mouth and parking it on the side of his plate. 'If your dad's an earl, aren't you a bleeding lord or viscount or something?'

'No, no. I could be, I suppose – except that I'm the youngest, and there isn't a viscountcy to give my brother as a courtesy title. He's just Lord Wymark and I'm just "the Hon.", though I don't use it if I can help it.'

Cynthia sat quite stunned by these revelations.

'And what about your stepsister?' Jacky asked.

'Ah, well, you see, she's Lady Sophie – there's no rhyme or reason to it. It's all very complicated . . .'

A silence descended on the table as Freddie digested this latest piece of information. Rupert was oddly gratified that Freddie seemed aware not only of the Hookes but of some of the ramifications of titles.

He was even more intrigued to find, after lunch, when Freddie took him aside for a family chat while Jacky and her mother cleared up, that in Freddie's den – which chiefly consisted of a bank of filing cabinets and a very bare desk – there were well-thumbed copies of *Who's Who* and *Debrett's Guide to the Peerage*.

Freddie made Rupert look himself up under the Hooke family name in both books. Rupert was able to point to his name in Debrett as 'Hon. Rupert Hooke, *b.* 1960'.

'Amazin', bleedin' amazin'!' declared Freddie. 'Well . . .! You'd better take our girl to meet your people, Rupe – and damn quick! After all, she'll be marryin' into the bleedin' aristocracy, won't she? And as I know too bleedin' well, you don't just marry a girl, you marry the whole bleedin' family! I mean to say, you should see Cynthia's mother, talk about a fuckin' dragon . . .!'

'I hadn't really thought about it that way,' Rupert replied calmly.

'You'll find out soon enough, my lad,' added Freddie, a trifle ominously. Changing the subject, he asked Rupert if he was interested in cars. 'That your MGB outside?'

'Yes.'

'Used to like 'em once. Always wanted one, thought they looked a treat. Then I got one. I mean! Bleedin' battery's under the back seat, innit? Any bother and you 'ave to 'aul the fuckin' seat out! And it's open to the road, almost, so you get all this corrosion and that. Honest, I'd 'ad it up to 'ere with MGs by the time I was finished. Never bought a British car since. Not worth it.'

'There is that,' Rupert agreed.

'You met Mark? No, 'course you 'aven't. He's my boy. Jacky's brother. He's a car maniac.'

'Is he in the trade?'

'In a manner of speakin'. Loves tearing 'em apart and stickin' 'em back together again. You'd like him. He should've been here for lunch, but he's like that. Always off on some little errand. Never know what he's up to half the time.'

Rupert vaguely realized that some people thought that he himself was 'like that', for similar reasons.

'I'd like to meet him,' said Rupert.

'So, you're all right then?'

Rupert wasn't sure what Freddie meant.

'You and Jacky. You'll be okay?'

'If it's all right with you.'

' 'Course it is. She's got 'er 'ead screwed on. Knows what she's doing. Always has done. So good luck to you. And anything you need, anything you want, you get straight on to me, my son, and I'll see you right.'

'That's very kind of you,' said Rupert.

The two men went back down to the lounge where Jacky and her mother were deep into girl talk over the coffee and chocolates. Freddie scooped up a handful and offered the box to Rupert who declined.

'Ah, here's Mark,' said Freddie, jumping up almost as soon as he'd settled on to the sofa. He went out and brought his son in, rapidly telling him Jacky's good news.

Mark greeted his sister in friendly enough fashion, if not with hugs and warmth, and then turned to meet Rupert. He didn't shake him by the hand but said, 'Pleased to meet you.'

'Me, too,' answered Rupert.

Mark was about twenty-six and had obviously just emerged from the vicinity of a car engine. He had his father's bullet head but topped with longer greased hair. He wore a motor-racing top, scuffed jeans with the knees scooped out, and very dirty old trainers. He was smoking and continued to smoke. Every ounce of charm seemed to have been scraped

99

off his personality. Rupert did not like the look of him one bit. Could he really be from the same stock as Jacky?

'Rupe 'ere's got an MGB-GT!' mocked Freddie, as though this was a huge joke that Mark would enjoy sharing.

'Ha,' was the limit of Mark's comment on this.

'And he's the son of a bleedin' earl!' Freddie added. 'What do you make of that, boy?'

Mark found nothing to comment on in that. It was a consideration completely outside his world and meant nothing to him.

'Uh-huh.'

'Well . . .' Freddie seemed to relax now for the first time. Mark sat down uneasily, not saying anything, and obviously wishing he was elsewhere. Rupert and Jacky were also wishing they could be off alone together.

Rupert kept thinking to himself, so this is family life, this is what I'm marrying! But he also tried to tell himself it didn't matter that he felt uncomfortable. After all, he wasn't going to spend his life with these people. They would be in the background.

He caught Jacky's eye, as if to drink in her support. She smiled reassuringly. The remarkable thing about her was that although she was patently one of this family, she was equally capable of being at her ease in very different company. She was also blessed with the kind of looks which meant that, though she was clearly a Moore, she could pass acceptably in a different social world – as a Hooke, even. She was someone very special.

'When did you first meet? Tell me that,' asked Cynthia. 'Let's hear the whole *Woman's Own* bit!'

Rupert explained. 'I have an old friend – we were at school together – called Henry. He's a dreadful fixer, isn't he, Jacks? He laid on a trip to a club and we were both of the party.'

Jacky nodded.

'What sort of club?' asked Freddie.

'The Carillon in—'

'I know where it *is*,' Freddie butted in, snappily, almost being rude to Rupert for the first time.

Rupert stopped short and hesitated.

'We went on from there,' he added, to round off the would-be anecdote. Then he felt he'd put his foot in it, because it sounded as though they'd gone straight off to bed together, which was certainly not the case. Once Rupert had been quizzed by the mother of an earlier girl friend as to whether he had sampled her cooking. 'Only at breakfast,' he had replied, plunging all present into embarrassed coughing.

'You go much to the Carillon?' Freddie persisted, interested.

'No, 'fraid not,' said Rupert. 'I'm a hopeless gambler. And I just don't have that kind of money. My friend Henry does, fortunately, and bankrolls me from time to time. We'll always be grateful to him, though, won't we, darling? Without him, we'd never have met.'

Freddie continued to pursue his line of thought: 'How much does it cost to join the Carillon? A year.'

Rupert had no idea, and another of those family silences descended on the five of them. Mark did nothing to relieve it, but stared sullenly into the fireplace where the artificial log was half on. He was keen to get back to his cars.

'I think we ought to be getting back to town,' Rupert quietly suggested when a suitable moment presented itself. 'Thank you for the lovely lunch.'

'Nice to meet you, Rupe,' said Freddie, looking him somewhere near the eyes for only the second time, but making no attempt to stay his departure. 'Let us know when the wedding's to be. We'll 'ave a big 'un.' He squeezed Jacky quite soppily.

'That's most kind of you, Mr Moore,' said Rupert.

'Freddie, *please*. Call me Freddie.'

'Anyway, most kind.'

In another few minutes, the ordeal was over. Rupert and Jacky were heading back west.

'Thank you for doing that, love.' Jacky touched Rupert's forearm on the steering wheel. 'You were a big hit. They really liked you.'

'You think so?' How can you tell? I felt a bit of a prat most of the time.'

'No, you weren't. It'll be just as bad when I meet your dad and mum.'

Rupert didn't respond directly.

'I still think,' he eventually remarked, 'it would be best if we could have a quiet wedding on our own. The thought of my lot and your lot getting together is pretty horrendous.'

Jacky felt disappointed but reluctantly agreed with him. 'You should have told me you come from a posh family. What am I supposed to do? Curtsey to your mother all the time?'

'Nothing like that. I didn't think it was important.'

'Of course it's important if your dad's a bleedin' earl!'

'I mean, I don't think it *should* be important. You're you and I'm me, and that's all the matters, surely.'

They drove on in silence until Jacky said, 'My dad'll be awful put out if he can't pay for a posh wedding, the whole bit – specially now he knows about your dad. That's my old man, I'm afraid.'

'We'll have to see.'

Jacky wanted to know when she would meet Rupert's folks.

'How about after we're hitched?' Rupert replied.

'So you're sticking to it – the registry office?'

'I think so, darling, don't you? I'd explode if I had to go through with the whole white wedding bit. Why not a wedding just between ourselves? After all, we're the important bit.'

Jacky thought quietly to herself and then smiled. 'All right, have it your own way – but I'll moan about it for ever!'

'Please,' Rupert pleaded, 'I couldn't stand that . . .'

'Only joking.'

'I liked your mum.'

'That's all right. You're allowed to do that. What about Freddie?'

'I'm working on that. He's a bit of a tornado, isn't he?'

'Yes, but he's my dad, and he's the only one I've got.'

# CHAPTER 10

After his surprisingly agreeable encounter with Duncan at Castle Cansdale, Alec had gone on to Huddleston and stayed the night with Hugo and Molly in a very good mood indeed.

'Duncan has found a way of continuing my allowance from the estate,' he confided to his elder brother as they sat together before the log fire. 'There's an element of *quid pro quo* but I'm very happy with it. I'm to organize the archives and write a guide book.'

'Oh, are you?' Hugo replied huffily. 'Well, that'll keep you out of mischief, I expect.'

'What mischief's that?'

'Never mind. You know what I mean.'

Hugo told Forager and Admiral, the wolfhounds, to lie down in front of the fire because they were blocking the heat where they were. Both dogs obeyed meekly, taking up most of the hearth rug in the process.

'I have to say,' Alec went on, undaunted by his brother's crustiness, 'that Duncan may have a point about opening the house to the public. Like you, I've always seen that as a last resort – marking its end as a family home, first and foremost. But I think in this day and age, he's probably right. It's a way of raising the money to keep the place in trim. It'll enable him to get the proper grants and such. As long as he doesn't go too far, I think it could be the best thing in the long run.'

Hugo stroked his nose and ran a rather frail hand through the hair on the right side of his head. He sighed.

'I haven't changed *my* mind, I can tell you. But let's not talk about it. I'll only get angry. Anyway, I'm glad you've got something out of it. I know the little bro. sometimes has a hard time.'

Alec was touched by his brother's last remark. The note of reasonableness was rarely to be heard on Hugo's lips.

'I had dinner with Rupert very recently,' Alec said. 'A very jolly time.

He seems to be doing very well at this money-making lark. We talked of all sorts of things.'

'Well, you are privileged, to be sure,' Hugo said ironically. 'I can't think when he last came home.'

'We talked of that, too. I think it's a complicated reaction to his circumstances. He adores Castle Cansdale but keeps away because he knows it's all Duncan's. There's not much love lost between those two, as perhaps you know.'

'What's the reason, d'you suppose?'

'Different mothers? I think there's some unease on that score. He thinks Duncan treats Molly badly. But I don't want to be a stirrer.'

'He's quite right, or course. Duncan is certainly guilty of that. But I wish someone would point out to Rupert that staying up in London, and keeping himself to himself, is no way of curing that problem. Did you find out what he was doing with himself?'

Alec smiled. 'I think he's melting maidens' hearts all over the metropolis. Or if he's not, there's something wrong with the damned maidens!'

'Be specific.'

'How can I be?'

'Well, I hope he takes care of himself. This AIDS thing is frightful – though I suppose it might put a stop to all the promiscuity.'

'Really, Hugo, if you think that . . . I've no doubt that Rupert is as careful as he is discreet. He's an intelligent boy, even if he didn't go to the university. I think he's quite capable of looking after himself.'

'But you think he's putting himself about, do you – with the opposite sex?'

'Good God, Hugo, you *are* an old humbug! With his looks and charm, he'd be a fool not to. Now, wouldn't he? Have you forgotten what it was like, Hugo?'

The Earl stood up, disturbing the wolfhounds, and fumbled about looking for the drinks tray away from the light.

'I don't know what you mean, Alec,' he said from the discreet shadows. 'I can't speak for you, of course – and thank goodness – but I'm not going along with the view that we all fornicated when we were young and so it's all right for the present lot to do the same. It simply wasn't true in my case, and I'm very hurt you should even suggest it was.'

Alec shrank ever so slightly within the wings of the leather armchair, so as not to have to meet his brother's eyes. Then, on second thoughts, he leant forward out of the light and stared into the gloom where Hugo stood.

'For heaven's sake, Hugo, get me some sherry quickly.'

'I thought you'd had enough of that with Duncan.'

'There you go again! Still being big brother. You haven't let up since we were boys together. Always the responsible one. Always the figure of rectitude. Well, you can ease up, old fellow! Besides, I'm simply not taken in. Nor ever have been. Just because you've been married for years and years you've got in the way of thinking you were always pure in such matters. But you weren't. So come off it!'

Hugo came back into the light of the fire and peremptorily handed Alec a glass of sherry that was only half full.

'It's just as well Molly isn't with us,' he said sitting down again. 'I don't like mucky talk. There's too much mucky talk these days, and there's too much mucky goings-on. Duncan, it goes without saying, is quite incorrigible. Sophie, I'm not so sure about – though I was told the other day she'd been described by Billy Wiltshire's boy as a "Deb". D'you know what that means?'

'Not a debutante, I presume?'

'No. Short for "Debenham" – as in "Debenham and Freebody". I think you get the imputation?'

Alec laughed. 'That's lovely. I must remember that!'

'It's not funny, Alec! It's *filthy* that anyone should say such a thing about my daughter. I'm sure there's not a word of truth in it, anyway.'

'Oh, Hugo, you're quite impossible! What does it matter? We've all done it at one time or another – the family, everybody. Just because you read the lesson in church on Sundays doesn't mean you can pretend you never did it!'

'But I didn't!'

'That's not what I've heard. I bet if Toby was here he'd have a tale to tell about what you got up to before the war!'

'Toby Blair? Lord Blair of Flaxmoor as he is now (and have you ever heard of anything so ridiculous?). He would tell you nothing, because there's nothing to know. We haven't all led lives of debauchery and filth of the kind you have, Alec.'

The voices of the two elderly brothers had been rising steadily during this exchange. Forager stood up and stretched his legs, as though sensing that someone was about to enter the room. In a moment, Molly put her head round the door.

'You all right, you two?' she inquired. 'I'll have dinner ready in ten minutes.'

'Thank you, dear,' said Hugo. His wife's appearance reminded him to keep his voice down when talking with Alec on such disagreeable topics.

When she had gone out again, Hugo spoke a touch more reasonably.

'I take your point, Alec, but let's talk no more about it. It won't get us anywhere.'

There was a pause. Alec continued staring into the flames and wishing there was more sherry in his glass. But he was nicely warmed now and a little sleepy. He had a horrible feeling that wherever they were to have dinner would be freezing cold. Despite all Molly's valiant efforts, Hugo had brought with him from the castle a determination to suffer.

'Going back to Rupert,' Alec said, intent on being conciliatory, 'whatever your fears, I think he may be about to make it legal.'

'What's that? Get married, you mean?'

'Exactly. He told me there was some girl who was very special. Quite a big name in her own way, I believe. A model or some such thing.'

Hugo gasped. 'A *model*? For heaven's sake, can't he do any better than that!'

'There's no reason to suppose he *hasn't* done very well for himself. One just doesn't know.'

'And you think it's imminent?'

'I got that impression.'

Hugo said no more on the subject but merely grunted – as he now increasingly did about everything.

A day or two later, after despatching Alec back to London, Hugo decided it was about time he himself should pay one of his infrequent visits to the dreadful metropolis. Accordingly, he steered the Silver Cloud in the direction of Craswall, where he parked at the station, and caught the train up to London.

He did not enjoy the ride – having to share a First Class carriage (and not even his own compartment) with businessmen using their portable phones. He couldn't concentrate on reading, and the ink on *The Times* came off on his hands so that he was forced to make use of what they would insist on calling the 'toilet'. How different it was to travelling in his great-grandfather's day. The 5th Earl Hooke had had his own train which would steam up and down the Great Western Railway and deposit him conveniently at Bourton station. That, like so much else, had long since fallen victim to expenditure cuts.

Hugo watched the countryside rushing past. He enjoyed doing that. He also quite liked taking a meal on a moving train, so he had lunch. Even so, he would have preferred to drive. But he loathed the motorways and could no longer cope with the traffic in London.

On arrival at Paddington, he took a taxi to the Athenaeum where he would stay for a couple of nights. The rooms were no more than cubicles, but the bathrooms were vast, Victorian and cold. He felt at home in them. He could have gone to the House of Lords and collected his attendance allowance but as he had not spoken since his maiden speech in 1947 there was some doubt whether the clerks would recognize him and sanction the payments. He didn't have anything very much that he wanted to communicate on the issues of the day – though if there had been something on inheritance tax he would most surely have put in a word.

With the doggedness of the old, Hugo stuck to his plan. This was to see Rupert and tell him a few home truths. His younger son was thus bidden to the Athenaeum for drinks, before being taken to Wilton's for dinner.

Rupert presumed that this rare London meeting with his father must have something to do with the way in which he had distanced himself from the family. Hugo began with a carefully thought out piece of diplomacy. He was affable to the boy, greeting him warmly. He made it plain that he didn't really mind Rupert's noticeable absences from gatherings at Castle Cansdale, or now from Huddleston.

'Your mother and I would like to see more of you, but we quite understand how busy you are.'

Rupert shifted slightly in the worn leather chair, crossing and uncrossing the pair of faded blue jeans he'd put on with his tweed jacket. He had been wearing his suit all day at work as usual, but he made the change just to unsettle the waiters at the Athenaeum and at Wilton's. Or so his father concluded – though Hugo was determined not to show that he had noticed.

'So, how goes it?'

Rupert tried to answer this awkwardly generalized inquiry. 'Okay. Busy, busy.'

'Good. Glad to hear it.'

Silences filled the gaps, as in all the family conversations Rupert could ever remember having – even the Moores were not immune, he had found. A clock ticked, and sundry bishops, or men who looked as if they ought to have been bishops, snored beneath their newspapers.

Hugo had apparently decided not to whisper, though Rupert felt obliged to do so. Then Hugo pretended not to hear, cupping his hand round an ear to catch what his son was saying – which wasn't very much.

Hugo remembered he must be diplomatic and beamed at the boy. He really was very good-looking. No wonder Alec had jumped to conclusions about the effect Rupert must have on girls. But he had no responsibilities, after all. He had an easy, if privileged and confident, air. It was very impressive, and even his father worried about being taken in by it. But he must not lose sight of his objective.

He held back until they had adjourned on foot to Wilton's. Then he could wait no longer. 'Your Uncle Alec came to see us the other day,' he began.

So that explains it, Rupert thought. He waited for his father to brandish whatever unpalatable fact had been conveyed by that likeable but infuriating middleman. Yet he had to wait. Shrinking from his purpose, Hugo sidetracked himself.

'You know he's in cahoots with Duncan now?'

Rupert said that he did not.

'Your brother, as you may have gathered, is threatening to turn Cansdale into an amusement arcade.'

Rupert merely nodded, determined not to get embroiled in all that.

'As you know, I've always been against it, but Duncan can do what he likes with the estate now, more or less, and that's what he wants to do. Anyway, he's nobbled your Uncle Alec to help him with the history and all that, though God knows he could've asked me. What do you think?'

'I can't see it doing any harm, Father. And if it gives Uncle Alec something to do, it can't be all bad, can it?'

'That's what you think, is it?'

A silence followed while father and son consumed Wilton's lobster with the close attention its likely cost warranted.

'Your brother is behaving distastefully, as always,' Hugo eventually went on. 'Mucky business,' he snorted. 'Got this woman in the village. Been carrying on with her since before he went to the house. Met her on the show committee. Wife of an architect.'

Rupert asked his father how he knew all this – more to stop the flow than to elicit further information.

'Your grandmother is the fount of knowledge. Knows everything that's going on. Sits by her phone all day and fishes these unpalatable nuggets from her cronies.' Hugo laid down his knife and ran a rather weary hand over his forehead. 'Anyway, the upshot is, the woman's expecting.'

Rupert was quite surprised by this. But it was only to be expected that if Duncan fouled up his own nest he would set off an earthquake at the same time.

'When's it due?' he asked aloud, though this was surely the least relevant aspect of the matter.

'March, I believe. We've only just heard, of course.'

'She's going to have it?'

'Yes. She's not one to do anything about it, apparently.'

This was not the kind of conversation Rupert had ever had before with his father, let alone about his brother; at least it was novel.

'He really is the limit.' Rupert felt this was the least he could say in the circumstances.

'He's a blighter. Should be concentrating on the hand-over, and he's off seeing this woman all the time. As for Joanna and the girls, he seems to have no time at all for them. He's mean with money for them as it is, and now I suppose he'll have to shell out something when the baby arrives.'

'What'll they do with it?'

'The baby? Lord knows. Give it away, I hope. I've never met the woman – though I'm told I have – so I can't say.'

'Ah, well,' said Rupert as though to conclude the matter. He only succeeded in rounding off the diversionary topic of his brother's misdeeds and directing Hugo's attention to himself.

'Now, your Uncle Alec mentioned something about you and a girl. Seemed to think it was serious and you might be getting engaged. I hope she's suitable.'

So that was it! No wonder Hugo had been building up to it gradually.

'It's true,' Rupert offered quietly. 'There is someone. I think I rather . . . love her. In fact, I know I do. And yes, we will get married, though I don't know when.'

'But is she suitable?'

Rupert gestured that he did not know how to answer the question.

'You know what I mean. Is she suitable?'

'Of course she is. You'd love to have her as your daughter-in-law.'

'What about her family? You've met 'em?'

'Yes, I have. They're all right. They live in Essex. Quite well-off. Her father has lots of little businesses.'

'Doesn't sound right to me,' said Hugo severely. 'And she's a model – is that it?'

'She is, yes, and very successful at it.'

'Can't have you marrying out. It just won't do. Actresses, singers, tarts – they're not for marrying. I think you should pull out. How far are you into this?'

'We're unofficially engaged, if you like.'

'Her parents know?'

'Yes.'

'But you didn't think it was right to tell your mother or me?'

'You seem to have found out.'

Hugo stopped, realizing he was being too rough. He tried another tack.

'What is it that you've got against us? You never come to see us. You didn't even show up on my birthday. You're not *embarrassed* to belong to the family, I trust?

Rupert kept quiet. He simply could not begin to explain.

Hugo started again. 'There's such a thing as duty and obligation, you know. If you're born a Hooke, you can't just go your own sweet way. All right, you're not in Duncan's position. As things stand, you won't inherit the title or the estate. But you're still a Hooke. And it's just possible that you could inherit in some way one day – or your children might. One can never tell these days what may happen. So that's why its important you should marry the right sort of woman. Which this one you say you've set your heart on quite clearly isn't.'

Rupert was boiling. 'I'll do what I like, Father! You've got no hold over me. I don't have to have your approval. That's old hat.'

'I'm only trying to think what's best for you . . .'

'Oh, no, you're not! Don't give me that. You're leaning on me. None of that means anything any more. People get married now because they actually *like* each other, you know.'

Hugo looked wearily at his son, but said no more. The waitresses could see there had been an argument at the Earl's table. The old man seemed almost on the verge of tears. Little did they imagine the precise nature of the dispute, or that it was between a father and his favourite son.

'Rupert,' his father began again, 'it's very nearly Christmas. Won't you come and spend it with us at Huddleston? Your mother would like that. It'd be good to have you back in the family once more. See Sophie – you still like her, don't you? And, perhaps, by then you'll have got over this girl, and we can all be friends again.'

Rupert sat looking at his food, having stopped eating long ago.

Then, sharply, he stood up, pushed his chair back, threw his napkin on the table and said, 'This is ridiculous, Father!' He walked out of the restaurant.

Christmas came and went without Rupert's putting in an appearance down in Wiltshire. But he did phone his mother, from Brentford, where he was spending Christmas Day with Jacky and the Moores. There was to be no reconciliation with home for some time yet.

Meanwhile, a completely unexpected reconciliation had taken place at Castle Cansdale. And Lady Sophie Hooke found herself being drawn into a precarious relationship, albeit a working one, with her brother and his wife.

The name Waterwheel had been adopted by the design partnership Sophie worked for because the offices were in the Old Mill on the Bourton–Craswall road. The mill itself had been completely restored and the wheel turned idly within a large glass case, providing a backdrop for the reception area and shop. Sophie was reasonably diligent in her work, though fully aware that her name on the letterhead and her connections throughout the county were her principal attractions to the company. During the hunting season she might miss a couple of mornings a week, but would make up for them by working on Saturdays.

It was on such a Saturday in the New Year that Sophie looked up from her cluttered desk, full of fabric samples and furniture catalogues, and saw that Joanna Wymark had found her way to the open-plan office area and was heading towards her.

Her sister-in-law was not quite as incongruous in this setting as she would have been had she come in her usual country clothes. That morning she had at least put on a two-piece and might even have run a comb through her hair.

'Joanna,' Sophie cried, 'this is a surprise! Like some coffee?'

Sophie and Joanna hadn't spoken to each other since Christmas and even then nothing had been said about Merrilee Bridgewater's pregnancy. Talking now to her sister-in-law, Sophie had at first to tread carefully. But Joanna came straight out with it.

'Things are all right again with Duncan. I thought you'd like to know.'

Sophie's eyes narrowed in disbelief, but her first reaction was to chortle, 'Thank God for that! What came over him?'

'Well, you know that Merrilee he was carrying on with?'

'Of course I do. We're neighbours now – and Roger's working on a house with us.'

'Oh, is he? Turns out she got knocked up by some other bloke.'

'What? Not Duncan?'

'No. She'd been carrying on with them both at the same time. Right old scrubber. Anyway, it's the other feller's kid she's expecting. So Duncan's chucked her over and come back to me.'

'That's super!' Sophie's apparent enthusiasm successfully disguised all kinds of nagging questions that occurred to her – like how did Merrilee know which of her lovers was the father of the child she was expecting? And why should Duncan return so rapidly to Joanna with whom only recently it had appeared to be all over?

'It's all very lovey-dovey between us again,' Joanna chirped on happily. 'We're even back in the same bed,' she added with a rather forced leer, such as Sophie had never known her make before.

'My!' Sophie replied. 'Then perhaps he's over his mid-life crisis or his male meno, or whatever it was.'

'Hope so. Anyway, the upshot is, Duncan wants me to help with doing up the house. I'm very pleased.'

Sophie wondered whether her brother's need to have someone – anyone – to sort out the house for him might have had more than a little to do with his going back to Joanna. It would be just like Duncan to disguise a practical need with some emotional smokescreen.

'Well,' Joanna went on, 'as you know, Sofa, I'm absolutely hopeless about such matters. So, like I said to you before, I was wondering if we could involve you and your people in the effort?'

Sophie hesitated fractionally at committing her colleagues and herself to a course which would mean being sucked into Duncan's turbulent world, but conceded that, yes, there was probably something they could talk about there.

'Oh, good,' said Joanna. 'That'll be jolly, won't it? Keep it all in the family, too!'

'Yes,' said Sophie, with a nervous smile, 'I suppose it will.'

'Will you spread the word then? Ask your chums? I expect we'll have to have a great big meeting at the house, won't we? So you can get an idea of what needs to be done.'

'And how much it'll cost,' added Sophie cautiously.

'That's Duncan's department, not mine. Must fly. Thanks for the coffee. Delish. Got to get my hair done.'

My God, Sophie thought, her *hair done*! She really is back in the land of the living. Aloud she asked, 'Where do you go?'

'There's a girl at Split Endz in Craswall I've been told about.'

'Meg, is it?'

'Yes. You know her?'

'She does mine.'

'Well, there you are! Got to have it done for a photo.'

'A photo?'

'Yes, there's a man coming this afternoon to take Duncan and me. In colour. It's for the brochure.'

'What brochure?'

'For the house. You know, "Lord and Lady W. invite you to visit them at their very charming home in the heart of Wilts." sort of thing.'

'It's all systems go then?'

'Seems like it.' And Joanna rattled out of the office, apparently with a new lease of life and with new purpose.

Sophie looked at her watch and wished that lunchtime would come so that she could push off. Not that she had anything in particular to look forward to. Billy Wiltshire's boy might have dubbed her a 'Deb', but the likelihood of anyone making free with her body that weekend was distinctly zero.

# CHAPTER 11

'I gather the park was done by Capability Brown,' said Alastair Bevis, gesturing vaguely.

'Who else?' Duncan chortled. 'You find me a park around here he didn't do and I'd be most surprised. Must have been worked off his feet, that chap. "Availability Brown", more like!'

Bevis dutifully tittered.

'Ah, here she is! Come on, my love.' Duncan waved to Joanna who was hovering on the step at the front entrance. Solicitously, he went and took her by the hand and led her across the gravel drive. 'Darling,' he said, 'this is Alastair Bevis.'

'How do you do,' said the tall man in a suit but with a smart new oilskin over it. On his head he wore a deerstalker. 'And may I introduce Miss Valerie Taylor from ShakesPR Ltd, one of our associate companies. Lord Wymark. Lady Wymark.'

'Good,' said Duncan heartily, not terribly sure what the woman was wearing high heels for on a job like this. 'Where's the photo chappie?'

'He's already setting up his stuff. Can you see?'

Indeed, about a quarter of the way down the Fair Mile, there was a man doing something like that.

'Pity about the weather,' said Joanna looking upwards. It was quite mild for January, but there was a blustery wind, and although it was only just after lunch the light was not very strong. 'Don't you need sun for snaps?'

Alastair Bevis knew when he had to be indulgent to the client and forbore to point out that when you were paying a photographer like Jervais Richmond, you didn't just get snaps.

'It'll be all right, for the ones of you,' he replied diplomatically. 'He'll have to come back another day to take the other exteriors. The sun'll give a lift to that wonderful honey-coloured stone.'

'Can he really take us from that distance?' Duncan asked, with a puzzled frown.

'Oh, no. We need to go down the drive to him. He'll then be able to angle it so that the castle shimmers in the distance behind you – like a stage backcloth.'

'Excellent,' said Joanna, 'that's a brilliant idea!'

'That's what we're paying Mr Bevis for, dear,' said Duncan.

They decided to ride down the drive in Mr Bevis's shiny black Range Rover, lest Joanna's hair get disturbed by the wind.

Duncan had put on a greenish tweedy suit, pale blue shirt and a dark red and blue tie. Joanna, hair done, wore a blue silk blouse that she had bought the day before and a dark blue skirt. She had applied a good deal of make-up to dampen down the fires that usually lit her cheeks, and had inserted a pair of golden earrings which she hadn't worn since her wedding day.

'That's better,' Duncan had said, when he first saw her outfit – meaning it as a compliment.

Jervais Richmond soon had the pair taking turns to sit on a large oak chair he had brought to the location with him. First, Duncan stood behind the chair with his hands on Joanna's shoulders. Then they changed position and Joanna stood with her elbows resting on his shoulders while he sat.

'That's the one,' Richmond purred enthusiastically from behind his Pentax. He had rigged up a battery of lights to make sure that the lord and his lady stood out in the foreground of the picture. Mr Bevis and Miss Taylor were detailed to hold up white reflector boards to give the lift that was required to their subjects' chins and necks.

'Very Hollywood, eh?' Duncan laughed, enjoying the attention.

Then, at just the right moment, the sun came out and illuminated Castle Cansdale behind them.

'That's it, that's it!' Richmond trilled. 'Wonderful, wonderful! You know what they say: God's the best lighting gaffer . . .'

The picture that emerged from the session was a triumph of art. Lord and Lady Wymark smiled confidently in front of their home, and looked as in love as they had been (presumably) on the day they married. It was a very reassuring, winning pose, and Alastair Bevis was convinced it could be used in all the forthcoming publicity for Castle Cansdale.

'Lord and Lady Wymark extend the warmest of invitations to visit them at Castle Cansdale, home of the Earls Hooke for over two hundred years . . .'

Duncan and Joanna would be seeing much of Mr Bevis, Mr Richmond, Miss Taylor and their various colleagues over the next few months. Mr Bevis was co-ordinating the launch of Castle Cansdale as what he called a 'main arena player' in the stately homes business. He prodded Joanna to come up with plans for restoration work, particularly on the worn fabrics and murky pictures in the rooms that would be opened to visitors. He prodded Duncan to establish concessions for a gift shop, a garden centre, a craft workshop, and made him think seriously of a nature reserve in the park. But Duncan didn't really favour the idea of having lions running about and, besides, Bath had surely cornered the market for all that over at Longleat long ago?

Mr Bevis came up with a whole list of money-making ideas. There was much talk of laying on conference facilities, and he was keen to have visiting Americans able to dine with the Wymarks – if not actually stay the night (preferably in a haunted bedroom). Just now, as Jervais Richmond completed his work, Bevis asked, 'You have a haunted room, I hope?'

'No, I don't think so,' replied Duncan, 'but, if pressed, I'm sure we'll be able to find one!'

'Good,' said Bevis. 'Every little helps.'

'I'll get Alec on to it. See if he can dig up some ancestor who ought to be wandering around in his nightshirt, even if he isn't!'

'I haven't heard from Mr Hooke,' Bevis noted. 'I think he's getting on with the guide, but I'm not terribly sure.'

'Don't worry. I'll make sure there's no slacking.' Duncan sounded suitably menacing. 'Uncle Alec made off with a whole taxi-load of books and papers, so I expect something out of him soon.'

'Good. We're still on course for an Easter opening.'

'God, so soon!' Joanna exclaimed. 'Can't be ready by then, surely?'

'Lord Wymark', said Valerie Taylor, the PR woman in the high heels, 'I wonder, has Alastair said anything to you about *publicity*? We really should be *seeding* some stuff in the papers already – you know, Nigel Dempster's diary, that sort of thing. Are you doing anything newsworthy in the next few weeks?'

Duncan just about knew who Nigel Dempster was and what kind of diary he wrote, but offhand he couldn't think of anything that would interest him.

'Lady Wymark, too,' Miss Taylor persisted. 'Any ideas you have would be most welcome. You'd be amazed how a story involving your good selves will set people rushing along to see your home. On the off chance of seeing you, you see.'

'What do you want us to do?' Duncan asked jokily. 'Have an orgy? Get divorced? A juicy murder would be just the ticket, I suppose?'

Valerie Taylor laughed along with him. 'No, no, nothing like that – but every little helps. All grist to the mill.'

'We'll have to think, won't we, dear?' Joanna concluded rather guardedly. 'There are limits, surely?'

'Quite', said Mr Bevis soothingly. 'It's got to be the right sort of publicity.'

'But just think,' Valerie Taylor went on, 'just think what it did for the Spencers at Althorp when Diana married Prince Charles. No one had heard of it before; now everybody wants to go there.'

'Althrup,' Duncan mentioned casually.

'Sorry?'

'They sometimes call it "Althrup", not "Awlthorpe". Same trouble as "Woburn" and "Wooburn". Nobody ever knows which it is. At least they can all say "Castle Cansdale".'

'But there is a slight problem there,' Mr Bevis put in. 'I'm glad you raised it. I'm just worried that people will flock to Castle Cansdale – and they will flock, have no worries on that score – expecting a real castle. You know, one with a drawbridge and battlements.'

Duncan said he could see no problem.

'Not a problem exactly,' Mr Bevis fluttered on, 'it's just that Valerie and I and one or two others on the team have been trying to come up with a form of words – a slogan if you like – that'll encapsulate the Castle Cansdale experience without in any way misleading people.'

Valerie Taylor rattled off some of the already discarded attempts at providing that experience with a selling line: 'Much more than a castle . . . a family home'; 'There's nothing you can't do at Castle Cansdale'; 'Not so much a castle, more a stately home', and so on.

'We'll find the right one eventually, don't worry,' Bevis reassured. 'We shall, of course, submit our final selection for your approval.'

'Don't you think we ought to go indoors with these people?' Joanna suggested, not before time. The wind had already restored her hair to its more usual wildness, and it was spotting with rain. 'Cup of tea, perhaps?'

Jervais Richmond declined, so they bade him farewell and said they looked forward to seeing him again when he'd brought some more sun with him.

Back indoors, Joanna was all for having the tea in the kitchen, as they were still waiting for the new butler to arrive and it was the cook's day off. But Duncan sensed that the type of discussions they were having with Bevis Associates and ShakesPR Ltd would more fittingly be conducted in the Drawing Room.

He led the visitors off along the corridors, through the Saloon, and waited a considerable time for Joanna to arrive from the kitchen bearing the tea tray. On it were mugs of tea, the tea bags still floating in them.

'No one takes sugar, I hope?' she said. 'Seem to have run out.'

If Mr Bevis or Miss Taylor did take sugar, they didn't let on. Bevis was much more concerned at the inelegance of Joanna's service. Mugs and tea bags were not what lords and ladies were supposed to use. Afternoon tea must always be drunk out of the best china. Equally importantly it must surely be Earl Grey or Lapsang Souchong. But he'd have to broach the matter carefully, make subtle suggestions. After all, the clients always thought they knew best. There had already been a tussle over the photograph. Joanna wanted her three daughters to be in it – more with a view to cementing the born-again family feel, probably, than for any other purpose. Bevis was horrified. Those ugly little sisters with their blushes and their braces would do nothing for Castle Cansdale's image. He'd had to work very hard at scuttling that little proposal.

'Jolly good name you've got for your company, Miss Taylor,' Duncan told her. 'ShakesPR Ltd! How did you think of that?'

Valerie Taylor smiled graciously: 'Yes, it is rather good, isn't it? In fact, it's got nothing to do with the Bard at all. Originally we were going to call ourselves Stately Homes PR – S-H-P-R, you see – and then we thought it'd be fun to shove it into ShakesPR!'

Joanna failed to see the subtlety of this and was rather wishing the visitors would go. Then she could get out of all the unaccustomed finery she was wearing and back into her sloppy Joes. She felt, too, that Duncan was being taken in by these PR smoothies. He was playing at the stately homes game as with a new toy. Ever since he discovered that this is what you had to do these days if you were going to open your doors to the public he'd been in a state of excitement.

'You don't just put up a notice saying "Queen Elizabeth slept here" and hope for the best,' he had already told Joanna, quoting Mr Bevis. 'These days, it's very big business. All these chaps have degrees in marketing, you know.'

Joanna was sceptical. Even she was aware that, like lawyers, consultants could be a slippery lot. While they drank your tea, they were charging you an hourly rate for the privilege. Joanna wished that Duncan would be more sensible, otherwise he'd spend in advance all the money he was supposed to be going to make from the project.

'I'm not sure about this "heritage trail", you know,' – he was randomly picking on points that worried him – 'I mean, I'm not sure we have that much heritage really.'

'By the time your uncle has finished his research we'll be all right on that score,' Mr Bevis reassured him.

'Maybe. And do we have to have guided tours? I'd hate to have to go on one myself.'

'Perhaps we should reconsider. There's very little difference in costings between having tour guides and letting people wander from room to room. You've still got to have someone on duty in each room to keep an eye on things and answer questions. It's up to you to decide what you're more comfortable with really.'

'I'll think about it.'

'I wonder if you've thought any more about that idea of mine for the stables?'

'What was that? Remind me.'

'A video experience, tracing Castle Cansdale's history, using slides and music and so on.'

'Ah, yes. But how expensive would it be?'

'I don't have the costings to hand,' Mr Bevis purred. 'That would be undertaken by one of our associate companies.' For once he refrained from adding, 'In this business you only get what you pay for' – which was one of his favourite mottoes.

'Perhaps we should think about it then,' said Duncan. 'Will you let me have an estimate?'

'Most certainly, if that is what you want.'

'What d'you think, Jo?'

Joanna hadn't expected to be asked her opinion about anything.

'Don't see why not,' she replied, without giving the matter much thought. 'As long as you leave enough stables for me . . .'

'Of course, of course,' Mr Bevis said. 'I think we had earmarked one wing for conversion into public conveniences but, yes, yes, we can be flexible. Or we can put it somewhere else in the Spring Lodge complex.'

'Isn't that where the gift shop's going?' asked Joanna dizzily.

'No, no, it's all on the plan. You'd better have a copy. Here, it's in what was the land agent's office.'

'And where's Colin Blakiston going to go?'

'Up in the roof somewhere?' Duncan suggested.

'By the way,' Joanna added, still flattered that any attention was being paid to her views at all. 'I've had an idea for the gift shop.'

'Really?' Mr Bevis pricked up his ears, not totally sure what to expect. It was always dangerous when the client started having ideas.

'Yes, I was thinking about place mats.'

The consultant reached for a print-out of the two hundred or so products that were destined to adorn the shelves of the gift shop. 'Ah, I thought so, here they are – place mats, three sizes.'

'What's on them?'

' "Wiltshire Craft" is how they're described. They'll be very nice, I assure you, though I do believe, in all honesty, they're made in Birmingham!'

'Well, I was thinking,' Joanna went on, 'you know some people eat off place mats with old prints on them, why don't we do some with the house on?'

'Good idea, darling,' Duncan beamed. 'I know just the thing. Sophie gave Father a picture for this birthday – Waterman, or some such name.'

'Ackermann, I suspect,' suggested Bevis quietly.

'Yes, that's the fellow. Must have a word with Sophie, see where she got it from.'

'This is your sister?'

'Yes, Joanna's getting her to do a bit of work on the curtains and chairs – or at least to give us an estimate. She works with some local people. What are they called – Cartwright's?'

'No, Waterwheel, dear,' Joanna corrected him.

'Waterwheel, I've heard of them,' said Bevis. 'Excellent reputation.'

'Provided they don't charge too much,' added Joanna.

'Ah, well, you get what you pay for . . . !'

The discussion wandered on in an agreeable spirit until Joanna suddenly stood up and announced she must go and look after her horses. Alastair Bevis and Valerie Taylor departed amid promises of further meetings soon. Duncan continued to beam happily. Perhaps Miss Taylor's high heels were not so inappropriate after all. In fact, she had rather beautiful ankles. His plans were coming along. He was on the right track. It was all going to be very good fun.

Hugo, naturally, wasn't so sure. He did not know the exact details of what Duncan was plotting for the house and the estate because nobody ever told him anything. Marjorie picked up whispers, but they were mostly garbled to the point of gibberish by the time she had relayed them to her son.

The worst thing about relinquishing Castle Cansdale had been that it all but removed Hugo's purpose in life. If he had no house and lands to own, what was he there for? Time was hanging heavily on his hands. Molly had made Huddleston relatively comfortable, despite the cold and damp, but it was a matchbox of a house compared with what they had been used to.

Hugo fretted. He had nothing to do, nobody to order about. He became ruminative, gradually convincing himself that his time in the great house had been a golden age – a golden age Duncan was bent on ruining.

As Sophie became more and more drawn into Duncan's plans, she tried to soothe her father's worries and became a sort of unofficial go-between.

'He's quite a different person nowadays,' she told Hugo when she had popped over to see him one day, and Molly was out of the room making tea.

'I find that hard to believe.'

'No, really, Daddy. Since he left that Bridgewater woman and went back to Joanna, it's been amazing. He has her in on all the meetings and asks her opinion. It's bizarre!'

'And is she any help?' Hugo murmured doubtfully.

'Yes, Daddy, I think so. I mean, it was she who got me and Waterwheel involved. She doesn't know much about design, but at least she knows she doesn't know and has the wit to ask.'

'Glad you're involved, Sophie, anyway. Can you exert a restraining influence? Stop Duncan from putting in big dippers, lion tamers . . .'

'Daddy, it's not going to be like that! Very restrained, really! There'll be none of that. In fact, I think you'll be quite proud of it when it's all finished.'

'It has to be good' – Hugo sounded as though he was squeezing a concession out of himself – 'if he's involving the family. If he's got you and Alec helping him, that is good, I agree.'

'I'm not sure about Uncle Alec.'

Hugo commented by closing his eyes and faintly stirring with his hands.

'I expect he'll turn up trumps in the end,' Sophie said hopefully.

Hugo changed the subject.

'I saw Rupert before Christmas.'

'Yes, I know, Daddy. You told me.'

'Did I?' Hugo shifted in his armchair and looked at Sophie a little more closely. 'He wants to marry someone unsuitable.'

'What's unsuitable?'

'He wants to marry out.'

'Have you met her?'

'No.'

'How d'you know she's unsuitable?'

'She's a model.'

So it's still on, Sophie thought to herself. She had heard various reports through friends that Rupert had gone soft on some such girl. As ever, he had managed to avoid coming down for Christmas, but Sophie still had her lines of communication open.

'What's wrong with that then?' she asked aloud. 'If he likes her, good for him. I mean, if I turned up and told you I was getting married to a . . . well, I don't know, a garage mechanic, you wouldn't mind, would you?'

'I wouldn't be too sure,' Hugo continued frostily. 'I love you too much, Sophie, to want to see you cast yourself away on a whim. Same goes for Rupert.'

Sophie always felt a tremble of embarrassment when her father used the word 'love'. It was difficult to take it from him.

'When are *you* going to get married?'

'When I find the right bloke,' was the ritual answer.

'Your grandmother says you've been seeing a lot of Billy Wiltshire's boy.'

'That's hopelessly out of date! I haven't seen him for ages.'

'He'd be suitable.'

'Which is probably why I won't marry him. Can't you see that?'

Sophie cut off this conversation and made moves to be on her way. She loved her father but he really was too tiresome on this subject.

To everyone's slight amazement, Uncle Alec did turn up trumps. In record time he produced a guide book which traced the fortunes of the Hooke family from the days of the 1st Earl right down to Hugo and Duncan, and included all the anecdotes that had accumulated over the years. He laced his account with small details from the account books and inventories of house contents he had found among the family papers.

He had even found a ghost. It dated from the first house there had been on the site – the one built in 1508 – and was surely due to walk again. All in all, he had accomplished everything that had been asked of him.

Alastair Bevis edited out the more arcane connoisseur's footnotes and sent the manuscript off to ShakesPR Ltd for turning into a full-colour illustrated booklet costing £2.95. On the basis of Uncle Alec's work, he was also able to persuade Duncan that £45,000 on a video show to be continuously run in a stables cinema would be a wise investment. Duncan gulped, but agreed.

Everything was roaring along, the Easter Saturday opening date was being promoted far and wide. It was decided that the restoration work would have to be conducted on an ongoing basis, while the public was being admitted; to attempt to complete it beforehand would mean delaying the opening for at least a year.

As winter ended, all that was needed was a *coup de publicité* of the kind devoutly wished for by Valerie Taylor of ShakesPR Ltd. The weeks passed and nothing emerged, but when it came, it was exactly what she had had in mind. Lady Sophie's hand in marriage wasn't sought by any spare royal. Neither oil nor buried treasure was found on the Cansdale estate. It was something of a more domestic nature that ensured that Castle Cansdale received a bevy of mentions in the pages of the popular press.

Merrilee Bridgewater gave birth to a boy ten days before Easter. There was no doubt that Duncan was the father. For a start, the child had the Hooke family nose. It gave the lie to Duncan's mollifying remarks to Joanna about his mistress having had another lover. Duncan was the father and there was no getting out of it.

It was Roger Bridgewater, who assumed the role of negotiator. He turned up at the house right after the birth and berated the Lord Wymark in no uncertain fashion. This took Duncan completely by surprise as he had assumed the man he had cuckolded was a weakling. Merrilee's husband excelled himself, dropping hints of paternity suits with great aplomb and generally shaming Duncan with a valiant defence of his errant wife.

'Oh,' was Duncan's immediate reaction. 'Well, if there's no question, there's no question. What d'you want me to do about it?'

'Just acknowledge the boy's yours, that's all.'

'What? Not pay for it?'

'No, he can be adopted. Merrilee and I are past bringing up any more children. Both of ours are away from home now.'

'Would there be any chance of seeing it – I mean, him? I'd like to, you know. You see, I've never had a son . . .'

'I don't really think that'd be wise, do you, Lord Wymark? And I don't know what Merrilee would think.'

'It's a bit, you know, ironic, eh? Three daughters, needing an heir, and I get a son this way!'

'He can't inherit your title, I do know that much.'

'If you say so. It is possible in some cases to legitimize a kid after the event, but I'd have to marry the mother, and I don't think that's on in this case, is it?'

'Certainly not.'

'Pity, though.'

Duncan was not, of course, one to take no for answer when it came to the question of his seeing the boy at Craswall Hospital. So he pushed his way in. He was entranced by the small replica of himself, and someone on the hospital staff put two and two together and told the papers.

The heart-touching story of the heir-less lord who had had a love-child was soon spilling over out of the gossip columns and on to the feature pages. Tabloid photographers bribed their way into the hospital to snatch a picture of the infant. And, round about this point, Roger and Merrilee Bridgewater decided they couldn't bear to part with the child after all. Duncan had to agree to pay for the boy's upkeep, and straightaway put his name down for Eton. Raymond Bridgewater was christened by the Rev. Dutson at St Michael and All Angels – though, on that occasion, Duncan had the grace to keep away.

It was a merry tale which only served to confirm the view that relations between lords of the manor and their villagers were still very much as they had always been, even in the late 1980s.

Valerie Taylor of Shakes PR Ltd and the beautiful ankles had got what she wanted, a newsworthy, media star as the owner of a stately home. The public would come pouring in on the off chance of catching a glimpse of the randy noble lord.

# CHAPTER 12

'You'd look lovely in Highland sweaters. Ever thought of modelling?'

Rupert laughed at Jacky's suggestion, but rather liked the idea of earning a bob or two by showing off his good features.

'It may come to that, you never know.' He gave her a kiss. They were about to be married and their finances were a frequent talking point.

The fuss in the press over Easter about Duncan's indiscretion had increased Rupert's desire for a quiet wedding. Somebody would be bound to make the connection and he could do without that.

His father's earlier heavy-handed attempt to stop the match had served to convince Rupert both that Jacky *was* the right person with whom to spend the rest of his life and that it would be wise to present the marriage as an established fact to both sets of parents, so there could be no more interference.

So, in mid-April, at Chelsea Old Town Hall, the knot was tied. The male witness was Rupert's old friend, Henry Rowlandson, who had, after all, brought the couple together in the first place. Jacky asked her agent, Maddie Shapiro, to be the other witness.

Henry whisked all four off to the Mirabelle that Saturday lunchtime. Then Rupert and Jacky walked back to the mews flat off Lowndes Square, which would become their first home, and made their first love of married life.

They surfaced again about six o'clock in the evening and wondered what precisely they had done. There were no doubts about the marriage, but both felt guilt about the secrecy. Now the deed was done, they felt a tremendous urge to tell their families of their new status.

So, risking wrath on all sides, they each rang their respective parents. Jacky went first. Inevitably it was Mrs Moore who answered the phone.

'Guess what, Mum? Rupe and me got married!'

After only the very slightest of pauses, Cynthia shrieked with delight,

'Oh, my darling girl!' and had a little mope into the bargain. 'Without telling your dad – he'll skin you!' But not a word of condemnation of their having done it this way. Rupert, she just managed to get out, was a 'lovely, lovely man' and Jacky was a 'darling, darling girl'. Cynthia had to speak to Rupert and tell him how proud she was. He was nicely overwhelmed by the torrent of good-hearted emotion that poured out of the phone.

Then he had to ring Huddleston and tell his parents, suspecting that the reverse would be the case. Again, it was the mother who answered the phone. She always did; Hugo never, if he could help it. It was about the only thing he had in common with Freddie Moore.

'Mummy, it's Rupert. I've got some news I hope you'll like.'

'What is it, dear?' asked Molly cautiously, reaching the right conclusion just a fraction of a second before Rupert told her.

'I hope you won't be angry, but I have a wife.'

Again, the tell-tale pause before the joyful outburst. 'Darling! And is it . . .?'

'Jacky. Yes. I know Father'll be furious.'

'Well, never mind if he is. It's too late, isn't it?' She chuckled. Her beautiful voice over the line instantly conjured up her face before Rupert's eyes. He heard her put her hand over the mouthpiece and call out to Hugo. There was a conversion lasting almost half a minute. Then Molly came back on the line.

'I think it's going to be all right, dear. He says he knew you wouldn't listen to him. Sends his love to you both.'

Rupert was rather startled by his father's acquiescence. It made him feel a rat for having done it so secretively.

'Should I have a word?'

'I don't think so, dear. Let him think about it. But he says you must come and see us soon.'

'We'll do that all right. Very soon. And, Mummy – I'm sorry if I've not been very good at being around. But it'll all change now. You'll see.'

'Of course it will, dear.'

Rupert felt a great sense of release as he put down the phone. Emerging from a family 'situation' like that was quite wonderful. It was going to be all right. He had done the proper thing.

Very late on the evening of their wedding day – Rupert and Jacky had stayed at home in the flat, keeping themselves to themselves – the phone rang and it was Freddie Moore.

He, too, sounded almost incoherent with delight, though he did threaten to be a little boring on being cheated of paying for a reception. In what sounded like an order, he told Rupert they would have to let him throw a party soon to celebrate.

'You'll 'ave to bring that mum and dad of yours along, too,' he added.

'Well, I'm not sure about that, Freddie . . .'

It was a meeting Rupert found it hard to imagine ever taking place.

Duncan was rather enjoying the notoriety he had achieved through the newspapers. If it seemed to show that the tradition of aristocratic goings-on was still alive in the deepest shires, then that was no bad thing. He could put up with any amount of tut-tutting from the old hens of Hooke country when he realized that a different set of people was looking on him in quite a new light. The tag of randy old goat applied to a balding middle-aged man in his early forties could not do him any harm. Especially if it brought in the punters.

That it most certainly did. Right from the first day Castle Cansdale opened its gates to the public, on Easter Saturday, there had been a steady stream of visitors in cars and coaches making for the latest tourist attraction. The visitors spent their pounds, consumed cream teas, bought their place mats, and much else, at the gift shop, and went home again. There was every chance that the house's normal running costs could now be turned into trading losses which could then be set against other estate income. He had made the right decision.

Besides, neither Duncan nor Joanna found it any great hardship to have to vacate some of the rooms during visiting hours. In fact, they were so disinclined to use them anyway that the ropes often remained in position after hours. So it was a fiction that the rooms the visitors trekked through were part of the 'truly lived-in family home' that Mr Bevis's brochure claimed. To be sure, Duncan and his family lived on the premises, but in what was virtually a flat on the first floor. They rarely strayed into the 'museum areas' as Duncan took to calling them.

If anyone took a proprietorial interest in the rooms now, it was Sophie. She disapproved slightly of her brother's neglect of rooms which – when she had lived in the house with her parents – had genuinely been used and cherished, as they had been continuously since the house was rebuilt in 1838. That was a tradition that Duncan had ended.

As Sophie oversaw the redecorating and restoration work, she soon noticed how the tide of visitors was literally leaving its mark. Waterwheel had to swathe the fading curtains in see-through coating so that sticky fingers would not hasten their demise. Tapestries, too, had to be similarly protected. Protective covers had to be placed over the priceless carpets in the Gold Library and the Salon.

This was woman's work, in Duncan's eyes, and as Joanna seemed incapable of getting anything right in that department, he was happy to let Sophie assume the role of chatelaine. She had virtual carte blanche to get on with whatever had to be done without his always having to be consulted.

Sophie noticed a change in his attitude, however, when she started bringing along one of her fellow directors from Waterwheel, an American designer and artist called Glenellen Summers. Duncan was obviously taken with this arty lady, to such an extent that he managed to manufacture a degree of interest in the finer aspects of flock wallpaper, carpet weaving, and picture restoring.

His sister sighed inwardly at the inevitability of it all. Sophie wondered how long it would be before Duncan bedded Glenellen. Well, at least she was a divorcee, so the adultery would be only one way.

Glenellen looked very much the artistic type. She wore a medieval smock whose design was based on a fourteenth-century Italian print in the V & A. She had Titian-red hair that tumbled right down her back. Her face was serious-looking and delicately pale and freckled. And she was American. All of these traits should have counted against Glenellen in Duncan's book. He liked a strapping woman (the fact that he hadn't married one was beside the point); he couldn't stand wimsy-pimsy types. But he was quite clearly fascinated by Glenellen Summers.

At first, she affected not to notice his attentions. She was intrigued to be dealing with a real live English lord, as any American would be, and simply adored the opportunity to work at Castle Cansdale. But she had heard, like everyone else, of Duncan's carryings-on and was determined not to be added to the list of his conquests.

Sophie was amused – and at the same time faintly appalled – when she happened to overhear Duncan's lumbering attempts at making conversation with Glenellen about tapestry cleaning.

'You mean you actually *wash* them?' he was heard to say.

'Yeah. You put them on a stone floor – one that you can irrigate – and then you pour on water and a little gentle soap. Then you tread the tapestry.'

'Like grapes?'

'Exactly. I tie sponges on my feet.'

'I should like to see that!'

'Finally, you rinse it all out, and hope the colours hold fast.'

'And if they haven't?'

'You touch it up. I take polaroids so I have a record of what they looked like.'

Glenellen fished in her bag and took out a packet of photographs.

'See – here's the Aubusson we took from the Smoking Room. See how bright it came up. And that's the water we took out of it. Just *look* at that dirt!'

126

'Good grief. The grime of centuries! Tobacco, too, I expect. You really are a clever girl.'

'That's what you pay for, sir.'

Duncan had never met anyone who talked like this before, nor had he ever met a woman who had such expertise in an area beyond his own. He found it curiously arousing and began to wonder how he could detach Glenellen Summers from the company of his sister, Sophie.

In the end, he did manage to get her on her own, without Sophie, and suggested she might care to come to tea on the following Sunday afternoon. As the invitation was issued in the form of 'seeing us at home without all the tourists about', Glenellen assumed that Lady Wymark would be present. It would be a social occasion and quite above board.

'Is there anyone you'd like to bring with you?' Duncan asked, hoping for the answer No.

'No. I'm just me. Fanny'll be with her father Sunday.'

'Fanny?'

'My daughter.'

'Oh, I see. Single parent, eh? Good.'

Duncan felt quite exhilarated by her acceptance, and began to work out how he could turn the meeting to his advantage.

Man and wife as they now were, Rupert and Jacky were due to spend that same weekend at Huddleston with Hugo and Molly. They were both a little tense at the prospect, not knowing how they would be received.

Jacky, of her own accord, had abandoned her short skirts and put on a more sensible skirt and top – nothing too dramatic. About the only showy thing on her entire person was the diamond wedding ring that Rupert had bought.

Her new mother-in-law was tense, too, and paced up and down when the young people were late arriving for tea on the Saturday.

'I wish you'd stop that,' Hugo told her.

'They're not going to come, you know,' she told him. 'Why should this time be any different? A leopard doesn't change his spots when he gets married.'

'Do sit down, woman.' Hugo looked up from the book he was trying to read. 'If he comes, he comes, and if he doesn't, he doesn't.'

'No need to snap.'

'Sorry, dear.'

Another fifteen minutes and there was the sound of a car drawing up and the rusty front gate being opened at the end of the rose garden.

'Here they are!' Molly bobbed up and tried to catch her first glimpse of the girl. She succeeded. Instantly, any reservations vanished. They made a lovely couple, she thought. She was a beautiful girl. There was absolutely no doubt about that. And so sensibly dressed.

Molly rushed to open the front door before they could knock.

'Well, hello,' she called out cheerily, finding that they had not even reached the door yet but were bending over roses by the path.

'Mummy,' Rupert said, coming up and kissing her, 'this is Jacky.'

Molly did not say anything but let her new daughter-in-law kiss her, too.

'What a lovely girl, to be sure. Welcome to Huddleston. Hugo's hiding inside, I'm afraid.'

Indeed, Hugo was pointedly not making any fuss. But the other three spent so long among the rose bushes that he became irritated. He was, in spite of all, curious to see what Rupert had thrown himself away on.

He walked to the front door and stepped out.

'There you are, there you are!' he called out, remembering to be friendly and forgiving.

He made straight for Jacky and after a little performance of changing his stick from one hand to the other, he shook her by the hand.

'How delightful to see you, my dear,' he said, with even a faint hint of a smile.

'Pleased to meet you,' Jacky replied a little shyly, trying not to call him 'my lord'. ('Don't call him anything,' Rupert had told her when she asked.)

Hugo's reservations appeared to vanish instantly. Of course, it was obvious why Rupert had fallen for the girl. She was lovely. Had he been over-hasty in the way he had tried to halt the match? She would be a splendid addition to the family.

Over tea and scones, Jacky didn't dare say a great deal and Rupert didn't care to. Neither Hugo nor Molly had much to say either. It seemed they just wanted to look at their son and daughter-in-law. Look and look. Not talk. Long silences punctuated the tea-pouring and scone-munching. It did not matter. There was an agreeable feeling in the room. Jacky loved the atmosphere of the old house and she was intrigued to note which parts of Rupert's looks he had inherited from each of his parents. The Earl and Countess were quite normal really. She felt reassured and happy.

Yet Rupert and Jacky had to do something for the rest of the weekend, so to fill in time rather than because they really relished the prospect of meeting more relations, Rupert suggested they pop over and visit Marjorie at Stoke.

The Dowager Countess seemed to be putting on the frosty act at first, just to give Jacky a bit of a fright, but soon the Amontillado was uncorked, one bar of the electric heater turned on, and the old thing became quite animated. Jacky had apparently passed whatever test Marjorie had put her through.

'Tell me, dear – about your job. You're a fashion model, I believe?'

'Yes.'

'Do you take your clothes off?'

'Grandma!' Rupert cried.

'Well, does she? I only want to know.'

'They try to get me to, but I don't,' Jacky answered serenely, when she was allowed to.

'That's all right then. Young people find it very difficult to keep their clothes on these days. Very different when I was your age. We used to pile them on!'

Marjorie Hooke chuckled at the distant memory.

'And what does your father do, my dear?'

Old habits died hard, and to Marjorie this was still the most natural question in the world to put to a young person.

'He's a businessman. You know, bit of this, bit of that.'

'I see. And you have family?'

Jacky wasn't quite sure what the Dowager was getting at here. 'There's my dad and my mum and my brother Mark.'

'I see. And do you keep in touch with all your uncles and aunts?'

'Oh, no!' Jacky exclaimed. 'Dad scared them off ages ago!'

'Very wise,' Marjorie told her, rather surprisingly. 'There's a lot to be said for doing it. Relations are a liability – though they do have their uses when you're an old crock like me.'

Jacky decided she would like Marjorie. It was much easier than she had feared, getting to know Rupert's family. She had got hold of the wrong idea. That was partly Rupert's fault. He had painted his family as such a gallery of grotesques that anyone would have feared entering their citadel.

Just before Rupert and Jacky departed, Marjorie rummaged about on one of her many small tables, found a thick vellum envelope and handed it to Jacky – who noticed that written on the outside in a stately but shaky hand was the name 'Jacqueline'. It was a second or two before she connected this with herself as nobody had called her by her full name since nursery school – not since she was a little girl and misbehaving, in fact.

'It's for you, my dear. It has been in the family for many years. The late Earl's mother wore it on her wedding day.'

Jacky took out a gold bracelet – slightly dim in colour – and quickly slipped it on her wrist, adjusting the small lock that clasped it.

'Oh, thanks, Lady Hooke. It's lovely. Isn't it, Roo?'

'That's very sweet of you, Grandma.'

'A pleasure, my boy. Are you taking Jacqueline to the house?' Rupert knew she meant Castle Cansdale.

'We hope to go tomorrow.'

'Well, if you look at the painting of Countess Kitty, you'll see she's wearing that same bracelet.'

Jacky didn't know what to say. She was dimly aware how important this sense of continuity was to the Hookes. Nothing in her own family home dated back further than yesterday. She was thrilled. The gift also seemed like a token of admittance to membership of the Hooke family.

In the evening, to save Molly having to do any cooking, Hugo drove the four of them to the Craswall Arms at Stroke and they dined in the new restaurant there. It had recently been decorated on a Castle Cansdale theme and the manager had been fishing for a visit from the Earl and Countess for several months.

Hugo did what he could to ignore the use of the family coat of arms on the menu and on the carpet, and the fact that there was something called a Wymark Bar in the pub part of the hotel. He let the manager bow and scrape them all the way to a special table by a recently revealed Elizabethan fireplace.

It was only when Hugo had waded through all the fancily named creations on the menu and ordered a bottle of wine that his eye fell on the place mats. They were all the same. Each bore a view of the old Castle Cansdale, taken from the Ackermann print Sophie had given him for his birthday. He sighed inwardly, and vaguely wondered how the print had come to be used in this way.

When the food came, Hugo wanted to complain about the vegetables.

'What are these things? Never seen them before.'

'It's just the shape they're cut in,' said Molly, mollifying.

'But they're not cooked!'

'It's what they call *nouvelle cuisine*, Hugo.'

'Oh, is it? Well, I'd say it wasn't cooked.'

Rupert laughed out loud at his father's cultivated crustiness. Jacky was beginning to like the old man more and more. It wasn't hard to see through his act. And she could see that he once must have been very handsome. Quite a one for the ladies, she imagined. That was where Rupert had got it from. She wondered what Duncan and Sophie were like. Tomorrow she might find out.

In retrospect, it was perhaps ill-advised of Rupert and Jacky to turn up at Castle Cansdale without warning Duncan and Joanna in advance. Rupert had not been back to the house since Duncan took over the previous

October and he had assumed that the easy-going ways of Hugo's day still obtained.

It came as something of a shock for him to find himself having to queue even to get through the gates at the North Lodge. There was nothing for it but to crawl behind everyone else towards what was being sign-posted as the Visitors' Car Park. It was only when they were about to have to pay entrance money for 'House, Gardens and Hooke Historical Experience' that Rupert was recognized by Arthur Latham who used to work in the estate office and was now a full-time car park attendant.

'It's Master Rupert, isn't it?' he said, touching his cap.

'Hello, Latham. Yes. How do we get to the front these days? This is my wife, by the way.'

'How do, miss. Well, sir, you'll find it a bit difficult getting to the front with your car. Better go round by the Spring Lodge.'

'Very good. Can you let us through?'

Latham obligingly unhooked the iron chain to allow the young gentleman to drive past the large notice saying 'PRIVATE ROAD'.

'Didn't used to be like this,' Rupert murmured, a little put out by the changes that Duncan had wrought. 'Father might have warned us . . .'

This was unreasonable of Rupert as his father hadn't been back once to Castle Cansdale since Duncan took over.

Jacky was rather quiet while all this was going on. She was stunned by the sight of the house itself, rising like a giant almond cake out of the Capability Brown landscape. No wonder it always seemed to dominate every conversation in the Hooke family.

'Don't they have a doorbell?' she finally asked, at a loss to understand what her husband was hesitating about.

'They do, but that's not really how things work.'

'Don't you go in the front? Where is the front?'

'Oh, all right, we'll walk round.'

It took a good few minutes, but when they did get to the front they found a queue of visitors.

'We're not going in with them,' Rupert said rather flustered but attempting to rid his remark of any distaste. 'We'll have to go the kitchen way after all.'

They pounded all the way back to where they'd started. Both were beginning to be hot and bothered.

'I'm sorry, Jacky. I'm afraid you're beginning to experience the effect of Duncan even before you've met him.'

'Do I *want* to meet him?'

'Got to be done.'

Having gone past another notice saying 'PRIVATE', Rupert found his way into the old kitchens and discovered them to be occupied by a foreign-looking man in his shirtsleeves.

'Yes,' the man inquired, looking up from the Sunday paper he was reading while he smoked a cigarette.

'Hello,' said Rupert.

'Is private, sir. No visitors here.'

'Yes, I know,' Rupert went on, blushing ever so slightly. 'I'm Lord Wymark's brother. Rupert. And this is my wife. Jacky. We just called on the off chance someone'd be at home.'

The Mediterranean-looking man rose slowly, put his newspaper aside, laid his cigarette in an ashtray, and slipped on his jacket. He had obviously decided that Rupert was sufficiently important to be addressed in formal wear.

'I'm not sure he's in,' said the man, who must be the new butler, Rupert concluded. 'I go see. Take a seat, please.'

'All right,' said Rupert and gestured to Jacky that they should.

They sat looking at their fingernails, as if in a waiting room. It was very apparent that Duncan's refurbishment programme was leaving the kitchen area to last, as it wasn't seen by the public.

In a minute or two, the butler returned.

'Not convenient. You come another day.'

'Oh . . .' Rupert might have been very angry had he really felt it mattered. It was Duncan all over. How typical of him to snub his younger brother and his new sister-in-law! Well, it was important for Jacky to see the unacceptable face of the Hookes as well as the other.

'Let's go, Rupert,' she said hurriedly, not wanting a fuss.

'No, well, but we ought . . .'

Rupert failed to finish his sentence because he'd had a thought.

'Well, good afternoon then,' he said to the butler. 'We'll go.'

He ushered Jacky out of the kitchen and shut the door behind him. But instead of heading for the door to the yard, he put a finger to his lips and signified they should tiptoe in the other direction.

When they were out of the butler's hearing, Rupert said, 'I'm buggered if I'm going to be sent packing by Duncan. We'll jolly well find where he is. Or Joanna.'

He led Jacky from the downstairs area to the ground floor. They crossed the Saloon on the opposite side to where visitors were gawping upwards from behind their rope barriers.

Then Rupert had another thought. It stood to reason that the family wouldn't be in the ground floor rooms while they were open to the public. They must be up in the first floor 'flat' he'd heard about. Rupert remembered perfectly well how to get about the house, though

132

with over a hundred rooms there was plenty of scope for opening the wrong door.

That was precisely what he did. He thought that the Green Bedroom – where Edward VII had once slept, and not alone, when Prince of Wales – was sufficiently grand to have been turned into a living room for the 'flat'. He turned the handle and peeped in.

There was a muffled sound – a voice, a woman's voice. Then Duncan's unmistakable voice rang out: 'Dammit, who is it?'

'Oh, sorry, it's only me, Rupert.'

'What the hell do you want?' Duncan's very red face glared at him from the bed.

Rupert saw at once that the woman in bed with Duncan was not Joanna. The Titian-red hair proved that.

The woman raised herself up to see who the intruder was and slowly covered a small breast.

'Er, hello,' Rupert said, covered in embarrassment, still stuck to the spot. 'I've brought Jacky to meet you.'

'How d'you bloody do, Jacky!' Duncan roared. 'Now, for God's sake, bugger off!'

Rupert pulled a face, and pushed Jacky out of the room.

They crept down the stairs once again, not saying anything, and then slipped over the ropes to exit the visitors' way rather than have to go back anywhere near the kitchen and risk meeting the butler.

As they went through the house, the room attendants vaguely realized who Rupert was, but couldn't account for his presence. At last, Jacky and he tumbled out of the visitors' exit.

'I'm awfully sorry,' Rupert said at last. 'I suppose we'll never hear the end of that.'

'Never mind, love. Why don't we go to the Hooke Historical Experience – whatever that is?'

'I've no idea, and I'd rather we didn't, my love, because they'll only want to see our tickets. And I'm bloody well not paying money to see my own bloody family!'

Jacky took him by the hand and kissed him. 'Settle down, love. Forget it. Let's go back to your dad's.'

It only confirmed Hugo's worst fears when Rupert recounted the unfortunate encounter with Duncan. He was curious to work out who the woman might have been, though no doubt Marjorie or the Rector would soon have the information to hand. He was appalled at Duncan's unfeeling reception of Rupert and Jacky. It only went to show.

'Well, dear,' Molly said to Jacky, 'you've had a baptism by fire, and no mistake. I expect Rupert warned you – what we're like as a family, I mean. I'm only sorry you had to find out the hard way.'

'I don't mind,' Jacky replied, cheerily. 'Families is families. I've got one too.'

The Countess was reminded by this of something else she must say. 'We really must meet your family,' she said. 'I'm not sure we could put them up. We don't have the rooms we used to, and I'm trying to manage without a housekeeper. But perhaps your mother and father would like to come for the day? Hugo and I would love to meet them.'

Hugo's unsmiling stare was taken as confirmation that he shared this view.

Jacky wasn't entirely sure how Freddie and Cynthia would respond to such an invitation but said she would find out.

'Is it worth a try?' Rupert asked her again as they drove home to London.

'If you can bear it, darling, so can I.'

'Okay, then. It might be rather amusing actually.'

'A right barrel of laughs and no mistake!'

Rupert looked at her, to see what she meant. She smiled and removed the doubts from his mind. Or most of them.

# CHAPTER 13

Sophie had been away for the weekend when Rupert and Jacky came down to Hooke country, and so she had still to meet Rupert's bride for the first time. Nine or ten days later – and it was now the second week in May – she was bending over her desk at the Old Mill, trying to make the computer terminal tell her what she wanted to know about progress on the Castle Cansdale account. She tried, first, without referring to the instruction manual – which she couldn't understand anyway – and, by so doing, threatened to erase Waterwheel's entire records. She then tried following the manual, but soon gave up in despair.

'God, Glennie, I'll never get the hang of this bloody thing!' she cried. 'What's wrong with good old pen and paper, I want to know?'

No reply came out of Glenellen Summers' office, so Sophie got up and put her head round the door. Glenellen wasn't doing anything – simply staring into space, with her feet up on the desk.

'You all right?' asked Sophie.

Glenellen still didn't speak but dipped into her bag, fished out a packet of cigarettes, and lit one.

'Do you really *like* Duncan?' she asked eventually, drawing deeply on her cigarette, and then exhaling a great cloud.

It was Sophie's turn not to speak. She entered Glenellen's office and plopped down on the chair of prize-winning design which she found to be devilishly uncomfortable. She considered what Glenellen was expecting by way of an answer.

'Put it this way,' Sophie finally formulated a response, 'I probably don't *dislike* him as much as everyone else.' She added a nervous little laugh.

'Good,' said Glenellen, brightening. 'That's what I'm feeling right now.'

'He's been on to you?'

'No, no. Just wondered, that's all. I expect people don't understand him. In his position. That's what I think.'

'That's very good of you,' Sophie told her, unsure what had prompted this unusual support for Duncan.

'I think in a very real sense he *is* Castle Cansdale,' Glenellen announced.

Sophie again hesitated before agreeing with what sounded to her like West Coast psycho-babble. 'Could be,' she allowed gently.

'I think we should give him all the support we can. And not charge him over the odds, either. I think Waterwheel should look on the Cansdale work as a prestige project. Do you agree?'

'Okay,' said Sophie, puzzled by this change of heart in Glenellen. Usually she would go as high as she could in charging the company's blue-chip clients. 'But it's hard for me, Duncan being family and all that. If you want to go easy on him, you'd best discuss it with Bill and Dickie' – naming the other directors of the design partnership.

Sophie felt a sudden urge to get away from the complications of working life. 'Do be a darling and show me how to work my terminal,' she said. 'It's driving me up the wall.'

'Oh, okay.' Glenellen swung her legs off the desk, lit another cigarette and soon had Sophie in touch with the computer files she wanted to see.

'By the way,' Sophie said, 'I'm riding this afternoon, so I won't be here. Can you take my calls?'

Glenellen hadn't yet found a way of expressing her irritation at the way Sophie was always buzzing off to hunt or to do things with her horse. She might claim to make up the time after hours, but Glenellen wasn't so sure she did. Still, it was the penalty they had to pay for having a 'name' like Sophie on the board.

On this occasion, however, Glenellen did find it in her to remark obliquely, 'You really like your four-legged friends, don't you?'

'Yes, I do,' Sophie replied defensively, in a very staccato voice. 'Yes, I do!'

'I'll take your calls, sure, but I may have to go over to the castle.'

Sophie didn't make any comment. As she gathered up her handbag and fished out the keys for the Golf, it occurred to her that Glenellen's remark about the horse was just the sort of thing Duncan would say. When he slagged off Joanna for her hunting, he usually blamed her 'four-legged friends' or 'anything on four legs'.

Fancy that, she thought. Glenellen's turning into Duncan's representative. Oh dear, if it went any further, it would be bound to end in tears.

She spun the Golf out of the Old Mill car park and with a marked lack of guilt at being about to play hooky on a working day headed through Bourton Cansdale and over to Hagger Farm on the Stoke road. That was where she now kept her horse. She took a look at Karberry, her chestnut mare, and made sure she was ready for an outing. Then she slipped into the adjoining cubicle to change out of her designer dungarees and into her riding kit.

Boots, breeches, coat, ruff and cap on, her hair clipped in place, and she was transformed. Karberry was soon saddled, Sophie mounted her and set off for a ride along the bridle ways that criss-crossed the gently rolling hills to the north-east of Bourton Cansdale.

It was a cloudy day but quite warm, even for May, and Sophie enjoyed the delicious peace of the countryside, especially with a steady mount like Karberry beneath her, and her riding habit so comfortable and well fitting. She let her mind wander vacantly from subject to subject, winkling out worries that afflicted her and finding them easier to put at rest now she was engaged on this soothing activity. The gentle rising and falling, the steady clip-clop of Karberry's hooves on the solid earth were reassuring – that she was right in what she did, in the life she lived.

She also felt deliciously alone. She was not one of those people who always had to be with other people. She had never shared a flat with other girls, as was inevitable if you lived in London. Even when she had lived at the castle with her parents, it was big enough to enable her to lead the kind of separate existence she craved. Now that she had her own cottage in Bourton, the same applied. She was alone and it did not bother her. In the old phrase, she liked the pleasure of her own company.

As she cut through the nature reserve which ran round the southern edge of Hagger Farm, she paid attention to the louder birdsong, the teeming noise of insects and small creatures within. She rode deeper into Sniggs Wood – delightful name – which was one of her most favourite places on earth. The light filtering through the trees gave it a misty quality. It had all the advantages of a storybook landscape with none of the dangers.

She found herself at last in the heart of the wood, stopped and dismounted. She fixed Karberry's bridle to a branch and crouched down to look at a bird's nest which had been left perilously exposed by the parent of the very young chicks cheeping within. The mother must have gone to find food.

Sophie was touched. She pulled the horse away so as not to put off the returning mother and went out of the clearing. She looked about her to make sure that she was truly alone and slipped Karberry's reins over a branch.

Sophie half-closed her eyes and moved back slowly through fallen leaves until she was leaning against an oak. There was the softest touch of a cooling breeze on her face. The sounds of the wood receded from her consciousness. She dug the heels of her riding boots either side of the tree to steady herself. She slid to the ground, almost faint. She crouched down there a while, until gradually once more she was aware of the birdsong, the smell of the bark, and of Karberry who patiently stood by.

Sophie had been thinking of a man. Not any man in particular. Just someone strong. A fantasy figure with whom she could share her life.

Then she felt ever so slightly ashamed, and apprehensive in case any one had seen her so alone. She briskly straightened her riding costume, slipped Karberry's reins off the branch, and climbed back in the saddle.

They went slowly together towards the light beyond the trees at the edge of Sniggs Wood. They moved so slowly and cautiously together that the shock when it came was all the more sudden and alarming.

A bird flew up right in front of them. It had been on the ground, well camouflaged, guarding its nest. Now it shrieked and fluttered; beat its wings in dreadful animal panic. Karberry reared up. Sophie clasped the reins to the mare's neck. But so unexpected was the move that she lost her footing in the right stirrup.

The horse reared again.

'No, no!' Sophie screamed, feeling the most terrible wrench as she fell back from the saddle with her left boot still caught in the stirrup.

This can't be happening! she told herself. It's so sudden! She knew she must either scramble back into the saddle or release her foot. But it was too late for either. Karberry, dreadfully flustered now, was starting to gallop. She dragged Sophie along by one leg, her rear scraping the rough ground of the wood.

She felt a dreadful stabbing pain in her ankle. She feared more injuries, gashes and blood, as her face came dangerously close to stumps of gnarled wood that lay in the horse's path.

But then, almost as quickly as it had begun, Karberry's panic subsided. She had dragged Sophie only ten or twenty yards and stopped in a clump of nettles. The stings bit into Sophie's face and hands, but it was less bad than what had gone before.

Was it possible for a horse to feel remorse? The way Karberry looked back down at her mistress as she lay in that humiliating position, splayed out to one side, her foot still held in he stirrup, it was possible. Or perhaps the mare had no idea what she had done. Sophie felt fury at the horse's docility now. Cursed it for not being able to understand.

The pain momentarily receded. Sophie struggled to extract the boot from the stirrup and finally succeeded in doing so, all the time acquiring more nettle stings. Her left leg fell to the ground. The pain returned a hundredfold. She cried out, beginning to wonder how she was ever going to get home in this state.

Sophie lay for several minutes, sobbing and feeling utterly sorry for herself. She lay in a cradle of nettles and looked up at the sky peeping through the trees at the edge of the wood. It appeared wonderfully free, the sky, and she really felt quite cross with it. She closed her eyes, hoping for release, then she opened them again. The sky had been partly blocked out by a human form. A man was standing near her.

'I suppose you're not all right?'

Any normal person would have asked, 'Are you all right?' or 'Is anything the matter?' Sophie thought, even though there plainly was. This man was different. She tried to sit up and take a better look at him, but every way she moved the stabs of pain shot up from her ankle.

'I don't know about horses,' the man asked. 'Is it all right?'

'Don't worry about the bloody horse,' Sophie winced. 'She won't bite.'

'Broken anything?'

The man stepped forward and Sophie registered that he was possessed of a fine head of dark hair. He wore a dark green corduroy suit – not real countryman's gear, she thought. But he pushed through the nettles, apparently lacking any fear. Then she saw that he was wearing an incongruous but usefully thick pair of gloves, even on a day like this. He bent down close and Sophie noticed he was wearing glasses. He slipped off one glove and held her hand.

'I said, is there anything broken?'

Sophie noted the assertion, the slight impatience in his voice. She wasn't used to that.

'Don't *think* so,' she muttered. 'Twisted my ankle. Bloody painful.'

The man smiled ever so softly for the first time. He approved of a woman who swore.

'Could you hop on one foot while I lead your horse? Have we got far to go?'

'Not frightfully.'

'Could I throw you over the horse?'

'No, you could *not*! I'm not a sack of potatoes. But I can sit on it. Side-saddle, sort of.'

The man helped her do this. She yelped and swore as he did so.

'Go on,' he said, 'make as much noise as you like. Don't mind me.'

At this, naturally, Sophie shut up. He took the horse's reins and tugged them. The small procession started off.

'Where are we going?'

'Hagger Farm, straight down this way. Can't miss it.'

'That where you live?'

'No. Just keep the horse there. Live in Bourton. You know it?'

'I've just moved into Sleepy Cottage.'

'Oh, really? Haven't seen you. I'm Sophie Hooke, by the way.'

The man didn't appear in any way impressed by this revelation. 'I'm John Tarrant – by the way.'

Sophie wasn't in a mood for more information. She couldn't begin to wonder what a man like this was doing in Hooke country. Couldn't work it out at all. But one did not pump new people for information as soon as one met them.

John Tarrant, though reticent in one sense, apparently had no such qualms himself. He kept on probing.

'You're a Hooke Hooke? The castle people?'

'Yes. True.'

'But you don't live there?'

'No. Like I said, I've a cottage.'

'You didn't.'

'I *did*!'

'No, you said you lived at Bourton. Nothing about a cottage.'

Sophie took a breath. But talking, even arguing, kept her mind off the pain, so she let him continue.

He asked her if she rode much.

'Depends what you mean by much.'

She was quite capable of paying him back in similar coin if he wanted to be argumentative.

'You hunt?'

'Disapprove, do you?'

'Why suppose that?'

Sophie couldn't say. She had just assumed.

'As a matter of fact,' he said, 'I don't really care either way – except when I'm paid to! I don't believe it's necessary for pest control, or any of that. But if people want to do it, and do themselves ghastly injuries, that's all right by me. And as for the antis, I think they're every bit as mad as the hunters.'

'Well, I'm glad we've got that sorted out!'

Tarrant glanced up and noticed the mocking look. He was a serious type, Sophie thought. He needed teasing.

'Don't you work then?' she asked even more provocatively.

This really seemed to rile him.

'Of course, I do. Just because I go for a walk in the afternoon doesn't mean I don't work. I could ask the same of you – don't *you* work?'

'Yes, as a matter of fact. I work for a design company called Waterwheel. But, if you must know, I was sort of playing hooky when I fell.'

'Waterwheel, eh?' It was impossible to tell whether the name meant anything to him.

'So what do you do,' Sophie said,' if you don't mind my asking?'

'I write.'

'Oh, that explains it.'

'Explains what?'

'Your not working in the afternoon. And the way you look.'

This was again provocative and Sophie knew it. John Tarrant chose not to be baited.

'If you say so.'

Hagger Farm came into view and they continued in silence right up to the stable door. Then Sophie became very authoritative, with only the odd wince to show she was still in pain. She slid off Karberry's back and steadied herself against the wall on one leg. Then she proceeded to give Tarrant a stream of instructions – how to take the horse's saddle and harness off, where to stow them, how to make sure the mare had enough to eat. Lastly, she told him that her dungarees and car keys were in the next box and asked if he would help her hobble over to the Golf.

'You're not going to drive that thing,' he told her firmly. 'You'll never manage it.'

'You've a better way to get me home?'

Edgy would have been the best way to describe the encounter. There was considerable mutual suspicion. John Tarrant felt uncomfortable at the mere thought of being with anyone from the Castle Cansdale clan. Without knowing anything about them, he presumed they represented a bastion of privilege.

Sophie, in turn, was deeply suspicious of anyone claiming to be a writer. Writers were anarchic and usually difficult. This one seemed to conform to type.

It was the spiky questions and answers that were the most curious feature of their encounter, however. In a way, they had both met their match in each other.

Claiming not to be put out, Tarrant firmly resisted Sophie's suggestion that he drive her home in the Golf.

'Probably not insured for me to drive,' he asserted, correctly. 'You'd better wait till I get mine.'

Sophie muttered a comment under her breath and when he looked quizzical said aloud, 'Nothing!'

If Tarrant wanted to be prissy and correct that was all right by her. She'd just have to sit and wait and suffer while he was away.

About half an hour passed before he returned in a Mini that had clearly seen better days – when presumably some other driver had been at the wheel.

John Tarrant drove Sophie to her Bethany Cottage and hesitated by the door.

'You could come in for a cup of tea,' she said, rather ungraciously, still balancing on the foot that was unhurt. 'Or something stronger?'

'I won't, thanks. Is there any more I can do?'

'I don't think so. You've been an angel. I don't know what I would have done if you hadn't popped by.'

At Sophie's charitable change of mood, Tarrant knew that he must stop needling her.

'You could give me a hand off with my boots, if you like.'

'Of course.'

He stepped over the threshold.

'Mind your head on the beam,' Sophie warned a fraction of a second too late.

While Tarrant rubbed his forehead, she lowered herself gently into one of the easy chairs before the fireplace and lifted up her unhurt leg towards him. John seized the still shiny leather boot by the mud-encrusted heel and toe and yanked it off with one movement.

'There! You enjoyed that, didn't you?' Sophie smiled for the first time since they'd met. 'Now the other one – and be careful.'

John took the injured foot a little roughly after that last remark and gave it a yank.

Sophie yelped. 'Beast!'

When he hesitated, she bossed him with, 'Go on, go on! Get it over with . . .'

She rolled around in agony while Tarrant wrestled with the boot. Finally, it came away. Gingerly, Sophie removed the white sock on her foot and revealed a dark blue and red bruise all round the ankle.

'Doesn't look broken,' Tarrant offered.

Sophie harrumphed. 'You could've fooled me. Anyway, thanks for everything. You've been a brick. I'll be all right now.'

'You'll see a doctor?'

'Of course, I will.'

They had known each other for less than two hours.

Sophie heard no more from John Tarrant for ten days. She found she was rather disappointed by this. It was unsatisfactory when a man came into your life suddenly and exited as quickly – particularly when he had the peculiar qualities John Tarrant had. It was something to do with his not being in awe of her. She had come across that awe in almost every man she had ever encountered. It wasn't just her manner, which she knew was on the forthright side, it was that they were all so bloody aware of who she was. And, frankly, though she was quite happy to make use of all that when it suited her – as at Waterwheel – she found it a terrible bore when it interfered with personal relationships.

So, as she lay at home recuperating from the accident, she found her thoughts repeatedly turning to John Tarrant. She wanted to find out more about this curious man. What sort of writer was he? Why was he living in the country? Did he have a wife? Sophie wanted to know, and without bumping into him again she would never find out. About the only thing she managed to get right was his age. He looked as though he was just on forty, a year or two ahead of her, and so he was.

Just before she hobbled back to work at Waterwheel she rang up her grandmother. The Dowager Countess fed Sophie gossip in exchange for one or two pieces from the younger woman, until Sophie popped the question.

'By the way, Grandma,' she said, 'I want some information from you. There's a man in Bourton called John Tarrant. Have you heard of him?'

'Yes,' Marjorie answered without hesitation, 'I do believe I have. He's moved into Sleepy Cottage, hasn't he – where Doll Bullman lived? She died in January, poor thing.'

'What else do you know?'

'Why, dear? Is he going to be another of your conquests?'

'I was hoping he'd do the conquering . . .'

Her grandmother laughed merrily at this. 'I'm trying to remember what I've heard, dear. I think he writes for a paper. Could it be *The Times*?'

Sophie correctly divined that her grandmother was simply mentioning the most obvious paper, though she was more of a *Telegraph* and *Express* person herself. But it did raise the unfortunate prospect of John Tarrant being a *journalist*. They'd had quite enough experience of that breed of late, what with Duncan's spot of notoriety, and Sophie wasn't sufficiently aware to be able to differentiate between the various types.

'The Rector says he holds strong opinions. That I do know.'

'Sounds like him,' said Sophie, almost disappointed at the news.

The call moved away from its prime purpose. Marjorie began to enthuse about Rupert and his new wife. This, so Sophie realized, was no more than a coded message that she ought to get a move on and wed herself.

'Have you met Jacqueline?' Marjorie inquired.

'Not yet.'

'I think she's a delightful girl. Rupert *has* done well. Your father's being his usual self, of course. Doesn't think she's one of us, or some such. But he's always been a fool in these matters. Marry for love, it's the only way. I hope you'll do the same, Sophie dear. And don't wait any longer for Mr Right to turn up – or I'll not be here for your wedding!'

Sophie's grandmother added the titbit that Jacky's family was due to descend on Hugo and Molly at the beginning of June. 'I believe her father's a very successful businessman,' she confided. 'They live on the wrong side of London, of course, but one shouldn't hold that against them.'

Sophie noted the snobbery breaking out and let it wash over her. It was just Grandma's way. She was too old to change.

'I must meet them,' she said. 'I can't wait to see what Rupe's found for himself.'

'You'll like her, Sophie. Mark my words.'

After they rang off, Sophie mulled over what her Grandma had said. If Rupert could break out of the straitjacket Hugo had sought to impose on all of them – that of marrying 'well', in the social sense – why couldn't she? Was this the restriction which had held her back all these years, until she was almost on the shelf? Was it now too late to make amends? No longer would she have to restrict her view to chinless wonders with the right family background. She could spread her wings and land where she liked.

Would it matter if she fell for John Tarrant? If it came to it, that wouldn't be 'marrying out', would it? He wasn't a scrap metal merchant's son, or such like. He didn't sound as though he came from the 'wrong side' of London. He was perfectly presentable. Classless perhaps rather than anything else. Hugo couldn't possibly object to him – unless those 'strong opinions' conflicted with his own.

Or unless John Tarrant turned out to be some kind of impostor. Sophie took the matter into her own hands. She rang him up, invited him round, and soon they were seeing each other regularly.

# CHAPTER 14

For most of the journey down the M4, Freddie Moore had nothing to say. He smoked quite heavily and gripped the wheel of the Mercedes while the countryside sped past. He was a little resentful at having been turfed out of his Sunday morning bed and the traditional routine, but even he was curious as to what precisely he would find when they finally met 'this Earl person'.

He also considered it an opportunity. You never knew. All of life was an opportunity and Freddie tried never to forget that.

Cynthia Moore was actually and admittedly nervous. She fiddled non-stop with the diamond stud in her fingernail and wondered whether she ought to take it off before she broke it. She had made Freddie stop the car soon after they'd started so she could take her coat off.

'It'll get hellish creased if I don't,' she said. The cream coloured affair was laid reverently on the rear windowsill of the car and not before her son, Mark, had ribbed her that it looked like a wedding coat.

'Well, perhaps it is, young man! Seeing we didn't *have* a wedding for Jacks . . .'

Mark was sitting in the front passenger seat next to his father, eager to get his own hands on the wheel. Freddie drove very fast just to show his son he was quite capable of it. But then, he always drove fast. As ever, Cynthia shrank on the back seat, not daring to look at the road as her husband aggressively sorted out less eager drivers than himself. Her nerves about the meeting that lay ahead were compounded. Otherwise, of course, it was going to be like a dream come true. Her Jacky getting married to a really nice class of person! And now she was going to meet a real live Earl and Countess. It was a pity they didn't live in the castle any more, but there was talk of their popping over to take a look later in the day.

Rupert and Jacky made their own way Huddleston. Having survived one visit to her in-laws very pleasantly, Jacky was now nervous only on her

145

parents' behalf. Freddie was bound to put on his rough-diamond act; Cynthia would probably talk too much to cover her nerves; and Mark – well, Mark would be sullen as always. Jacky was surprised that he had even said he would go.

'Stop worrying, darling,' said Rupert, turning from the wheel of the MG and resting a hand on Jacky's leg. 'It'll be all right.'

'I know,' she answered brightly, 'I know. And when it's all over, we'll never ever have to do it again.'

'That's the spirit! And if it's ghastly, there'll only be us to know. Not like a wedding.'

'True.' Jacky gave a little smile and ran her fingers through the blond hair that she was wearing longer these days. Another mile of motorway slipped beneath the wheels before either of them spoke again.

'You think they'll get to meet your brother?' Jacky wondered.

'Of course. Don't worry. Duncan's not too bad really. It's just when we went, it was a cock-up all round. In more ways than one.'

Jacky laughed. 'Are you sure you don't know who he was bonking?'

'I dread to think who it was. Chances are he'll have kicked her out of his bed by now anyway.'

As it turned out, the two cars bearing the Freddie Moores and the Rupert Hookes both arrived at Huddleston within a few minutes of each other. Freddie had followed the sketchy instructions Rupert had written out for him and managed to arrive first. The Moores were still sitting in the Mercedes, trying to summon up the courage to dismount, when Rupert and Jacky drew up behind and saved them.

There was a bustle of handshakes and kisses as the two families introduced themselves to each other in the drawing room at Huddleston. Hugo, naturally, contrived to be a minute or two late before making his entrance. Jacky noticed her father bounding up to him, determined to be first with the outstretched hand. Hugo shook it, reservedly, and peered with a bland, aristocratic look at the small, eager man. 'Well, here we are then. Fancy that.'

'I can call you Hugo, can't I?'

'Yes, of course. Do that. Call me Hugo.'

'And you can call me Freddie. Only fair.'

'All right. I shall call you Freddie, if you like.'

Cynthia clung to Molly's hand for rather longer than the Countess might have wished and finally gave her a kiss, as though to underline their status as the two mothers in the case.

Jacky had to push brother Mark into saying proper hellos. He was soon off on his own, however – looking at pictures of racehorses on the walls and regretting they weren't motorcars.

'Must have a photo,' Cynthia decided with a little shriek. 'Mark, get my flash out of the car, will you?'

Mark went off and returned with the equipment after a very long interval – such a long interval, indeed, that he must have had a good poke round the rest of the house on the way. He then took the picture which would no doubt end up suitably framed on the Moores' bar in Brentwood.

Eventually, Hugo was reminded that, lacking a butler, he was supposed to be offering drinks to his guests. He distributed enormous tumblers of dry sherry regardless of people's individual preferences. Cynthia began to wonder, if they didn't run to a butler, who was going to cook lunch? Molly didn't appear to be giving the matter much thought.

About one o'clock there was the sound of another vehicle drawing up outside. It was a car with Sophie in it, but she was not at the wheel. John Tarrant had driven her over in his Mini. Sophie was still limping slightly from the riding accident.

'Oh, good,' cried Molly, relieved. 'They've come, so we're all here.'

'Who's that?' Cynthia asked, not having expected anyone else at the festive lunch.

'Rupert's half-sister. And a friend. I haven't met him.' She lowered her voice and confided, 'Someone new!'

'That's nice,' commented Cynthia, as Sophie hobbled into the drawing room, wearing a skirt rather than dungarees or jeans, her stepmother was pleased to see. Molly Hooke strained to catch sight of the man Sophie had brought with her. She had pretended he was more of a chauffeur than anything else, but Molly could see through that sort of talk.

John Tarrant was very cool and collected as Sophie stood leaning on her stick, pointing at her mother, father and Rupert, and then – though she hadn't met any of them before – at the Moores and Jacky. In the end, it was only Jacky she actually shook by the hand, as being the most significant addition to the family group.

Molly reminded Hugo that the newcomers might want drinks too. When these had been poured, she beckoned John Tarrant to her side. She was intrigued by this new friend of Sophie's as he was patently not her usual type. For a start he wore glasses which marked him out as a townsman – as did the clothes, which though countrified and tweedy bore the air of having been designed by a city tailor with a view of what a country gentleman ought to wear.

'Sophie tells me you've been most kind to her since she had her little accident.'

John coughed modestly and turned his full attention to her ladyship. 'It was nothing. I could hardly have done anything else. She was just lying there.'

'But even so . . .'

Sophie came nearer. 'He was brilliant. Weren't you, John?'

'No, I wasn't. I couldn't have left you there, so I didn't.'

Sophie steadied herself on his arm.

Molly noticed, and saw how excellently unembarrassed John was. In a flash, she saw that he was Sophie's lover. It wasn't something she liked to give much thought to – her stepdaughter's sex life, especially one which now involved a man negotiating her sprained ankle – but the situation was so totally clear there was no avoiding it.

'You hurt your foot then?' Cynthia rather pointedly asked, pushing in slightly, trying to assert that she still existed.

'Yes,' Sophie told her briskly. 'Fell off my horse.'

'You ride, then? My, I've always wanted to do that. How lovely!'

'Yes, it is.'

Hugo was still being quizzed remorselessly by Freddie, the more noticeably so as Hugo did not return the compliment and ask him about his own life and works. So it came as a considerable relief when Mrs Powers, the housekeeper, came in and told Molly lunch was ready. The attempt to save money by dispensing with staff had been short-lived.

The group walked through into the dining room and Molly sat everybody where she wanted them, apparently off the top of her head but in fact consciously memorized from the piece of paper in her pocket.

At one end of the table, Hugo found himself flanked by Mrs Moore and Jacky; at the other end, Molly had bravely put herself in the company of Freddie Moore and John Tarrant. This meant that Sophie and Rupert could sit next to their respective partners, while Mark was inserted between Sophie and Cynthia almost as an afterthought.

The Earl was rather more gracious to Cynthia Moore than he had been to her husband. She was a chirpy little thing, he considered, but in no way offensive. And so he unbent to her a fraction. That was when he was not taking long looks at Jacky. He liked her more at this second opportunity and even felt a slight stirring in his old loins – not so much at the thought of her, but at the thought of Rupert and she having made a match. She was a beauty all right. It was all very satisfactory, now he came to think about it, and he slightly regretted having taken steps to try and prevent the marriage.

Molly made little headway with Freddie. She really could not talk to him at all, so when he had exhausted his patter on the excellence of Jacky and how lucky Rupert was to have married her, she almost despaired of sustaining any other topic of conversation. For the rest of the meal, she favoured John Tarrant who was sitting on her left.

'Now tell me,' she began, 'I gather you're a writer. How fascinating. And what exactly is it that you write?'

'Journalism,' John answered a touch curtly, as though to cut off her avenue of inquiry.

'I understand. But is it books or *newspapers*?' The way she said the second word alerted John to the consequences of admitting to it.

'Sometimes books, occasionally newspapers. I used to be on *The Times*' – he noticed a slight lessening of apprehension at this – 'but now I freelance. Mostly magazines, some papers.'

'You write *columns*, is that it?'

'Exactly. From the country – articles, book reviews, and occasional political pieces. That kind of thing.'

'Excellent. I shall look out for your name.'

Freddie, who had been chomping away without speaking, pricked up his ears at the mention of *The Times*.

'Been to Wapping then?'

'No, I haven't, actually. I left before all that.'

'You live out here now?' Freddie asked, as though Bourton Cansdale was a remote out-station from which a journalist would have to send in his pieces by cleft stick.

'Yes. I decided I could do what I do just as effectively here as in the Big Smoke. So I bought a cottage and moved here. I can fax my stuff up, or send it direct from my PC. And I don't have to work in a ghastly office. Spent years of my life trying to get away from that. I'd had enough.'

Freddie wasn't sure what kind of criticism this was. Did dislike of an office in the smoke reflect badly on the whole of London? For once, he decided to let the matter drop. But he gave John a steady look – their eyes did not meet – and this was supposed to express that he was reserving his opinion.

'These political pieces you write,' he asked, 'who are they for?'

'The *Mail* mostly.'

'Ah, good paper! Read it myself. Get it for Cynthia.'

But John wouldn't let him off that easily. 'So what's your line, Mr Moore?' he asked, almost a touch menacingly.

Freddie trotted out his litany about being a businessman and John was no wiser than if Freddie had claimed to be a company director. It was only when Freddie mentioned the 'property and so on' that John pricked up his ears. He said nothing but stored the information away.

Molly pressed John as to whether he rode or hunted, now that he had moved to the country. Neither, he replied, though he had written a feature about it for the *Mail* quite recently. 'In the end, I came out against.'

'Hugo will be pleased!' Molly exclaimed triumphantly. John wondered how his views would be of the slightest interest to the Earl. And then he realized that the warm – or cold – embrace of the Hooke family was being

149

extended to him. He was being sized up – to see if he was suitable for Sophie.

Molly couldn't quite fathom how, if John had come out against hunting in his article, he could consider being friendly with Sophie. But then, Sophie only seemed to go along for the ride, so perhaps it didn't matter.

Freddie declared that he was also anti-hunting – passionately so, he said. John recognized the tone of voice in which this view was expressed. It was as though they were all passengers pinned in the back of a taxi by the prejudices of the driver.

'You know what I think,' Freddie was saying, 'I just don't understand how people, calling themselves human beings, can do that sort of thing to a poor, defenceless little creature. Tearing it apart, and that. And for sport! I mean, I can hardly credit it. Why there's no law against it, I just don't know. It's obscene. Know what I mean?'

Sophie had already had her attention drawn to the sensitive topic of conversation, but was determined not to have a discussion about it at table. That would be too boring. She noticed Jacky shoot a look at Freddie as though his daughter had registered that he was straying into a field with a bull in it, and wanted to head him out again. But she did it in a kindly fashion.

Poor girl, thought Sophie, having that bore for a father.

It came as a relief when Molly scotched all chance of a full-scale debate on the subject by signalling that they should adjourn for coffee. After twenty minutes of this, Hugo startled everyone by announcing that they were all going out into the garden to play croquet.

The proposal was so preposterous that any remaining tension was instantly abolished and, amid shrieks of laughter and cries of 'I don't know the rules', the whole gathering moved onto the lawn. Hugo, who had only a very basic knowledge of the game himself, started dividing people into teams and telling them what to do.

Freddie soon established himself as a natural croquet player. He had the requisite viciousness needed to make his opponents lose rather than aim to win himself. He almost recommended himself to Hugo on these grounds alone. Molly, on the other hand, was keen that her guests shouldn't in any way be discomfited. She ran about uttering encouraging cries of 'Subtle shot!' whenever anybody tapped ball with mallet and failed to budge it, or 'Forceful shot!' when they hit too hard and despatched the ball at speed into a flowerbed.

Sophie did not play, because of her ankle, so John took this as a suitable reason to excuse himself, too. Games – certainly of this kind – were not his forte.

Mark managed to disappear altogether, either to tinker with his father's car or to 'strangle a few chickens', as Freddie joked to Hugo.

The game proceeded and, with a little help from Hugo, Freddie won. He saw this as a triumph either of his class or of his natural talent. Hugo gave one of his rare smiles, happy that his idea of the game had not been as foolish as it might first have seemed.

They were back indoors for tea by four thirty. Sophie asked whether the visitors from Brentwood were going to make a pilgrimage to Castle Cansdale.

'You really must see it,' she told Cynthia, 'you'd love it.'

'I'm sure.'

'We'd better warn Duncan in advance,' Rupert urged.

'Oh, yes, do that,' said Molly with a serene smile. So Rupert went and phoned his brother. He was not at home. Joanna answered Rupert's request for a visit in fairly horrified tones. She had no idea where Duncan was or when he would be back, but by all means Rupert could bring over his in-laws for a look. 'It's open to the public anyway this afternoon,' she added in a none too kindly way. 'Last admission half past five.'

And so a tour party consisting of the Moores, Rupert and Jacky, Sophie and John set off in a three-car convoy to Castle Cansdale This time Rupert knew how to avoid the queues and the car park, and they drove right up to the Spring Lodge without trouble.

Freddie bounced from his car, his eyes out on stalks. 'My God,' he exclaimed, 'I knew it was big, but this is a palace and a half! What do you think, Cynth?'

Cynthia, slightly overcome at the thought of her Jacky marrying into a family that had such a noble pile in it, could not find the words to answer.

'Come on,' cried Sophie, in her best organizing voice, 'let's not hang about.' She stomped off as fast as her injured ankle would let her.

The party breezed past the kitchen where the Mediterranean-looking butler had been so obstructive to Rupert and Jacky on their previous visit, and swept upstairs to the Saloon.

Members of the public who had paid their admission fee must have wondered what the motley crew was that appeared on the wrong side of the rope barriers: one or two aristocratic types, yes – and the other people . . . rather like themselves.

Sophie pressed on, heading for the family 'flat' on the first floor, with Rupert trying to wipe any doubts about the manoeuvre from his mind. Finally, she burst in upon Joanna who was sitting on her own with show jumping on the television. Quick introductions were made and the absence of the three Wymark daughters explained.

'Why don't you just look round yourselves? See the house, then come back here and I'll lay on some tea?'

'No need for that,' said Sophie, keen to head off any more embarrassing time spent sitting around with the Moores. 'Just had some at Mum's. Must be going soon.'

'All right, whatever you like – and I'm sorry Duncan's not here to say hello, but that's his way, I'm afraid.'

Sophie assumed the role of tour guide as she was the one who, of the present Hookes, cared most for the house. She was perhaps a trifle over-detailed in her descriptions of the redecorating and designs, but that was her job, after all.

Cynthia beheld everything in wonder and fortunately kept her cries of 'I bet this takes a spot of dusting' to herself. Even Freddie was unusually absorbed. He was especially appreciative of the vast silver service on the dining table.

'Bet that costs a bob or two to insure.' He had chosen John as the recipient of this remark.

'I'm not sure,' Rupert cut in. 'I'm not sure it even is insured. I mean, it's priceless – irreplaceable, really.'

'Still,' said Freddie, in his most knowing voice, 'you can never be too careful these days.'

The party strolled through all the rooms and predictably was most struck by the Gold Library.

'When Mummy and Daddy and all of us lived here, we really used these rooms,' said Sophie to Cynthia. 'Not like now. Duncan and Joanna made that decision.'

'Fancy,' said Cynthia, who was now more anxious to get to the souvenir shop, but was denied the visit because it was well past closing time. She would like to have bought a few postcards or a tea towel to show her friends.

Still hobbling bravely, with John for physical as well as moral support, Sophie eventually led them back to Joanna's room to say farewell.

'Is there a little book I could buy?' asked Cynthia.

'Buy! No, you must *have* one,' cried Joanna. 'You must have Uncle Alec's guide book. It'll tell you all you need to know about us. And some more! I'll get Lopez to find you one.'

The Spanish-born butler, so named, was summoned and with some speed fetched a copy. The look on Freddie's face as Joanna uttered her command with a mixture of authority and casualness was one of complete astonishment. Jacky, meanwhile, was staring at the floor, rather hoping it would swallow her up. She was still accustoming herself to the idea of organizing servants.

By the time they had sauntered down to the cars, Lopez had procured Uncle Alec's guide to Castle Cansdale and Cynthia delightedly accepted it.

'I hope you like the picture of Duncan and me on page twenty-four,'

Joanna said. 'It's probably the nearest you'll get to seeing him anyway!'

'Funny woman,' whispered Cynthia as she climbed back into the car with Freddie and Mark.

'What a bloody marvellous place, though,' Freddie enthused. 'I mean, would you believe it!'

In the following car, Rupert was muttering to Jacky, 'Almost over, darling.' He gave her a surreptitious kiss.

With John and Sophie bringing up the rear, the convoy set off back to Huddleston for the final round of farewells. They had to drive from the Spring Lodge round to join the road from the front of the house to the North Lodge exit. It was a broad sweep taking the path away from the back of the house and was out of bounds to visitors' cars, although they were free to walk in that area.

In the opposite direction the path was well brocaded with 'PRIVATE ROAD' notices. And what should come roaring up at speed in that direction now but Duncan in his Volvo. He flashed his lights and sounded his horn, but there was no room for two cars to pass on the path without one spilling on to the grass.

That was what Duncan did, but not without drawing up alongside the first of the 'trespassing' cars – which turned out to be the Moores' Mercedes. His face was crimson with annoyance. 'Who the bloody hell are you?' he yelled. 'This is private property. Can't you read? Get the fuck out!'

Freddie could give as good as he got and tossed back a few of his own expletives.

Duncan slammed his foot down and the Volvo shot off at speed again – so quickly, indeed, that Duncan was probably unaware of his sister and brother in the two vehicles to Freddie's rear.

'Nice fuckin' bloke, and no mistake!' Freddie shouted as he drove on again.

'That was him, that Duncan,' Cynthia said confidently from the back seat. 'He's just like the picture in the book.'

'Well, whoever he fuckin' well is, that's no way to behave. People like that deserve to be taught a lesson.'

When they were back at Huddleston, Molly asked innocently whether they had seen Duncan.

'Oh, yes, we saw Duncan all right,' Sophie quickly and diplomatically intervened, and though glances were exchanged all round, no further comment was made.

'I'm glad,' said Molly, brightly.

After yet another cup of tea with Hugo and Molly, the Moores finally made their farewells and headed back to London at about seven o'clock, duty done.

'So that was your brother?' John Tarrant commented when he and Sophie were at last free and he was driving her back to Bethany Cottage. 'He seems as much of a shit as everybody says.'

'He's got a short fuse, it's true,' Sophie answered, as ever reluctant to slam her brother. She added: 'You'd get on well with him, actually. You both speak your mind. He likes people who do that.'

John wasn't so sure. 'He'll hear I'm a journalist and think I'm a Trot or some such.'

'Well, aren't you?'

John knew it was a joke – though, like him, Sophie didn't have the way of signalling jokes in advance with a smile. He'd already told Sophie of his humble origins, his grammar school education, the inevitable period as an investigative journalist, then writing the odd piece for the old *New Statesman*.

'Why don't you just shut up?' he said, taking one hand off the wheel and squeezing her arm with it. 'I can't *wait* to get you on my own . . .'

Sophie was glad of the hint. There was something quite extraordinarily unsexy about being with relations.

It occurred to her that she had been John's lover longer than any other man's she'd ever known – even if it was less than a month since they first met, and the injury had caused them to get off to a slow start. If only she could get that wretched ankle better there'd be no limit to what they'd get up to!

'I've got a very long memory,' John suddenly announced, off on a very different tack.

'Have you? Good for you.'

'Yes. And, if I'm not mistaken, your little brother – or stepbrother, should I say? – has married into a very interesting family indeed.'

'Interesting? I thought ours was supposed to be the interesting family.'

'Quite possibly. But the penny dropped at lunch when our lovable Cockney sparrer, Mr Moore, mentioned property. He's been inside, you know.'

'What?' Sophie turned quickly to look at John. 'In prison?'

'Exactly that.'

'What for?'

'I'll have to dig out the cuttings.'

Sophie gave a big sigh. 'Good old Rupert! Trust him to walk into something like that.'

'I may be wrong, I'll have to check. I'm not usually.'

'No, I know that, John.'

They were outside Bethany Cottage now.

'You're coming in, aren't you?' said Sophie.

'You try and stop me.'

154

# CHAPTER 15

Uncle Alec had seldom enjoyed anything as much as he had writing the history of Castle Cansdale. To dig around in the dusty past was, for him, an exceptional pleasure. The fact that it was the past of his own family only gave it added lustre. He had expanded the text for the illustrated guide into a full-length book which would be published the following year.

How miserable it must be for my elder brother, Alec thought, not to derive as much pleasure as I do from his inheritance. As for Duncan, he wasn't so sure. Perhaps he did get pleasure from it, perhaps he did not, but both father and son appeared to be more afflicted by the burden of inheritance than fired by enjoyment of it. That was Alec's prerogative. He was capable of simple enjoyment. He had no responsibility in the matter.

But Alec still wasn't sure how he might continue to earn his small stipend from the Hooke estate in the years to come. Duncan wouldn't be wanting a new guide book written very often, if ever again. But Alec was hopeful that Duncan would go on behaving in a kindly fashion towards him. He had seen how downright stingy his nephew could be to Joanna and the girls, but he was quietly confident that he would continue to be regarded as a special case: as an ally in the family.

The most important thing, though, was that Alec had been given carte blanche to visit and to stay at Castle Cansdale. It was all he could wish for, though he told himself he must make sure neither to go too often to be a nuisance, nor so seldom that Duncan forgot about him. Being under an obligation first to his elder brother and now to a much younger nephew was unfortunate, but that was the system into which he had been born and in which he had elected to stay.

That morning in June, Alec had risen at eight, as usual, breakfasted on freshly-ground coffee and newly-delivered croissants, and spent half an hour in a hot bath reading the *Telegraph*. Then he had dressed in his customary brown velvet suit and gone to his desk. He straightaway answered the one invitation he had received by that morning's post – a cultural reception at the French embassy; there were no personal ones for him today. He still received invitations to the odd At Home, the occasional dinner party, but so many of the people he knew were dying off. He sent off for single tickets in the next booking season at the Royal Opera House and even found himself ringing to inquire about returns for Glyndebourne – but that was always such an expedition.

He would go to these operas on his own, probably. His supply of widows and divorcees was beginning to bore him. Even at his age, if he went with a man, he couldn't stand the assumptions people made. As for the young friends of either sex whom he was willing to treat, well, they probably found him an old bore now and were too busy pairing off to spend time with him. What did they want with a doddery old fellow who would reach his three score and ten the following year?

Towards midday, having achieved very little in terms of real work, Alec let himself out of his small apartment in South Audley Street. He walked about half a mile in light rain which spotted his tinted glasses. It was a walk he usually took once a week. He went northwards, over Oxford Street, and into the area of squares and streets beyond.

When he reached the large white terraced house he did not pause to see if anyone was observing him. It did not occur to him to do so, for who would know who he was anyway? He went down the steps, lightly touching the black iron railings with an elegantly-gloved hand, and rang the bell of the basement flat.

There was no reply for quite some time, but he knew better than to ring again impatiently. He did, however, look at his watch to check the time. Eventually, the door opened and a small man of Middle Eastern appearance, aged about fifty, came out quickly and thrust on a pair of dark glasses as soon as he saw the other man waiting.

Alec quite understood why the Middle Eastern gentleman behaved like this. He half-smiled back, as though to reassure the other man, though he would rather not have been made aware of a previous customer. A small, elderly woman, perhaps nearer his own age, waved him in without speaking. Inside the flat was a kind of waiting room with red plastic-covered armchairs which Alec shrank from sitting on. Instead, he stood waiting, smiling slightly.

In time, Maxine appeared wearing a dressing gown of loud green silk. Her brown hair was up and she was smoking a long cigarette in a holder.

'Good morning, my dear,' said Alec, holding out his hand to be squeezed. 'Or perhaps it's after noon. Yes, it is. My, you are nice and warm.'

'Still my same old Alec, eh?' Maxine answered, allowing Alec to brush the back of his hand across her cheek.

'Not so old,' Alec pointed out, a touch disappointed at Maxine's choice of words.

' 'Course not, dear,' she said rapidly. 'Nothing wrong with you, is there?'

'No.' Alec smiled, sheepishly, as though he was a small boy being paid a compliment.

'Expect you'd like to come in?'

'Rather.'

Maxine escorted him down the corridor towards the bedroom as she had done many times before.

'Must show you this,' she said, taking him a little deeper into the flat and closing the door to what she realized was an off-puttingly domestic scene of kettles and unwashed mugs and plates in the small kitchen. She proceeded to open another door and switched on a low light.

'Finished at last, it is – my dungeon!'

Alec could see a lot of shiny equipment in the half-light. Wooden crosses with leather bonds and metal buckles; manacles attached to the walls; hard-looking wooden chairs with restraining gear; and on a medical trolley an assortment of whips, masks, bits and harness. Alec was more amused than excited by this display of the equipment of a dominatrix. It wouldn't give him pleasure, he knew that. He was perfectly clear in his own mind exactly what would.

'Very pretty, dear,' was all he said.

Maxine had known he wouldn't really be interested, but she was always saying that variety was the spice of life, and like all the best salesmen she believed in showing off every facility available.

She let Alec into her more usual workplace. There was a double bed with a single fresh sheet on it, various pillows and cushions. There was a mirror on the headboard and another on the ceiling.

'You sit yourself down,' Maxine suggested, in a homely fashion. 'I'll go get dressed. Won't be a sec.'

She left the room. Alec did nothing to prepare himself, merely gazed at the backs of his hands and tried to avoid catching his reflection in the mirrors. There was an air of calm and patience about him, none of urgency.

Soon Maxine re-entered the room in her costume. She strode forward, hands on hips, and stood a few feet away from Alec, her legs wide apart.

Alec smiled and gave a quiet sigh of satisfaction. He sniffed audibly to catch Maxine's newly-applied scent. He ran a hand over what remained of his hair, slipped off his glasses and laid them carefully on the bedside table.

Then, remembering that he would need them to see properly, he put them back on.

It had taken a long time to get to this point. When he first started coming to Maxine she had over-acted, kept trying to play all those terrible old tart's tricks with him, kept coming out with the same old hoary phrases of encouragement that only had the reverse effect on a man of Alec's refinement. Now, finally, she had learned that he did not want fake orgasmic moans, play-acting, or posturing of any kind. No words must be spoken. That she was wearing her costume was, for him, enough.

He tentatively put out his right hand and gazed up at the handsome body that loomed above him. The light caught his tinted glasses. He touched her costume at the hip and then slowly, very slowly, ran his hand down the sheer silk of the stocking on her thigh. The four inches that this move covered took an eternity, but for him it was one of exquisite pleasure.

His fingers at last came to the top of the green suede thigh boot and he continued the downward journey of his hand.

He stopped abruptly, a pained expression on his face. 'You've forgotten—'

'Sorreee, darling,' Maxine apologized and strode quickly out of the room, returning in a moment with a pair of long green arm gloves made of satiny material.

Poor Alec. Maxine was still capable of making mistakes. The experience was still not quite perfection.

She stood once more before him. The principal boy pose was now complete.

He could not remember when the obsession had first got to him. He supposed that he had first noticed the strapping thighs of principal boys in pantomime in the late 1920s, before he had reached puberty. Even then he could remember being thrilled by the magical sight of a brisk, confident woman in male garb. Perhaps if he had ever had a marriage that lasted longer than his brief one to the Polish Countess he would have indulged the obsession with his wife. It was certainly after that disastrous interlude that he began to pursue his enthusiasm in earnest.

During the pantomime season he would attend as many as he could in the hope of satisfying the craving, if only visually. In pursuit of his fantasy, how many tawdry, unfunny, meretricious versions he must have sat through of *Dick Whittington, Puss in Boots*, and *Cinderella*! He would travel all over London on the off chance of catching sight of a thigh-slapping principal boy, and felt sadly cheated when he was disappointed. If people ever came to hear of his going to so many pantomimes, he said he was an enthusiast for the genre. Indeed, he had written a little book on its history which gave him an excuse to undertake the most delicious research – much poring over old photographs – and an ideal cover for his yearning.

Now, finally, he had found the perfect way of satisfying that craving. Maxine looked stunning in the long green boots that he had bought for her. They hugged her thighs so splendidly that he was sometimes left gasping at the mere sight. The long gloves had a similar effect on him. The rest of her costume – the tunic, the ruff, the little hat – he could manage without. He was in thrall to the experience and knew precisely what form it should take.

He gazed. He occasionally touched. And Maxine stood, earning her money a good deal less energetically than with any other of her clients. There were no problems about condoms or AIDS or any of that. The only connection between them was the finger that Alec sometimes allowed to touch her thighs – softly touch, as though he was expecting to receive an electric shock; whether orgasm was reached, even Maxine was never quite sure.

After twenty minutes, Alec was the happiest man in the world. He paid his pounds – which made a £190 dinner at Scott's seem like value for money – and bade Maxine his usual courteous farewell. He took a taxi back to his apartment, a happier man.

He felt no guilt, no shame, no sense of anti-climax. None of the sadness that man and animal were supposed to feel after intercourse. Maybe this was because he had not had intercourse in the accepted sense. There was nothing wrong with this thing that he regularly did, he told himself. It was a purely private pleasure. If people did not understand it, then bad luck to them. He was happy because of it and would continue to enjoy it for as long as he could afford to.

Down in Hooke country that same month, Sophie woke up one morning and realized her ankle was better.

'Thank bloody God for that!' she thought. Now life could resume. She rang John and told him she wouldn't be needing his ever-so-kind lifts to work any more; she could now drive herself round the customary circuit to the Old Mill, to Castle Cansdale and back to the office. She might even be able to start riding again.

'I was hoping you might have got over that,' John said in that infuriatingly direct way of his.

'Oh,' said Sophie, cautiously. 'Not really. Just because you take a fall doesn't mean you give up riding. It's the price you have to pay sometimes.'

Now it was John's time to say, 'Oh.' Ah, well. Perhaps the next time she fell would clinch the matter.

'I hear what you're thinking,' Sophie told him with matching directness, but quite sweetly. 'But don't ask me to give up that pleasure. Please.'

John didn't ask her, and never raised the subject again. Curiously enough, however, it was from that day that Sophie's interest in riding began to wane.

The morning of the cured ankle was a bright, gentle June day and Sophie's heart was light as she drove out of Bourton and headed for the Old Mill.

'How's the ankle?' asked Dickie, her co-director, socially rather than necessarily as he could see she was no longer limping.

'Beautiful,' purred Sophie, and swept on through the reception area and shop with its endless sound of water trickling round the wheel behind the glass, and up to her office.

It was not often that she was the first woman in the building. Usually, Glenellen Summers was there at the crack of dawn as though she was still on American time, but not today. Sophie turned on the computer and found what she wanted without any trouble. This was, as ever, the schedule and costings for the Castle Cansdale project. It looked as if it would go on for years, so bills had to be sent out regularly to Duncan.

Glenellen did not show up until coffee time. Perhaps Sophie thought, she had gone straight over to the castle to check on one of her renovations. But no. One look at Glenellen's face showed she had been crying. She said nothing but rushed into her office and slammed the door.

Sophie pulled a face at Dickie and felt self-conscious and guilty about her own high spirits.

'What's up with her?' asked Dickie, not content to let Glenellen suffer.

'I've a pretty good idea,' Sophie said softly, 'and I wouldn't be surprised if isn't something beginning with D.'

'Ah,' Dickie said, as though there was no need to say more.

It was common knowledge by now around the company that Glenellen had, unforgivably, been screwing the client. It was, of course, one way of keeping the client happy. The only trouble was, would he still be a client when the screwing came to an end? But in Duncan's case that wasn't really a problem. Duncan could no more sever his links with Waterwheel now than Hugo could get the estate back from him. Waterwheel had orchestrated the renovation programme completely, and there was no one else who could possibly take it over. Besides, there was the link through Sophie.

No, if there was to be trouble between the castle and the Old Mill, the only removable part was Glenellen herself. She would have to be taken off the job and work on another project.

Sophie, still full of morning directness, managed to wait five minutes and then went into Glenellen's cubicle without knocking. She quietly closed the door behind her. The American was sitting at her desk, tears streaming down her face, almost threatening to extinguish the cigarette she was puffing at.

'He's a fuckin' asshole,' was how Sophie received confirmation of her suspicions.

'You're not the first to say that,' she replied.

Glenellen told her tale. Duncan had promised they would go away the previous weekend. There was some wonderful hotel in Dorset she had read about in a magazine. If they went there, they could be safely on their own without interruptions. Castle Cansdale was impossible. 'The corridors are busy as a freeway,' said Glenellen. Her digs in Craswall, which she shared with her daughter, were not conducive to gentlemen callers. She was getting desperate for a place where they could make love in peace and Duncan had become impossibly vague whenever she asked him if there was a cottage free anywhere on the estate.

'Then, goddam it, if he didn't stand me up! He said he'd stop by my house on Saturday afternoon and we'd go to the hotel, but he never showed. I tried calling the castle but all I got was Joanna. She sits on the phone, you know, like a dragon. So that was that. No fucks Saturday night. Then tea time on Sunday afternoon he comes over. No word of explanation or apology. Wanted to jump me in a field or some such. I told him he'd have to jerk off after shitting on me like that. So he went.'

'Sunday afternoon, you say? I think we caught the tail-end of that hurricane. We were over at the house with Rupert and his wife's people. Duncan came belting up and gave Jacky's father an earful. Thought he was trespassing.'

'He's a rat.'

'You didn't say anything yesterday, or the day before.'

'You know me, Sophie, plucky old Glenellen. I sat on it. Then I went to the castle first thing this morning to see how the gold-leaf treatment was taking. Soon as I got in, there he was in the Saloon. Cuts me dead. Wham! Just like that. As if I'd never known him. Never existed. How can people *do* that?'

'You come from a family like the Hookes, it's in the blood.'

'What, behaving shittily?'

'Aristocratic disdain. The opposite of *noblesse oblige*.'

'But you're not like that.'

'Oh, I can wither when I want to.'

'Well, I tell you what I call it. There's a thing in wine-making called "noble rot" – that's what Duncan's got. And it's started in his brain or in his cock.'

Sophie laughed. She wasn't going to start an inquisition about what would happen next or how Glenellen would feel about continuing to work at the castle with Duncan blowing in and out. She simply said she was sorry.

'I know he's a shit. That's like saying fire burns. But he's my brother and I have to forgive him for most things he does. That's family, too . . .'

Glenellen made no reply, but seemed to signal that she understood, and could see what a difficult position her brief fling with Duncan had put everybody in.

She lit another cigarette, took a tissue to her eyes, and tried a smile. 'How's *your* lover?' she asked.

Sophie's eyebrows rose at the word. She didn't quite think of him in that way yet, though it was true 'boy friend' would have sounded a bit silly at their age.

'Oh, fine. I put him through a baptism of fire on Sunday. Took him home. Molly loved him at first sight. That's because he's interested in me and she, in her stepmotherly way, has begun to get desperate. He's marvellous, anyway, and sails through anything like that. He can talk to anybody. Such a hoot in contrast with Jacky's family. I mean, she's super, no trouble there – I can see why Rupert fell for her – but the father and mother! I know one shouldn't mock, but it was too much. The mother had a diamond stud in her little fingernail! Probably the height of fashion in Essex or wherever they come from. Then there was an awful brother who moped about like a lost handkerchief. And then Daddy dragged them out on to the lawn to play croquet!'

Glenellen could appreciate that this was a peculiarly English form of torture you dished out to guests you didn't want to see again.

'And then, to cap it all, John said he recognized the father. Thinks he's been in prison. He's finding out what for.'

'Do you think Rupert knows?'

'Shouldn't think so. I expect our Freddie keeps it dark, claims he's gone straight, put all that behind him. But, I mean, what a hoot!'

Glenellen lit yet another cigarette from the stub of the previous one. 'You know, Sophie – and don't get me wrong – you come from quite a family. It just goes on and on. Never a dull moment. You amaze me.'

'It is rather like that, isn't it?' Then Sophie quickly took the glee from her tone. 'I'm only sorry you've, you know, been a little hurt by it all.'

'I reckon I'll live. And I hope your John does, too. I hope the other Hookes don't drive all over him.'

'Don't worry. I won't let them. I'll keep him all to myself. Besides, he's big enough to look after himself, you know.'

\*     \*     \*

For some reason, there had been a lull in Jacky's modelling engagements in the two months since her marriage to Rupert. It was almost as if the news had got out and had mysteriously affected her attractiveness to clients. So now Maddie Shapiro was chasing her and wanting her to go on more 'go sees' – the endless round of casting sessions with photographers, editors and advertising agencies. Jacky seemed to be playing hard to get.

'Can't have you sitting at home all day,' Maddie told her, having summoned Jacky to the tiny office off Hanover Square. 'Everything all right?' The leading question could have referred to any number of fields of concern.

'Oh, yes,' Jacky answered with a hint of coyness, thinking that Maddie was asking about her marriage.

'Good, dear. Well, I must say this, you're looking absolutely super. You've got a glow about you, Jacky. I don't know what it is, love – you're pregnant, you're on the pill – whatever it is . . .'

Jacky looked innocent and gave no confirmation of any of these possibilities.

'. . . in other words, you're radiant.' Maddie smiled as well as she was able from behind the enormous horn-rimmed glasses with which she so successfully hid her own once-glamorous, now middle-aged features. 'Just as well – there's some lovely jobs coming up. How's your diary?'

Jacky fished in her bag and vaguely mentioned August as a time when Rupert was talking of a belated honeymoon.

'Quite right, too,' Maddie said, insistently. 'It was a shame you didn't have it at the time. But I can understand, dear. Now you find out from Rupert what you're going to be up to,' Maddie rattled on. 'Then we can plan. There's no point my sending you off on go-sees if your availabilities aren't there.'

Jacky knew she sounded vague, as though her life now revolved around Rupert, and it was true; she had lost her hunger for work. The lure of trips to Africa, the West Indies, the Seychelles had begun to fade soon after she had met Rupert.

There was something else she felt, too – something she couldn't find words to explain to Maddie, who probably wouldn't have understood anyway. Jacky wouldn't work topless or in the nude anyway, but she was beginning to have inhibitions about giving her body to the camera at all now that it belonged, in a sense, to Rupert. When she told him of this, he – naturally – said it was nonsense. He wasn't jealous of other men ogling his wife. Rather liked it, in fact. And, after all, she was well hidden beneath layers of furs, expensive frocks, and gorgeous underwear. But she continued to feel this way, nevertheless.

'I'll do whatever I can,' she said at last, sounding bolder than she felt.

'That's lovely, darling, I'll be in touch with you in no time,' said Maddie.

Jacky picked up her bag, gave Maddie one of her biggest smiles, and headed out of the agency. In the waiting room were four girls she did not recognize. She assumed they were aspiring models trying to get on Maddie's books. They looked at Jacky enviously, instantly recognizing her from the large photos that were sprinkled prominently on the agency walls and on the narrow staircase up from the street. But the presence of the future competition was a reminder to Jacky that if she slackened her grip on work, there were plenty coming up to elbow her aside.

When she was back down in Hanover Square, she felt free, as though her visit to Maddie Shapiro had been an ordeal. She gave in to the temptation to do some shopping and spent three hundred pounds on a couple of items spotted as she comprehensively reviewed every fashionable shop in South Molton Street. Then she took a taxi back to the flat off Lowndes Square, tried on the new clothes in front of Rupert's ridiculously small mirror, and left the bags and wrapping paper all over the floor.

They were going to find a bigger and better flat. They were agreed on that. She would rather have had a house, but prices were so dreadfully high. Visiting Huddleston and Castle Cansdale had made her 'house broody'. She didn't really know what Rupert could afford. He didn't earn that much – in fact, her earnings as a model in the year up to their marriage had been rather more.

Then she had an idea. Surely her father would help them find somewhere – just as he had found her the little flat in Paddington?

And then a shadow fell across her thoughts. Of course Freddie Moore would do the decent thing by them, if asked. The trouble was, he was a bit too keen on doing the decent thing these days. Every favour carried with it a certificate of obligation.

# CHAPTER 16

If Duncan could be said to be running a family business at Castle Cansdale, trying to make money out of his family's history – as well as providing employment for sister Sophie and Uncle Alec (among others) – then Freddie Moore wasn't far behind him.

It wasn't simply a case of making sure that his darling daughter Jacky was properly looked after by Maddie Shapiro and taking a share of the proceeds of her exploitation – for Freddie was co-owner of the agency. Freddie also employed his son Mark as an assistant in his multifarious enterprises. Mark was the heir apparent.

Just to look at them, it was obvious they were father and son. Jacky, on the other hand, derived most of her features – and all of her allure – from her mother. Mark might have been good-looking if he had wanted, but apart from a small ring in his left ear he didn't seem to care much about his appearance. His hair, though fashionably short at the sides and all piled up on top, was either greased or, when not, had a matted look. Recently he had grown a moustache which didn't go too well with the hair. His clothes were those of a man who thought shopping a waste of time.

Freddie disapproved of the earring – thought it was a nancy touch – but Cynthia told him he didn't have to look at it if he didn't want to. Besides, it wasn't half as bad as some of the things they'd worn when they were growing up in the sixties.

Mark had left school at sixteen (eleven years ago now). He had had the usual ambitions to be a musician, a racing driver, a computer programmer, but faced with the national employment picture – and coupled with a lack of real fire in his belly – his father found him jobs to do. First he was an office boy, a messenger; then he was his dad's chauffeur; now he was increasingly used by Freddie as a kind of trouble-shooter.

Mark seemed to prefer the company of other men without, Freddie devoutly prayed, getting up to anything overtly homosexual. People

165

tended to be wary of him, if they weren't scared off altogether. He had a short fuse.

Freddie had that temper, too. Faced with a rival under the same roof, the effect on him was to cut back on his own temper and let Mark take it out on other people for relief. This relief was necessary because Freddie and Mark operated on the borderline of legitimate business and outright crime.

Freddie's companies – property, travel, video shops, garages – were always run on a day-to-day basis by other people. His business method was to put a good manager in charge and let him get on with it. But at the first hint that the manager was not delivering the goods or was on the fiddle, Freddie (or Mark) would be down on him like a ton of bricks.

Freddie spent most of his time sitting among the filing cabinets in the otherwise sparsely-furnished den at Dorset Avenue, waiting fireman-like for reports of conflagrations which he would speed to put out or send Mark to deal with. Freddie was a great one for issuing stern warnings once only. And never shrank from firing people on the spot. No one ever took him to court for wrongful dismissal.

He also provided powerful back-up to his more loyal managers on the difficult business of debt collection. Freddie thought he knew a thing or two about that, and now Mark was getting wise in the necessary ways. Freddie took reasonable care these days, but it was still a grey area. When did the extraction of payment on a legitimate debt become extortion? Were there legitimate ways of teaching people a lesson? In many cases what was simply good business practice to the likes of Freddie was crime in the eyes of the law.

Freddie's fortune was established when he had been his son's age, in the late sixties. Starting from nothing, he had acquired capital in the heady days when to have a cheeky, chirpy Cockney manner was sufficient to get you anywhere. For Freddie, this had not meant his becoming a film star, photographer or pop singer, it had led him into property renovation, acquisition and selling, when prices were minuscule compared to what they would become.

This was not to say that Freddie accumulated his money unobtrusively. He was not averse to publicity; it was all the thing in those days. He rather fancied himself being dubbed a 'tycoon' but he didn't have many engaging qualities, nor could he boast of making actual millions as some could.

He did his best. He liked to go to the fashionable clubs. He acquired Cynthia who looked sensational in a mini-skirt, but it hadn't all happened the way he had wanted it to. There had been the unfortunate time spent relaxing at Her Majesty's pleasure. That was when Cynthia had had to keep the companies ticking over for him while sheltering Jacky and Mark from any stigma that might attach to their father's imprisonment. It had been a tough time for them, but it also meant that when some of the bigger fry started crashing about them, Freddie was left with his small but sound business intact.

Now he was just over fifty, Freddie had lost a smidgen of his chutzpa, a small part of his push, but he still loved a deal, a bargain, a golden opportunity. It was in his blood, this drive, with an eye to the main chance. It was probably a reaction to his own very humble background and to his father's complete lack of any sort of drive or ambition. His father had been an 'interior decorator in Islington' when neither job nor place had any of the fashionable associations they later acquired.

By dint of the same reactive process, neither Mark nor Jacky really had the hunger their father had. They had grown up in comfort, they had lacked for little, and so they took the good things in life for granted. In Jacky, this hadn't done her much harm.

'She's landed on her pretty feet, ain't she?' Freddie would beam proudly when he discussed his daughter's marriage, which was often. It was true, she had been blessed by God with remarkable looks. She had sailed serenely into modelling and had done very well, even if, unknown to her, Freddie had pulled as many strings as he could to ensure her success. She was a bloody marvel though. She didn't ask for or expect anything, and yet she got things just the same.

Mark was a disappointment in this respect. Freddie would never express this out loud to him, though occasionally he did to Cynthia. Still, Mark had got the message. He knew that he had not made his mark, was riding on his father's fortunes. He really ought to assert himself in some way. The way in which he chose to do so came as a surprise to Freddie – though by all the rules it should not have done.

It was a day or two after the Moores had been to Huddleston and Castle Cansdale. Freddie was still reeling from the experience: that he, humble Freddie Moore from Brentwood, was now connected through marriage to all that . . .

'Y'know, boy,' he said, 'it's a bleedin' miracle, if you ask me. I'd never have dreamt, not in my wildest. What a place, eh? Well, both of 'em, but specially the castle. Fabulous! I'd give anything to have a place like that. A few horses, a few dogs, me favourite cheroots – I'd be as happy as Larry.'

'Some chance,' Mark told him, down as ever, his voice grating as usual.

'Oh, come on, my son – you've got to dream a little. It's come true for Jacky, hasn't it? Marrying a real toff!'

'Hasn't got any dosh. Doesn't live in a castle.'

'So what? She's on to a good thing there, with that family. They look after their own, you know, once you're one of them. Did you see that bracelet she got? The gold one? If that's not worth two grand, I don't know

167

anything. And she got that as a signing-on present! I bet there's more to come.'

'Well, Jacks is Jacks, so what's it all to me?'

It was unusual for Mark to express any bitterness in words. Freddie looked at him, saw how unappealing his son was with his hair, that earring, and that stupid moustache – which he'd presumably grown to make himself look older.

For one of the other odd things about Mark was his boyishness. He looked about ten years younger than he was. Freddie couldn't account for this retarded look. It didn't do Mark any good. To make his way in the world, he needed to look more of a man, so that people would respect him. Yes, respect was the word. It was very important in their line of business.

Freddie bounced up from behind his desk and moved round to where Mark was shifting about in an office chair. His father jabbed at him with his finger, in an emphatic way, never actually touching him.

'Listen, boy, don't ever let me hear that again. That's envy or jealousy, if you ask me.'

'But it's true, whatever it is. You're always going on about Jacks. Jacks this, that and the other. The sun shines out of her arse, the way you go on.'

Freddie could see that Mark had a point. He did go on about her – but given what a pudding Mark had turned out to be, was that so surprising?

'Change subject,' he snapped. 'There's going to be no family barneys in this house. We're a happy family and it's going to stay that way. And if we're not, I'll knock your bleedin' block off.'

Having lifted the edge of the curtain on his feelings, Mark went back to being silent again. Freddie sat down and resumed his patter. Talking of family barneys had made him think of Duncan. He had picked up the odd word or two about this odious man's behaviour and had taken an instant dislike to him after the brief exchange in the park at Cansdale.

'Have you ever set your eyes on such a shite as that brother of Rupe's? Isn't he just *typical*? That's what I hate about the bleedin' aristocracy. They behave as if they own the place. Trouble is, they bleedin' do, often enough!'

Freddie was rather pleased with his little joke, but maintained his serious, pugnacious look. 'He's obviously on the boil all the time. Jacky says he's got some little totty on the side. You know what I think of that sort of thing. And he crashes about. I tell you, if I'd moved a bit quicker I'd have rearranged his face, the way he went at me.'

'You still could.'

'What's that?' Freddie was genuinely startled by Mark's interruption.

'You could still push his face in. Find a way.'

'Nah.' Freddie waved his stumpy hand dismissively. 'Wouldn't help

Jacks, would it, if I went and biffed her brother-in-law? It'd be terrible. Upset her. And we'd never have anything more to do with them.'

'That's all you're worried about, isn't it? Hobnobbing with those gits.'

'What if I do? Got on very well, in my opinion. No trouble at all.'

'There are other ways of getting square.'

Freddie was again brought up by what his son was saying. It was just the kind of challenge that he, Freddie, would normally have laid down.

'What do you mean, boy?'

'Did you notice what I noticed, at the castle?'

'Whaddya you mean?'

Freddie drummed his fingers, impatient for Mark to get to the point now that he'd started.

'It'd be a pushover. If you wanted any of those pictures, or the silver, or anything, you could just walk in and pick 'em up.'

His father stopped drumming and looked Mark full in the face for the first time that morning.

'You off your head? You've never done what I'd call a job in your bleedin' life and you want to steal the bleedin' crown jewels! Come off it, mate!'

'I was being serious.'

'Look, son, you can't go bleedin' robbing the other side of the family, just because they're loaded. Chances are you'd be picked up the minute it was done. Stands to reason.'

'No, it doesn't, Dad. We'd be the last people they'd think of. They wouldn't believe we'd do it to the family, like you said.'

Freddie started fiddling with the papers on his desk, folding them into shapes, smoothing them heavily with his worn thumbs, being fussily but unnecessarily neat. He was thinking.

After a long silence, he said, 'Nah. Nothin' doin'. I'm not going to harm anyone connected with your sis', even if it is a shit like his lordship. And I'm not going to do the job myself either. I've kept my nose clean for six years now and I'm not starting again. That's final.'

Now it was Mark's turn to make the dramatic pause, after which he said simply, 'There's nothing to stop me doing it.'

Freddie looked more composed than he had done for months, on the outside at least. On the inside, he was buzzing.

Well, why not? If Mark could pull it off, he'd have proved himself. It was a wide-open target, so with the right kind of help it shouldn't be too much trouble. Freddie also felt the old tingle of excitement that had been missing from his drab money-making activities for so long now. Just to be on the fringes of a job would get the old adrenaline going. The money wouldn't matter. The excitement would be enough.

169

Freddie did not give a direct answer to Mark's question, but asked – quietly for him – 'What happened to that booklet your mother got?'

'I think it's in the lounge. Or on the bar.'

'Well, fetch it for me, boy. Fetch it.'

Mark slipped downstairs and was soon back with the guide book which was then put to a use its author had never thought of.

'What was you thinking of then, boy?'

'I was wondering what's in that temple thing? It's separate from the house, isn't it? Might be easier to get into it.'

' 'Old on, 'old on. You mean the Pantheon?' Freddie found the page devoted to it and read: ' "The Pantheon was erected in *circa* 1810 to house the Roman statuary collected by the 3rd Earl. It was he who commissioned the building of the present Castle Cansdale though he died before it was completed." Nah – you don't want any of that rubbish. Lumps of marble.'

'Just a thought.'

'Now, here we are,' cried Freddie, flicking through the pages and then slamming the book open flat with the palm of his hand. 'Thought there was a map.'

Mark came round the desk and stood behind his father as Freddie ran his finger over the ground plan.

'We went in through the back, didn't we – by the kitchen? Then up these steps here, coming into the Salon, right?'

Mark nodded. 'I think so. It's a rabbit warren down there.'

'Rabbit warrens are a darn sight more useful than a bloomin' desert. I mean, one thing you could never do is come at it through the front door. Or the windows on the ground floor. Too open. Flat as a pancake. You just couldn't get near without being seen, or making a noise on that gravel. If you're going to get near, it'd have to be somewhere near the Spring Lodge – which, if I'm right, has trees and sheds and things all round it.'

'Right.'

'You spotted no security?'

'There was an old burglar alarm on the back of the house. Rusty tin box on the wall. Might be a fake. Mightn't be switched on.'

'But there weren't infra-reds in the rooms, or in the display boxes?'

'Not that I saw.'

'That's bleedin' odd, innit? Some of that stuff is fuckin' rare. I mean, look at that silver.' Freddie flicked through the booklet until he came to a photograph of the Dining Room. Then he turned up the description of the Salon. 'Now, 'ere you are, boy, look 'ere. "Portrait of Countess by Sir

Joshua Reynolds" – you could do quite well with that. "Small Self-Portrait by Rembrandt".'

'Rembrandt? Let's see.' Mark all but snatched the booklet out of his father's hands. 'Oh, yes, I remember that. It's *very* small.'

'Nothing wrong in that. Easier to take away. But you don't want to get mixed up with that big-name stuff. You'll never get rid of it. Much too well known to those what knows.'

Freddie licked his thumb and rapidly flipped backwards and forwards through the pages.

'I agree most of this stuff's far too big. Look at that – "Van Dyck representing War and Peace". And "Charles Ist on a horse" – fuckin' gi-normous. No use at all. And look at them! "Pair of seventeenth-century K'ang Hsi vases on top of a black lacquer commode"! Far too big, far too big. What you need is silver snuffboxes, gold watches and jewellery. Portable stuff, like. Or – now, look at this – this is also in the Salon, in those display cases: "Beautiful green and gold dinner service made in Vienna . . . other services in lavender and white, festooned with blue flowers, from the Sèvres factory".'

'What's the Sèv-res factory?'

'Search me. But, 'ere you are, "The Harlequin service from Sèvres, each individual plate of a different design".'

'I don't want to be lugging plates about. They weigh a ton. I'd only drop them.'

'You'd have to find out which was which, just take a few. Read a few books. And you'll have to go back. On your own. Take a shufti. Make sure no one clocks you.'

'Okay.'

'And then you do it – properly, mind!'

'What's "properly"?'

Freddie feigned exasperation. 'You find someone who wants the stuff. Individual items, specific like. Not any old thing you can lay your 'ands on. Bespoke, if you like. Then you find yourself an expert. You can't pull a job like this on your own. I always thought the perfect job was one you did yourself, so no one else knew. No one else could blab. But you gotta have help with this one.'

'You know anybody?'

' 'Course I bleedin' do! I'll just have to have a think. But, like I said, you're doing this on your own. I'm taking a back seat. God help you if you fuck it up! I'll never speak to you again, even if you are me bleedin' son!'

For once, Mark had a light in his eyes. He would show his dad what he could do. It was the perfect opportunity for a big set-piece. He would not get caught. It would be fail-safe. A piece of cake.

'Dad,' Mark asked, pausing momentarily before rushing off to get started, 'what about Mum? Will she know?'

'No, boy. She never knows. What the head doesn't know, the heart doesn't grieve over. She never knew in the old days. That's the best way. She'd only worry herself silly, try to stop you. So, no, she's got to be left in the dark. You'd better put this booklet back where you found it. *Exactly* where you found it. She'd notice otherwise. She's quick, you know. So, not a word.'

'Okay, okay.'

'Now, piss off, and don't tell me anything until you've made some headway.'

Mark nodded and left. Freddie stood up and went to look out of the window at the scene of suburban tranquillity that it presented. He sighed, stretched, opened the window, and stuck his head out. He was getting on. Robbery was a young man's job. How fantastic that Mark had suddenly discovered his gumption! Freddie had despaired of his ever doing so. Perhaps he'd turn out all right after all.

A stately home job! He'd never tried anything like that himself. His had been urban crimes, where the logistics were all bricks and mortar and sashed windows and forced entry. All you had to fear was a passing bobby on night duty. Well, no fear of a passing bobby at Castle Cansdale. Freddie began to imagine what it would be like – casing the joint with the night air of the country in your nostrils, the stars up above, shinning up a pillar to a casement window.

Who was that geezer who used to do jobs like that? Raffles, that was it. Or Cary Grant in that Hitchcock film? Classy type of robber, and always got to bonk the mistress of the house.

Freddie's imagination began to run away with him, and he began to feel he would like to be involved. It would be too good to miss. He wouldn't say anything to Mark until the lad had got it sorted out. But Freddie decided he wasn't going to pass up the opportunity. His biggest difficulty would be restraining himself from taking over from Mark.

He pulled back from the widow, sat down by the desk once more, and looked up a number in his well-thumbed address book. He dialled the number and only had to wait a couple of rings before it answered.

'That you, Brian? Freddie . . . How you bin? . . . Yes, long time . . . well, this and that . . . the usual. Say, I'm not *asking* you, but just tell me, what's silver like these days?'

The man he was calling replied at length. Freddie grunted as though he was interested only in the broad gist, not in the detail.

'And china, cups and saucers – the best?'

The man wanted to know if he meant porcelain, *good* porcelain.

'Yeh, yeh, if that's what you call it. And pictures. You know, old masters. Peter, Paul and Rubens – that sort of thing.'

The man gave further considered opinions.

'Well, I don't know,' Freddie concluded. 'But I might just know where I could get a little. No, I'm not telling you, okay? Now listen, my kid Mark's doing this one. I'll get him to ring you. That okay? He's in charge. Don't take him for a ride now, will you? I'd be bound to hear about it. Okay, Brian. He'll be calling. Take care.'

Freddie sat, drumming his fingers once more on the desk. Then at last he stopped thinking of the Castle Cansdale project and turned his attention to the heap of papers in his in-tray. He read them intently for ten minutes. Then he yawned and stretched. This was so boring compared with what Mark was about to do.

He shot up, put on his golfing windcheater and went out of the den, locking the door behind him. Cynthia was out, shopping or playing tennis or whatever it was she did to fill her days, so he locked up and put on the burglar alarm. He wasn't going to be caught out at his own game.

He started up the Mercedes and drove slowly across to Battersea where he had to give a verbal thumping to the manager of one of his garages. He left it at that these days. Once upon a time he'd occasionally had to give someone like that a smack in the mouth. He'd only whacked hooligans, but the rumour had got about that he was into violence. On the whole, Freddie was proud of what he'd been able to do in the old days and the way he'd done it. He'd kept crime in the area down and controlled what people got up to. But nobody would ever believe you when you said that now.

Today he felt he'd got his message across to the man in the garage. It helped that people knew he had a record, so they were a little less likely to try it on. There was something in having a past if it meant people automatically respected you that little bit more. So he hadn't had to do any thumping. Just straight talk. But it still wasn't as much fun as a really good heist.

# CHAPTER 17

'I had to go and speak to Duncan,' Sophie said to the back of John Tarrant's head. He was sitting on the floor of Sleepy Cottage, leaning against her knees. Most of the time they spent together they ended up at Bethany Cottage but that Friday night in late June she had come to him.

Sophie ran her fingers through his hair and then removed his glasses.

'Why?' he asked simply.

'To sort out the Glenellen business, of course. How those two could even start screwing each other when this was bound to happen, I just don't know.'

'They're not talking, that it?'

Sophie stopped stroking John's hair and found a safe haven for his glasses. 'Yes. Glennie couldn't do her work at the house without talking to D. And since they'd had a tiff, he was pretending she didn't exist, that he'd never set eyes on her, let alone been on top of her. Impossible situation, for all of us.'

'But Sophie sorted it out – the go-between?'

'That's one way of putting it. I fixed a time to see Duncan, all very formal, and told him he was being quite childish and making life very difficult for all of us at Waterwheel.'

'And?'

'Well, Joanna had to come in just as we got started. She was in one of her lovey-dovey moods – and there's nothing more grotesque than that, frankly. The sight of horsey old Jo playing kittenish and lamb-like with Duncan is a bit hard to take.'

'So the prodigal has returned?'

'As far as Joanna's concerned, yes – yet again. I don't know why she falls for it, but she does. She actually pointed out while I was there that Duncan had said he'd never do it again. And she *believes* him! Anyway, as

174

far as she's concerned, they're together again, and all's right with the world.'

John, who had noticed Sophie's use of the word 'horsey' in a pejorative sense and took this to be an encouraging sign that his small campaign to unsaddle Sophie was paying off, gave a pretend cry of weariness.

'God, they deserve each other, those two. I suppose they'll carry on, on and off, to the crack of doom?'

'Exactly. Anyway, I got Duncan to promise to speak to Glennie and have it out with her. So with luck she will be able to keep on at the house. But it's driving me bonkers having to rush around playing agony aunt all the time!'

'Never mind,' said John, trying to look up at his lover, but she was behind him. 'Worse things happen at sea.'

'You always say that.'

'Oh, dear. Not getting bored with me, I trust?'

'No fear!' Sophie pushed him forward with her knees, leapt out of the chair, and lay down beside him on the hearth rug. 'Not bored with you. Can't get enough of you.'

She positioned herself on one elbow and gently lowered her lips on to his as his head sank backwards to the floor.

'You're happy then?' he said, after they had kissed.

'God, yes. I don't know what I'd do without you. Best thing ever happened to me, falling off that bloody horse.'

John fished for a further compliment, whilst pretending the opposite. 'I bet your people don't approve of me. They're very polite, but they must have twigged we're together a lot. And they can't really be pleased you've ended up with riff-raff like me.'

Sophie was beginning to feel randy now and didn't want John to get all talkative.

' 'Course they think you're all right,' she whispered. 'No trouble at all. If there's any riff-raff around it's to do with what's in Rupert's bed, frankly, not mine. You can see they're in a terrible jam over that – don't know how to cope with it. But that doesn't affect you. They haven't a *clue* what we get up to, or what you mean to me. So, you shouldn't think about them for a moment.'

John reacted against Sophie being on top of him and with a sudden movement changed places. Something she had said seemed to trigger off a great urgency in him. He pinioned her arms over her head, on the floor. She was devastated by what he said next. It was so sudden.

'I'd love to tie you up.'

It wasn't so much the proposal itself as the unhesitant way in which John expressed his wish that did it for her. Sophie couldn't remember ever having been with a man before who had been so direct in his demands – and who did not take for ever and a day to express them.

'God, you know you can – anywhere – here, now,' Sophie said, staccato, but swallowing her words in anticipation.

'Have you had it this way before?'

'No, but I've . . . wanted it.'

'One so old' – John couldn't resist the joke – 'and so conventional.'

'Oh, come on, John – do it for God's sake! What with?'

John pressed a finger to her lips, pulled Sophie up from the floor, and chased her up the narrow cottage stairs.

In John's bedroom was an old Victorian brass bed with rails at top and bottom, ideal for the purpose to which it was now to be put.

John swept off the duvet and then turned to Sophie who simply stood there, looking pink and dazed. He helped her undress, even down to pulling off her tight jeans rather as he had once pulled off those riding boots after her fall.

'Got some tights I can use?' asked John.

'In my bag.'

John slipped downstairs and found the brand new spares which Sophie apparently carried about with her.

She, meanwhile, sank naked on to the bed to wait.

John came back up and rummaged around in the chest of drawers until he found another two pairs. Sophie didn't begin to think what they were doing there.

'Lie further up,' he told her gently but firmly.

He nimbly tied her wrists together and to the bed-head. Then, opening her legs, he used the remaining pairs of tights to fix them to the bottom of the bed. Then, almost as an afterthought, he took a pillow and pushed it under Sophie's rear.

'Oh, hurry up, please!' she said urgently, her body already aroused by the restraints on her arms and legs, by her vulnerability to whatever this lover chose to do with her.

He quickly shed his own clothes and climbed on the bed over her. It was a long time before he took her. He agonizingly licked every place in her body that could give her pleasure. Finally, he drew himself down across her – down her lips, her throat, her breasts, her fetchingly curved stomach. Then, with a suddenness that made Sophie gasp, he was between those famous thighs.

They did not take long after that. Both had been on the brink, even before he entered her.

They both lay shattered, until Sophie said to him, eventually, 'Make me one promise, John.'

'What's that?'

'Don't ever marry me. A fuck like that wouldn't be possible, not if we were married . . .'

Although it was early days yet, John had already thought about marrying Sophie. But he wasn't put off by what she now said. He knew what she was getting at. It must surely be hard to make the bed – or any other domestic chore – with someone who'd just tied you *to* the bed.

'I promise,' he told her. But he did not take his promise as legally binding. It was just love talk.

'That's what I'd call a designer fuck,' Sophie sighed. 'How do you decide which it's going to be: one of those or just an ordinary one?'

John didn't know what to do with these post-coital teases. 'It seemed like a good idea at the time . . .'

'Oh, J., please, never leave me. You're the best thing I've got. Promise.'

'Of course I won't ever leave you,' said John, sounding rather sensible after such exertions.

But he meant it.

That same evening in late June, about a hundred miles away, an already-married couple had just enjoyed a comparable experience. But in their case it had been achieved simply with their bodies and their imaginations, and no additional aids to enjoyment.

Rupert and Jacky had, unknowingly, managed to disprove Sophie's view that the heights of pleasure were impossible to achieve in marriage. But then, they had only been married a comparatively short while, they still shared Rupert's bachelor bed, and they had certainly not been doing any domestic chores previously. They had been celebrating – with champagne, of course. One of Rupert's new rules was that they must never run out of the bubbly stuff.

'There was a French king, you know – don't ask me which – whose motto was, "A chicken in every pot". Well, mine is "A bottle of champers in every fridge"!'

So they had drunk, and they had skipped the food, and it did not seem to have spoiled their lovemaking one jot.

As to what they were celebrating – apart from having survived another week – Jacky had just earned her largest ever fee for a day's modelling. Maddie Shapiro's blandishments had at last led her to accept an engagement, and Jacky's brief absence from before the lens had done wonders for her earning capacity: £1,200 had come her way – less, of course, Maddie's twenty per cent – for having been up since dawn on a shoot in the New Forest. The only drawback was that the wild ponies lacked her own considerable professional discipline. They seemed quite unable to take direction from Jervais Richmond – the photographer of Castle Cansdale had now turned his lens on Jacky, though he was unaware of any connection between his model and the Hookes.

Rupert was immensely pleased by Jacky's success. He did not feel envious, nor was he going to insist she kept her nose to the grindstone (or her shoulder pads to the wheel, as he more felicitously expressed it) – though there was no escaping that it was jolly useful being married to such a big earner. All he asked was that Jacky's work shouldn't tire her too much and interfere with their daily lovemaking. The daily bout was Rupert's way of keeping their marriage alive, so he said. It was quite the reverse of a routine, he insisted. Routine was when you did it on certain set days and at certain set times. Doing it every day was not like that at all. He needed to make love once, if not twice, a day and he wasn't going to do so – he assured his darling wife – other than with her assistance.

'And which school of thought does Jervais Richmond belong to?' he inquired of Jacky. 'The Not Before or Doesn't Matter?'

Jacky pretended not to know what he was talking about. She had, perhaps unwisely, told him once that some of the photographers who trained their lenses on her form believed that models shouldn't have sex the night before a shoot.

'Like footballers before a match? Why ever not?' Rupert had asked.

'They say it takes some of the shine off you!'

'Quite the reverse I should've thought. Could do wonders for you!'

'I'd say Jervais was a Don't Know,' Jacky at last gave her view. 'I'm not sure he's really very into girls – or guys. He's supposed to be better at buildings. And they don't bonk the night before, so there's no problem.'

Rupert was delighted that Jacky was back on form. Her well-paid outing that day seemed to have revived her interest in the job.

'So what do you think about when you're being photographed?' he asked.

'Oh, Roo, that's the oldest question in the book. What do you think about when you're venturing capital, or whatever it is you do?'

He didn't mind her pretending not to understand what he did for a living. She could act the pea-brained model when it suited her, but he knew she was not. In fact, one of the things Rupert had become aware of since they were married was that Jacky had both a brain and a will of her own. She wasn't prepared to be ordered about – and, having met her parents, it was quite clear to Rupert from whom she had inherited this trait.

'I've been thinking,' Jacky changed the subject suddenly.

Rupert said nothing, but grasped the fingers of her hand to show that he was listening.

'I want you to tell me if it's true. What happens if Duncan and Joanna don't have any more children? Who'll be the next Earl?'

'Ah,' Rupert said, and turned on his left side to face her. He could not see straight into her eyes, so addressed her breasts instead. 'You really want to know?'

'Yes, I do.'

'Well, it all depends. If Duncan dies before me and doesn't have a boy – a legitimate one, that is – and the chances are he won't now, though you can never be sure, then the title comes to me.'

'That's what I was thinking. You never really said that before.'

'Maybe not. If we have children, and we have the boy that Duncan hasn't got, the title goes to him when I die. But who's to say Duncan'll die before me? It's a bit of a lottery, and that's why I try not to spend too much time thinking about it.'

'Mm,' said Jacky, hoping not to sound as though she had been too calculating.

'And, of course, as I say, Duncan may not have finished yet. Though given the way he seems to stick himself into everyone but Joanna, perhaps he has.'

'What about the little boy he had by that woman in the village?'

'Can't inherit the title – unless he marries her, and that's pretty unlikely, I should think. Could inherit some of the estate, but there'd probably be a fight.'

'It makes me nervous,' said Jacky. 'It means so much hangs on having babies.'

'You mustn't worry. What will be, will be. There's nothing we can do about it. Ours might be all girls, like Duncan's. Then they'd really have to dig around the family tree.'

'What if Sophie had a baby, a boy?'

'Doesn't count. And if Duncan and I fell under a bus tomorrow, it would go back to Uncle Alec. And, from what one knows of him, he's unlikely to marry again and produce an heir. I prefer simply not to think about it – it's snakes and ladders!'

But Jacky couldn't get the idea out of her mind. She hadn't given Rupert's position a moment's thought before she married him. Now she had had dealings with the Hooke family, she was becoming more aware of her role. She hadn't just married Rupert, she had enroled in a great scheme of things.

She let her restless thoughts take another direction. She started to ask Rupert about houses. In a way, this was related to having children. It was to do with ownership and nests, sharing and security. Having walls of your own around you, having a roof over your head. Before she married, she would have said all that was unimportant. As long as Rupert and she had a little hole to go home to, to be together, that was all that mattered. But now she was more aware of the importance of bricks and mortar. She had also learned from her exposure to Huddleston and Castle Cansdale just how beguiling houses could be.

'So put it this way then,' she said, ever more awake and brisk while Rupert still lay in post-coital languor, 'and I don't really mind what happens, so long as I keep you, and never mind if we have boys or girls or none at all – do you ever think you'll succeed Duncan, and get the castle?'

Rupert pulled himself up on to the pillows, and made sure the bed-clothes adequately covered his naked body if he was to talk seriously.

'I'll tell you something, Jacky. I've not said anything before, but I ought to now, I think. I know we've been down to Cansdale a couple of times very close together since we married, but before that I used to avoid it no end. Used to get me into hot water, but I had a reason. I couldn't bear to be there knowing it would one day pass to Duncan, not to me. You see, I love the place – much more than he does, I'm sure.'

'Why didn't you say so before? I didn't know it had that effect on you.'

'It does. And it doesn't end there – the complications. You see, Dad's made the estate over to Duncan under some silly scheme his lawyer came up with. If Dad lives for another six years then Duncan won't have to pay any inheritance tax. But it's all a bit dicey, and from what I've been able to find out, it's the wrong scheme. Dad's solicitor's a bit past it and doesn't know what he's doing.'

'But your dad hates Duncan so much, he'd do better to pop off and lumber him with the tax!'

'You'd think so, but then Joanna and the kids would land in it. Duncan's stingy enough as it is. And, chances are, the estate would have to be broken up, and Dad sees it as his duty to prevent that.'

'I see what you mean. Perhaps we're well out of all that. If you can't have the castle, we ought at least to have our own house!'

'Exactly,' her husband agreed.

'Oh, Roo ... darling.' Jacky moved over and rested her head on Rupert's warm shoulder. She reached up and gently stroked his cheek. 'Trouble is, we sell here and put it with the money from my flat, we still won't have enough for a house. You know what houses cost in London. What can we do?'

'Get out the begging bowl. We can get quite a good joint mortgage, especially if you get a few more jobs like today's!'

'A semi in Surbiton?' Jacky wondered, a little sadly.

'Might have to be. A bungalow in Brentwood?'

'Not that, please! Perhaps my Dad'll help.'

'Mr Property, you mean?'

'He'd do anything for me – within reason.'

'That's what I worry about.'

'Rupert!' She pinched him near his hips which made him double up.

Rupert had already established his father-in-law as a joke figure in the demonology of the marriage. He knew that Freddie and Jacky ran a mutual admiration society, so he had to make his lunges gentle enough. He sensed that Freddie needed to be dealt with cautiously at all times. John Tarrant might be on to why, but he and Rupert had barely exchanged words at their first meeting.

Jacky knew, of course, about her father's chequered past, but had only hinted about it to Rupert. It was not from guilt that she did this. She did not think it necessary to tell him everything. She loved her father and what it was not necessary to say did not have to be said.

She would talk to Freddie about finding them a house.

Hugo and Molly were also side by side, having an early night, but in adjacent, not adjoining beds. That had been their way for several years now. It was so much more convenient. Hugo tossed and turned in bed at the best of times and sharing a double bed with him had long proved impossible. Molly herself slept only a few hours a night and spent the rest of it reading detective novels, so it was distracting for Hugo to have the bedside light on so near to his head.

Nor had they been 'having a cuddle', as Hugo for so long had euphemistically referred to sex. These days that took place only on birthdays or other significant occasions, and on holiday if it wasn't too hot.

No, they were in bed early that Friday evening because Hugo had been feeling unwell. They were installed by nine thirty, so eager was Molly to embark on an Agatha Christie, completely oblivious of whether this was the second or third time she had read the book, and totally unable to remember who did it.

Hugo, rather to his wife's annoyance, appeared to be neither reading (something he did not enjoy at the best of times) nor trying to get off to sleep. He lay with his pillows piled high, breathing rather heavily, his arms on top of the counterpane as though modelling for a medieval tomb.

'Close your mouth, Hugo,' she said to him with moderate kindness in her voice. 'Take your medicine before you forget.'

'Yes, dear,' he replied grumpily.

Molly worried every time Hugo had one of these minor illnesses nowadays. He wasn't a good patient. Increasingly, his complaints weren't really illnesses at all, simply signs of old age. She tried hard to forget that there was a reason why Hugo should be kept alive – it was a grubby, calculating reason, of more benefit to Duncan than anyone, so not worth losing any sleep over – but in her heart of hearts she had begun to accept that Hugo wouldn't be with her for much longer. She was younger than he. The chances were, being a woman, that she would outlive him anyway. It worried her, the uncertainty of not knowing what would happen and the certainty of knowing that when death did take him away, she might not be able to bear it.

'I think we should go abroad,' Hugo suddenly announced, and with his eyes shut.

Molly allowed her half-moons to slide off the end of her nose and on to the bosom of her nightdress where they were restrained by the chains. She was quite annoyed by this sudden interruption of her reading.

'For a holiday, you mean? But why abroad, dear? We haven't been abroad for ages.'

'That's as good a reason as any.'

'You mean for a holiday?'

'What other reason would there be?'

'Oh, Hugo, don't sound so *tragic* about it!'

Hugo did not rise to this bait, but gave one of his pauses and then cleared his throat.

'I think it would make me feel better. The sun and the warmth would be good for me. I'll never get better in this old barn, especially this rotten summer.'

Hugo was riding one of his more recent hobby-horses. He was convinced that Huddleston was damp – which it was, though hardly more uncomfortably so than the cold that used to trouble him at Castle Cansdale.

'Very well then,' said Molly. 'Where shall we go?' She knew that the task of organizing the trip would fall on her. Hugo did not readily come up with a suggestion, so Molly felt obliged to kick off. 'We haven't been to Nice for years, have we?'

'Not going there. Spoiled it, they have, according to the paper. Can't see the sun for blocks of hideous flats. And all the women sunbathe with their thingies out.'

'You'd like that, dear. Give you something to do with your binoculars.'

Hugo did not answer – as always his most effective way of expressing disapproval.

'I was thinking more of Italy,' he eventually said.

'The Cipriani at – what's that place? – Asolo! I'd love to go there again. That room with the terrace. I wonder if we could get it again?'

'No. I wasn't thinking of there.'

'Well, what *are* you thinking, Hugo? Out with it.'

'I think we ought to go and find my father's grave.'

Oh, so that was it, Molly realized. He had resurrected this old worry after his chats with the Rector. He wouldn't be able to rest until it had been resolved.

'I've never been to Sicily,' she said.

'I have,' he said.

'Doesn't it get frightfully hot in the summer?'

'Can't remember.'

'When shall we go, if you're so keen? It'll be booked up.'

'How about early September? Shouldn't be too bad then.'

Molly said she would get on to the travel agent in Craswall next day and scribbled a note to remind herself.

# CHAPTER 18

Down the length of Italy, at the very toe, the town of Reggio di Calabria lay glaring across the Straits of Messina at an island casually sleeping in the heat haze. It was as if the toe of Italy wished to boot Sicily away like a football – as well it might, with all its lingering, festering, age-old problems.

The President of the Republic of Italy had issued an unprecedented demand for action against the Mafia. A prosecutor in the flyblown port of Trapani had alleged that once more no one had any idea what was happening in the power structure of the Silician underworld.

Within a year of the Palermo 'maxi-trial' in 1987, after which 347 Mafiosi had been convicted and there was hope that the organization was at last beaten, the advantage was crumbling away. The Mafia families were regrouping. A fresh fight for domination was under way. It was going to be very much as it had always been for the 'honoured society'.

Benino Noto was one of the oldest of the Mafia prisoners in Reggio di Calabria gaol. He was in his early seventies now and over the years he had acquired a reputation for invincibility. They had tried to shoot him, more than once, but he had outwitted them. He had prospered, joylessly, but now he had suffered his first real defeat. Charged with conspiracy to murder – his alleged victims were a magistrate and a chief of police – and with drug-trafficking, he had been given a prison term of eight and a half years. That was for Mafia membership and drug-trafficking. The evidence from *pentiti* – repentant former Mafiosi – had failed to make the other charge stick.

But to be in prison for any length of time was worse than death for Benino. He had always believed he would die peacefully in bed or with a bullet in the back of his head. He had never for a moment imagined it might be in prison. But at the trial – the one with the prisoners lined up against the bars of a cage in the courtroom, in Palermo – he had been given this terrible sentence.

For a man of his age, it could mean that he would never live to enjoy his freedom again. It was impossible. Why had those bastards in Rome suddenly decided to meddle in Sicilian affairs? The bosses had run the island for as long as Benino Noto could remember. It was as natural for a Sicilian to do things this way as it was to use the air to breathe. The fools in Rome had overreached themselves. Just another example of their contempt for the south.

But he sensed there was little that could be done. He could appeal against his sentence, and was in the process of applying for leave to do so. He could wait for another earthquake in Reggio to break down the prison walls. He could wait for forgiveness. Or, in the old Sicilian phrase, he could wait till the horse rode on the back of the man.

Benino Noto moved slowly, with a dark and sinister dignity. He still carried himself like a boss – they would never strip him of that quality. He placed the cheap wooden chair against the side of the table. His sun-beaten hands, worn now, made sure this arrangement was safe with unexpected gentleness and care.

Then slowly he stepped on to the chair.

The slide on the observation hole of the cell door shot briskly across. Benino did not turn to look. He did not want to see the guard's eye looking inquisitively, contemptuously up at him. So he continued with what he was doing as though nothing had happened.

Now he was standing on the table, his fingertips grazing the rough cement on the cell wall. If he stood on tiptoe, he could glimpse the corner of the roof of another cell block. It was nothing worth getting excited about, but it was all he could see of the world beyond. Above it was the ravishing deep blue of the sky over towards the Straits of Messina. He had never noticed the sky till he was in prison. It had always been there for him. But too bright. To enjoy it was what other people did.

The observation shutter on the cell door was closed as briskly as it had been opened. The guard had satisfied himself that Benino was not about to top himself. Benino stood, staring up and out of the window for a good five minutes before, again with slow deliberation, he climbed down once more.

What else was he to do? He did not read – could just about, but did not. He sat on the edge of his bed, not sprawling like the younger prisoners did, but almost religiously. His mind was a blank. He did not know how to deal with this way of life. Nothing had prepared him for the blankness, the emptiness of his days. It was a living death. And yet, in time, he would start scheming again. If he could not live in the world, he could still make the world dance to his tune from a prison cell.

The following day, a Sunday, if it was a Sunday – he lost track of time so easily – Benino Noto expected that his son, Alvaro, would come to visit him. He was never sure. It was such a long drive from Palermo, even using the autostrada. Then he had to cross the Straits on the ferry. Much better that Alvaro should do useful things back home. The Noto family must keep its share of the heroin smuggling that went on between Sicily and the United States. The Greco family, the Corleonesi families, the Altofonte mob – none of these rivals must be allowed to steal a march on them.

And yet, Benino wanted to have news. He wanted to know about the family. It was so cruel to have such power, to have so many dependent on you, and then to have it taken away.

He wanted to know how Alvaro was doing now that he was the effective boss of the Noto family. The transfer of power was not as it should have been. Benino had been kept on remand so long before the trial, not knowing what would happen, that he had not, could not have, acted with the speed and decisiveness that was expected of him. And so he had learned that Alvaro had taken charge. Alvaro had visited him in gaol in Palermo, soon after his arrest, and presented it as an accomplished fact.

Benino had not been happy, had withheld his formal assent. Alvaro was not right for the role. He was not one of them, he was an outsider. Never mind that he had been raised in the family traditions, he was not *of* the family. He was not of Benino's blood, and that was important.

Benino had three sons and two daughters, all married now, in their thirties and forties, and busily producing grandchildren for him. Alvaro, though at fifty the oldest, was in addition to the children he had had by Consiglia. Benino always tried to avoid calling him his 'son', for Alvaro was not his son, but sometimes the word slipped out.

It had been one of those things. The marriage to Consiglia had been arranged because it was a good one, but the price had been that she was pregnant by another. Benino had bowed to the wishes of his father and her father, and accepted the strange imposition.

It was not a secret that could be kept. There was no great dishonour in being with child on your wedding day in Palermo, even fifty years ago. The priest had been open-minded. Dishonour only came if the mother had been raped. So Benino had acknowledged that Alvaro was his son, for form's sake, but no one in the quarter of Palermo where both families lived was taken in.

Alvaro was palpably *not* the son of his father. He was tall, had light-coloured hair, and did not look like a Sicilian. It was not long into his child-hood, and shortly after the war when all those British and American soldiers had been on the island, that he became known as *L'Inglese*, the Englishman.

Consiglia was filled with shame. How had her secret escaped? Benino knew the facts of the matter, but how had the neighbours and friends found out?

'You have betrayed me,' she told her husband. 'Made me feel small. Why have you done this thing?'

Benino had not moved to touch her or hold her. He treated her like dirt. He only took his pleasure with her when he wanted to get her with child. Then it was rough and short. It hurt Consiglia, just as it hurt when she gave birth. There was no pleasure for her, not even in that corner of her life.

'I have not told anyone,' he spat at her. 'I had no need. The world knows. Your shame walks before you.'

Consiglia, already looking older than her years, felt tears on the way. She drew a black-draped arm up to her face and prepared to wipe away the tears her husband so hated her to shed.

And so it had gone on. She had raised the five children fathered by Benino with as much love as she gave to the bastard she had been given by the Englishman at the Hotel La Torre all those years ago. She cooked the food, she looked after the house, and she kept quiet as her husband rose high among the Mafia dons.

The anguishing thing was that Benino's activities never seemed to improve their lives. There never seemed to be any more money to spend on clothing for the children. They never had a better house. The activities seemed to have more to do with defeating rivals, defending territory, than making life more bearable.

Consiglia favoured Alvaro. He was the eldest, he was her special responsibility, but this was not approved of by Benino. He never missed an opportunity to upbraid his wife if he noticed she gave the bastard a larger portion of food, or if she was seen to be fussing unnecessarily over his clothes. Benino would give her the edge of his tongue, there and then,and Alvaro would shrink from acknowledging his mother's kindness. It was more than a boy could do to stand up against such a father. The house was full of anger and tears all the time he was growing up.

It was only when Alvaro left school, started working in the docks at Palermo, and acquired a slight measure of independence that he began to appreciate quite how cruel his father's treatment of his mother was. He could not understand why it happened. What had Consiglia done to deserve it? What, in particular, was there about his own relationship with his mother that seemed so to anger Benino?

Once he had boldly and bluntly put the question to his father.

'You are too young to understand,' he was told. 'When you are old enough to show respect, you may learn. But not till then.'

So Alvaro continued in ignorance. Of course, he was used to being teased about his strange looks. He accepted the nickname of *L' Inglese* without understanding it. And he continued not to know the true story of his birth. It was only when he started to show an interest in the dark, beautiful girls of

# A Family Matter

Palermo that he began to wonder about the mystery of his origins. He almost worked it out for himself. He must have another father, whom he resembled. Somehow he had been absorbed into this alien family.

In time, Alvaro himself married. Maria was a schoolteacher, not from a Mafia family, and deeply religious. Benino had allowed the marriage, perhaps because he still considered Alvaro unimportant. It did not matter whether the boy made a good, dynastic marriage or not. He could marry whom he liked – provided she was not the daughter of Benino's enemies.

Maria produced two children, a boy and a girl. Alvaro was inordinately proud of them and made sure that Maria lavished her love upon them. He treated her almost as an equal. It was a rare and almost a dangerous thing to do in that land.

Because Maria was an outspoken, free-thinking woman, she had no hesitation in remarking on the way Alvaro's father treated his wife.

'Why does he do that? It is not natural.'

'I do not know. I cannot ask.'

'But you must find out, Al. How can you ever be at peace if you do not?'

Alvaro made a wide gesture with his hands. 'I will know some time – even if it is after they are both dead.'

Although he loved Maria, Alvaro was worried by her. As he saw it, there was no other way to exist in Palermo than the way generations had done. This meant subscribing to the codes of honour and behaviour that were passed on from generation to generation – like *omertà*, the vow of silence. He understood these rules and saw they were just as good a way of life as any other. But he worried that, if he played his rightful role in the affairs of the Noto family – and did the sometimes cruel things that were required of him – Maria would object.

And so she did. It was after one of Alvaro's regular 'rebellions' against his father that he was summoned from his work at the docks. He had been told, with no mincing of words, that he was to attend on Benino during his lunch break.

Alvaro sensed at once what this meant. He did not hesitate, and presented himself at the family home as he was bid. He was struck by Benino's calmness. His father was almost smiling, was gentle in his movements, almost stroked Alvaro on the arm as he guided him into the darkened room, away from Consiglia and one of Alvaro's sisters who still lived at home.

'I have not asked you to do anything for me before now,' Benino began, looking at Alvaro steadily.

'Yes, you have,' the younger man spoke up, 'many times. I have done many things. Always when you asked—'

Benino made a gesture with his right hand, turning it palm up. It stopped Alvaro's talk.

'You misunderstand. Let me tell you a little story. You have heard me speak of the Greco madman?'

'I think so – in the Greco family, who have the gasoline franchise?'

Benino nodded. 'It is the gasoline which is at stake. They have been talking to Domenico at the Monreale service station. He told me. They have offered him big money to go over to them.'

'They're moving in on—' Alvaro was going to say 'your' but changed it to –'our patch? They can't do that.'

'Of course not. Domenico is a fool even to talk to them. Which is why I am now asking you to do something for me. You are willing?'

Alvaro nodded, without thinking. There were some things you did not allow yourself to think about.

'I do not want to hear of Domenico ever again.'

Benino was looking at his son very hard. Alvaro felt dry in the throat.

'I understand,' he said, standing up and pushing the chair away behind him with the heel of his boot.

He said nothing else, but turned quickly, went to the kitchen, exchanged cold pleasantries with his mother and sister and left as quickly as he could.

He was shaking and covered with sweat. He had been given the order to shoot and kill Domenico. Domenico was one of the corps of *picciotti* or foot soldiers, the little men who did the dirty jobs, and consequently of no importance. It was Alvaro's first such contract. He knew his father was testing him. He must not fail. Or, rather, he *could* fail – but then he would be out of the family. His father would make sure of that.

Alvaro returned to the docks in a daze. He couldn't make head or tail of the dockets he was supposed to be checking. He told his supervisor he had a fever and must go home. The supervisor could see there was something up and let the young man go, fearing what Alvaro's father might do to him if he refused the request.

Alvaro thus had all the time in the world to worry about such matters as where to get the right gun and the right ammunition, and how to make sure he killed the right man, and how not to get caught.

Maria spotted the change in him that evening, though she did not ask what had caused it. But she could tell he was brooding over something and she later observed he did not sleep at night but lay on the rough sheets bathed in sweat.

Alvaro obtained a gun and took a bus to Monreale to see if he could catch sight of Domenico and, if possible, work out a neat way of killing him. And kill him on the spot, if he was able.

It was much easier than he had feared. In fact, it had all the hallmarks of a family execution. Alvaro made no effort to disguise himself, banking on the fact that no one in Monreale would know who he was anyway.

189

He managed to gain access to Domenico's office at the back of the garage without being spotted. Domenico was seated at his desk with his back to the door. Alvaro did not shoot him immediately. He had to be sure that this was the correct victim. He wanted to look him in the eye as well.

Alvaro purposely kicked over a bucket in which Domenico had been stubbing out his cigarettes. The man turned anxiously to look. With both his hands, Alvaro made a relaxing gesture and came round so that he stood facing Domenico across the paper-cluttered desk.

Their eyes met and Alvaro knew he had found his victim. It seemed to him that the man knew what was happening. Not all the details, perhaps – not who his visitor was exactly. He began to rise as Alvaro reached inside his jacket for the gun.

Sheer panic shot through the man. He put his hands before him to fend off his death. Alvaro squeezed the trigger. The force of the bullet was like a fist under Domenico's jaw. He was thrust backwards and up. His face exploded in red and white. One of his eyes simply disappeared. Alvaro almost turned aside at this moment, but stuck to it. He pumped three more bullets into the man's neck, heart and groin.

There was a smell of cordite mingled with flesh such as Alvaro had never known before. He was riveted by the sight of the body before him, from which life was so rapidly fleeing.

He left quickly. Already he could hear people coming, cries of 'What is it? Domenico, what is it?' But he had found his route out of the back of the garage earlier and had left a door open. In a matter of seconds, he was clear of the scene, his heart now throbbing with triumph, a grim satisfaction in his head.

He ran quickly to the cloister of the church in Monreale and lost himself among the visitors. Then he ran down the hill and hid in an orange grove.

When his pulse was almost back to normal, he came out of the grove and caught the bus back to Palermo. He did not report to his father. He would find out soon enough that his wish had been fulfilled. Alvaro went straight back to his flat. Maria noticed there was something different about him. She made him coffee and gave him one of the small almond *biscotti* he was so fond of.

Then Alvaro chased the children out of the door, took her to bed and made love harshly. Maria did not know why and allowed herself to enjoy it.

Alvaro had proved himself – to himself and to his father, and he felt an unbelievable satisfaction in this. It was not something he would ever forget, this first 'useful job'. It was not to be his last.

The trouble was, he eventually told Maria. The vow of silence was supposed to extend to his wife, but he did not see why this should be. She was beside herself with anger. Why did he have to do what everyone else did?

How dare he risk the lives of his children – and his wife – by doing such a thing? It took many weeks before Maria would be quiet on the matter. She even risked telling the priest at confession – always a dangerous thing to do.

From then on, Alvaro decided he would not tell her when he had to do one of Benino's special jobs. But whenever he made love to her in that harshly enjoyable way, she lay and wondered what he had been doing just before.

Alvaro did indeed turn up the next day at visiting time. It was an imposition, the journey to Reggio, but how much worse if Benino had been imprisoned further north, in Rome, or Milan even.

At three o'clock, the old prisoner was taken from his cell and marched to the interview room which was the size of a chapel. Down the middle was a ceiling-high grille – to prevent anything being passed over from visitor to prisoner. There was no table for each side to lean on. Apart from the grille, there had to be clear air between the parties.

Alvaro bowed and mimed kissing the hand of his senior. Benino was glad, thinking that the gesture showed proper respect to him as a *capo*, a Mafia boss. Perhaps his 'son' had seen sense.

The younger man saw at once that his father was distracted. He had had the fight knocked out of him. He spoke vaguely, almost as if he was on some sort of medication. Perhaps he was. His heart had begun to give him trouble at the time of the trial. It wouldn't be beyond the prison authorities to give him drugs to keep him down.

'I have something to tell you.'

Alvaro was struck by Benino's sudden matter-of-factness. His father leaned forward as if to whisper, but then realized he would be reprimanded by the guards if he was seen to be uttering intimacies to his visitor. So he spoke strongly, as though not caring who heard – though such was the clamour from all the others in the room there was little chance of this.

'I have something to tell you, Alvaro. I have been thinking.' He almost smiled. 'I have plenty of time to think these days. And sometimes I do. I have had time to think of an old matter that concerns you.'

'Tell me what it is, Benino.' Alvaro had always shrunk from calling him 'father', just as Benino had always avoided referring to him as his 'son'.

'You should know one or two things. So that you can do what must be done.'

Alvaro blinked, and stared as hard as he could at the older man's lips.

'I'm going to tell you what I have not told you in all your life. Not in fifty years. You are that old?'

'A little more than that, Benino.'

'Yes? Well, this is what I have thought. You are not my son. But I think you knew that already?'

191

'I have always tried to behave like a true son of yours, but yes, it comes as no surprise. Yet I am my mother's son?'

'Of course. There is no doubt of that. You have a certain look, do you not? I must tell you. She was already with child – expecting you – when we married. I have never bothered to hide that. You could have worked it out for yourself. You know your birth date and our marriage date.'

'Yes. So, you are going to tell me who my father is?'

'No, I cannot, for I do not know. But I am telling you now that you must find out who it is.'

'Will that be hard, Benino?'

'I cannot say, but you have many people who can help you. Wherever he may be, you must find him.'

Alvaro paused before replying. 'But . . . I wonder, do I wish to know my father? I have always looked on *you*—'

'You must, of course. Not to know it for your own satisfaction, but so that you can do what must be done.'

'I do not understand. Why must anything be done?'

Benino looked irritated at his son's stupidity.

'There is honour, there is duty. That man dishonoured your mother. Raped her most cruelly when she was a young girl of eighteen. That is why you must do it. For your mother's sake. Your family's sake. It is necessary.'

The words reduced the surrounding hubbub to silence in Alvaro's ears.

'You mean, I must *kill* . . . my father?'

Benino actually smiled now. Alvaro was horrified. Surely no one waited fifty years for revenge? It was the family code that revenge must always be quick – and silently accomplished. And what good could it possibly do, except please Benino who seemed to have devoted his long leisure hours in prison to thinking of old scores to settle?

'But why?' Alvaro felt so unsure of himself, he had to ask the question.

Benino shook his head. 'So that I can call you my son, and you can call me your father. And if you are to be the head of the family, that has to be done.'

'Head of the family?'

So, Benino might finally pass on the baton, give formal consent.

'You see, it has to be done.'

'But who is my father? Why wasn't this dealt with at the time I was born?'

Benino made to move back to his cell without giving a reply, but the guard indicated he must stay until the end of visiting time.

The two men, father and son, sat staring at each other through the grille for a while in silence, the sound of excited talk, laughter and some tears echoing around them.

'You had better talk to your mother,' said Benino sourly.

192

# CHAPTER 19

'I know nothing, my son.'

Alvaro was angry at his mother's reaction to the question. He repeated it.

'Who was my father – my *real* father?'

Consiglia Noto turned her head away so that her eyes were hidden by the thick black hair now streaked with grey. She went and sat on the hard wooden chair and stared at the crucifix on the wall.

Alvaro knew that he must be gentle with her. Was it possible that he had never known her smile? Never seen a break in the hard lines of her profile? Did she have to look so like a martyr?

He moved to his mother's side and pulled up a bench to sit on.

'You say you know nothing,' he began. 'That is only because you think I, too, know nothing. For all my life to this moment it was true. I did know nothing. I only had the sneers to listen to. From school I had them, and after, too, at my work. I was always the one on the outside because I looked so different. I always had the nickname, *L'Inglese*. I always wondered why. You never told me. Only now, when I'm fifty – fifty years of age – does my father, the man known as my father, tell me I am not his son. I deserve to know all the truth, *mammina*.'

Still the old woman showed by the defiant lift of her nose that she would not tell him anything.

'Well, I must tell you then.' Alvaro spat twice into the palms of his hands to get rid of the dryness, and then he went on. 'You know what Benino wants? He wants me to find the man who took your body. And then I must kill him. Do you understand, *mammina*? It has come to this. After all this time, and now he demands it.'

Consiglia seemed troubled by this information. Her son could see the struggle that was going on within her.

'It is so long ago,' she finally murmured huskily. 'It is not important.

193

You are a man now. I was a young girl then. It is a long time ago.'

'But Benino says the man must pay – as if it were yesterday he did this thing.'

'He may be dead, anyway,' Consiglia suggested sharply. 'So many things have happened. He went away. There was a war. He could have died in that . . .'

'Did he seem like a soldier? Was that who he was?'

Consiglia did not answer the question.

'He was, of course, an Englishman – that goes without saying?'

Consiglia nodded wordlessly.

'A visitor to our island, was he? And you let him have your body? Did he pay you?'

Consiglia slapped his face. He recoiled surprised and shocked.

'I am sorry. I should not have said that. He did not pay you.'

She nodded agreement and met his eyes with hers for the first time. Then she spoke.

'There is no need for anyone to kill him. I had you, my son. I was able to look after you, with Benino's help. There is nothing to pay. I was blessed by God that I could look after you. I forgive the man.'

'But you know that is not how things are on this island, among our people. A man who does what he did must pay with his life. I have that contract. That is why I must know who he was.'

Slowly his mother shook her head from side to side.

'Surely you know who he was, *mammina*? You must tell me. I must do it for another reason. I have seen how Benino has treated you all these years – and how the family has, too. They treat you as dirt. You have paid, dearly, for any sin you committed, but they have made your life a misery. No woman should suffer as you have done, year after year, for all this time. The man who made that happen to you must pay the penalty.'

'No!' Consiglia moaned.

Alvaro was getting nowhere. His mother continued to stare upwards at the crucifix, pulling her clothing about her restlessly. Alvaro was uncomfortable on the hard wooden bench. He disliked the perpetual gloom in which his mother liked to reside.

There was a knocking at the door and in came Gina, one of his married sisters.

It was Gina who looked after their mother most. Alvaro knew he must stop talking now. He could not pursue the questions while his sister was in the house. He waited, nodding occasionally, while the two women exchanged small talk.

He thought hard to himself. Should he tell his wife Maria of Benino's command? She was so clever she would know what to do. But she would no more approve of a murder than his mother. He would have to be careful. He could not afford to have another outburst from her like the one they had had before he started withholding information of his 'business' activities. He could imagine how she would react to a scheme which involved killing someone Alvaro did not know, in a foreign country, and who – to cap it all – was his father. She would think it unforgivable in God's eyes, and – her favourite word – obscene.

Then Alvaro had an idea. When he was once more on his own with his mother he would tell her that Maria did not wish him to lift the contract – she wanted him to do it. There was a kind of bond between Maria and his mother. It was as if they both knew they were outsiders in the Noto family. They did not believe in doing things the way the family had always done them. Of course, Maria was cleverer. She was a teacher. But they were close.

When Gina went, and it had taken her a long time – Alvaro had almost had to stand with the door open to get rid of her – he returned once more to his questions. Consiglia delayed him a moment more by fetching a small bowl of black olives in oil and herbs. She set it down between them on the kitchen table.

'You know,' Alvaro began again, laying siege to his mother's pride and stubbornness, 'I have to tell you this: Maria thinks this is important. As soon as I told her of Benino's wish she said, "That you must do". She sees the rightness of it.'

Consiglia gave her son a certain look. Slowly, she put a black olive in her mouth and chewed it. She did not speak until she had put the stone on the plate.

'You don't speak true,' she said, finally. 'Maria would never agree to it – I know that. She is not a killer, like everyone else.'

'No, I assure you, *mammina*, those were the very words she spoke to me – "That you must do". Ask her for yourself!'

The mother looked puzzled, but did not say she would or would not.

Then Alvaro had another idea. 'Would it make it better if I promised not to do it myself?'

His mother brightened almost imperceptibly. 'There is a way?'

'Of course, there is always a way. Besides, the man may be in England. How would I ever manage to find him myself? I do not speak the language very well, though I speak some. I have never travelled. What would I do?'

'If you promise not to have anything to do with it, that is different.'

'Of course I promise, *mammina*.' No promise was more easily given. 'And I mean it.'

'Good.'

'Well?'

'I cannot tell you now. I must think. I must find something. Then I will tell you.'

In some relief, Alvaro swept up out of his chair, picked up his hat, and gave her a wave. 'Next time, then.'

Alvaro drove the car down into the centre of Palermo. He was meeting Carmine Agnello who looked after the drug side of things for the Noto family. It had been a long-standing engagement. They were to dine at the best restaurant in Palermo. They knew it must be the best restaurant because they were paid good money to protect it. Well, they weren't getting paid for doing quite that, but they had always a peaceful time there and never had to pick up the bill.

They did not talk much about drugs this time. Carmine Agnello did not mind. He was proud of the clever system he had established for routing the heroin on to America, but he did not like the drugs himself. They were for fools, for desperate people.

Alvaro came straight to the point.

'You have been to England?' he asked. Carmine nodded. 'What is it like?'

Carmine lit up one of his American cigarettes. 'It is not like Sicily,' he said drily. 'I can tell you that. It is not like America. You know what America is like?'

'No, I do not, except what I see on the movies. I have not been to America.'

'I know you have not been to America. It shows.'

Alvaro bravely accepted the snub and said nothing.

Carmine went on. 'England is very soft. It is not hard to do what you have to do there. You have not been there? Even though they call you *L'Inglese*?'

'No. I have not been there. But I want to know what it is like. How easy is it to do our work there?'

Their main course arrived, accompanied by an ingratiating manager. They pushed aside the stuffed sardines they had begun with and the manager quickly removed their plates. Neither of the men he waited on passed any remark on the newly-arrived *pesce spada* – fat, white swordfish, nicely grilled – and he shrank away nervously.

'It is easy, what you ask. There are people there, in England, some of our own people – but mostly not our own people. Different families.'

Alvaro called for another bottle of Corvo to give him strength. He told Carmine in the most general terms what he wanted to do in England.

'You have special business to do?' Carmine came back almost at once. 'I understand. You do not wish to do it yourself?'

196

'You take the words from my mouth, Carmine. I cannot do it myself – how could I in a foreign land? In addition, I have made a promise to someone that I would not do it myself.'

'A promise. That sounds weak. Is it to your wife?'

Alvaro looked indignant. 'No, my wife knows nothing, nor will she. She is never told anything. I know my vow, and I do not need you to tell me my business. You forget, I am the head of the family now.'

'Since when?'

'I saw my father in the gaol in Reggio on Sunday. That was when.'

'I see.'

Alvaro was playing with fire, lying to Carmine like this, but he had sensed his mistake just in time. He made a respectful gesture with his hand away from his forehead and the difference between them was put to one side.

'I will tell you how things can be done in England,' Carmine continued matter-of-factly and rapidly. 'It is no use doing it through our present men. They have their work to do. You must use a sleeping one.'

'They are there, of course. Many of them?'

'*Si!* You had not thought of them, had you? That was a mistake, but that is what they are for.'

'How would I find one?'

Carmine gave a sigh of slight exasperation. Why was he having to tell a head of family this sort of thing? Such people were supposed to know. But he could not afford to be difficult.

'Perhaps you must talk again to your father?'

'He is not talking to me about this. He set me the task – it is a very personal matter – but he is leaving me to find out the detail.'

'I am sure he will help you to find a sleeper. He will have to go back through his memory. None of this is written down, so his memory is the only place it will be found. Only he will know of a sleeper who might help you. He won't have forgotten. The obligation is there, from the war.'

Alvaro could not remember much from that time. He had only been a little boy. Sicily had been devastated by the Americans and the British. They had used the island as a doormat for their landings. Then they had pushed up towards Rome. It was after these events that the families had begun to reassert themselves. There had been that fool, Salvatore Giuliano – some called him a saint, but Alvaro had always thought him a fool. Robbing the rich to feed the poor was all very well, but he was vain, and he had allowed himself to be killed. That was not a good way to do business.

'I think you are right,' Alvaro said. 'I have a memory of Benino helping

197

some men go to London. He paid for their fares. Allowed them to escape this place. I don't know how he did it.'

'Then they owe him respect,' Carmine insisted, stroking the side of his glass. 'You will be able to call on them. They must do what you ask of them. If they are not capable, their sons may do it. The debt can be passed on.'

'Good. That is what I wanted to hear.'

Gradually, a plan was forming in Alvaro's mind. He had never been an international operator. All his business had been done on the island. He had never even paid a visit to America. There were some Mafiosi who thought you could not rightly call yourself a man unless you had been to America and seen for yourself.

Yes, he was beginning to see a way forward. It did not matter that he would not do the business himself. People knew he had the capability. He had demonstrated that a sufficient number of times. It would be better if another man did it, especially as it had to be done abroad. Or, at least, Alvaro presumed it had to be done abroad. The man, his natural father, would surely never set foot in Sicily again? If he was alive, he would be quite old.

Next morning, he returned to his mother. She was sweeping out the kitchen when he arrived and had a caller – a neighbour, a foul widow draped in black whom Alvaro disliked. As soon as he appeared, Alvaro made sure she felt uncomfortable. She soon departed.

Then he began once more to tax his mother. Perhaps the passing of a day and night had done its work.

'You know, *mammina*, what we talked of yesterday?'

She nodded, but did not look away this time.

'I will make you a promise, with my hand on my heart. But even that is not necessary. I give you my word, as your son. Nothing more is needed. I promise you that I will not do what Benino has asked me to do. I mean, I will not do it personally. You do not have to ask why it must be done. You know how the honour of the family must come first. But I will not do it myself, and I hope that will satisfy you.'

Consiglia nodded and her son quickly added more to his sentence: 'And that you will tell me what I need to know. What I asked you yesterday.'

His mother stood up and walked away and sat down again in a dark corner, facing the wall, not looking at him.

Alvaro waited.

Eventually she began, in a very low voice. It had a hard edge to it, but it was almost as though it was her younger self speaking. She spoke for the first time of a terrible thing that had happened half a century ago and about which she had never talked since.

'This is not what a mother should ever have to tell her son,' she began. 'It is not right these things should be told. I had to tell them – when it all came out. My father, my mother, they had to be told. They were cruel. There was no understanding. I was treated like a fallen woman. And so I was. I have suffered for it to this day. What have I ever had to be happy about since? Not even my children have I been allowed to enjoy. I had you, of course, my baby – but you have not been happy and I blame myself for that.'

Alvaro did not move, did not want to take his mother in his arms and tell her that it did not matter, that it was all right. He just wanted her to go on. To tell him what had happened.

'I was only a girl. I worked at the hotel – the one on the headland, overlooking the harbour. You know the one, it has a tower. It was very grand. Still is, I imagine, though I have not been since then – since I was found out. I have been past it, many times, but I have never dared go in, not even through the gates just for a look.

'My father had got me a job as a chambermaid. It was my first work. I did what I had to do. I was still learning. It meant my getting up early and walking right across town. Sometimes there was a bus, but not always. I liked being at the hotel. It was so grand. I saw so many fine people who stayed there. From many countries they came, in their rich cars. Then there were the *fascisti* and one day even *Il Duce*. We weren't supposed to be seen – the staff – when visitors were about. But we did quite well. Of course, it was forbidden for us to have anything to do with the guests. That did not stop some of the girls. They would take money to go with the men, but I would not do that. Besides, I still had not given myself to a man.'

Alvaro sat listening, without moving. He was being consciously patient, wasn't going to hurry his mother in her painful memories. It would come, what he wanted.

'But then it happened. I had seen these Englishmen. There were three of them, almost my age I should have said. I made the beds in their rooms. They had two of them. One was a best room in the tower, with a balcony. I had seen their clothes – they had lovely clothes. Shirts such as you have never seen. And such expensive luggage – big cases and bags of the very best leather.

'They took no notice of me if I was in a corridor and they went past. I did not mind. I had my job, and my place to keep. Well, it was one of them. I think he was the eldest. He was handsome, the way an Englishman is handsome. His skin was pale, not like our people. He was tall. He was fair – I think he was fair, it is so long ago . . .'

Consiglia stopped and said no more. Alvaro did not want to prompt her, wanted just to wait for her to tell him what he must know.

199

'One morning, just after I arrived, I went into the garden. I don't know why I did. We were not supposed to go there. But I loved the smell and the pretty flowers. We never had a garden at home. I have never had a garden all the years I have been married to Benino.

'And he was there. Why he was there I do not know. Perhaps he had woken early and could not get back to sleep. We could not speak to each other. I did not have his language, and he did not speak to me in mine, even if he could. I can't remember how it happened, what happened next. I had no experience. I still do not really know about these things, even after five more children! But I had this wonderful feeling. He was demanding, the way men are. It just happened. It was my first time. I was not ashamed. Not at first. He went away that same day, I think. So I did not see him again.

'Then I was found out, in the normal way. My father was so angry. He went to the hotel. He used his influence. I dare not think what he must have done there, trying to find out who had done this thing to me. I think he felt the family had been disgraced. I had this child growing in me – you, my boy! – and I sat at home, behind the curtains, waiting. Then, one day, Benino was brought to see me. I was told he was to be my husband. Only later did I find out how good a marriage it was in my father's eyes. It enabled him to join with another family, to work together. They seemed glad that Benino should marry. So that was how it happened. And you, my baby, were the result. Do you understand?'

Alvaro remained oddly still. There were few men who could have been told of the circumstances of their conception without being to some extent intrigued, but Alvaro gave no hint. He just sat staring at his mother's back.

She turned to face him now, her tale told.

Alvaro asked her coldly and simply: 'Who was the man, this Englishman?'

His mother quickly turned away again, as though she could not bear to discuss these intimate matters if her eyes met her son's.

'My father found out. It was not very hard. I could tell him which room the man had been staying in. The name was in the hotel register.'

'And what was it?'

'It would mean nothing to you. It was a foreign name, of course. You see, he was a *milord*.'

'What?' Only at this information did Alvaro show any particular curiosity.

'Yes. He was a lord from England. There, that'll suit your pride, won't it!'

It certainly was not unpleasing to Alvaro. The natural son of an English aristocrat . . .

200

And then he remembered why he had been extracting all this uncomfortable information from his mother.

'What was the lord's name?'

'Questions, questions!' said Consiglia. 'I can never remember it.'

'You have forgotten? How could you have forgotten!' Alvaro sounded unpleasantly accusing.

'Yes, I have forgotten. But I know where I can find out.'

'Where?'

'The Bible.'

'How do you mean? What Bible?'

'It is in the Bible.'

'What – a name like Joseph or Moses? What do you mean, *mammina*?'

'No. Bring it to me and I will show you.'

The family Bible was kept in the glass case in the dining room, along with the best china and the souvenirs. He knocked a glass jug to one side, cracking it, in his haste to get the Bible out. He came back into the kitchen and thrust the large black book into his mother's hands.

Consiglia calmly opened the book to the inside of the front cover.

'Look,' she pointed. 'Have you never seen this, in all the years you have been alive? These are the names of your ancestors. They go back to 1843.'

'The name is there?'

'No. But look at this.'

She handed him a yellowing piece of headed notepaper that had been pressed between the pages all these years. It was from the hotel on the headland overlooking the harbour, the Hotel La Torre.

There was nothing on it except two words written in pencil, now fading: 'LORD WYMARK'.

Alvaro slowly and quietly pronounced the two words, but could not manage the second. It came out sounding like 'Veemark'.

'There you are, my son. Now, do not say anything more about this matter. I do not wish to know what happens next. But I shall say a prayer for you.'

Alvaro slowly and quietly folded the piece of paper, put it in his pocket, and departed from his mother's presence without a word more.

# CHAPTER 20

Uncle Alec's scholarly volume recounting the history of Castle Cansdale and its occupants was due to be published the following year. The announcement of the forthcoming publication alerted an influential television producer to it and Alec's existence.

Jack Rivers had recently left one of the big TV companies and set up as an independent producer. His first project – which he had eventually succeeded in selling to Channel 4 – was a series about Britain's historic homes and their owners. It was hardly a new idea, there had been any number of such series in recent years, and so he needed a novel twist to make the thing work.

It was when he was researching a whole list of castles, famous and obscure, and reading round the subject, that he visited the Hooke family seat and came across *Castle Cansdale – A House and Its Heritage*, the guide book by the Hon. Alec Hooke. He found mention of the forthcoming bigger book and obtained a proof copy from the publisher.

Although scholarly in format, it was written in a quirky style, full of little jokes and anecdotes, and very far from the dusty and matter-of-fact tomes Rivers had sampled elsewhere. He was struck in particular by one of Alec's sentences which stated what had, indeed, become one of the themes used to market Castle Cansdale – that it was 'more than a castle, it was a home still lived in by the same family'.

This gave Jack Rivers the title and connecting thread for his whole series. *An Englishman's Castle* would visit those stately homes with the word 'castle' in their names, which were still used as family homes. Rivers quickly drew up a list including Castle Howard, Highclere Castle, Saltwood Castle, Saltney Castle, Arundel, Broughton, Belvoir and even Windsor – though he doubted whether the owner of the latter would be willing to perform before his cameras.

It was only right that Jack Rivers should add Castle Cansdale to the list.

202

It had the advantage of unfamiliarity, having only been open to the public for just a few months, and it did seem to have an interesting family living in it. Rivers soon made the connection between the owner of Castle Cansdale and the randy Lord Wymark who had so recently appeared in the gossip columns of the popular press. It would do no harm if he was to show his face before the cameras.

Indeed, so intrigued was Rivers by what he had heard of the Hookes that he quickly put out a feeler to Uncle Alec, met him for lunch (rather more modest than Alec was used to, though Rivers Productions paid for it) and, being so taken with the old man's whimsical charms, invited him there and then to appear as the presenter of *An Englishman's Castle*.

'Oh, my dear chap!' Alec purred in mock horror. 'You have absolutely no idea what you'd be letting yourself in for! I'd look frightful in these glasses. And, I have to tell you, I've never appeared on the television in my life!'

Rivers wasn't worried by the glasses. They could always be prised off him. He had a hunch that Alec Hooke would turn out to be a natural television performer. He was anecdotal, enthusiastic, eccentric but not wildly so, and – more important – he would be acceptable to the aristocratic owners of the homes which were to be featured in the series.

In no time Alec had overcome his purely polite reluctance and been signed up. *An Englishman's Castle* was to be filmed all round England in an intensive schedule during July and August. Uncle Alec adored the fuss that was made of him. They didn't seem to be paying a great deal of money, but there was always a nice car to take him to the various locations. And they always put up at the best hotels and treated him like – well, like a lord. It was a form of paradise for him, visiting great houses, looking at priceless works of art, and chatting to their owners on more or less equal terms.

Jack Rivers was equally delighted with the way Alec came across on camera. 'This man'll go up like a rocket,' he told one of his colleagues. 'He's a natural. Remember Barbara Woodhouse with those dogs, Arthur Negus and the antiques? I bet Alec'll end up the same. People love an expert, especially when he's dotty. I tell you, I'm going to have to sign him up for another series before he gets expensive!'

Alec was aware he wasn't doing badly at the broadcasting and rather dreaded it all coming to an end. The TV crew with whom he worked so closely for two months was like a happy little family. They were full of jokes and horseplay, which only served to disguise a happy competence and serious professionalism, and it would be tragic when they eventually had to split up at the end of the video-recording and go their separate ways. Besides, Alec had fallen in love with a blonde, twenty-four-year-old production assistant who wore the tightest skirts he'd ever seen. He never found the nerve to tell her, though.

Now there was just one more programme to do before the final wrap. Jack Rivers had saved it till last, although it might just as well end up first, or in any other position in the series, when the programmes were shown. This was the episode dealing with Castle Cansdale. In a sense, it was going to be the trickiest programme of them all to do for the simple reason this was the house Alec knew most about. He brimmed with so many ideas that if Jack Rivers had included every detail Alec wanted, he would have had a three-hour programme on his hands.

There was also the delicate situation – which Rivers only gradually became aware of – concerning the edgy relations between the two major branches of the Hooke family.

Alec was as frank on the subject as he could be. 'Well, you see, Jack, my nephew's the owner now. Purely for tax reasons, you understand. My brother Hugo had to move out. So, if you like, you've got a bit of a cuckoo in the nest. It wouldn't matter, except that Hugo hates Duncan. *I* don't – I get on perfectly well with him, and with Hugo, but there is, er, a bit of a situation. I mean, I can see from your point of view you *ought* to include Hugo – might make a rather good point, being cast out of his inheritance for beastly tax reasons – but if you wanted to show him wandering about the estate, well, I don't think he's set foot in there since last October. I suspect he's not talked to Duncan much in that time either. In fact, I know he hasn't.'

Jack Rivers rather liked what he heard of the family conflict. Wouldn't it make good viewing if the rift could be made to spill over on to the screen?

'There's really no problem, Alec,' he said, reassuringly but artfully. 'If your brother lives somewhere else, we can talk to him there. He doesn't have to meet Lord Wymark. We can cut the two together – if we have to. Might even be more effective if they don't meet.'

'That's all right then.'

'Surely. But you don't think there'll be any trouble with either of them, about appearing at all, I mean?'

Alec was confident he could persuade both Hugo and Duncan to appear, and so it turned out. The camera crew swarmed over Castle Cansdale for a whole week at the end of August. Alec was shown chatting to Duncan in any number of choice settings, and Duncan seemed genuinely to enjoy it. As far as he was concerned, Uncle Alec had more than earned his stipend for the next few years by bringing in these TV johnnies. It would all be excellent publicity for the house. A good TV mention was worth at least a couple of thousand on the admissions, or so Miss Taylor of ShakesPR Ltd assured him.

Jack Rivers left the interview between Alec and Hugo until the very last day. The Earl's plans to visit Sicily were going ahead, and a flight had been booked in early September, so the interview would fit in very nicely. Rivers wasn't too worried if it didn't take place at all, in fact. There was probably some poignancy to be extracted from an old codger who'd been kicked out of his ancestral home in order to save his son tax, but Rivers wasn't too sure that viewers would grasp all that, and besides, he had more than enough to fill a programme from Lord Wymark. Duncan had come over well in his interviews, giving more than a hint of his fiery temperament, and nicely alluding to the activities which had won him such attention from the press.

Now, at the end of the last week of August, the TV crew had only to drive the short distance from Castle Cansdale to Huddleston to record the interview with Hugo, and then that would be the end not only of the particular episode and of all the location shooting for the series. But a rare call from his step-mother to Duncan meant these plans took a dive.

'Duncan, dear, it's Molly.' Duncan froze and his usual hot-blooded response to everyone and everything was stayed as a terrible inevitability dawned.

'What is it ? Something up?' Duncan went straight to the point.

'Your father's not too well, I'm afraid. Nothing to worry about, I don't think. But I've had to cancel our Sicily arrangements. And he can't possibly do this TV thing Alec's put him up to. Can you tell the people? They're with you, aren't they?'

'Yes, been here for weeks, it seems. You're sure it's nothing serious?'

'I don't know, do I, dear? He's not been himself for a some time now, and late yesterday he suddenly took a turn for the worse. The doctor's quite clear he mustn't travel or be disturbed.'

'I'll come right over.'

Duncan put the phone down before his step-mother could say anything to discourage a visit from him. He shouted news of the cancelled interview to Uncle Alec, Jack Rivers and the crew, leapt into his car and headed – for the first time in recent memory – to Huddleston. So unfamiliar was he with the route that he lost his way and was reduced to asking a woman in the lane the way to his father's house.

Molly opened the door to him.

'Be gentle, Duncan. He really isn't well.'

'Yes.' Duncan was non-committal, and pushed past her not really knowing where he was supposed to be heading.

She took him up to the bedroom where his father was lying, listlessly, not reading, not sleeping, just feeling sorry for himself. For a moment, Duncan feared the worst. His father was wearing some pallid pyjamas, which together with his white skin and greyish-white hair made him look near to death. He was also sitting with pillows ranged behind his head and his hands out in front of him on the top tartan blanket as though ready to receive the last rites.

'Hello, Father.'

'Oh, it's you, Duncan.'

'Yes.'

'You only come when I'm ill.'

Even Duncan knew he must bite his tongue at this.

'Never mind about that, Father. Molly told me you are ill, so I came right over. That's all right, isn't it?'

After a moment's pause, Hugo agreed it was.

'Thought I was going to pop off, did you?'

'Never crossed my mind. Just wanted to see how you were.'

'Mmm.'

There was another pause. Duncan made himself comfortable in a chair by the side of the bed. He was prepared to sit this one out. Never mind what his father threw at him, he would take it, just this once. The main thing was, his father must survive. A lot depended on it.

'The TV people were disappointed, of course,' said Duncan, making conversation.

'Who were?'

'The TV people, and Uncle Alec – they were expecting to do you today.'

'Were they?'

'Yes. You'd agreed, hadn't you? Uncle Alec's going to be a TV star, so they tell me. Good for him.'

'I don't remember anything about it.'

Duncan looked at Molly and pulled a face. The old man was putting it on. His son instantly went back on his resolve to let Hugo say what he liked.

'Father, stop acting gaga! You're all there, and you're not going to pop off either, are you, you old sod?'

Hugo perked up at this challenge. He rearranged himself on the pillows with Molly's help and smiled weakly.

'Of course not, you stupid boy. Though I've a good mind to. Serve you right, that would, wouldn't it! If I went now, that'd teach you a lesson, eh? Think of the mess you'd be in!'

Duncan growled, 'It's not just me, you know, who'd suffer. It wouldn't be good for any of us. It would probably mean the end of the house.'

'Yes, I am perfectly aware of that. I'm certainly not hanging on for you.'

Duncan felt a certain guilt at letting their feud ramble on, though he did not accept responsibility for it. It was frightening, though. His father seemed poised on a knife-edge. He looked as though he could go at any moment.

'Father,' he began. 'I feel I ought to . . .' He was going to say 'make amends', but that was unnecessarily contrite. Instead, he substituted, 'I have not always been as I should be – I'm sorry . . .'

Hugo felt this was deeply embarrassing. How *lowering* for his son to have to say such a thing!

'Phooey!' he exclaimed. 'Don't be such a hypocrite, Duncan. You know you're only interested in your own advantage. You don't feel sorry for me in the slightest. And you'll be a damn sight embarrassed when I get better having said what you just did!'

Duncan knew his father was right, and said nothing more on the subject.

'What shall I tell Alec and the TV people?' he asked feebly instead.

'They'll just have to wait – if they can be bothered.'

After this, Duncan chatted inconsequentially for about twenty minutes, but he was a troubled man. If anything, his problem lay rather in an excess of feeling than in any lack of it. When he could take no more of it, he bade goodbye to his father and cornered Molly who had gone out into the drawing room.

'He's going to be all right, isn't he?' Duncan demanded, desperate for reassurance. The descent of the earldom upon his shoulders was the last thing Duncan wanted at that moment; it would mean the most God Almighty battle with the Inland Revenue.

'I mean, nothing to worry about, is there?'

'Nothing more than usual,' Molly replied unhelpfully. 'You've got to realize, Duncan, that your father is an old man. Seventy-one's not much by some people's standards but he's decided it is. I don't think there's anything really wrong with him – if Doctor Russell's to be trusted. Just old man's things, blood pressure, and so on.'

'Good.'

'A little rest and he'll be up and about again. He's improving already. When he's in bed he gets lots of fuss made of him and he likes that.'

'Right. Sorry you're losing your holiday, by the way.'

'We'll fix it again when he's better.'

There was the sound of a car drawing up outside and Duncan quickly kissed his step-mother and made off, rather frantically, to avoid whoever it was arriving.

'Oh, it's the Rector,' announced Molly, who was adept at catching glimpses of visitors through net curtains.

207

'Oh, God,' Duncan muttered. 'Must dash.'

When the front door was opened, he wasn't able to execute avoiding action as swiftly as he might have wished.

'How do you do, both of you,' said the Reverend Dutson, dispensing with any use of titles. 'Just thought I'd see how the patient's coming along.'

'He'll be glad to see you, Padre,' said Molly.

Duncan bristled at the use of his father's name for the clergyman. He had always disliked it.

'Keeping well yourself, Dutson?' he inquired pointedly.

'Yes, I am, thank you.' He gave Duncan a steady look. Duncan was relieved to see that it contained no hint of prejudice. It was odds on that the doughty Reverend wouldn't exactly be in his supporters' club when the time came for Hugo to shuffle off.

'Was just on my way,' Duncan said loudly, pushing towards the door. 'Why don't you go and cheer the old bugger up.'

'Oh, I shall,' said Dutson, unfazed.

'Yes, well . . . 'bye, Molly.' He came back and gave her an impulsive peck on the cheek. Then Duncan at last achieved his freedom.

He drove home with exemplary slowness, frightened to the marrow that his father would die. He would spend the next few days in fear of a phone call from Molly informing him that it was all over.

He could not bear it. Could not bear the system in which so much depended on mortality.

As soon as Channel 4 started showing *An Englishman's Castle* in September, viewer reaction was exactly as Jack Rivers had predicted. It was a happy coincidence that there was an absence of new soap operas and major mini-series the week the first programme was aired. More than one national newspaper critic devoted space to the curious but entertaining figure of the Hon. Alec Hooke. He was profiled in some of the posh Sunday supplements. Even the tabloids gave a merry chortle at the latest enthusiastic eccentric to hit the small screen and Alec quickly found himself something of a 'name'. People came up to him in the street and asked him questions, taxi drivers waved at him. He even received well-mannered fan mail on good notepaper written largely from the south coast of England. He revelled in it. Fame was something new. He derived great satisfaction from this late flowering in the evening of his days.

He had lived, if not a blameless life till now, then at least a life that should have been of no concern to anybody but him. It had been an almost totally private life and, like many another innocent coming into television for the first time, he felt entitled to have it remain so. On that point, he was wrong.

Back in South Audley Street, Alec realized he had neglected to make any visits to Maxine for several months. He had not missed her sexually – he had found a satisfactory substitute in, first, the prospect of fame and then in fame itself – but now he quite naturally fell back into the rhythm of his visits north of Oxford Street.

Maxine was professional enough not to show that she had noticed her client's desertion. Once more she donned the costume of his craving – the principal boy tunic, the svelte silk stockings, and the clinging green suede boots that so intoxicated the Hon. Alec Hooke.

He was surprised – and delighted – when Maxine revealed that she, too, was following his TV series. TV crossed all boundaries. Alec discovered how strange it was, the people who saw you. They were never the people you thought you were addressing. They were anyone and everyone. Even a prostitute like Maxine watched what Jack Rivers had assured Alec was classified as a form of 'adult education'.

Maxine once more stood while Alec gazed and gently fingered her thighs, enjoying whatever gratification he derived from suede and skin. Then she bid him adieu, though not without first relieving him of the usual bundle of twenty pound notes. That was the only gratification she experienced, though it was possible she received more of a *frisson* from relieving a celebrity of his money than she got from the average punter.

And she talked about him to others – not with any malice or guile. She just talked. She was hardly aware that she was doing it, so natural was it to chatter about the clients she'd pleasured that day. She tended to be on first-name terms with most of them, their full identities did not count for much.

Except that Alec was now famous. Maxine did not see her link with him as a way of earning any additional money, but there were those who did.

# CHAPTER 21

Cynthia had just returned from a trip to the Moores' flat at Puerto Banus when Jacky broke the news. Freddie had not gone with his wife this time, and so maintained his customary pallor. Cynthia's skin was a golden brown colour – 'all over, too', she would confide, with a nudge.

The news that Jacky was expecting her first baby filled Cynthia with delight. Next day she came rushing up from Brentwood to Knightsbridge to visit her daughter – and do a spot of shopping, too. The wedding to Rupert had been sprung on them, but a grandchild was an event which she would be able to anticipate for every one of the months that were still left to run till the birth the following May.

'What's it going to be then?' she chirruped, kicking off her shoes, parking her bronzed legs on the sofa, and making herself completely at home in the flat off Lowndes Square.

'Give us a chance, Mum! I shouldn't think it knows itself just yet.' Jacky was not the slightest bit envious of her mother's colour. Ever since the modelling had started, Jacky had been very cautious of the sun. Her gentle complexion was her stock in trade. When a tan was required, it came out of a bottle. Some of Mrs Moore's probably came the same way.

'I think it'll be a boy, don't you?' Cynthia went on breezily.

'Haven't really thought. You're only saying that because Dad would like one.'

'No. I think it *will* be, that's all. Just got a feeling.' Her mother smiled. 'And how are you, love – all right?'

'Of course, Mum, of course.'

'I bet he'll be a lovely little feller. I mean, you and Rupe are a smashing couple, so with your brains and his looks, it ought to be!'

'Mum!'

'Is he pleased?'

'You bet, couldn't be happier. Especially coming from his family.

210

They're into breeding in a big way. It's what keeps them going, I suppose. So I'll get lots of brownie points, whether it's a boy or a girl!'

'It's what keeps the human race going, dear, and no mistake.'

'It's more complicated than that, Mum. Rupert was telling me. You see, it's all to do with sons and heirs. His brother's got no sons, only girls, so when he goes it's just possible the title and the house might come to us – if we're not in our graves by then. And if we had a little boy – well, it'd pass on down to him!'

'Gracious!' Cynthia Moore's hands shot up to her cheeks. 'You mean, he becomes a lord, and you a lady, and you both go to live in the big house?'

'Don't get too excited, Mum! It'll never happen. For all we know, that Duncan'll stop playing around long enough to have a boy by his wife, and then we'll be nowhere.'

'Still . . .' Jacky's mother wasn't going to be cheated of her dreams. 'Fancy!'

Another thought struck her. 'So you'll not be able to do your modelling, eh? 'Cept for maternity wear.'

Jacky laughed. 'I can go on doing it for a month or two. I've already told Maddie and she understands. In a way, it's a pity. Things have been going rather well lately. Lots of work. But babies and modelling just don't mix!'

The phone rang. It was Freddie stuck in a traffic jam near the Embankment. Knowing that Cynthia was going to visit Jacky, he had thought he would do the same – especially since he had never actually been to Rupert and Jacky's flat. It was another hour before Freddie came bounding into the flat. His delight at seeing his darling daughter, and at her news, was tempered by the circumstances in which he found she was now living.

' 'Ere,' he announced flatly, almost as soon as they had dispensed with the preliminaries, 'when you moving out of this dog kennel? Won't be room for three in 'ere.'

'There's no hurry, Dad. This is just where Rupert lived before we got married. A bachelor pad. Of course, it's a squash with all my frocks and everything, but it's not too bad.'

'Come off it, girl! You and Roop can do better than this. 'E's used to living in castles, not matchboxes. You must be making a bomb between you, too. Maddie told me how you've been coining it lately. A thousand quid for standing around all day with a pout on your face – I should be so lucky!'

'Leave her alone, Freddie,' said Cynthia. 'You know there's more to it than that.'

'Yes, Dad, I don't earn that every day and you know what Maddie takes out of that.'

'Only teasing, only teasing.' Freddie walked round penitently on the worn sheepskin rug. 'Still, you ought to get somewhere a little bigger. What you going to do about it?'

'We've talked about it . . .' What with one thing and another, Jacky hadn't yet broached the subject of her father helping them out with a house. Now here was the opportunity.

'Ain't those Hookes got places in town you could 'ave?' asked Freddie.

Jacky explained as best she could how Rupert didn't like to ask and how he wanted to remain independent of the family as far as he could. Besides, although the Hookes had a great house and lots of land, they never seemed to have any cash. What property they'd had in London had long ago been disposed of to meet pressing bills.

'Yeh, well,' said Freddie, affecting to have heard that sort of reasoning before. But he saw an opportunity. If the Hookes were being stingy with the newlyweds, perhaps this would be his big chance? He could show them how he had a bob or two *and* knew the right thing to do for his lovely daughter – and son-in-law.

'I reckon you'll want a property,' he declared, 'to call your own. Somewhere nice. Where's nice, Jacky?'

Well, at least he's not telling me, she comforted herself. But he was offering to help – just as she'd hoped he would when Rupert and she had first talked of the possibility three months before.

'There's lots of nice parts,' she said aloud. 'Trouble is, prices are unbelievable. A phone booth costs half a million round here.'

'No, seriously,' Freddie pressed on. 'Where are we talking about – down Fulham way? Putney? Kensington? Where would you like? Never mind the cost.'

'Well, anywhere, Dad. Doesn't have to be a castle. Just a nice house. We're not fussy.'

'Look, Jacky darlin', you deserve the best. Right? You're my daughter, so it goes without saying. I'll see you okay. You tell Rupert to give me a bell. We'll soon 'ave you sorted out.'

'We haven't got much to put towards a house.'

'Shuddup! Stop making problems, girl. I've said I'll help.' As an afterthought he added: 'And I want you in there, with it all nice and shipshape, before you have your little event.'

That evening, when Rupert came home from the City, he was quietly relieved to find that Freddie and Cynthia had paid a visit in his absence. He'd been spared all that. Then Jacky began, excitedly, to tell him of Freddie's offer to help find them a house.

'I think he wants to buy us one – or most of one, depending on how much we can put in. I know it's silly, but I think he sees it as his way of keeping up with your lot.'

Rupert gave a little chuckle, having already reached a similar conclusion. But he felt uncomfortable at the thought of having to deal with his father-in-law. However much they wanted – and needed – help if they were to buy a decent first house, did they really want to be indebted to Jacky's father? There was nothing worse than that kind of family obligation, Rupert thought. He also wondered just what Freddie might think was a suitable house for Jacky and himself. A semi in Sidcup?

'Well, I don't know,' he eventually said, rather quietly. 'Nice of him to offer, and all that, but I feel we're being pushed a bit.'

'It'll be all right, Roo.' Jacky sat down by him and took his hand in hers. 'He's not as bad as he sounds. And we do need somewhere bigger and better than this.'

Rupert managed to look sad at this unintentionally harsh remark about his old pad.

'Oh, lovey, don't look so miserable!' cried Jacky, pecking him on the cheek and fingering the points of his collar.

'Sorry,' he said, kissing the hair on the top of her head. 'If it was Hugo offering to do all this, I'd still feel the same. Parents don't half know how to manipulate! But don't worry, I'll talk to Freddie. I'll do it, tomorrow. We'd better start looking around, hadn't we, get lists from the estate agents?'

They went out for a meal, as almost every evening now. Jacky said she would start to cook properly when she had a real kitchen at her disposal. For the moment, anyway, she only pecked at her food – the constant discipline of her job. Rupert ate and drank for them both.

In the mild October evening, they decided they would walk to their favourite brasserie. Jacky couldn't help but relay more of her father's observations.

'Dad says we're missing a treat on the telly.'

'What is it? We never see anything, do we?'

'It's your Uncle Alec. He's doing something on Channel 4.'

'I did hear a mention. We ought to take him out for a meal, so you can meet him. You'll like him; he's a nice old thing. He was always taking me out to dinner before you and I got married. P'raps he thinks I don't need feeding any more!'

'Well, Dad says he's been wandering about these castles on TV. It's a series. Dad wasn't too sure if it was him at first. But then he thought, with a name like Hooke, he must be a relation. Said he saw a resemblance to your dad.'

'I suppose there's a bit of one. I don't know what it's all about, this TV thing. It's so long since I heard from Mummy and Daddy. I haven't had the gossip.'

'Well, when are you going to tell them about me being pregnant?'

'I ought to give them ring. See if they're all right. But why don't you do it?'

Jacky sensed the buck being passed, but knew she'd have to pluck up the courage to speak to them herself one day.

'Oh, okay,' she said. 'I hope I get your mum, that's all. Your dad makes me nervous.'

'Don't worry. He never answers the phone if he can help it.'

Next day, Jacky did summon up sufficient courage to phone Huddleston. The housekeeper answered and Jacky was able to ask for Molly after all.

'Nothing the matter, is there, dear?' was Molly's first inevitable reaction to receiving a call out of the blue from her daughter-in-law.

'No, no, no,' replied Jacky hurriedly. 'Not at all. It was just that . . . well, Rupert thought I ought to see how you were.'

'Um. Well, I'm glad you rang because Hugo's not been well, you know.'

'Oh, I am sorry.' Jacky couldn't bring herself to say 'Mother' or 'Lady Hooke', so ended the sentence rather abruptly.

'In fact, for two or three months now.' It sounded like a reprimand.

'Not serious, I hope?'

'No, not really. He's up and about again now, but we had to cancel our holiday.'

'Oh, that's terrible.'

'Perhaps we'll go somewhere sunny for Christmas. And how have you two been keeping?'

'That's really why I'm ringing,' Jacky ventured bravely, still somewhat in awe of the upper-class tones that wafted at her down the phone lines, however beautiful the voice. 'You see, I'm expecting a baby.'

Molly's manner changed in an instant. It was all sunshine and peals of happy laughter now. She wanted all the details, and then she couldn't get off the line quick enough to tell Hugo.

'Oh, by the way,' Molly added as a final question, 'do you have a television?'

It seemed a peculiar question to ask anybody these days but, come to think of it, Jacky couldn't remember noticing whether the Earl and Countess had a set and she was pretty sure they'd never set foot in Rupert's flat.

'Yes,' she replied, 'of course.' And then, for no apparent reason, added, 'Just a small one . . .'

'Have you been watching Rupert's Uncle Alec?'

'No,' Jacky admitted shamefully. 'We only just heard. My dad told me yesterday.'

'You ought to try and catch it. It's *An Englishman's Castle* on Sunday nights. You've missed most of them now, I'm afraid. Next Sunday's the last, but it's all about Cansdale. You might find it fun. Hugo was going to be in it, but had to pull out when he fell ill. Duncan's in it, of course.'

'Oh, lovely!' Jacky exclaimed. 'I'll tell Rupert. We'll certainly give it a look. Can't wait!'

Rupert's duty call that morning – which he made from the office – was to his father-in-law. He didn't find it easy talking to Freddie, especially about the matter in hand, but the other man sounded in good heart, still evidently pleased on account of the expected baby. He even suppressed some of his natural ebullience when faced with Rupert's quiet, laconic voice on the line. Freddie was also, though he would never admit it, still very much in awe of any member of Rupert's family.

'Actually,' said Rupert, 'we've had an idea. We're beginning to think about somewhere in Docklands.'

'Right!' said Freddie. 'Docklands it is. You start looking, and get on to me pronto soon as you see something you like.'

Freddie was rather taken with the idea. He knew, of course, that that was where all the yuppies headed for these days – and his daughter and son-in-law probably fell into that category, though Freddie wasn't sure whether Rupert needed to be upwardly mobile exactly. But the thought of their moving eastward across London pleased him. Docklands would be a fitting halfway house between the worlds of the Hookes and the Moores.

Rupert and Jacky didn't start looking in earnest until the weekend. On the Saturday, they drove around the converted wharves and warehouses, and the newly-built developments, but only looked from the outside. On Sunday morning, Rupert crawled out in his best scruff to buy the *Sunday Times* and the *Observer* to see what properties were being advertised. It was while waiting his turn in the newsagents that Rupert had an opportunity to study the headlines in all the Sunday papers.

When his turn came to be served, he told the shopkeeper, 'Oh, and I'll have this one too.' He tucked a copy of the *News of the World* inside the other papers and bravely refrained from looking at it while he walked back round Lowndes Square to the flat.

Jacky was still in bed, half dozing.

'I don't know what this is,' Rupert said, coolly, plopping the papers down on the bed so that the *News of the World* came out of its protective covering. 'Not very nice, I expect.'

'What d'you mean?'

Jacky stirred and sat up. She took the tabloid and with her first glance saw a photograph of a face she recognized.

It was Rupert's Uncle Alec. 'TV CASTLE MAN IN SEX SHOCK,' shouted a headline.

Rupert still didn't seem to want to read the story, so Jacky greedily read it to herself.

'You don't half have 'em in your family!' was all she would say on finishing.

Rupert had to read it now. It was certainly a shock, though not in quite the way the paper meant by its headline. He had never really thought much about Uncle Alec and sex. It wasn't that he thought there was anything funny about Uncle Alec. He had simply assumed that whatever drives Uncle Alec had once had must now lie dormant, as he assumed they did in most men knocking on seventy.

But this was something else. The exposé seemed based on the assumption that it was wrong for a man who had recently established a reputation as a mildly eccentric TV personality – and had thus gained access to millions of viewers' homes – to pay out money to a prostitute. It was not clear what the money was paid for, whether for performing depraved acts with the woman or merely for watching. Maxine, the prostitute in question, had apparently declined all blandishments from the paper to describe her sessions with the Hon. Alec Hooke, though it was revealed that he had been going to her 'for over a year'. That seemed the only real offence. Presumably, she had been indiscreet in talking about her celebrity client and people to whom she had spoken had carried the information to ears eager to hear.

The paper laid it on with a trowel. The front page report carried readers through to a centre page spread where the potential embarrassment to Uncle Alec was at its deepest. The paper had acquired photographs of Alec from the series *An Englishman's Castle*. He was shown hobnobbing with the titled owners of the homes finally selected for the series. It was the ultimate disgrace, of course, that the degenerate old codger had recently set foot inside Windsor Castle and thus desecrated a home of Her Majesty the Queen. Fortunately he had not met her.

'There's a mention of Duncan,' Jacky said, after wading through the entire piece, with Rupert looking half-interested over her shoulder. 'Says they're on tonight. Says how he carries on, too.'

Rupert sighed. It didn't matter at all, this stupid report – and yet it mattered a lot. He bore the name Hooke, too. He could live with the jokes that would inevitably follow, but what about Hugo and Molly? They didn't deserve to be dragged through this.

'Poor old Uncle Alec,' he said finally. 'He's a sweet old thing. Last person in the world they should've done it to.'

'Perhaps you should ring him up. Say you're sorry.'

'Yes, that's a good idea. I bet he's lying low, though.'

'You don't know until you try.'

Rupert duly made an attempt to ring his uncle, but without success. There was no reply from the Mayfair flat. He could be anywhere.

'Well, I'm sorry,' Rupert said.

'It's not your fault. It's no skin off our noses. It'll die down. These things always do.'

'I hope so.'

But Rupert continued to worry. Why was it that his family had this self-destructive urge?

'Dirty old man!' Freddie Moore chortled. 'Why didn't we meet 'im when we went to the castle, that's what I'd like to know? I thought he had a bit of twinkle in his eye, on the telly. Always patting the bums of all them statues and the like!'

'Rupert likes him a lot, I think,' Cynthia put in from the other side of the bed. It wasn't every Sunday that the reading of the newspapers produced a sensation so close to home.

'Well, Rupert's going to 'ave to be careful!' Freddie could only see it as a huge joke. 'Loada goats he's related to. I hope Jacks can take it!'

'Freddie, don't say that. Not nice.'

'Where's the boy, then?'

'Didn't hear him come in,' Cynthia said. 'Still asleep, I expect. What's he up to these days? Been acting strange. Not saying anything.'

'I dunno,' Freddie lied. 'You know our Mark.'

'I sometimes wish I didn't.'

'Come off it, Cynth. That's no way to talk.'

What neither Freddie nor Cynthia knew was that Mark had spent Saturday a good deal closer to the Hooke family seat than most members of the Hooke family. He had visited Castle Cansdale once again, this time as a paying member of the public. Having driven down on the Saturday afternoon, on the Saturday evening he had crept back into the park. He spent until the small hours sitting in the scrub about two hundred yards from the Pantheon at the rear of the house, simply observing what happened – whether there was any visible security procedure, what time the lights went out, whether there was any late-night coming and going of cars.

It was a lonely vigil, though not as cold as it might have been, what with October so mild that year. By the time he finished, he thought he had observed just about every form of nocturnal wildlife. There were bats and owls in the air, and from all around him came sounds of scratchings and strange cries. For most of his vigil he was extremely nervous. Worrying about being surprised by humans was as nothing to the fear of some creature suddenly leaping upon him.

Mark could tell there was a delicious side to being out in the cold night air but he was too intent on the task in hand really to enjoy the experience. He could have done with company but not everyone would want to spend a Saturday night this way. He was determined to do the job right. The best way of achieving that was to do it all himself.

As the clock in the tower of St Michael and All Angels struck three in the distance, Mark looked at his watch in the dark and dragged himself to his feet. As silently as he could – why *did* leaves have to make so much noise when you stepped on them? – he retraced his steps across the park to the North Lodge exit. Instead of going through the gates which could still have been observed even at that hour, he cut back to a path which led to a gate three hundred yards further along the high brick wall that ran round the park. There he recovered his car, drove it for about eight miles deeper into the countryside, and turned into a wood clearing. Then he curled up on the back seat and slept soundly till well past daybreak.

Had Mark returned to Castle Cansdale later on the Sunday he would have encountered a curious spectacle. In the late morning, he would have observed a motley collection of cars ignoring the 'HOUSE OPENS 1:30' and 'PRIVATE' signs and making their way right up to the front entrance where they disgorged a gaggle of Fleet Street journalists and photographers. These were those who came in the wake of the *News of the World* article – the rest of the British tabloid press trying to compensate for their late start on the story. They had concluded that as Alec Hooke was not apparently at his London flat, he might be at the Hooke family country seat, or somewhere near it in Hooke country. If he wasn't there, well, there was nowhere else to look. They had also concluded that, even if the whereabouts of the Man of Shame could not be established, they should at least be able to prise a quote or two out of the media-friendly Lord Wymark.

In this, they were only half right. Lopez, the butler, answered the door and found out what they wanted. With agonizing slowness he conveyed the message to his lordship. Duncan, who had been alerted to Uncle Alec's fall from grace, sent down a message to the assembled pressmen that he would speak to them after he had had his lunch. So they departed for the pub in Bourton Cansdale to await this press conference.

Duncan took the precaution of getting Valerie Taylor, the hard-nosed woman from ShakesPR Ltd, to tell him whether he was wise to do this. She told him he was, but asked if Duncan had actually spoken to his uncle.

'No. Don't know where he is.'

'Well, just be nice about him, that's all. Don't rock the boat, and don't forget to mention tonight's programme.'

'Oh, my word, yes. I 'spect the whole country'll be watching!'

Indeed, that very afternoon brought an extra wave of visitors who had been reminded of the house's existence by the piece in that morning's paper. It was all good for business, Duncan reassured himself – particularly pleased that this time round it was not his own sexual exploits arousing such intense, but useful, curiosity. What would things be like after they'd shown Uncle Alec's programme about Cansdale? He anticipated a busy week ahead, with the tills merrily ringing. What a shame the house would be closed as usual on Monday and that Tuesday afternoons were reserved for connoisseurs.

# CHAPTER 22

Luigi Corsini could not always quite make out what the guide said. He spoke very firmly and clearly – that wasn't it. The problem lay with Luigi's lifelong difficulty with the English language. He had lived in Britain now for forty years and yet he still found all those odd expressions very hard to understand.

For most of the time it did not matter. At home with the family he spoke nothing but Italian, of course. In his Soho restaurant, most words the customers said to him were Italian anyway. The rest he could get away with. The only problem came with the income tax and the VAT forms, and all the social security rules and regulations. Luigi simply could not cope with these and paid an accountant to sort them all out for him.

He hadn't wanted to listen to the guide anyway. The fact that he had to be shown round Castle Cansdale by one had come as a surprise to him. He'd have much rather gone round on his own. But he happened to go on a Tuesday afternoon and Tuesday afternoons were reserved for connoisseurs and connoisseurs had to be chaperoned.

Despite his problems with the language, Luigi Corsini had had no difficulty in establishing where Lord Wymark lived. He found out in the most obvious way open to him. He knew that one of his most regular customers at La Principessa was a man he called Mr Harry. Whether Harry was his surname or his Christian name, it had never occurred to Luigi to find out. He was always 'Mr Harry', and sometimes even 'Signor Harry'.

Whatever the case, the fat man liked his food and always lunched alone. He would arrive with a bundle of the day's papers and the first edition of the *Evening Standard*. Always he would be given the corner table to sit in, from which he could observe the rest of the clientele. Luigi assumed he was a journalist on the basis that he carried lots of newspapers. The fact that Mr Harry spoke with a Scots drawl might also have seemed to confirm this, but Luigi was probably not sufficiently aware of the North British hold on what was once known as Fleet Street to make the assumption.

Mr Harry would be able to help him, though – of that there was no question. He knew everything. So at the end of his lunch, Luigi offered him a complimentary glass of *sambuca*. When the coffee beans were alight, Luigi pulled up a chair at Mr Harry's table and sat down.

'You know many important gentlemen, Mr Harry,' he said. 'I ask you question.'

'Go right ahead, Luigi. I'm all ears.'

Luigi frowned at this unfamiliar expression.

'Never mind,' said Mr Harry, seeing this. 'Tell me what you want to know.'

'Yes. I have important customer dine here the other day. He called Lord Veemark.' This was not in fact the case, but Luigi was not totally without cunning. He hadn't been born in the poorest part of Palermo for nothing. 'You heard of him?'

'Oh, my God, yes. He's all over the papers this morning. Very much the man of the hour. Never met him personally. But everybody's heard of him. You do mean *Wymark*, I suppose?'

'Yes, the Lord Veemark, *si*.'

'Was on TV last night. There's been the most frightful hoo-ha about his uncle – dotty old fellow called Alec Hooke. Has a TV show about castles.'

'Excuse me, Mr Harry, what is this hoo-ha?'

'Fuss, row, shemozzle – call it what you will. Been in a spot of scandal. So has Wymark. Always popping in and put of bed with country wenches, as I recall. Randy old sod.'

'And this Lord Veemark – he live in London?'

Mr Harry was in expansive mood and was glad of an opportunity to air his knowledge of aristocratic trivia. Another glass of *sambuca* would not have gone amiss either, so one was fetched.

'No, no – well, he may have a pad, for all I know, but chiefly he has this castle down in Wiltshire. Programme about it on the telly last night, like I said. It's not really what *you* would call a castle, not like the . . .'

Here, Mr Harry tried to think quickly of an Italian castle that was well known and actually looked like one.

'Well, such as they have in France – on the Loire, you know. What I mean is, it doesn't look like one – but it's very grand. From the pictures I've seen, anyway.'

'I understand. I go take a look?'

'Why not, Luigi? It shouldn't take you long to get there down the motorway. You've got a car?'

'Oh, yes. But I have to leave it at home. In Soho not possible to park.'

'Too right. Well, you tootle off down the M4 – it's somewhere near Craswall or Swindon. Make a nice day out. You take your wife and the *bambini*?'

Luigi, oddly, dismissed this suggestion rather sharply, but he agreed he would make the trip one day. Or maybe not. It would all depend.

The restaurant owner had probably only understood about two words in every three that Mr Harry had sprayed at him through rather ill-cared-for teeth. As a result, Luigi had a jumbled picture in his mind of tellies and hoo-has, country wenches (who were all ears) and randy old sods, and still hadn't quite got the information he wanted.

'You tell me the name of his house. Is possible?'

'Yes It's Castle Cansdale. Not hard to find I shouldn't think. Big signs up everywhere. You pays your two pound fifty and in you go, I expect.'

For the first time, Luigi Corsini managed a smile from below his moustache with the silver streaks. 'Castle Cansdale,' he said to himself, trying hard to remember the name, and called for yet another glass of flaming *sambuca* for his informant.

'I thank you very much, Mr Harry,' he said.

'Pleasure, old fruit. Come in often, old Wymark, does he?'

Luigi lost his smile for a second or two before regaining it. 'Oh, all the time, signor, all the time.'

This was another little fib, but Luigi knew he must put a little camouflage over his probings.

'Mostly in the evening, you see,' he went on. 'That's why he not here this lunch.'

'Ah, yes, that would explain it, wouldn't it?'

Luigi moved uncharacteristically fast and on the Tuesday made sure his Number Two could take charge all day and prepared to drive out of town. After a good deal of trouble he found out where Castle Cansdale was located. It was not marked on his tourist map of south-west England (printed before the house had been opened to the public), but he managed to find it and saw that he could get there and back within the day.

When he reached the North Lodge gate after much twisting and turning down country lanes and getting stuck behind tractors, Luigi drove straight past the notice which gave the opening times and prices of admission. A minute or two later he was sweeping across the park towards the noble pile which stood quietly and enigmatically in the late October sunshine.

He missed the turning for the car park and so drove right up the path to the front entrance. It seemed the natural thing to do. He only half-understood the notice saying 'PRIVATE'.

It was quite a relief stepping out of the Alfa, his bulk having been crammed in the small driving seat all the way down from London. Luigi reached into the glove compartment and took out a large pair of dark glasses. He threw his heavy blue overcoat over his shoulders and loosely hung a yellow scarf round his neck. Then he made for the front entrance to the house.

Miss Wardlaw had quite a shock when the door opened and Luigi came in. She was chatting to one of the other guides, Mrs Carter, and with a reflex action stuffed away the copy of the *Daily Mail* which they had been poring over. It contained an article about the Hooke family following the Uncle Alec revelations. Somehow it did not seem quite right to let visitors see that guides were at all interested in such scandal. Miss Wardlaw shot up from her chair as though she had been caught out in some nefarious enterprise. She was even more flustered by the appearance of the strange big man in the suit, coat and dark glasses.

'Is it for the connoisseurs'?' she asked in a shrill voice.

'I see the castle, okay? I pay you?'

'Yes, you do. It's five pounds on connoisseurs' days.'

Luigi remembered what Mr Harry had said about 'two pounds fifty' and wanted to tell him how wrong he was. But he paid up and made a move as though to start looking round.

'It's a *guided* tour,' Miss Wardlaw insisted, firmly but politely. 'The guide will be with you shortly. I think I can see some other people coming. Perhaps you'll wait here, please.'

Luigi felt trapped. He didn't fancy being shown round by someone jabbering a language he could hardly understand. All he wanted to do was take a quick look, make sure that Lord Wymark did live here, and if possible obtain a better photograph than the ones Mr Harry had shown him in the papers. But Luigi realized there was no escaping now. He would have to grin and bear it. He was also dimly aware that he mustn't draw too much attention to himself. Catching sight of his reflection in a large gilded mirror by the door, he slipped off his dark glasses, smoothed his hair, and waited as inconspicuously as he was able.

A group of five Americans arrived within a few more minutes. Luigi thought they must be genuine connoisseurs, if he understood the term correctly, though in fact they were ordinary tourists who had upgraded themselves because they couldn't wait another day until the house was open to the guide-less general public.

They were finally joined by an Englishman of refined appearance who actually was a connoisseur, and then by the guide, a grey-haired, stockily built man in a rather good suit. In fact, he was the retired headmaster of the school in Stoke Cansdale but Luigi thought he might have been a soldier once, so erect was his bearing.

Reg William was a considerable performer and prided himself on being the best of the Castle Cansdale guides. Everybody could hear what he said and he stumbled over not a single word in all the two-hour tour. Reg William had two phrases that he used a great deal. Whatever object or painting he pointed out tended to be either 'absolutely rare' or 'quite superb', and sometimes even both. But still, Luigi Corsini found it diffi- cult to follow him.

Luigi had never been a great connoisseur of porcelain, and the twenty minutes Reg William spent expatiating on the wonders of the Hooke collection were rather wasted on him. Those plates wouldn't last five minutes in La Principessa, he thought. His interest was only briefly stirred when the guide pointed out a rather lifeless plate and described it as having a 'tobacco leaf' design.

'Five thousand pound one like it fetched recently at a most important auction. Quite superb, I think you'll agree.' The Americans and the solitary Englishman murmured their agreement.

He wasn't much impressed by the Italian old masters either, though he sensed he should have been. All he wanted to see was a picture of Lord Wymark and possibly a glimpse of the man himself.

Reg William dragged them upstairs and downstairs and seemingly pointed out every painting, sculpture and carpet there was to be seen. The two rooms Luigi most enjoyed were the Gold Library and the Dining Room. The former had never failed to impress anybody yet. The silver dining service in the latter had the Italian's eyes out on stalks, though he could have done without the detailed exposition of the Hooke family portraits lining the walls there. He felt they would have been improved by a good wipe with a damp cloth.

The guide now began to get a touch matey. He wanted to know where his connoisseurs came from so that he could perform a trick of relating their country of origin to some picture or object or anecdote from the house's history.

Luigi wasn't going to play. He felt sure that if he said he was Italian the man would go on at embarrassing length. So he just said 'London', and that was that.

In the Drawing Room, the guide pointed to a TV set and the video, 'which Lord Wymark and Lady Wymark use, just like you or I do'. The Americans chuckled, but Luigi remained unimpressed. He still hadn't worked out how to use his own video yet.

After an hour and a half, most of which was lost on Luigi, the guided tour looked as if it was coming to an end. He still could not understand where Lord Wymark fitted in. Then he discovered there was yet another place to visit – the Pantheon, where all the classical statuary was kept and which was a short walk across the grass to the north-west of the house.

'Not usually open to the public at this time,' Reg William assured them, 'but as you're connoisseurs, it is.'

Luigi thought it looked as though the Pantheon was falling to bits. They had much better ones in Italy. Reg William knocked rather solemnly on the high wooden doors and a female voice cried out, 'Come in.'

Inside, there were individual dust sheets over each marble statue and bust, and it took a moment for the visitors to locate where the female voice had come from. Eventually, they spotted a mass of Titian-coloured hair tumbling over the edge of a tall scaffolding tower upon which a young woman was lying on her back. She was painting the ceiling, or rather restoring it, as the guide quickly pointed out. It was the group's privilege as connoisseurs to talk to her and interrupt her labours.

The girl, wearing paint-stained T-shirt and jeans, swung down the tower, pushing her long hair back into a kind of snood to protect it from paint splashes.

The Americans and the Englishman asked her questions which she answered conscientiously. The Americans were quick to note she had an American accent and soon confirmed that she was indeed one of theirs. As though to cut off this interesting avenue of discussion, Reg William moved towards Luigi and suggested that he, too, must surely have a question.

Luigi was flummoxed. The technicalities of paint and plaster were not for him. So he asked the question, the only question, he wanted answered: 'Where is Lord Wymark?'

Glenellen Summers coloured and made an embarrassed gesture with the paint brush in her hands. Who was this stupid man – touching her on her most vulnerable spot? She regained her composure quickly enough. He wasn't to know. Probably quite an innocent question. Reg William saw Glenellen's discomfort, wasn't totally ignorant of the reason for it, and gallantly came to her aid.

'Ah, you're looking forward to your cup of tea!' he said to a baffled Luigi.

'Am I?' he said. 'Yes, a cup of tea. Why not?'

The Americans chuckled, as if a cup of tea would certainly not go amiss with them.

'I should have mentioned earlier, it is usual – or, rather, it is always our hope – that at the end of the connoisseurs' tours our visitors should take tea with Lord and Lady Wymark in the Gold Library, but I'm afraid to say that today's it's not possible, as both of them are away.'

There were sighs of disappointment from the Americans, a politely non-committal look from the Englishman, and relief from Luigi. He most certainly did not wish to meet Lord Wymark face to face over a cup of tea.

'Will we see picture of him?' Luigi asked plaintively.

The guide smiled, 'Oh, I think we can manage that. There's one in the guide book. We may even be able to do better than that. Now come along. It really is tea time.'

Glenellen was already winging her way back up to the top of the scaffold, relieved to be rid of the dumb visitors.

Reg William duly led the connoisseurs back across the lawn and into the Gold Library where tea had now been set out for them. Lopez was on hand to deal with the silver teapot. There were plates of cucumber sandwiches cut into the slenderest of pieces and a stand full of sliced fruit cake. The atmosphere continued to be a touch uneasy and Reg William wondered what it would have been like had his lordship managed to be present. Duncan usually behaved quite well on these occasions – when he could manage to attend, that was – and her ladyship tried very hard to be knowledgeable. She was learning. But one was never quite sure who would rub up whom the wrong way. Perhaps discretion had kept the Wymarks away today, in the light of all the revelations currently filling the papers.

To break the silence, Reg William crossed the room to Luigi and said, 'I think I can find you a picture of his lordship if you'd like to follow me.'

Luigi put down his plate, cup and saucer and followed the guide to the Smoking Room – which had been excluded from the tour – and waved him in.

'There. Rather good little painting, isn't it?'

'But – is a boy!' exclaimed Luigi.

'Oh, yes. And that's his sister, Lady Sophie. There's a half-brother, Mr Rupert, but he's much younger. Wasn't born when this was painted. Quite superb, don't you think?'

Luigi wasn't going to be fobbed off.

'You have another picture?'

'No more oils, I'm afraid. There is one of his lordship when he attained his majority, but he keeps it upstairs in the family flat. There's *photographs*, of course.'

'Yes. You show me photograph. I like that.'

'Ah, I see. I misunderstood you. I thought you were interested in paintings.'

Mr William took Luigi even further away from the tea party in the Gold Library which was now being entertained solely by Lopez. Eventually, the guide opened a door into the Music Room and there, on a table were colour photographs of all the family.

'There he is, with her ladyship. It's quite a good likeness. You'll find it in the guide book in the shop on the way out, if you want.'

Luigi stared hard at the bluff figure in his country clothes. It was hard to work out why he needed killing. But the order had come from Palermo and he had to carry it out, even though he had no experience of such matters.

Luigi peered a little closer, as if memorizing the details.

Reg William went on about the other photographs. 'Those are his three children – all girls – and that is Lady Sophie, and that is Mr Rupert with his wife. They married quite recently. And that's Lord Wymark's father and mother, the Earl and Countess.'

But Luigi only had eyes for his future target.

'Quite a well-known chap, he is,' said Reg William amusedly. 'I'm surprised you haven't seen his picture in the papers.'

'I don't read the papers,' Luigi said flatly.

The two men walked back to join the others in the Gold Library. Luigi was first to leave, though he did stop to pick up a guide book on the way out. He drove up to London, thinking hard.

John Tarrant spent his one day a week in London in the usual manner. He drove to Craswall, caught the train, and then demolished his pile of newspapers and magazines before arriving at Paddington. Then he began his rounds of those magazine and newspaper offices where he was still in favour. In Dean Street he had a pub lunch with an old friend to whom he imparted gossip on the Alec Hooke affair – the 'inside view', the friend was given to understand. This was followed by a quick visit to the London Library to change his books, and finally he went to the offices of the *Evening Standard* in Kensington High Street.

'Can you do me a favour, Chris?' he said to one of the sub-editors with whom he had once worked in another place.

'Up from Barsetshire?' said the sub who, in spite of his job, retained a literary frame of reference.

'Yes, and I can't wait to get back, as usual.'

'Don't know why you bother, John. You could fax your stuff up now. Or phone it from your PC – if you've got one.'

'I've got one, I've got one,' said John. 'Trouble is, if I never came to town people would forget I existed. And there's other reasons. I know I can sit at home and research with a database over the phone, but it doesn't help with everything. There's a hell of a lot of stuff you can only find in the good old cuttings. That's why I'm here. Can you help me?'

'I shouldn't,' said Chris. 'But how?'

'Can you get me into your cuttings library? No hassle about passes, or what I'm doing it for?'

'Okay, but you can't take them away, of course. You'll have to sit down there and go through it.'

'Fair enough.'

'What is it? Dirt on the Hookes? I saw your piece in the *Mail*. You setting up as their spokesman or something?'

'Well, I do live quite close. In fact, very close.' But John was much too sensible to start dropping hints about Lady Sophie.

'Are they all having it off, like they say?'

'No more than most, I shouldn't think. In fact, there's some doubt whether Uncle Alec can get it up at all.'

'Oh, "Uncle Alec", is it? You *are* well in.'

'No, everybody calls him that. I think if you were to tax this Madame Maxine with the true impartiality for which your organ is famous, she wouldn't have a great deal to say about his little visits.'

'Not our line of country, I'm afraid. We let other papers make that kind of allegation. Make a mistake and it's costly.'

'Quite so.'

'So what do you want cuttings on,' Chris asked, waving John towards the library, 'if it's not sex in the shires?'

'Crime, London, general,' John answered, lowering his voice.

'Would that be Crimes General, Crime Robberies, Sex, Fraud Squad, or what?'

'God knows. I want to find out about a feller called Freddie Moore.'

'Footballer?'

'No, that was Bobbie Moore. He's East End-ish. Got put away for something or other about twelve years ago. Property came into it. He's had his finger in all sorts of pies. One of those villains.'

'I'd say you're headed for a needle and haystack situation there, me old son, but you can but try.'

In the cuttings library, John was quite nostalgic as the smell of several decades' worth of old newspaper scraps hit him. Although the office was brand new, since the *Standard* had moved out of Fleet Street along with everyone else, they seemed to have ensured that the smell came with them. Nor would all the modern technology of shiny, humming computers ever replace that vast storehouse of seemingly dead information.

'Do you want any help?'

'Leave me to it, Chris. I don't mind the slog. Makes me feel I'm an investigative journalist!'

'That'll be the day!'

Chris told the clerk to give John Tarrant what help he could and went back to the subs' desk.

The most obvious short cut, looking for a file marked 'MOORE, Freddie', soon proved to be a non-starter. It did not exist, or if it had, someone had filched it and not replaced it.

'Tell me more about him,' the clerk said. Although his was a drudge of a job he hadn't quite lost sight of the thrill of the information chase.

'He's a small- to big-time crook. East End once, now south of the river. Lives in Brentwood.'

'And you don't know what he was done for? It *would* help, you know.'

'No, that's precisely what I want to find out.'

'You'd be better off getting into the Yard computer.'

'Not with my reputation. Haven't you read my pieces?'

The clerk didn't think he had. He wasn't even sure he knew who John Tarrant was.

'And you *think* it was twelve years ago?'

'Yes. I think. Could be wrong.'

'Well, why don't you look through these. This is Crime General, 1973–80. It's on microfiche.'

John sat himself down before the big screen and started feeding in the small, black, card-sized pieces of plastic. It was going to take a long time. He shouldn't have spent so long in the pub. He knew he would end up missing his train back to the country. It was always like this when you tried to dig out information in a hurry.

It took him half an hour to get through 1976–8, which was the period his folk-memory cell kept telling him was the target. His eyes were beginning to swim as they swept repeatedly over the screen. His back was beginning to give him jabs of pain, too, as he perched on an office stool.

After an hour, he knew he was going to have to give up. He was getting nowhere.

And what does it matter? he started asking himself. This wasn't *work*. Just idle curiosity. But how he wanted to solve the little mystery!

Then suddenly the words leapt out at him from the screen.

'Freddie Moore (39), a company director . . .'

John gave a silent whoop and read the short report dating from an edition of the *Standard* in May 1977.

'Got it!' he exclaimed, aloud now. 'Can I have a copy of this.'

'Sure,' said the clerk. 'You know how to use the photocopier? Found what you were looking for?'

'Yes. And how!'

John didn't tell him what he had found, and the clerk didn't really give the impression he wanted to know.

Giving Chris an enthusiastic pat on the back and profuse thanks, John Tarrant swept out of the newsroom, his scarf trailing behind him. He made a dash for the Tube, and caught his train from Paddington down to Wiltshire by a whisker.

God, there was nothing quite like finding information you'd been searching for! It made his whole trip to town worthwhile. On the train,

John bought a small whisky to celebrate and took the photocopy out of his bag to read again more carefully.

'Freddie Moore (39), a company director, was found guilty . . .'

He knew Sophie would be waiting for him at Bethany Cottage – if she hadn't stayed on late again at Waterwheel. It was his turn to go round to her. She might even have started cooking their supper by the time he arrived. The image of domestic bliss delighted him. It would soon be November. Logs in the grate, bonfires in the garden, candles flickering in the windows. So much better than London.

# CHAPTER 23

They were not the kind of visitors Alec Hooke was used to, but recently he had encountered a considerable number of people who were outside his normal acquaintance. The fuss over the *News of the World* revelations had died down by the following Sunday and Alec felt able to return to South Audley Street. He had sat out the journalistic siege with kind friends in Northamptonshire, but now he was back on his home patch and taking phone calls again.

His sudden fame and subsequent notoriety meant that he would have to have the phone number changed and his name taken out of the book. But that would take time and he was still vulnerable to calls from strangers. So it was that he feared the worst when he received a call from a Mr Moore who spoke with a rather rough accent. Probably another journalist, he guessed, and put on his most stubborn manner – which, it has to be said, would not have deflected anybody very much.

'Alec Hooke,' the voice told him forcefully, 'you don't know me but, in a manner of speaking, we're related.'

Alec took off his glasses at this claim and stared down into the phone mouthpiece as though that would help him recognize the speaker.

'Oh, really?'

'Yes. My name's Moore. Freddie Moore. My darling daughter married Rupert.'

'Why . . . yes – my oh my! I've heard nothing but the nicest things about her, though we have yet to meet.'

'Now, look,' Freddie pushed on in his best cut-the cackle mode, 'my lad – Mark – and myself, we 'appen to be coming down your way later on and we was wondering if we mightn't pay a call on you. Say how d'you do and that.'

Alec's heart sank at the proposal. It reminded him of those carpet-cleaning sales people who tried to pressure you into a quick deal on the grounds that they were in your area that day and, on the basis of the presumed honour this bestowed, would give you a special discount. He also saw more of his precious time being stolen. There had been so many demands on it of late, what with his fame and notoriety. Numerous invitations to go and speak to people, to open things, charities to help. If he wasn't careful, he would end up doing no actual work and become a professional personality. Apart from which, he would have no time to read. In a sense, Alec's whole life was geared towards that one goal of being able to sit quietly in an armchair reading a book. It sometimes seemed that everyone else in the world had the one goal of preventing him from doing so.

'Well now, Mr Moore,' he began to reply, courteously as ever, 'you will know that I'm a very old man!'

Don't give me that, Freddie thought – you've still got enough blood in you to get your leg over Madame Maxine whenever she takes your fancy!

'. . . and I have been under a – how shall I say? – a certain amount of pressure of late. I think you may know what I mean?'

'Exactly,' Freddie told him emphatically. 'That's the nub of it. That's why we want to talk to you, Alec. We – that's my boy and me – think we can help you there.'

'Oh.' Alec couldn't imagine how anybody could help him out of that hole. He had resolved that the best thing to do was lie low and say nothing. He certainly wasn't going to try suing the paper or anything like that. The matter would blow over in due course, as it showed every sign of doing already. The bloodhounds had selected another, much more juicy, target and had left him to lick his wounds. 'Well . . .'

'Promise you, it won't take a jiff, Alec. Know how busy you must be. But, being as we're *family*, I thought we might be able to help.'

'Very well then . . . Freddie. In an hour or so? You know where I am?'

Freddie told him the exact address which was, of course, available to anyone who cared to look in the phone book – but it surprised Alec that Freddie knew it so readily.

Father and son arrived promptly at eleven thirty. They entered Alec's cosy book-lined flat and couldn't help looking round at it rather as though casing the joint, though this was not at all their intention.

'Do come and sit down,' Alec waved Freddie and Mark before him and decided from the look of them that he wouldn't offer them any hospitality beyond a seat.

'Nice place you got here,' said Freddie. 'Worth a bob or two, eh?'

'I think it will turn out to have been quite a nice little investment,' Alec smiled – without adding, 'when I'm dead', for he had no intention of ever moving again.

'Saw you on the telly,' Freddie enthused next. 'Bleedin' marvellous!'

'It amazes me how many people did! I thought there was so much for people to watch these days – so many programmes to choose from – that no one would see my little spot. But there you are!'

'Didn't see them all, mark you,' Freddie added. 'In fact, the only one we really saw was the one about Castle Cansdale. 'Ad to see that, of course. You gave that Duncan quite a going over, didn't you?'

'You think so? Oh, well, that wasn't really the intention. Just a friendly chat. He is my nephew, after all. We're quite close in fact.'

'You like him then – do you – that Duncan?'

Alec paused before replying. He glanced at Mark who sat, quiet as ever and exuding an air of impatience, then back to the father. What was this man doing, barging in here with his dominant deodorant, insinuating disagreements into the Hooke family?

'Yes, I think you could say I do like Duncan. Within the family – and perhaps you've heard some of this from your daughter – he does have a slight reputation for divisiveness. But I have never found it so. I don't suppose you've met him yourselves?'

Mark looked away. But Freddie wasn't in the business of holding anything back.

'Unfortunately, we have,' he said loudly. 'Not very friendly, he wasn't. What I would call a jerk, if you'll pardon the expression.'

'Hmm.' Alec pressed the tips of his fingers together. 'I'm sorry you have received a bad impression of him, but you're not alone so I wouldn't worry about it. Now then . . .' It was Alec's turn to hint gently at impatience.

Mark wished his father would get to the point. Neither of them was used to diplomacy of this order and Mark had only come along – had only involved his father – because he'd got stuck with his plans for the Cansdale job. Freddie wasn't supposed to be in on it at all. It was Mark's show, and his alone, but he needed help. Freddie had at least seen that there was the makings of some sort of deal in Mark's need for vital information and the possibility of 'helping' Alec in some way.

The problem was how to spell it out without giving the game away. It would be negotiating under wraps, without the kind of threats that Freddie usually employed. He stumbled on, not really sure what he was aiming at.

'Yeh, yeh, don't get me wrong, I'm coming to it,' he said. 'Now look here, see, I'm a blunt man, Uncle Alec – is it all right to call you that? That's what they all seem to call you. Right? Now, I know it's a bit funny like, me and us being mixed up with the likes of you, and all the other Hookes, but that's the way it is, isn't it? And – you know? – I have to tell you, we was very upset by what you was put through recently. As members of the family, we felt it a lot.'

'That's most kind of you. It wasn't really too bad, you know.'

Here Alec was not being entirely truthful either. He had been badly shaken by the affair and only his gentle demeanour could have fooled anyone otherwise. But what was it that this extraordinary little man, Freddie Moore, was trying to suggest to him? That he could somehow expunge the hurt? Maybe even exact retribution? And if so, what authority had he to do so?

'You see,' Freddie went on, getting a little more into his stride, 'I don't like anyone in my daughter's family being messed about. 'Specially now she's expecting.'

Freddie paused so that Alec could take this on board.

'Oh, how wonderful!' he exclaimed. 'A little one, eh? I had no idea.'

'So, what I'm saying is this,' said Freddie 'you tell me who's been bothering you, and we'll make sure it doesn't happen again. And, if it does, you just give the word and we'll sort 'em out.'

Alec didn't find it hard to keep a straight face. Although what the man was saying could have been comic, he spoke with such conviction that he sounded quite frightening. Alec did not doubt that if Freddie wanted to be his guardian thug, he could make a very good go of it.

'Come, come, Mr Moore, this is all very noble of you, and don't think it isn't appreciated, but, really, my little spot of difficulty is over now,' said Alec. 'The storm has passed, thank goodness. I don't expect to be troubled again.'

Freddie's face registered disappointment for a moment. 'But what you goin' to do?' He was on the attack again. 'What about that woman – that Maxine, she did the dirty on you, didn't she? Stands out a mile.'

'No, please! I really don't want to talk about it. It's all too embarrassing. I'm sure the woman in question is blameless. She was probably led into her indiscretion unawares.'

'You aren't half an old softy, Uncle Alec, if you don't mind my saying so! It wouldn't be no trouble for me and Mark to have a word with her, and her ponce. Make sure it doesn't happen again. Find out how many nicker she got for it.'

'No, no, as I say, I absolutely forbid you to have any such connection with her. I have no complaint against her and I, after all, am the injured party – if there is such a thing.'

Freddie was very put out by Alec's attitude. It didn't add up. He had a good mind to go and teach Maxine a thing or two, whatever the old codger said. Freddie felt hemmed in mentally, so as usual he burst out of the jam with an impatient switch of subject.

234

'Well, well, Mark's got a question for you, haven't you, boy?'

Mark sat up with a jump and was rather annoyed to be thrown in the deep end, just so Freddie could extract himself from a hole.

'Well, maybe . . .' He looked at his father with a scowl. 'You wrote the guide book, right?'

'To Cansdale? Yes, of course.'

'It doesn't have a very good plan.'

Alec's eyes twinkled unseen behind the tinted glasses. 'Oh, dear, another disappointed customer!'

Freddie crashed back in. 'What he means is, he's really interested in the *architecture*. Would love to know more about it. He's really keen on that sort of thing, ain't you, Mark?'

'Oh, well, in that case,' Alec said, rather relieved, and standing up, 'I've got some very interesting things you might care to look at.'

He went over to a mound of files that stood on his desk, in dire need of a cupboard, and fished among them. Finally, he produced a yellowing piece of parchment and tossed it playfully at Mark. 'There you are. Feast your eyes on that. I came across it too late for my guide book, otherwise I'd have included it, it's so spot on.'

'What is it?' asked Freddie beckoning to Mark to spread the parchment on the carpet.

'The original plan for the remodelling of the house in 1838. By Barry – you know, who designed the Houses of Parliament. The amazing thing is that the house as it stands is exactly the same as his first plan. Hardly a brick different. Isn't that odd?'

While Alec enthused about the plan, Mark had a very good look at it. There was a cross-section of the centre portion of the house, the one that contained the Salon. Immediately it answered one of his questions as to the precise location of the servants' quarters, kitchens, and so on, downstairs. He hadn't been able to work out whether they were the real ground floor of the house, or whether they were in what would have been the cellar anywhere else. They were half and half, but now Mark could clearly see the way the stairs connected the downstairs with the main part of the house. He had no trouble reading the plan. It was just like following a car engine diagram. You just had to use your common sense.

There were ground plans of each of the floors of Castle Cansdale, too, giving a clear room-by-room layout. The only thing omitted was the security devices – but it would have been asking too much of Barry to have predicted those in 1838.

Alec eventually handed the drawing to Mark for closer scrutiny. So pleased was he to have discovered someone interested in architecture that he prattled on about architraves and pediments, embrasures and slate lintels until Freddie quite glazed over.

'I suppose I might offer you a drink,' Alec then proposed, forgetting his reservations about the Moores in his enthusiasm. 'A little sherry, perhaps?'

Soon the threesome was getting happily merry on Tio Pepe. Then Freddie came to, and thought he and Mark had better be off. Alec took Freddie next door into his bedroom and showed him a rather happy little photograph of young Rupert in short trousers.

'A lovely little boy,' Alec said with a smile. 'He's still the same, of course – your son-in-law.' He emphasized the relationship.

'You should have a pic of Jacks for your collection,' Freddie assured him, squeezing Alec's elbow. 'You could have one of her modellin' – David Bailey, Lord Snowdon, Patrick Lichfield, they've all done her. If only they'd had a proper wedding you could have had one of 'em together. Perhaps my Cynth has a snap. I'll send it to you.'

'Oh, do that,' Alec chortled delightedly. 'I should love it.'

So the visit ended on a much happier note than had seemed possible half an hour before. Alec wondered whether he might one day actually manage to like Mr Moore – though he wasn't so sure about the son.

'Stupid old git,' Freddie said out of the side of his mouth to Mark as soon as they were down in the street. 'What did you make of 'im?'

'Soft,' said Mark, tapping the inside pocket of his jacket.

'What d'ya mean?'

Mark pulled the plans of Castle Cansdale an inch or two out of his pocket to show Freddie.

'Fuckin' hell, boy, you are comin' on, ain't yer? But what happens when he finds it missing?'

'He won't,' said Mark simply.

It was true. Alec Hooke was too disorganized to notice such a detail. He would only begin to wonder when he needed to refer to the plans again, and when would that be?

Sophie and John had been together now for almost a year and a half. To all intents and purposes, Sophie and her lover lived together as man and wife. It was an unusual pairing – at least as far as Hooke country folk could see. He was an outsider, not quite her class; she was slumming it, letting him wean her off her country interests.

This was true. But the process had begun before John came on the scene. She had 'gone commercial' by joining those design people down at the Old Mill. Now it wasn't just the hunting and the riding that John's influence had caused Sophie to abandon. She no longer mixed with the sets that went with these pursuits.

What she was doing wasn't quite 'done'. But she was getting on, poor thing, and at thirty-nine now it was perhaps inevitable that she would do things like that.

John was a perfect catch for her, however. He had a marvellous ability to cut through snobbishness and pretentiousness without offending anyone in the process. He was able to talk to anyone, neither looking up nor down at them. People respected him, but slightly out of fear. They had a feeling that he might put them in one of his articles, so they took pains not to rub him up the wrong way.

The upshot was that Sophie and John spent almost all the time they weren't working in each other's company. They didn't see much of anybody else. They liked each other to the exclusion of all others. John didn't seem to have many friends – certainly not ones who could be bothered to come out of town and visit him.

He had been married – rather a long time ago – to another journalist. She was now quite famous and, more often than John would have liked, would appear on the TV holding forth on abortion, women's rights, nuclear disarmament and the Green Party. His inclination was usually to turn her off, as he had done in married life, but Sophie risked a row every time by wanting to stare at – and listen to – John's former lover. According to John, his marriage had been a flop from the word go. They had never really been married, so little time had they spent with each other after tying the knot. They had lived together for years before that, but as soon as it was made official that was the end of it.

Sophie bloomed under his attentions. She behaved as though she had just discovered sex at her somewhat advanced age and wanted as much of it as she could have, as regularly as possible, in case it all evaporated tomorrow. John was happy to oblige. Sophie looked so much better that people remarked on it, not least her brother, Duncan. He felt a curious satisfaction at knowing his 'little sister' had found a soul mate and, as far as he could judge, was getting well serviced by John. Whenever Duncan saw Sophie coming up the drive to Castle Cansdale he was always glad. She was the one member of the family who never gave him a hard time.

Duncan didn't really know much about John Tarrant, had barely met him, but he seemed a sensible sort of chap and had certainly done what was expected of him when he came, valiantly, to the rescue of Alec – and of Duncan himself – when the rest of the British press was trying to eat them for breakfast.

Then one day his wife Joanna, re-installed in the marital bed for what she was convinced was for good now, said they really ought to have Sophie and John over for a meal. They didn't see enough of them. There was a danger that Sophie would end up merely as a paid retainer at Cansdale, through her Waterwheel involvement, and not as a member of the family. So the pair was summoned over for what Duncan insisted was an informal meal but which Joanna contrived to have in the Dining Room, with Lopez serving.

Sophie took the opportunity to dress up in a party frock which displayed her cleavage and legs to good advantage. John, as always, dressed with a studied dullness in corduroy, denim and shirt without a tie. He teased Sophie with the argument that it was what the package contained, not the wrapper, that was important, and she was quite happy to let him wear whatever he liked.

Duncan, too, was not one to dress up for anybody, but this time wore a baggy suit, rather at odds with his image and presumably designed to make him look younger and more fashionable than he was. Unfortunately, he had worn it out in the park that day and served drinks still with tares and blades of grass attached to the trouser legs. Joanna had tried very hard and wore a starched white blouse with a velvet skirt. For once, comments on her appearance were not spiced with irony. She looked the best she had done for years.

With no other women to distract him, Duncan spent almost all the dinner talking to John. He pumped him for opinions which John was naturally good at giving. They didn't sound too barmy to Duncan, so there were no scraps. The two of them covered world affairs, national politics, and ended up with the family, that most absorbing and never-ending of issues.

John, rather to his surprise, came to feel that Duncan was not quite the madman he was usually painted. He had, after all, taken on the enormous burden of Castle Cansdale and – in whatever unorthodox ways – seemed to be making a go of it. He wasn't too off-beam either in his views on the characters in the family, though John reminded himself that this was the man who had terrorized the countryside for miles around and was legendary for his volcanic outbursts. If not regard, then mutual respect was the outcome of their talks.

'Met my little half-brother, have you?' Duncan inquired at one point.

'Rupert, you mean? Yes, once – when his wife's people were down.'

'Oh, really? Never met 'em.'

'I think you did, actually – without realizing it.'

Duncan did not pursue the point, it wasn't important.

'She's a bit of all right, isn't she?'

'Jacky?'

'Yes. Trust Rupert to get himself well fixed up there. Wouldn't mind drinking from that trough myself. But there it is. Is he a yuppie?'

'Given that he works in the City and is – so rumour has it – contemplating a life with Jacky in Docklands, I think he probably is.'

'Funny chap,' Duncan opined, offering John a cigar and attentively lighting it for him. 'Not on the same wavelength, I'm afraid. He keeps away from here, and the further off the better, in my opinion.'

Sophie was trying to keep one ear on what her brother was saying while Joanna prattled on about her bloody horses in the other. When she understood him to be slagging off Rupert, she froze a little and tried very hard to concentrate on what Joanna was saying.

John was reluctant to get drawn into discussing family rifts and cast about for a topic that would divert Duncan. He soon found it. Despite his closeness to Sophie it was not something he had yet ventured to tell her. When he returned home from London after delving in the files of the *Evening Standard*, he hadn't shown her the cutting about Freddie Moore. Now, eager to change the subject and his tongue loosened by Duncan's claret and port, he decided to confide it to her brother.

'Yes, Jacky's all right. Not the bimbo you'd expect. Not by a long chalk, in fact. Quite foxy, I'd say. Certainly makes a packet. No, it's her father I'm not so sure about.'

'This chap I'm supposed to have met but can't recall?'

'Yes.'

'What's the matter with him?'

'Had a hunch I'd heard of him long ago, so took the trouble to look him up. I remember telling Sophie when I first met him I thought he'd been up to something fishy once upon a time. And was I right!'

'Come on, old chap, spill the beans.'

'Well . . .' John made no attempt to lower his voice, well aware that Sophie was still half-listening while Joanna chattered on. 'In 1977, he got sent down for manslaughter.'

'Good grief. The dreaded d-and-d?'

'Drunken driving? No, no. They had him up on a murder charge. He fancies himself as a bit of a landlord and apparently took it out on a tenant who was behind with the rent. But there was some jiggery-pokery among the lawyers and he got seven years on the lesser count. Didn't serve all of it, I don't suppose.'

Duncan laughed very loudly. 'D'you mean to say little Rupe has married into the criminal classes!'

Sophie stared at him and Joanna abruptly stopped her chatter.

'I don't suppose he knew,' John replied, more quietly. 'Why should he? I had to dig bloody hard to find out. More like the criminal classes marrying into Rupe, if you ask me.'

'But surely Jacky would have told him?' remarked Sophie without bothering to ask why John hadn't told her the news before.

'How can we be sure?' said Duncan. 'I'd be prepared to bet she didn't.'

'The little minx,' Joanna said.

There was silence at the table. John was beginning to feel that the Hookes' horrified reaction was as predictable as a caricature, but told himself he couldn't judge, not being a member of the family himself.

Then it all blew back in his face.

'Well, I hope when Sophie finally drags you to the altar you won't spring anything like that on us!'

'Oh, Duncan!' Joanna and Sophie chorused together.

Duncan was no fool. He may not have realized what he was doing, but his words very shortly precipitated the very step he had alluded to. The resolutions Sophie and John both had about not getting married began to dissolve as though they had never been. As far as Duncan was concerned, that was all to the good. It made up for the surprising nastiness of Jacky's father. And John, even if not quite 'one of us', was a good fellow and, heaven help us, was the first man to come along and make his sister so radiantly happy.

# CHAPTER 24

A few days after the dinner party, Lopez was on the long haul up from the butler's pantry bearing the customary pot of morning tea for Duncan and Joanna. Their bedroom was on the first floor and after crossing the Saloon, he had to go up another flight of stairs. He made the journey every morning and could have done it blindfold; he knew exactly where everything was.

That day, however, Lopez noticed that something was different. It wasn't that anything had been moved or disturbed, but it looked odd somehow.

His route took him past first the display case containing the medals and decorations of the Hooke family and then the cases with the porcelain and silver that were not on display in the Dining Room.

And then Lopez realized what it was. There was no reflection coming back at him from one of the display cases. In fact, there was no glass in it. And then, with a rather sickening blow to his stomach he realized there was nothing in the case. All the silver had gone.

He staggered ever so slightly and, responsibly, decided to put down the tea tray before doing anything else. Then he approached the case for a closer look. He put his hand out towards it, as though the glass was still in the frame. His fingers went right through. Lopez noticed, moreover, that there was no trace of glass left. The pane had not been smashed, but carefully removed in one piece.

His impulse was to run and shout, but he knew better than to do that. He took another look at the case, picked up his tray again, and continued in a dignified fashion up the flight of stairs and along the boudoir corridor to the Green Bedroom. He knocked gently and waited for Duncan's customary morning grunt. Not receiving it, he went in nevertheless and was dimly aware of the two people in bed, apparently in some kind of embrace.

Once again, Lopez put down the tray. He opened the curtains just a crack. Still trying not to look at his master and mistress, he said, 'Good morning, my lord, good morning, my lady,' as quietly as he could, and moved the tray to Duncan's side, as he had always been instructed to do.

'Excuse me, my lord, I may speak?'

Duncan, who had been pretending to be asleep for more than half an hour now in order to escape Joanna's attentions, yawned irritably.

'Well, what is it, Lopez?'

'I'm sorry, sir, but has been robbery, I think.'

Duncan was suddenly very awake. He sat up, leaving Joanna to fend for herself.

'Where? What have they got?'

'The silver, my lord. In Salon.'

Duncan leapt out of bed stark naked.

'Dressing gown, quick,' he barked. Lopez obligingly held it out for him.

Duncan ran down the stairs, barefoot, tying the garment round him as he went. Lopez followed at a more stately pace.

There was no mistake, the silver had gone.

'How the devil did they do it? I'll have to ring the police, drat it. Not supposed to touch anything, are we?'

Lopez apparently had no view on any of these matters, and stood silently by.

It took the police forty-five minutes to drive over from Craswall, which didn't go down at all well with Duncan who found himself incapable of eating any breakfast until they had arrived. The detectives quickly established that no one appeared to have broken a way into the house, though with so many doors and windows it was just possible they might have missed the signs of forced entry.

'Were the items insured?' a policeman asked.

'Not really,' Duncan replied vaguely.

'I see. Do you have any photos of them?'

'Oh, sure. They're in the guide book.'

'You don't have an alarm?'

'No,' said Duncan a little reluctantly. 'Well, we have one, yes, but it was always going off, so we tended not to switch it on. It was a real pain. Only needed a sparrow to fly past to set the bloody thing off. Drove us barmy.'

Duncan was less concerned about the loss than he was about the prospect of being forced now to do what he had so long put off: making Castle Cansdale secure. It would cost a lot of money.

'Well,' Duncan said, to no one in particular, 'could have been worse, I suppose.'

'They were professionals,' said the detective. 'I think we can be certain of that. Knew what they wanted – exactly – and only took that. Always a sign of amateurs if they grab everything in sight.'

'They won't be able to resell it, that's for sure,' Duncan stated confidently. 'Too well known, those pieces.'

'Depends how quickly they move, sir.'

'Well, you'd better catch them quick, hadn't you?'

The detective seemed much more interested in such tedious questions as when the silver had last been seen in place, whether the house had been open to the public the day before, were the staff reliable, and had they been vetted?

Lopez said he felt sure no one had noticed anything missing at closing time, or else they would have told him. But perhaps they simply hadn't spotted anything amiss.

By the middle of the morning the police had completed their interviews of the staff, noted the names and addresses of the castle guides, and left. Duncan at last had some breakfast and then made two phone calls. One was to Valerie Taylor at ShakesPR Ltd to get them busy with the publicity; they might be able to make some capital out of the loss. The second was to a security company whose name he had found in an old copy of *Country Life*. They appeared to specialize in systems for protecting stately homes.

Joanna hadn't seen Duncan quite so put out for years.

'Oh, Freddie, look.'

At breakfast the day after the robbery was discovered, Cynthia Moore passed the *Express* over to her husband and tapped it heavily with her left hand – temporarily without the diamond stud in the little fingernail.

Freddie made little noises while he read the report. But he said nothing. He did not know what to say. His first reaction was, 'Good old Mark!' but he knew that he mustn't let Cynthia know.

'Terrible,' he restricted himself to saying. 'Wonder who did that?'

'Half a million,' Cynthia commented. 'That's a lot, isn't it?'

'Well, I expect our friend Lord Wymark'll be chewing the carpet right now. And serve 'im bleedin' right!'

'You reckon? Probably did it himself to fiddle the insurance.'

'Yes, dear, quite like.' Freddie went back to his breakfast. 'Where's Mark?' he asked as lightly and innocently as he could.

'Still in bed, I suppose.'

Freddie was puzzled. Mark had been home the night before and the night before that, hadn't been away for several days, in fact. That was odd. Had Mark got someone else to do the dirty work? It was possible. That was one way of doing it. But, surely, he'd have said something? Or perhaps he wouldn't. Perhaps he really was keeping this one to himself. Mark had had to bring in his father to help get the plans from Alec Hooke, but he might still be determined to make the execution of the job one hundred per cent his own.

As soon as he decently could, Freddie swallowed the dregs of his last cup of black coffee, left the kitchen and went upstairs. He entered Mark's bedroom without knocking and asked him straight out, 'Did you do it, boy? Eh?'

Mark was dead to the world. There was no one quite like him, thought his dad – like concrete when he slept.

Freddie woke him and got an earful of abuse in response.

'You've done it, eh?'

'Done what?'

'The job! The Cansdale job. It's in the paper.'

'What is?'

'The silver stuff – half a bleedin' million, they're saying.'

Mark didn't speak until the light had dawned. Then he cried out, 'Fuck it! Some other bloody fucker's got there first!'

'What? Wasn't it you, then?'

'Nah. I wasn't ready to go yet.'

'Oh my bleedin' sainted aunt! And you'll never get in there now . . .'

The same thought did not occur to Luigi Corsini. He did not, after all, look at the British newspapers. Hadn't done for all the forty years he had been in the country. And even if he had, he would not have been able to understand much in them.

He found out about the robbery from his usual conduit. Mr Harry was in for lunch again at La Principessa towards the end of the week after an unexplained absence of a few days. As usual he had the corner table and manoeuvred his stout frame into the little chair, which he overflowed, and parked his bundle of newspaper and magazines on the side plate.

It was the *prosciutto con melone* today, followed by the *osso bucco*, and then the *zuppa inglese*. Just for good measure he thought he might as well have a bottle rather than a half of the red Corvo, all to himself.

Luigi waited until Mr Harry was well dined and wined before oiling up with his 'Everything all right, sir?' routine.

'Your friend's been in the news again,' Mr Harry announced.

Luigi didn't quite understand.

'Your *amigo* – in the papers – Wymark – Veemark . . .'

'Oh.' Now he understood, but failed to see why the newspaperman called Lord Wymark his 'friend'.

Mr Harry told him about the robbery. The original report had been amplified over the past couple of days. It wasn't very important news, the valuables were not that interesting or hugely valuable – it was just another burglary. But the story was made more interesting when the basic item was tricked out with reminiscences of the Hooke family's other recent exploits. Uncle Alec was mentioned – even quoted in a comment on the history of the silver – and Duncan's rumbustious life style was again alluded to.

Mr Harry detected a lack of interest on Luigi's part. Perhaps his enthusiasm for Lord Wymark had waned? Perhaps Lord Wymark had not been to dine lately? It wasn't clear why Luigi had ever had an interest in him in the first place. The chat moved on to other subjects. Mr Harry did not receive a complimentary *sambuca* that day.

In fact, Luigi Corsini had registered what he had been told. It was not good news that Castle Cansdale would now have policeman scrambling all over it looking for a robber. It might inhibit him in what he had to do. That was already taking far longer to accomplish than it should have done. There would be questions from Palermo soon about why he hadn't carried out the contract.

But Luigi had a problem. He knew everything about his victim now, but that wasn't all he needed for the task. He needed a gun to do it with. These English with their stupid laws! It was so hard to get a gun. He had had one, of course. He had smuggled it into the country many years ago, but it had been stolen . . .

Well, they would just have to wait, those people in Palermo. He would do the job, but not today. Not even tomorrow. Maybe the day after that. It might take weeks. They would just have to be patient.

When the Dowager Countess picked up news of the robbery she expressed the view that it wouldn't have taken place but for opening Castle Cansdale to the public. That gave potential burglars a chance to 'case the joint' – she relished the phrase. It was only to be expected that there would be more such incidents following Duncan's move.

But she did not express the view to Hugo or Molly. She responsibly did not wish to provide her son with ammunition against her grandson. In fact, Marjorie Hooke provided the opportunity for an element of reconciliation between them the following week. She died.

Though it should not have done, it took everyone by surprise. The family had just taken for granted that she would always be there. No particular illness had sounded a warning note. Marjorie had remained her plucky self right to the very end, her delightful personality still shining out of an increasingly bent and stiff body. This to her was the cruellest blow, not to be able to walk with the wonderful erectness she had exhibited for so long.

In the final two or three months, though, she had stopped initiating telephone calls herself and relied on others to call her and keep her amused. Sophie was one of her most regular callers by phone and in person. The last time they had talked was when Sophie called to tell her grandmother that she and John had decided to reverse into marriage, so to speak. The news was greeted with predictable delight.

'My dear girl, and about time, too! I thought he would fall for you as soon as I heard about him.'

'I think I rather fell for him, actually . . .'

'Well! have you spoken to the Rector? When will the wedding be? It will be in church, I trust?'

'Of course, Grandma. We haven't fixed a date yet. Next spring, probably. And you must be there.'

But it was not to be. Nor did Marjorie ever set eyes on John, though she had formed a good impression of him from what she had read of his articles. It no longer seemed to bother her that Sophie was, in a sense, 'marrying out'. As long as the girl was happy, that was the main thing now.

The funeral at St Michael and All Angels, Bourton Cansdale, was a relaxed, almost happy affair. The church was nearly full – not only of family, but of people from all over Hooke country. There was an unspoken feeling that, quite apart from being the wonderful old thing she had been, the Dowager Countess deserved to be given a proper send-off. She had always carried herself as she was supposed to. She was an aristocrat, but with the common touch. People did not think they would be able to say the same about some of the younger Hookes.

Hugo took his mother's death very badly. After his own recent illness, the reminder of mortality depressed him. Next month, in December, she would have had her ninetieth birthday. She had been cheated of it by just a few weeks. Hugo, mournfully, doubted very much whether he would last until that age before he joined her.

Dutson, the Rector, gave a happily-phrased address in Marjorie's memory. Hugo and Duncan read passages from the Bible that had been selected for them. In the front pew with the Earl and Countess, Duncan and Joanna and their two eldest girls Josephina and Serena sat the sad but now very familiar figure of Uncle Alec. Rupert and Jacky shared the next pew back with Sophie and John.

Sunlight shone through stained glass, the organ jerked the odd tear, and Hugo couldn't stop glancing at his father's memorial and wondering when he would ever get round to dealing with that unfinished business. Marjorie would be buried just beneath the 7th Earl's memorial. What a shame she would not actually be lying next to her husband's body.

Afterwards, at Duncan's suggestion, the family and a dozen or so other mourners went back to Castle Cansdale for drinks. It would be the first time Hugo had set foot in the old house for over a year and he felt decidedly uncomfortable at the prospect.

Molly drove the Silver Cloud as Hugo wasn't too sure he could manage it these days, and they sailed up to the front entrance past the forest of little signposts that had grown since their time.

Drinks were served in the Salon and, inevitably, one of the main talking points was the empty glass case that still bore the remains of fingerprint powder the police had sprinkled on it so liberally.

Molly made sure that Hugo didn't start lecturing Duncan on his responsibilities but, as it turned out, Hugo wasn't in a mood to make capital out of the misfortune.

'It was bound to happen sooner or later, especially with the public trooping in and out. Only thankful we survived all our time here without losing anything.'

Duncan, who was on his best behaviour just then, told his father about the new security system arriving that very week. It was costing a fortune, but it had to be done. All display cases would be fitted with shatterproof glass and sensors connected to a master control. On the outside of the house there would be lighting which would come on automatically if there was any movement during the hours of darkness. There would also be television cameras and infra-red devices surrounding the house.

'And if that doesn't work, nothing will,' said Duncan, sounding as if it was all a terrible burden.

'It's necessary these days, I suppose,' his father said. 'But tell me – show me – what you've had done.'

'You may not recognize some of it,' Duncan warned.

And off they went, slowly following the tourist route, with Duncan pointing out the cleaned tapestries, the re-upholstered chairs, and the new wallpaper matched as closely as possible to the original.

'We've got a long way to go yet, but I think you can notice a difference.'

Yes, Hugo had to admit, it was an improvement.

'You've done very well,' he even allowed.

Duncan smiled to himself. Perhaps the old man was coming round. How useful funerals were if they allowed you to heal old wounds like this.

It was a time for catching up, too. 'I must say, your Uncle Alec is looking pretty rough after his, er, ordeal,' Hugo remarked.

'You think so? I thought rather the opposite: how well he'd managed to come through.'

'Silly ass,' said Hugo. 'Fancy getting mixed up in all that.'

'He's entitled to have a woman if he wants, isn't he?'

'Not sure that he is. But I didn't mean that. Meant all that TV nonsense.

What'd he want to go and do that for? Showing off in public. Shouldn't have done it.'

'Why not? You're an old sourpuss, Father! He's rather good at it. And, anyway, it did wonders for us. We've been getting so many visitors we hardly know what to do with them.'

'Always thought he had a screw loose,' Hugo went on, doing his favourite trick of ignoring points he didn't want to hear.

Duncan made a gesture of mock despair which no one saw and led his father back to the Salon. He deposited him on Sophie and John, knowing that they would be able to make conversation with him. Hugo said he supposed their wedding would be the occasion of the next family gathering.

'When'll it be? I need to know. Got to arrange the finances, you know.'

John told them the date they had just agreed with the Reverend Dutson for the following April.

'You'll be wanting the full show, I expect – marquee on the lawn, that sort of thing? You'd better ask Duncan if you can have it here. There's hardly room at Huddleston.'

'Yes, there is, daddy,' Sophie piped up. 'The croquet lawn's quite big enough for a tent.'

'We'll have to decide,' John put in, soothing as ever. 'It might be a good idea to have it here. Facilities and so on.'

'It's not the Coronation, you know,' Sophie teased.

'Or it could be a christening, I expect.'

Sophie blinked, wondering what her father was talking about. But Hugo was simply pursuing his own line of thought. What he meant was that if his daughter's wedding was not going to be the next family event, the baptism of Jacky's expected offspring might be.

When they had made the mental leap to this new concept, Sophie was the first to skirt the dangerous subject of Jacky's father.

'That'll be an interesting show, won't it?' she said, giving John a look. 'Can't wait to meet her divine ma and pa again . . .' She ended up with a mild guffaw.

Hugo looked sideways as though to hide the suggestion of a smile that played upon his own lips.

'Aren't you presuming rather a lot?' John said, all seriousness. 'Who's to say they'll have the kid baptized at all?'

'Of course they will,' said Sophie, firmly. 'We're going to be married in church—'

'Blessed,' John quietly corrected her.

'Same thing, really – so why shouldn't they do things properly?'

Her father noted the sparky way Sophie and John talked together, and saw how well they coped with each other. They were going to be all right. He turned and looked over to where Rupert and Jacky were chatting animatedly with Alec Hooke. What a pretty thing Jacky seemed, especially now she was pregnant. He felt very fond. Soon each of his three children would be married.

He saw Duncan grasp Joanna by the arm and steer her towards Rupert, Jacky and Alec. The gesture seemed rare enough to be remarkable. Yet again, Hugo was being supplied with evidence that all was not as bad as he liked to make out. Gingerly, he considered the possibility.

Molly was already fussing about what they should do for lunch. Duncan had even threatened they should all go into the visitors' canteen and have a bite there. But this had not gone down well with anyone and so plans were afoot to set off for the Craswall Arms at Stoke Cansdale.

Before that, Duncan had a little catching up to do on the drinks and poured himself a stiff gin and tonic before moving over to join Uncle Alec whom he greeted warmly.

'Everything all right with you?' Duncan asked.

'Just fine, just fine,' Alec responded gamely, 'and I'm all the better for meeting this dear girl for the first time.' He gestured at Jacky standing by him. 'A pity it had to be at Mummy's funeral but I've been waiting for a long time!'

'Can't say I've had much experience myself,' Duncan leered. 'In fact, old Roo's been keeping her pretty well tucked away – and not surprising!'

Rupert flinched, but decided not to remind anyone that on the two occasions he had tried to introduce Jacky to his half-brother, Duncan had behaved abominably. Nor was Rupert going to enter into a justification for his absences from most family gatherings before this one.

Duncan as ever was unable to resist flirting with a pretty woman, especially when he knew it would annoy her husband. He also knew it would annoy Joanna who stood uneasily at his side in the group.

'What's it going to be then?' he asked, pointing at Jacky's swollen form.

Jacky blushed and turned, as always, to Rupert.

'Triplets,' Rupert joshed his brother. 'All girls.'

'You bugger!' Duncan frowned, seeing the joke was upon him and his inability to produce a male heir. But he laughed as well as he could.

'I wonder,' he mused. 'So much depends on the father, wouldn't you say?'

'How do you mean?' Rupert asked, taking his brother more seriously than was meant, suspecting that some sort of dart was being hurled in his direction.

'I sometimes wonder if the father doesn't dictate whether the baby's a boy or a girl. You see, I like women so much, that's why we've got three girls!'

Joanna pulled a face 'Don't talk rot, Duncan.'

Sophie and John, as though sensing that Duncan's danger level was rising, came over to join the larger group. Molly half listened, more interested in the time and wondering why no one was interested in organizing lunch.

'Well, one only has to look about one, doesn't one?' Duncan went on, obviously the worse for gin. 'Look at Hugo, what a fine father . . . look at me . . .'

His inspiration running out at this point, Duncan caught Uncle Alec's eye and saw that he was embarrassing the childless old chap. Floundering, he seized once more on Jacky.

'Now you, my dear, have got the most amazing father – what's he called, Freddie? – or so I'm told, never having had the honour.'

Rupert chivalrously threw in the comment that if either of Jacky's parents was amazing, it was surely Cynthia, from whom Jacky so clearly derived her looks.

'Ah, there again, haven't had the pleasure,' Duncan went on. 'But it's this father I'm so terribly fascinated by.'

Sophie swallowed, realizing where this was leading them. Duncan was spoiling for a fight.

'What are you getting at?' Jacky asked, spikily, at last.

Don't, don't, John Tarrant found himself thinking, you'll only regret it!

'What I'm getting at, my little darling, is that from what I hear, your daddy seems to have had a bit of a colourful past. Am I right? Uh?'

At the interrogative grunt, Jacky blushed deeper, felt trapped, hated this man for the way he was taunting her.

'I don't know what you mean,' she said quietly, meaning for him to shut up and not explain.

'Surely you must,' Duncan roared on. 'I think Daddy knows what it's like to be detained at Her Majesty's pleasure. Am I right – or am I right?'

'Forget it, Duncan,' Sophie ordered her brother coldly. 'There's no need.'

But Duncan wasn't going to be stopped. He shook off the real and imaginary restraints on his shoulders. 'Killed a man, so we're told.' He turned to John now. 'Isn't that right?'

'Don't bring him into it,' Sophie hissed.

'Isn't that right?' Duncan persisted, turning back to Jacky. 'Well, either you know or you don't know, dear!'

'What's going on, Duncan?' asked Hugo, coming over. 'It's time we were leaving, isn't it, Molly?'

250

Jacky was on the verge of tears and Rupert put a consoling arm round her.

'Lay off, Duncan!' Sophie told him sharply.

Joanna pulled him away by the sleeve of his jacket.

Once more Duncan had succeeded in souring a family gathering. Having done the right thing in bringing his father back to the house and winning him over to what was being done there, he had now spoilt it all by upsetting Jacky.

Uncle Alec tried to be consoling. In an attempt at chat he told a tearful Jacky that, funny as it was, he had actually met her father recently. And her brother. 'We had a very jolly chat,' he exclaimed. 'About architecture mainly.'

Jacky was too upset to grasp the full meaning of this strange report. It wasn't long after, when Rupert had managed to get Jacky on her own, that he asked her what Duncan had meant.

'It's true,' she sobbed. 'He did time. For manslaughter.'

Rupert was shocked.

'But why didn't you tell me? Why only now?'

Jacky sobbed all the more into his shoulder. She couldn't explain. It would only spoil everything.

In the end, they didn't go for lunch with the others to the Craswall Arms. Rupert offered Uncle Alec a lift back to London. They travelled in silence. Why was it there always had to be some incident like this whenever the family got together?

251

# CHAPTER 25

Rupert found it difficult to get the words out when he spoke to his father-in-law, but speak to Freddie it was unfortunately necessary to do almost every day now. They had put in a bid for a house in a new Docklands development called, ironically, Castle Wharf. The new house would give Rupert and Jacky a great deal more room. It would be handy for Rupert's work and the riverside site provided an ideal place in which to live. Rupert had cobbled together a package of financing and mortgages but it would not work without the significant contribution promised by Freddie. There was no chance of any matching help from the Hookes.

But the revelation that not only had Freddie been to prison but that he'd been sent down for manslaughter had come as a terrible blow to Rupert. He might have joked that his father-in-law behaved like a bit of a villain but the fact that Freddie had indeed been one – might still be, for all he knew – was outrageous. There was no other word for it. Here was a man he had to deal with, had become involved with, on a family basis, on a basis of trust, and with one blow that basis had been shattered.

At first it even threatened his love for Jacky. She hadn't told him, hadn't hinted or warned him that there might be any form of skeleton in the Moore family cupboard. As Christmas approached, Rupert found it very difficult to summon up much good will towards Jacky's family. He even wondered for the first time whether he had made a mistake in marrying her.

They kept chewing over the subject, endlessly.

'Of course, I knew he was inside!' Jacky cried – she seemed to be in a permanent state of tears these days. 'Bloody hell, your father can't be away from home five years and no one notice.'

'I thought it was seven years,' added Rupert rather brutally.

'Five years with remission. It's something we had to live with. That's why I won't hear a word against my mum. She was a bloody marvel, the way she kept us going all that time.'

'You still could have told me,' Rupert suggested.

'Well, I didn't. Why should I have done? Why spoil it between us. There's a law about people who've been in prison. After a while it doesn't count against them any more. So why not with my dad?'

'I know, Jacky, but you can't exactly ignore the fact that a bloke's been up for manslaughter – once you know.'

Tears ran down from cheek to chin. Jacky dabbed her face with a damp piece of tissue. She was getting to the pitch where she just wouldn't say any more.

'It really screws up the house,' Rupert said despairingly.

Jacky felt obliged to speak again.

'Why should it? If he's going to lend us a few quid, we should take it. Money's money, never mind what he's done in the past. It's not dirty money, you know. He's straight now, I'm sure of that.'

'How can you be sure? He's hardly likely to tell you if he's not, is he?'

'I just *feel* he's okay. You've got to believe that.'

Later that week, the deed was done. Rupert's purchase of the Castle Wharf property started to go through and he secured Freddie's contribution. When the cheque arrived, Rupert held it as though it might burn his hand off. He tried not to think how Freddie might have acquired the money and banked it the same day he received it, to forestall further misfortune.

When that was done, he told Jacky that her father must be a forbidden area of discussion from then on. He told himself he would have as little to do with Freddie as possible, though he knew that was going to be difficult.

The child grew in Jacky and it was hoped they would be installed in the house well before the spring, in time for the birth of their baby. The wound inflicted on their relationship slowly began to heal.

Mark Moore wasn't aware of the exact details of his father's financial help to Rupert and Jacky. He would have been pretty angry if he had known how much it was. And he would have completely failed to grasp why his father was doing it – a mixture of sentimental devotion to his darling daughter and a means to continue exercising a hold over her.

In fact, Mark wasn't all that interested in money as such. He had what he needed. It would be nice to have bought the BMW or the Porsche he felt he deserved, but money was not what motivated him. He did not have expensive girl friends to entertain. He got bored when he went on holiday. He lived at home, so had no great expenses there.

His reason for continuing to gnaw at the Castle Cansdale project was because it had become an obsession. How to do it, how to plan it, how to bring it off. It was a challenge. The money would be fine, if he ever got it, but that was beside the point. He wanted to prove himself to his father. He wanted to get some kind of kick out of doing it. And he wanted to teach those stuck-up Hookes a lesson.

But now everything had been thrown back into the melting pot by the silver robbery. He asked around in the London area but couldn't discover who had pulled off that job. A gang from the West Country or one specializing in country house raids, most likely. Whoever it was had really fucked up his chances, but Mark was not inclined to give up. He went back to puzzling it out with a will. He would have to make another visit to Castle Cansdale to see what, if anything, had changed. He was beginning to worry that someone might recognize him if he kept going back there. He bought a pair of glasses from a junk shop, ones with weak lenses, in the hope that they might help disguise him. Then once more it was down the M4 to pay admission to the house he one day hoped to enter for free.

He was depressed by what he saw in the gathering dark of the cold December afternoon when he was one of only half a dozen visitors. They had moved very fast, and now the house was bristling with security devices – TV cameras, sensors, pressure pads, he spotted them all. He had been shafted by fate, there was no doubt about that.

But all was not lost. Mark made a note of the name of the new security system and seized the opportunity of visiting the downstairs part of the house which, as luck would have it, was open to visitors that week. He wandered down the tunnel-like corridors, peering into wine cellars, beer cellars, washrooms, storage rooms, butler's pantry, kitchen and all. What a bit of luck, he thought to himself, that he had the original plan of the house – the one he had eased out of Uncle Alec's possession. It helped make everything clear.

There would be no point sitting out in the park during the night this time. That would not help him with his problem. Also, it being early December, he wasn't too keen on freezing his arse off, crouching about like a poacher.

Mark headed back to London and put in a call to Manorial Security. He told them he was interested in having a system installed urgently. A brochure would do to begin with, and he gave them a post office box number his father often used. He didn't give his own name either. He said he was 'Rupert Hooke', though he neglected to point out the final 'e'.

While he waited for the brochure to come through, Mark started chatting to the contacts Freddie had given him. They told him the best thing he could do would be to nobble someone in Manorial and slip him a few quid to spill the beans on circumventing their systems.

But Mark thought that too risky. Whoever he nobbled would squeal eventually. He wanted a way of circumventing a security system from the outside, so that no one would know – only him. He was making a fetish of keeping his plans to himself. Like Freddie said, the best job was the one that didn't involve anybody else. Then nobody could rat on you. Mark wondered if the best job of all might be the one where everyone else did the work but no one knew who was in charge of the operation. But that was fantasy. Leave it to the film-makers.

Mark chatted to any number of villains, plied them with drinks. He soon realized he had a terrible disadvantage. He had never been in prison. That was where you learned the trade. That was the college of crime. But he had not been inside, yet, so that was that. He also found the shadowy figures with whom he spoke deeply suspicious of a lad who clearly had ambitions but had not been blooded.

A recurring theme in the advice he nevertheless received was that there was no point in attempting to disable a security system yourself. You never knew when even the most lackadaisical of owners might decide to do a spot of monitoring. The chances were that you would be noticed if you found a way to cut the cable, so to speak. No, the method was to make it appear to the owner that there was something wrong with his system so that he himself turned it off.

'Worked very well on a job down Peckham way,' one of Mark's informants said. 'Tobacco warehouse. What we did was set off the alarm. Nothing fancy, no cameras, just a bell. Not difficult – even you could do that! Then we waited quarter of an hour and along comes the bill, has a chat with the night watchman, and goes away again. We wait five minutes and set it off again. Twenty minutes later, back comes the bill. Not so pleased this time. Are they ever? Chats to the bloke. Back to the barracks. By this time, it's one thirty, two in the morning. We sets it off again. This time the cops don't come. There's obviously a fault with the alarm, so the geezer turns it off. We see the little red light go out, and in we goes. One of our better ones that.'

'Aren't they wise to it by now?'

'Nah. Anything for a good night's sleep.'

Mark went off and spent a lot of time thinking how he could make whoever monitored security at Castle Cansdale do the same. But there you were talking about TV cameras. You couldn't creep up to those and smash them with a hammer or drop a bag over them. How did you make them go on the blink?

He would have to find out.

★      ★      ★

'God no,' said John as he and Sophie began to draw up a list of invitees to the wedding.

'Don't want to upset Rupert and Jacky,' Sophie told him.

'It's not necessary. They're not close family – yours or mine. And they'd cause a nasty stink.'

' 'S'pose so. Just thought I'd ask.'

And so the names of Freddie, Cynthia and Mark Moore were struck off the list. In any case, it wasn't going to be that big a wedding. It would be in white, with all the trimmings, but not too many guests. John and Sophie were getting on a bit, so it seemed a touch indecent to go the whole hog. John's previous marriage prevented that anyway. It had been a very long time ago, but the Reverend Dutson put his foot down, as he was entitled to, and wasn't to be swayed, not by all the moral force of the Hooke family who provided him with his living. John and Sophie would have to get married first in Craswall registry office. Then they could have a service of blessing at St Michael and All Angels. The invitations would be sent out just as soon as Christmas was over.

Other plans were also marching forward. Glenellen Summers insisted on making the dress for Sophie. Waterwheel would decorate the church and the marquee. Duncan had taken up Hugo's suggestion that the reception be at the castle rather than Huddleston. It was going to be quite an occasion.

Saturday, 21 April, was four months away. Although the wedding would hardly alter John and Sophie's situation as they had been living together for over a year, there was the inevitable anticipation and excitement. What a time it was turning out to be for births, marriages and deaths. Jacky expecting, Sophie and John splicing, Marjorie lately dead. Thank God there were no divorces in prospect, thought Molly – who seemed to be taking on her late mother-in-law's role as monitor of family affairs. The only possible candidates for divorce had been Duncan and Joanna, but that – following the latest reconciliation – was a divorce that 'would not now take place'.

They made it clear they were getting tired of waiting. Benino Noto in his prison cell in Reggio di Calabria had far too little else to worry about, unfortunately. Having so belatedly come round to putting out a contract on the man who had once dishonoured his wife, he was now consumed by irritation that his order had not been carried out.

Benino found it hard coming to terms with loss of power. At one time, he had simply had to raise his little finger for something to be done; now he was staring at a tiny spot of bright sky through his cell window, incapable – or so it appeared – of getting even the simplest task done in the world beyond.

It was even more infuriating when Benino read in the papers about what was happening in Sicily. The families were still in the process of reconstituting themselves. Those traitors who had deserted were being hunted down and ruthlessly punished. There had been over fifty killings in the gutters of Palermo that year alone.

The settling of such an old score as Benino had might have seemed irrelevant and unnecessary in the current climate, but that was beside the point. He had made a decision. He had ordered Alvaro to make the arrangements. *And it had not been done!* It was the first time he had ever had to confront failure, and he did not like it one little bit.

When Alvaro came on his next visit, Benino wanted news of what was happening to the Noto family's affairs, but first he wanted to know about the contract on the Englishman. When Alvaro said, as he had done on previous occasions, that it was taking time, Benino shouted at him:

'Who's doing it? What's the matter with him? They think they can disobey me because I can't get at them from here.'

'No, Father, no.' His son signalled that they should not raise their voices. The security guard would only listen to their interview.

'I said, who's doing it? I want to know exactly.'

Alvaro lowered his voice until it was almost inaudible.

'A Corsini. Luigi Corsini. He is the one who is indebted to us. I do not know what the delay is. I will give him a reminder.'

'A sharp reminder,' his father shouted. 'He should know what will happen if he fails!'

'He knows that already,' said Alvaro. 'Rest, Father. All will be well.'

Then he proceeded to give the old man a recital of all the killings, betrayals, and other triumphs in which the family had been involved since his last visit. Benino listened with a distasteful look, occasionally letting out a yelp of frustration and anger.

'I fear trouble from America,' Alvaro said. 'They are just waiting – but not for much longer. They will move in, they will lose patience. The Corleonesi are egging them on.'

'You know what you must do, now you are in charge.'

'Yes, Father. I have much work to do. No time to sleep. There is so much going on. That is why I cannot spare too much thought for the Englishman business.'

'Don't say that to me,' the old man barked. 'Show a little respect. You know where your duty lies. Do it!'

★   ★   ★

One and a half thousand miles away, in London, it was understandable if Luigi Corsini was beginning to sweat a little. He had had too comfortable a life running his restaurant all these years. But now he had been given this unpleasant task to do by the Noto family. They seemed to think it was easy. He knew there was no getting out of it. He owed it to them for all they had done for his own, more peaceable, family. But the Notos did not understand his difficulties. He was not used to this sort of thing. Serving pasta was not the best training for killing people, however deep the ways of his homeland were supposed to be ingrained in its sons.

He wished the call had not come. Of course, he had a debt of gratitude to pay for their getting him where he was, but why did he have to pay this kind of forfeit? He had never killed a man before, though he didn't like to admit it, and so rusty was he in his familiarity with that side of life that he was still finding it difficult even to get hold of a gun.

One night, in the week before Christmas, La Principessa had a customer who did not wish to eat. He only wanted to see Luigi in the little office up the back staircase beyond the kitchen. Luigi knew as soon as he saw him that the man bore a message from Sicily.

Although Pietro Bonfiglioni lived in a comfortable stockbroker's house in leafy Surrey he ran the Mafia's British operations. Luigi had heard of him but never met him. The original contract to kill 'Lord Wymark' had been given to Luigi by another Italian. But he could guess why Pietro was now paying him a visit.

'My friend, I have a message for you from the island,' the short, ugly man began without formality. 'They are not happy. They want news that it has been done as they wished. What is the position?'

Luigi, feeling suddenly queasy, told the man about his visit to Castle Cansdale, how he had identified the target, but how he was having difficulty in getting hold of a weapon.

The man laughed mirthlessly and told Luigi he was a fool. Why had he not asked for help? There was no problem over guns.

'You are making excuses. When they say something must be done, they want it done yesterday. You should know that. A gun will be delivered to you tomorrow, and the ammunition. Then there will be no excuse.'

Luigi felt sick, and tried not to look the man in the face.

'You must not threaten me,' he tried to say bravely. 'It is Christmas. I am very busy in the restaurant. I will not take that sort of threat.'

'You will take it if you deserve it,' Pietro Bonfiglioni said calmly. 'If you do not perform, you will pay the penalty, and someone else will do the job. How long is it since you got this job?'

'I don't know,' replied Luigi.

'Is it not more than three months? Three months! Men have had their testicles cut for less!'

Luigi involuntarily lowered his hands for protection.

Pietro Bonfiglioni came round and stood behind Luigi and pushed a stubby finger painfully into the restaurant owner's shoulders. Then he turned to the calendar on the wall. It was of a girl with breasts like melons. She was a curious yellowy-brown colour, some would say her skin was golden. The man stubbed his finger against the dates. 'There, the end of the month, after Christmas. Saturday, the thirtieth of December. You do it by then, else you will hear from me again. You understand?'

'Yes, yes,' Luigi whined. 'I will do it. The restaurant is closed for a week after Christmas, I will do what I can . . .'

Early in January, and shortly after the Rupert Hookes had received their invitation to Sophie's wedding, Jacky was back home in Brentwood having lunch with her mother. There had been a pre-Christmas visit to Dorset Avenue with Rupert which had been very uncomfortable. Rupert had been so keen to spend as little time as possible with Freddie that they had even gone to spend Christmas itself with Hugo and Molly at Huddleston.

Jacky was doing almost no work now, with her baby due in May, and it would be a month or two before they took possession of the Castle Wharf house. They still got on well together, mother and daughter, especially with the baby to speculate about and plan for, but it wasn't long before Jacky once again expressed her unhappiness on a certain subject.

'Rupert still upset about that, is he?' Cynthia gave a sigh and said she was sorry. 'You really never told him?'

'No.' Jacky lowered her head. 'He nearly blew a fuse when he heard, and it's still difficult between us.'

'You kept it from him all this time? That was a bit daft, wasn't it?'

'You think I ought to have told him and risked losing him? That might have happened, you know.'

'But you knew he'd be bound to find out sooner or later, and now he has. Poor Jacks. Mind you, the way those Hookes carry on, they've got a nerve to complain about us.'

'They don't go around killing people, though.'

Cynthia looked at her daughter very hard and seemed most put out.

'It's a long time ago now,' she said. 'He doesn't do anything like that now. It's all in the past.'

'Oh, Mum.' Jacky went and buried her head in her mother's shoulder. 'Why did he do it?'

'He didn't really. It was an accident. He was set up.'

'But my *dad*!'

'I know, I know, and I was so glad when you got fixed up with Rupert. I thought that would take it all away. Draw a line under all that. You'd be somewhere else where the knowledge would never get to you.'

Cynthia was wondering how Duncan and John had found out about Freddie. Who'd told them? What were they up to? But she did not share her thoughts with Jacky.

As had always been the case, a pot of tea was used to revive spirits. Having got the matter off her chest again, Jacky perked up and sat away from her mother on the other side of the lounge.

Cynthia was proud of her, oh so proud! She recognized that her daughter had done so much more than she had managed for herself. Jacky's clothes were quality. Her appearance was immaculate – classy. You could buy one, but you couldn't buy the other. And she had a kind of bloom on her, too. Nothing to do with the baby, either. She had begun to talk a bit posh. The Brentwood vowels still sometimes came through, but it was more the subject matter and the words she chose – and the *look* she had in her eye as she said things. Her darling daughter had grown perceptibly away from her. They could still be close, but not quite as close as once.

'We'll not be going to Hugo and Molly's again until the wedding, I expect.' Jacky seemed to be reassuring her mother that there wouldn't be too much contact with 'the other side', but was in fact gently inquiring whether her parents had been invited or not. She didn't think they had been, but she wasn't sure.

'Is that Sophie's, you mean? That'll be a big do, won't it? When is it?'

'You've not been invited?'

'No. Why should we be?'

'Just thought you might have, that's all.'

'No. But I'll send them a card and a little present. When is it?'

'No need to bother with all that,' Jacky put in quickly. She anticipated her mother sending something rather embarrassing which wouldn't go down at all well with Sophie. 'I mean, better not. Not for their sort of wedding. It's on the twenty-first of April.'

'Whatever you think, dear.'

Brother Mark had ambled into the room during the last part of the conversation and greeted his sister in his usual semi-surly way.

She smiled back at him, unconscious of this, but noticed he made no attempt to kiss her as he usually did. Was it because she was pregnant or something?

'Who's getting married?' he asked.

'Sophie. You know, Rupert's sis,' Cynthia told him.

'Big do?'

260

'Quite big,' Jacky told him. 'Church blessing, then afterwards at the castle.'

'What date?'

'April the twenty-first.'

'Is that a Saturday?' Mark noted the date and wondered how it might be useful to him.

'Cup of tea?' his mother suggested to him.

He declined.

'Not out with Dad?' his sister asked.

'No, why should I be? We don't do everything together, you know.'

'Sorreee! Only asked.'

Jacky gave Mark one of her big smiles. But he could see that she had been crying, and there was a distance between them now.

# CHAPTER 26

'There's a Mr Hook for you,' the receptionist told the salesman. 'Will you come down or shall I send him up?'

She nodded into the phone and replaced it.

'If you'll take a seat, Mr Hook, he's just coming.'

Mark Moore, somewhat uncomfortable in the assumed identity of 'Rupert Hook' without the 'e', didn't acknowledge this information but threw himself down on the leather banquette. He stared at the display cases and at the advertising material on the low table before him.

The salesman, a man called Stubbs, was soon on the scene, hand outstretched.

'Pleased to meet you, Mr Hook. Why don't we go to the showroom? It's all in there. Everything you could possibly want.'

They walked down a glass-walled corridor through which Mark could see the workings of the factory. In a moment, they were in a large room, decked out like a trade fair stand with small raised platforms upon which various displays were mounted. Blown-up photographs and boards with advertising copy on them were lit by small spotlights. The carpet climbed up the wall behind the displays.

'Of course, I'd have been delighted to come and see you at your home, Mr Hook. It is a home you have in mind?'

'A factory. A small factory, actually.'

'Oh, I see. I wonder if we sent you the right brochure?'

Mark explained that it was a small engineering works. He couldn't say exactly what they made, he wasn't allowed to.

The salesman raised his eyebrows and purred, 'Yes, yes, I quite understand.'

'We need a round-the-clock guard, night and day. And it needs to be visual – not just the alarm.'

'Then I think we'll be thinking along lines like these, if you'd like to come over here.'

Stubbs took Mark over to a stand where two security cameras were mounted on plinths.

'These are the two basic Manorial models. This one is a straightforward line-of-sight model. It can operate in pretty low light, but we very much recommend the additional floods which can be made part of the package. As you can see, Mr Hook, the camera can be moved using a remote controller. It's quite similar to the ones the police use – you know, the type you see on buildings, used for motorway observation, and so on.'

'What's the other one?' asked Mark.

'That's the infra-red. It'll operate however bad the light or the weather – and at night, of course.'

'Seems more sensible to have that, doesn't it?'

'Right, right,' said Stubbs, as though immensely impressed by the client's decisiveness. 'I can see you know what you want.'

'Do they break down?'

The salesman laughed and hugged himself with his arms. 'What a thing to worry about! Frankly, it'd take a bomb to put one of these off. In fact, only last week one of ours actually survived a bomb in Belfast. It was the only thing left in one piece, and it went right on working! They're very, very tough – we use the strongest laminated plastics. And the glass on the lens is bullet-proof. Rather necessary these days.'

Mark seemed completely unimpressed, but the salesman saw nothing unusual in this. His customers were a tough lot. It was hardly a fun investment they were making.

'I'm worried they'd be interfered with,' Mark said, excelling himself as an actor now. 'I mean, what happens if someone shins up and pops a bag over them?'

'Well, I've never known that to happen – no, really, I haven't. Usually they're fixed on an arm, from the wall, and so high up you'd have to get at them with a ladder, as our service engineers and installers do. You'd be spotted doing that.'

'Not if you were *behind*.'

'Ah, yes, but with all-round surveillance, there are no "dark" patches, as we call them.' The salesman seemed rather pleased that he had capped that objection pretty well. 'And let me say, even if someone did get up to one, there are no controls on the actual camera. Everything is sealed within the case and can't be tampered with.'

'What about the cables then? They could be cut.'

'They could indeed but, there again, all cables are sunk into a fantastically hard tube which is about five inches thick where it's vulnerable. It's virtually impossible to cut it, and of course anyone would be seen trying.'

Mark was beginning to think that he was doing rather well in his assumed identity. He reckoned he had been quite clever to think of this way of getting the dope on Manorial systems. No one had had to suggest it to him.

'How much is it going to cost?' he asked casually.

The salesman knew that he mustn't start mentioning figures at this stage. 'That would depend on your needs and requirements, Mr Hook. First, we would have to send a surveyor round to your home—'

'Factory,' Mark corrected him.

'Oh, yes. I mean, so much depends on things like cable distance, where you're going to locate the monitors, and so on.'

'Do you think most people actually use the monitors – you know, all the time? Or do they just let it rip, as a deterrent, like?'

'It's not for me to say, Mr Hook. But we always install these systems in the hope that security guards, night watchmen and so on will be keeping an eye on them all the time.'

Mark walked away from the stand with the cameras and squashed himself in a smart executive chair made of leather and chrome.

'I don't suppose you've got any pictures of actual installations – in position, like? To give me an idea.'

'Well, you must understand, Mr Hook, that security is what we're about, so all our clients are guaranteed complete discretion on our part. We simply cannot divulge who they are.'

'But you must have a video or something. Everyone's got a video.'

'Yes, indeed, and you're most welcome to watch it. And there are these posed shots over here. That should give you a pretty good idea of what they look like.'

'It's funny, but I think I know one of your clients.'

'Really.' The salesman looked a touch embarrassed, not quite sure how he should handle this.

'Yes. What's that castle place near Swindon? I saw your name up there.'

Stubbs was an interesting shade of pink now.

'Yes, Castle Cansdale.' Mark plucked the name as if from the depths of his memory. 'Know what I mean?'

Stubbs couldn't get out of it. 'Yes, well spotted. Lord Wymark's place. That's only a recent installation. You must have been down there within the past month?'

'I have.'

Careful, Mark warned himself, don't go too far. You shouldn't have mentioned Cansdale. This prick's the type to remember.

'You really can't give me an idea how much this is going to set me back?' he asked.

Stubbs thought it odd that Mr Hook should be talking in terms of it setting *him* back, rather than a company, but he did what he could to give him an idea of the cost of units like the cameras.

'Phew!' Mark acted. 'So we're talking six figures, right?'

'Not quite. It all depends, of course. Maintenance contracts. Lines to the police. They all cost extra.'

'Well, I'll have to think about it,' replied Mark. 'Of course, I'm looking into more than one system.'

'Of course.'

'But I'll let you know.'

'Do we have your number, just so that I can keep in touch?'

'No, you don't,' said Mark, sharply. 'And we don't accept telephone selling.'

So saying, and having reduced the salesman to almost nothing, Mark turned and made for the exit with Stubbs bobbing and weaving behind him.

'Goodbye, Mr Hook,' he cried, as Mark reached the glass door in reception.

Mark stopped abruptly and turned as though he was going to set the salesman right about something. Then he went on again and out. He had almost corrected Stubbs about his name. That was a close one. You had to concentrate so ruddy hard on this acting.

'Your ladyship won't be needing these?'

'What are they, Rosie?'

'These clothes – they're for throwing out?'

Joanna got up from her writing desk and came to look at what the house-maid was on about.

'Oh, they're nothing to do with me. They're Duncan's. My bottom's not that big!'

'Sorry, I'm sure. Having a bit of a clear-out, is he?'

'Yes. I suppose he must be.'

Joanna had a rummage through the pile of clothes which her husband had presumably decided weren't right for him any more. There were two pairs of designer jeans, a baggy suit with shoulder pads (in which he had always looked ridiculous), and several rather garish ties. She had never really approved of Duncan's taste in clothes, especially during the last few years when he had wavered between conventional corduroys and cavalry twills and much more modern stuff. He'd been consciously dressing younger. It was a bit sad really, his trying to cling on to his fast-receding youth like that. Chasing after younger women had all been part of the same process, she supposed.

Well, perhaps he had finally got over that little mid-life crisis and regained his sanity. He had certainly been a hundred times more affectionate towards her lately. Of course, being Duncan, he still had his lapses. He would always be like that, she assumed. He was rather like a firework that some fool had unwisely brought indoors. People would rush for cover as it fizzed and spluttered, but if they only held on it would be all right.

'Oh, just get rid of them,' she told Rosie. 'Unless you want any of them yourself. Feel free. Perhaps they'd fit your husband?'

'Thanks very much, your ladyship. I think they might.'

Joanna had a momentary vision of Rosie's Tom – he was a gamekeeper – flitting about the park looking like a rustic clone of Duncan, and then forgot about it.

She went back to her writing desk and rather wished that Rosie would get a move on with the cleaning and leave her alone. Joanna was trying to write a letter to her daughter, Josephina, who had just gone back to Benenden for the Easter term and was having a tough time. Rosie would chatter while she did out the bedroom, and Joanna couldn't really do anything about it. It was ludicrous – here they were in a mansion with a hundred and something rooms and she couldn't even find a quiet place to write a letter. Of course, in the old days, one would have gone to the library – but it was full of gawping tourists now, so that was out of the question.

In the evening she found Duncan curiously attentive when she was knocking up a little light supper for them both in the small kitchen they had installed in the first-floor 'family flat'. Joanna was trying out a new chicken recipe she had come across in a magazine. For most of their marriage, her cooking had been a byword for awfulness but lately she had begun to try very hard. It was easier, of course, when she had to cook for only the two of them. She had never once cooked for a dinner party since moving into the castle. She knew she just did not have the right touch and, besides, there was a good cook on the staff for that kind of thing. But now that Duncan was being a bit more receptive – not to mention actually being at home more – she was discovering the pleasure.

As she was stuffing the bird with rice and apricots, she felt Duncan come up behind her and put his arms round her waist.

'Ow!' she shrieked. 'Stop it, Duncan!'

It was a natural reaction to being tickled, but she immediately regretted having behaved in so predictable a fashion.

'Oh, all right. But don't make me spill anything!'

Duncan returned to his groping, fondling her breasts while pressing himself against her. He kissed her on the back of her neck, through her hair, and made growling noises.

It was the Duncan of old, being attentive like this. What could have brought it on? She noticed he wasn't wearing his rather daunting aftershave either.

'Been having a clear-out, I see,' Joanna said, not to deter his amorous attentions but so she might have a little more freedom to finish stuffing the chicken.

Duncan pulled away, realizing how foolish he had been to go all sexy when she was fiddling about with that cold moist thing.

'Ah . . . yes,' he replied, distractedly. 'I thought why not? They didn't suit me. Better not to cling on, isn't it?'

'You're going to dress your age then?'

'No. I am going to dress as I've always done. Like I am now.'

Joanna didn't have to look to see what he meant. It was the cavalry twill trousers today with his hacking jacket, striped shirt and paisley cravat. Thank God he was out of those jeans, looking so silly with his bulges. He didn't have the legs for them either. Neither did she, but that was different.

'Good!' she trilled, rather overdid the peppermill on the chicken's breast, and popped the bird into the oven. 'Right, that'll be an hour and a bit.'

'Time for a sit-down. Want a drink?'

'Heavens, what's that you've got there?'

'Malvern with bubbles.'

'Good God, darling, what has got into you? I suppose you've given up booze along with your jeans?'

'No, of course not, just rather refreshing . . .'

'Well, I'm not bloody well going on the wagon with you! Open that bottle, for God's sake. I'll have to drink for two of us.'

'Just thought I ought to try and lose a bit of this tummy, that's all. It seems to have set in rather. I'm certainly not giving up the bottle. I'd die rather. But you know . . .'

'Heavens, darling, are you giving up anything else? You don't smoke, so that's out. How about sex? Is that part of your new routine?'

'Christ, no. More of it, if I can manage it.'

'With your girl friends, I suppose? Don't they call it the male menopause? I should think you're just the right age.'

'*No*, Jo!' He clutched her hand and brought her closer to him, so she had to look into his face as he spoke. 'I know I've been a bad boy. But that's all finished. I've just decided. I'll behave myself from now on.'

Joanna was quite bewildered by all these changes of heart. She had often accused Duncan of being a little boy, of never having grown up. She looked upon his love of motorcars and guns and gadgets, the gym equipment he had once invested in, even the hi-fi and the video camera as all part of that.

'Do I have to do anything? Give up my horses, or what? The

267

menopause'll strike me pretty soon, you know. I'll need something to keep me happy while that's on.'

'Perhaps it won't be too bad, darling. I mean, why should it be?'

'Well, I'm just warning you. If you want to get more sex in, you'd better get a move on.'

'Talking of sex,' Duncan said, 'you know Fruity McLaren, the chappy on Craswall council? He told me a story about Sam Butler, the town clerk. Smoked like a chimney – two packets a day. Anyway, his wife told him, more or less, she'd leave him if he didn't stop. Wasn't going to stick around if he chose to kill himself with the weed – usual charming ultimatum. So Sam turned round – or at least this is what Fruity claimed – and told his wife, "All right, I'll give it up if you promise you'll give me a poke every time I feel like a smoke"!'

'I don't believe it,' Joanna said in no-nonsense fashion. 'A little boy's tale, if ever I heard one.'

'Seemed rather a good idea to me . . .' Duncan sounded almost wistful, as though he'd been about to suggest something similar. 'I mean, what time's that chicken going to be ready?'

'Duncan! I've only just sat down. Haven't had a sip of wine yet.'

'Well . . .'

He looked so comically appealing she knew she couldn't say no. 'Better be a quick one.'

Duncan went through to their bedroom and turned on the bedside lamp and proceeded to strip off his clothes. Joanna could hardly keep up with him; he was already naked and between the sheets before she was out of her slacks.

They had to warm each other up before they could begin and this took several minutes. With the minimum of preparation, Duncan was then on top of her, pumping hard and managing to massage her small breasts at the same time. Joanna had gritted her teeth for so long when Duncan made love to her she was rather startled when she suddenly felt an old feeling flicker into life deep down inside.

She let out an involuntary cry – a warm cry so at odds with her usual brisk bossiness in bed that Duncan felt himself go particularly hard, as if it had been a vote of confidence in himself as a lover. He could hardly believe that Joanna actually seemed to be enjoying herself. It was almost with a sense of detachment that he observed her experiencing the most obvious – and certainly the noisiest – orgasm in a very long time. He came himself half a minute later and gasped 'We did it' in his wife's ear, before rolling over and falling asleep.

Perhaps he was selfish, perhaps he was too heavy the way he was lying on her, but Joanna didn't care. She had rediscovered what she had once known.

If Duncan was true to his word, they could have a very enjoyable time as they coasted into deep middle-age.

When Joanna abruptly became aware of the smell of chicken seeping in through from down the corridor, she gently roused Duncan and slipped from under him.

They had a warm and wonderful evening together. He deviated from his new regimen to the extent of three glasses of Rioja, but this was such an improvement on what would previously have been a whole litre bottle that Joanna didn't think it mattered. She was almost comically happy. If only life could be like this more often it would be marvellous.

She did not shrink, however, from being her usual outspoken self, even in this mood. As she toyed with the chocolate truffles which were supposed to be a more slimming alternative to a hot pudding, she couldn't resist asking Duncan what had really made him change his ways.

'There's a little voice in here,' she touched her temples, 'that's telling me there's a reason.'

'No, there isn't,' he said. 'Just kind of happened.'

'I don't believe it.' She coasted dangerously towards provoking him. 'I think you've been rejected by some totty.'

The expression on Duncan's face instantly told her she was right.

He came clean. 'Oh, all right, that may have had something to do with it. Damn it, of course it did! Brought it home to me. Never found any difficulty before.'

'Who was it, darling? You can tell me now. I won't mind.'

'You don't know her. Called Francine. Works at those estate agents in Craswall. Very fanciable. Dark. Lots of hair and a very fetching deep voice. Couldn't resist, but she turned me down. So that was it.'

'Did she say why? It is possible she might not have fancied you. Or there might be some women left who don't want to have it away with other people's husbands.'

'Oh, no. She made it very plain: I was too old. Told me where to get off. I always thought it was all right for chaps. The older you got the more you were on to a good thing. Whereas women have a harder time of it . . .'

Joanna kept looking at him, cool but dignified.

'But it was a bit of a blow. I expect I needed it, to make me see a bit of sense. Anyway, here I am.'

'Poor old darling. Well, it's nice to have you back. And if you can keep on making me happy like you did earlier, then that'll be wonderful.'

They sat in silence for a little while, no more words needing to be spoken. Then they stood up and started turning off the lights before going off to bed.

'Oh, lor',' said Duncan, just when he thought he'd finished, 'I'd better go down and see the burglar thingy's all right.'

'You really have to do that?'

'Lopez has to have a night off. It's only fair.'

'Still . . .'

Just as Duncan was about to descend to the Salon on his way to the downstairs area, he glanced through one of the windows at the rear of the castle and saw Lopez arriving back from wherever he'd been in his little Renault.

'Thank goodness for that,' he said and turned as though to go back to the first floor.

Then he thought, no, I'd better have a word with him. Make sure everything's all right. And so he went down the stairs and into the cold, dark shadows below.

He hated that dank smell they had never been able to get rid of. It wasn't as though this was a medieval castle with sodden dungeons and dripping ceilings, but it was eerie enough in its own way. Duncan remembered how frightened he had been of this part of the house when he was a little boy. Once, when he was about five years old, he had tested himself and crept down from his nursery on the top floor all the way to the kitchen and stolen a cake from out of cook's tin. He had been petrified all the way there and all the way back. But he had not made a sound, had woken no one, and the mystery of the missing cake had baffled everyone when it was discovered next morning. He had not been suspected. No one would have dreamt he could have got down there without disturbing the rest of the house.

It wouldn't be possible now – not that there were any five-year-olds loose in the house. The sensors were switched on inside the house when everyone went to bed. It only took a mouse to stir now for calamity to break out, with blood-curdling electronic bleeps and alarm bells ringing.

At the back door, by the Spring Lodge, Duncan waved to his butler as he made for his room in the separate block.

'Just checking up, Lopez!'

'Thank you, sir.'

'Had a good evening?'

'Just a drink at the pub. The usual, sir. Everything all right with you and her ladyship?'

'Oh, fine, fine,' Duncan whispered. 'Had a lovely time.'

It was rather a touching, innocent exchange of male intimacies.

'Well, good night, sir.'

'And you, Lopez. See you with the morning tea.'

# CHAPTER 27

More than two months had elapsed since the expiry of Pietro Bonfiglioni's deadline, but Luigi Corsini had yet to carry out the contract on 'Lord Wymark'. Slightly less than two months had passed since Mark Moore's visit to Manorial Security Systems, and still he had not made his attempt on Castle Cansdale.

The 8th Earl Hooke, in happy ignorance of both these plots, was in better spirits that he had been for a long time. He had made a complete recovery from the illness which had upset him the previous summer and autumn. It was the Countess's view that there had never been much wrong with him anyway. He was just depressed at getting old and at having to take a back seat while his offspring went their own sweet way. He had nothing much to do himself.

'You shouldn't have given up those committees,' Molly told him.

'They were such a frightful bore,' Hugo explained. 'And I don't count for much these days.'

'Don't be ridiculous, Hugo. You are what you are.'

'Not at all. Since we left the house, I've seen it in people, they're not as interested in one as they were. "What's he now, without a proper home?" – I know that's what they're thinking.'

Molly went and stood behind the armchair in which Hugo was fretting and smoothed his thinning, grey hair.

'But at least you're happier about the house and what Duncan's been doing to it. I noticed when we went back there after Marjorie's funeral you seemed a lot happier. It wasn't too awful for you, was it, darling?'

No, Hugo had to admit that it was not. In fact, he was now almost prepared to admit he had been wrong in objecting to Duncan's throwing it open to the public. That destroyed several centuries of exclusivity, to be sure, but perhaps in this day and age it was what had to be done. 'But why did Duncan have to upset Jacky about her father . . . Once he was just unpleasant to you, Molly, now he has a go at anyone who takes his fancy – the more vulnerable the better.'

'I can look after myself,' said Molly. 'Let's have some tea, shall we?' she rang for Mrs Powers to bring it. 'Now, what are we going to give Sophie and Douglas for their present?' She asked, ever the practical one.

'Oh, lor'. Search me. Cheque, I suppose. It'll set me back a bit, this whole affair. I hope this do at the house isn't going to be too costly.'

'Don't be such an old miser, darling. You've only got one daughter and when she's gone, you won't be called upon to do it again.'

Hugo realized he had slipped back into his old ways and tried to charm his way out of it.

'Yes,' he said, 'all the birds will have flown. Fingers crossed they'll be all right. Duncan seems to have settled down a bit – though without Mother to keep track of his doings, one can never be quite sure. And Rupert's little wife seems to be coming along well, doesn't she?'

'Don't think she'd be very keen on the "little wife", dear. She's a modern miss.'

'Well, you know what I mean. When's she going to have that baby? Not in the middle of the wedding, I trust.'

'No, not till May – four or five weeks later.'

'Wonder if it'll be a boy?'

'Now don't start thinking about that, Hugo. There's nothing can be done about it. Man plans, and God laughs – you know the saying.'

But Hugo was going to bother about it. After all, ensuring that the line would continue was the mainstay of his existence. It might not matter to most men, but to him it meant everything. His mind turned back to Jacky.

'What *was* all that kerfuffle about Jacky's father after the funeral? I didn't understand it at all – except that Duncan seemed to be stirring things.'

'Neither did I, dear. Something Duncan and John hatched between them, I think.'

'Seem to get on well those two, don't they? Were they saying he was a bit of a rough diamond?'

'I should've thought it was obvious he was. It's amazing what a sweet girl Jacky is, given her father – and that surly little brother of hers. I suppose it must be the mother's influence. As is so often the case!'

'Mmm. Well, I tried to warn Rupert, but he wouldn't listen.'

'Water under the bridge, Hugo. Must make the best of it. They seem happy together. I think he's very lucky.'

'Same with this John . . .'

Molly was going to get furious if Hugo went on rumbling away like this. She shot out of her chair, put her head outside the door and actually chivvied up the housekeeper. She was very good, Mrs Powers, but she was a bit scatty. Didn't get a move on.

'Coming, my lady,' a West Country voice called down the passage. In a moment, a small round bustling woman entered the drawing room and placed the silver tea tray down on the table. 'Sorry it's a bit late,' she said. 'Spilt a drop of water on my leg.'

'Hot water? Oh, poor Powers,' Molly exclaimed, while Hugo raised his eyes with exasperation.

When she'd gone, it was Molly who returned to the discussion.

'John is wonderful. Just right for Sophie. I know he's not what you might have liked, but they're devoted to each other. You can see it. He really looks after her. She's a changed woman since he came along. I must say, it's a relief not to have her out hunting. Just hope it's not too late for them to have children.'

'I expect I'll learn to like him,' said Hugo, ignoring the womanly speculation. 'Seems quite a sensible fellow. These bits he writes for the paper. Intelligent. But that's not everything these days. He's a bit *Left*, isn't he?'

'Thank you, dear. I think we've had enough of your pronouncements for today.'

'Where's the milk?' Hugo bristled. 'Really, that woman is hopeless. You deal with it, Molly.'

And Molly had to chase after Powers to remedy the deficiency.

In the small scullery, she discovered a possible reason for Powers' distracted behaviour. There was a man sitting at the kitchen table, having a cup of coffee. On hearing the Countess approach he correctly stood up and bid her good afternoon.

'Good afternoon, your ladyship.'

'Oh, it's Lopez, isn't it?'

She wondered what had brought Duncan's butler over to Huddleston. Was he on some errand connected with the wedding?

'Mr Lopez is on a social visit,' the housekeeper explained rather importantly.

'Good,' said Molly, and picked up the milk jug sitting on the table. Then added, 'I didn't know you knew each other.'

'Oh, yes,' Powers answered cheerily. 'Mr Lopez goes to the Craswall Arms on his nights off and we chat there. We've been doing it for many months.'

Molly was intrigued at this connection among the servants.

'That's lovely,' she said, retreating with the milk. 'Do come here to see Mrs Powers – whenever you like. Well, goodbye, Lopez.'

'She's very nice, really,' Mrs Powers said after a pause. 'They're both very nice really. He's a bit picky, you know, but not too bad.'

Lopez wasn't going to be drawn on the likeability of his own employer, and merely nodded.

Mrs Powers thought she was on to a good thing. Her husband had left her long ago and she had been in service ever since. Lopez, as a butler, was a figure she would naturally look up to. His Spanish looks and manner made him appear even more exotic to her.

Their small talk was of below stairs life. The housekeeper knew more than the butler did about what was going on in the villages of the Hooke estate. Lopez wasn't really a countryman at heart and was quite happy to spend most of his time at the castle. It was like being a waiter at one of those large country hotels. Your life was the hotel, and you were as cut off from the people and country round about as your employers were. So this was rather an advance for Lopez, to be out visiting even for an innocent cup of coffee. There wasn't much to talk about – though Mrs Powers had her ears open for any work that might be coming up at the big house. With a certain inevitability they chewed over the only other social occasion they had in common, the visit to the Craswall Arms the night before.

'I bet you don't like the Maidens Constable Special. You foreigners never do.'

Lopez produced a small smile from the depths of his rather tragic countenance and allowed that this was so.

'Your English beers, they are not my taste,' he explained. 'They are so bitter.'

' 'Course, they are,' Powers guffawed. 'That's why they're called bitter!'

'Now the lager, I can take. It is a sweeter beer, yes?'

'I like those too,' Powers admitted, and offered him one of the short-bread biscuits she had taken from the Countess's tin.

'You English and your biscuits,' Lopez frowned. 'Everything so sweet.'

'Well, make up your mind. You like sweet beers, what's wrong with a bit of sugar on your biscuit?'

Lopez took one.

They talked about the characters in the pub. Lopez was obviously ignorant who most of them were, although in many cases they were employees on the Hooke estate. But why should they know him? He was an 'indoors' person and, what's more, he usually kept himself to himself when he went to the pub. If Mrs Powers did not join him, he sat at a side table and read the Spanish newspaper that the newsagent in the village always had such difficulty getting hold of.

Having now acquired in Mrs Powers a knowledgeable guide to the surrounding countryside, he asked her who the young man was – the one who'd been sitting near them all the previous evening.

'Which young man?'

'He had spectacles and a moustache – like you call a Mexican moustache.'

'Oh, him. I've no idea. Never seen him before. Had a ring in his ear, too – is that the one?'

'Yes.'

Lopez tilted his head to one side and pushed forward his jaw, as though to show polite surprise that Mrs Powers did not know who he was.

'He seemed to know a lot about the castle. I took him for a man from the village.'

'No, I don't think so, dear. Sure I'd know if I'd seen him before.'

The butler felt the first twinge of anxiety, in case he had said too much to the young man.

'He was very interested in the house. Asked me much about it.'

'And you told him? Nosey parker, that's who he was. You have to watch out with people like that.'

'Well, I did not think about it at the time. He ask me all about my job. I tell him. I thought maybe he want to do a job like mine, or training, or something.'

'Fancy.' Mrs Powers was a little less than interested in the young man whom she could now dimly remember having hogged Lopez's attention when she had been trying to do the same.

Lopez continued to mull over the encounter. Perhaps he shouldn't have said what he said. But the young man had seemed so very interested in the security devices and genuinely concerned about the silver robbery last year. He had wanted to know whether the police had caught anyone or found the missing valuables, but Lopez had had to tell him they had not.

And then he tried to brush the thoughts aside. The security was supposed to be very good now. It was not a responsibility he had been told about when he was engaged as butler to his lordship. It had come up since the robbery. He felt it added to his importance. He was even paid another twenty pounds a week for 'additional responsibility'. But it was not a full-time job. During the day, one of the guides doubled as security man. But Lopez could not be monitoring the screens all night, nor was he supposed to. It was just a token thing.

After an hour of chat, Lopez thanked Mrs Powers for her hospitality and said he looked forward to seeing her at the pub the following week.

She gave him a little wave from the back gate, as he drove off in his Renault and then went inside to clear away the tea things.

Detective Constable Kenworthy's small radio was digging into his thigh and he tried to shift into a more comfortable position, but it was very crowded in the hole even with just the two of them there. He was a beefy character not best designed for crouching in muddy holes for round-the-clock surveillance. Trouble was, his colleague, Detective Constable Axe, was of an equal bulk.

They had been in the hole for three days now – or so it seemed. They had been relieved from time to time, but basically this was their pigeon and they were stuck with it until something happened. They knew precisely what they had to do. At the first sign of anyone approaching the little shack by the side of the river, they were to radio for reinforcements. These would come from the main police station, three or four miles away in the centre of Craswall.

Kenworthy and Axe were in the hole with another purpose, too. They were not just to arrest whoever came to the shack, they were to make sure that the half million pounds' worth of historic silver from Castle Cansdale wasn't stolen all over again.

The CID at Craswall police station had been dourly jubilant at its success in finding the silver stolen from Lord Wymark's seat just over five months previously. It was not detective skill which had done it, however – sheer good fortune. There had been a tip-off.

But that did not matter. Their stolen goods recovery rate would be improved in the statistics. The only problem was, how long would they – in the shape of Detective Constables Kenworthy and Axe – have to stake out the hiding place until the thieves came back to collect? They might leave it for months, though from what the police knew of criminal behaviour, this was unlikely. It was one of the rules of theft that people disposed of the goods as quickly as possible. But for some reason – perhaps the amount of publicity given to the Cansdale robbery – these thieves had decided to take a good long time about it. Perhaps the property was too hot, and so they had decided to let it cool off in this, albeit not very secure, shack on the river bank just north of Craswall.

DC Axe who was the less down-to-earth of the two policemen held an image in his mind of the silver plates, candlesticks and bowls lying ignominiously in a sack in the damp, foul-smelling shed. What a contrast to the magnificence in which they had been housed for so many years at Castle Cansdale. He had established that DC Kenworthy had not yet paid a visit to Wiltshire's latest tourist attraction and had little idea how magnificent the silver looked when displayed in the context of the great house. DC Axe assured his colleague that a visit would be well worth the trouble. It was just silly that the owner had done the usual thing – waited until he was burgled before having the security equipment put in.

DCs Axe and Kenworthy both knew that Lord Wymark had not yet been told that his silver had been located. It stood to reason. Everybody was a suspect in a case like this. No one was to know that there had been any movement until an arrest was made. Of course, if no arrest looked like being made, the picture would change.

That Thursday afternoon, the week before John Tarrant and Lady Sophie's wedding, the two detective constables both instinctively felt that something was about to happen. It was just after five o'clock, with the light fading and the prospect of another night in the bloody hole before them. Most of the people who passed along the river bank could be discounted. They were fishermen quite obviously going to take up their positions the other side of the road bridge. Or they were quite ordinary people taking themselves and their dogs for a walk. But the two characters approaching now immediately put Axe and Kenworthy on the alert.

The two lads, both aged about thirteen, were obviously killing time on their way home from school. They were larking about, unable to move an inch without pulling off a flower's head, chucking a stone in the river, or making some sort of noise at each other.

Then their eyes lighted on the shed. They pushed open the door. Cries of 'Pooh, what a stink!' and 'Retch!' were audible by the policemen who lay twitching in their hole twenty yards away. There was a long period of silence from within the shed. The two DCs prayed the two lads wouldn't find what was hidden there and desperately wondered how they could head them off without giving themselves away.

The boys came out changed characters. They made no noise now. They looked about them, up and down, the towpath, and saw nothing.

'Come on!' one hissed at the other.

'Yes, okay – but you explain.'

And then they ran off, over the bridge and towards Craswall, bursting with the secret they had to share.

'Come on,' said Axe, heaving himself out of the hole, 'we'd better stop them.'

'Right!'

The two DCs, holding their waterproofs about them, ran as fast as they could after the unwitting finders of the Cansdale silver. Their boots thudded on the cobbles of the sloping bridge, and then they were down the other side and in hot pursuit. But it was no use. The lads were nowhere to be seen.

The boys found their way to the local police station – not Craswall's main one – and were soon gabbling out their account of the silver they'd found in the shed by the river. The desk sergeant wasn't to know that they weren't supposed to find it. He had to satisfy himself that they weren't making it all up.

This all took time.

About twenty minutes later a beat constable was found and told to accompany the boys back to the shed. When he had done so, he radioed for help and sent the boys home They soon broadcast the news round their families and friends and dreamed of a reward.

When DCs Kenworthy and Axe returned from the main police station, they discovered the constable and learnt how the smaller station had effectively ruined their stake-out. It was all a question of the force getting its wires crossed – or, rather, one hand not knowing what the other was doing.

There was no alternative but to call off the wait for the thieves. The Cansdale silver was solemnly retrieved from the shed and locked up in the central police station. DCs Kenworthy and Axe slept in their own beds at last, but were pissed off that their efforts had come to nothing. The Craswall force had lost its chance of catching the thieves red-handed.

The Friday before the wedding was a scene of intense activity at Castle Cansdale. Vans and cars were drawing up at the Spring Lodge every few minutes bearing food, wine, flowers and additional catering equipment for Sophie's reception.

Lopez had to act as a traffic policeman as the various caterers and decorators went about their business, and tried to keep them out of the way of the paying visitors who were still being allowed into the house.

Glenellen Summers had insisted on decorating the route from the front entrance through the Salon and out to the marquee at the rear with baskets of flowers on mock Corinthian pillars, which Duncan was convinced would inevitably topple over and damage some of the guests – but he put his view to her nicely, and felt good with himself that they were now on speaking terms again.

Flowers were arriving to be transported to the church the following morning. Glenellen was also going to be arranging these and went along to St Michael's in the late afternoon to make sure the right vases were available for her displays. They weren't, so she had to summon up supplies from the Waterwheel shop at the Old Mill.

In the evening at half past six there was a short rehearsal in the church with the Reverend Dutson doing his best to appear organized and relaxed without his pipe in front of the altar. Sophie arrived with her hair half done. John was actually wearing a suit. The 'best man', a droll and very bachelor lawyer called Simon, turned up from London just in time to miss the rehearsal.

'Well, you try getting out of London on a Friday afternoon,' he explained. 'I tried to phone you from the BMW, but to no avail.'

'If I had one of those things, which I don't,' John gently pointed out to his friend, 'I expect I wouldn't have brought it into the church.'

Hugo was there, and actually looked as if he might be going to enjoy the following day's extravaganza. He couldn't let the occasion pass, of course, without taking John and Simon into the Hooke family chapel and pointing out his father's memorial.

'Fascinating!' Simon assured him. 'Of course you should go to Sicily and follow it up.'

'There you are, Molly – hear that?'

But Molly was giving her stepdaughter advice about her bouquet.

A message came through that John's widowed mother had arrived and was installed at the Craswall Arms. She would be dining in the Hooke Restaurant – feeling quite somebody, her son marrying into such a family.

That night, in a small concession to tradition, John and Simon got a little drunk together and slept at Sleepy Cottage. Down the road at Bethany Cottage Glenellen continued to fuss over Sophie, and even spent the night, just to see her through.

Back at Castle Cansdale, Duncan and Joanna were fussing over their daughters. Josephina, Serena and Christabel were to be Sophie's brides-maids. And then at about eight thirty, just when everyone had thought he'd got lost, a taxi arrived at the front entrance and the familiar figure of Uncle Alec stepped out clutching the case in which was his morning dress.

Lopez was everywhere, even at the door to take Uncle Alec's bags and escort him up to his favourite bedroom overlooking the Fair Mile, and then down to the Dining Room where Duncan, Joanna and the girls were about to begin the meal.

'How lovely to see you, Uncle,' said Joanna, leaping up and giving him a kiss. Then the three girls lined up to give him theirs, too. They quite liked their great-uncle as he'd been on television and talked to them as equals now they were growing up a bit. They knew there was something a bit funny about him, which they weren't supposed to know about. It had been in the papers, and was a bit naughty, but that was as far as their knowledge went.

Alec took his place at the table next to Joanna. Duncan decided that he wanted to talk about the house and his plans for further development, so all the females round the table fell silent except when it was necessary to call for the salt or pepper.

'Well, I've got it,' Duncan announced triumphantly. 'Just heard today. Rather a nice wedding present for *me*, I'd say!'

'What's that?' asked Alec, peering at his nephew through his tinted spectacles.

'Got the grant for redoing the stables. Seventy-five grand. Not bad, eh?'

'Oh, well done, Duncan! That's quite a coup.'

'You knew I'd put in for it?'

'I think you mentioned it when I was here for Marjorie's funeral. All you've got to do now is the ceiling in the Salon?'

'I don't know about "all", but it's certainly the last outstanding bit in the house that needs doing up. Then I expect we start all over again. Like painting the Forth Bridge.'

'Yes, too true, I'm afraid.'

Josephina, the eldest girl, boldly spoke up at this point. 'Great-Uncle Alec, I still haven't seen the ghost. I think you were fibbing!'

Alec laughed, Joanna reproved, Duncan beamed.

'Well, I've seen it, and I expect your father has, too.'

Duncan nodded, agreeing to anything.

'But d'you know what I've just discovered?'

The children looked ready to be suitably impressed.

'I was looking through some papers about the house – or, rather, the one before this one, in about 1783, long before you were born! – and I came across mention of a secret passage. Now, how about that? D'you think you could find a secret passage?'

'Yes!' the girls chorused, clearly excited at the prospect.

'Trouble is,' Alec went on, 'I can't figure out for the life of me where it might be. I don't know if it's in the bit of the old house they left in the middle of this one or not. And, d'you know – a frightful thing – I don't seem able to lay my hands on the plans they drew up when this place was built. I did have them, and very good they were, too, but I don't seem able to find them.'

'Never mind, Uncle,' said Duncan filling both their glasses. 'I'm sure it's not the end of the world.'

'I didn't give them to you, did I?' Alec inquired.

Duncan shook his head.

'Oh, dear. My memory's going, I'm afraid. I can't remember what I've done, or who I've met . . .'

'Can we get down now?' asked Christabel.

'Yes, darling. But you mustn't go looking for any secret passages tonight. You've got a big day tomorrow.'

'Coffee in the library,' Duncan told Lopez. 'Are you going to join us, Joanna?'

She said she just had to pop upstairs, and then she would.

'Come along, Uncle. I've been spending a bit more of my time in the Gold Library lately. Know what I found? Might appeal to you – some filthy old books!'

'Oh, my!' Alec twinkled, quite like his old self. 'I don't know anything about them, but my memory's not what it was, as I said . . .'

# CHAPTER 28

Benino Noto had been granted leave to appeal against his prison term and on New Year's Day he was released from gaol in Reggio di Calabria, pending the outcome of the appeal. Within hours he was back home in Palermo and picking up the reins of power that he had been forced to hand to his son Alvaro.

Luigi Corsini in London might have been relieved to learn that the originator of the contract on 'Lord Wymark' was no longer sitting in a cell brooding about settling an old score and now had other matters on his mind. But no one told Luigi what had happened. As it was, he was simply relieved that Pietro Bonfiglioni had not turned up to threaten him again – or maybe worse. In terms that Luigi did not care to recall, Pietro had given him a second deadline and one more chance to carry out the contract. That deadline had expired the night before.

The promised weapon and ammunition had duly been delivered, so that was no longer a problem. In January and again in February he went down to Wiltshire with the intention of killing the man. On the first occasion he found that his target was away for the day and on the second that security cameras and floodlighting had made the castle impregnable at night. Luigi resolved to carry out the deed – in broad daylight, if need be – just as soon as he could confirm his target's whereabouts. The only problem he really anticipated lay in making his getaway. The house itself was half a mile from the nearest gate. Then there were five miles of twisting roads to negotiate before he could be back on the safe anonymity of the motorway. If his deed were discovered soon afterwards, and if the police or anybody else responded quickly, he would most likely be caught. Luigi did not think that finding Lord Wymark merely by turning up on his doorstep would be too much of a problem, and he would deal with the danger of recognition by disguising himself as best he could. He had already obtained false number plates for the car.

When he arrived at Castle Cansdale around lunchtime on Saturday, 21 April, he was horrified to see scores of visitors swarming all over the place. On his previous visits, it had been a connoisseurs' day or in the winter, and so the house and gardens had been virtually empty. The trees had rustled, the wind blown, the house had dominated all in its dark, quiet way. All these people would make locating his target more difficult; and if he had to make a quick dash in his car, he might find himself stuck in one of the queues which so easily built up on the narrow roads around the estate.

Luigi admitted to himself that he was frightened. But he had been in this state ever since he was assigned the task. He knew that no sane person would carry out a contract in broad daylight surrounded by tourists, but he also knew that he had to do it today. He had run out of time, and Pietro had made it clear that he had run out of patience. Luigi knew what people like Pietro could do to your business, especially one like a restaurant, if they wanted to. He had seen it happen to others. He also knew that to defy the Mafia command, not necessarily wilfully but by default, could very well end in his own death.

Luigi paid for his ticket and parked his car with its rear towards the car park fence. He turned off the ignition, leant over to the glove department and extracted a small container of *antipasto misto* which he wolfed down, using his fingers. Then he picked up the flask into which he had decanted a little red Corvo and sipped the strong, heartening liquid.

In the afterglow, he began to tell himself that perhaps the various obstacles were not so bad after all. The main thing would be to carry out the shooting where it would not be discovered, and then to leave the grounds as casually as any other visitor. The normality of his movements would be his best disguise.

It was now three o'clock. Luigi had confirmed that Lord Wymark would be at the house by the simple expedient of ringing up and asking. Whoever answered the phone had done so courteously and, without giving anything very much away, had said she had a special reason to believe that Lord Wymark would be at home on that particular Saturday. She did not say what the reason was, but Luigi discovered soon enough when he walked over to the house.

The lawn at the rear – the one that led to the Pantheon – contained a large pink and white striped marquee. It was clear that a wedding reception was being held there and Luigi wondered whether he might be able to filter in among the caterers.

But access to the tent was going to be difficult. Visitors were kept well clear of the wedding guests by being channelled into the house near the Spring Lodge instead of the main entrance which was reserved for wedding guests. When these guests arrived from the church, having driven the long way round from Bourton Cansdale and up the Fair Mile, they parked their cars on the last hundred yards or so of the drive. The front of the house was kept free of vehicles so that the newly-wedded pair could be driven right up to it.

Luigi Corsini, unaware of these details, could only see that he was being restricted in his movements. He had been told that you could get in anywhere if you had sufficient confidence; but today there were more than the usual number of officious guides manning every gate and path, and Luigi's already fragile self-confidence evaporated completely. He began to feel a kind of deep, dull pain inside him. And he felt trapped. Could not work out what to do. He was absolutely on his own, with no one to consult about his dilemma.


Lady Sophie Hooke and John Tarrant had become man and wife at midday in the modest surroundings of Craswall Registry Office. A homely registrar, seated in front of a Canaletto reproduction, had done the necessary and wished them well, while ranked behind them immediate family from both sides had glanced warily at each other.

The Hookes looked sideways at John's relations and were apparently relieved to find they were quite normal. Mrs Tarrant was supported by John's younger sister, a civil servant, her husband and a younger brother. That was all. Glenellen Summers – who had worked wonders decorating the church, the marquee, and Sophie, was the female witness. John's friend, Simon the radical lawyer, was the male witness and performed the functions of best man.

After a light lunch at Huddleston, supervised with efficiency by Mrs Powers, the families were transported to St Michael and All Angels for the three o'clock service of blessing. Sophie and John travelled in a hired white Bentley which was slightly overshadowed by Hugo's Silver Cloud, driven by Molly.

There was always a good crowd for a wedding at St Michael's, Molly knew, but today it seemed bigger than usual. The marriage of anyone from the big house had always been an event in Hooke country and some people had travelled quite long distances to stand and watch.

Everyone recognized Lord Wymark, squeezed rather tightly into his morning suit. He looked a little redder in the face than some remembered, though at least he had his wife by his side. Opinions on whether his three bridesmaid daughters looked really attractive in their lemon frocks was divided.

A very audible murmur greeted Alec Hooke when he stepped out of the hire car with John's mother. His was a face from the television, which demanded that his autograph be sought; but he was also a figure darkened by newspaper scandal, so some people were reluctant to get too close to him.

A small cheer went up when the Earl and Countess walked through the lych-gate. The cheer had a timeless quality, it was the kind of cheer that could have been accorded to any of his ancestors over the past two hundred years. Hugo did not find it embarrassing, merely his due.

Then finally Sophie and John descended from the Bentley. Sophie was wearing a three-quarter-length white silk dress and looked ravishing. John had eschewed morning dress entirely. He wore a dark velvety suit and a stock with pin instead of a tie.

And so they went into the church to be taken through the service of blessing by the Reverend David Dutson. It seemed to have all the ingredients of a wedding service, even though it lacked the actual dramatic moment of marriage. Hugo joined in the hymns and kept his gaze away from the Hooke family chapel. He felt a sort of completeness; his third and final child had at last been married off. A good match, if not a good marriage. It seemed like an affirmation of his purpose in life. He felt unusually benign as a result.

Duncan sang the hymns loudly and his voice vied with the Rector's during the prayers. He had decided that this marriage was a very good thing. Sophie had done well to find John, John was a very good chap, and he, Duncan, was going to enjoy every moment of the day.

Jacky held hands with Rupert the whole time. When she had to sing a hymn, though, she let go and balanced a hymn book against her unborn child, due within the month. She felt slightly sorry that she had not had a wedding like this but had a pleasant feeling of the family being brought together by the occasion and made the closer for it.

Finally, after photographs outside the church, family and guests formed a long motorcade which made its way to the South Lodge and then drove triumphantly down the Fair Mile to the main entrance of Castle Cansdale – the letters of the Hooke motto '*In Hac Spe Vivo*' becoming more readable as they drew nearer.

Duncan had made sure that the Hooke flag was flying from the central tower. A light breeze tossed and furled it, and – as if on cue – the sun finally emerged from the clouds and bathed it in light as the happy pair arrived.

Luigi Corsini was beginning to feel very hot inside his heavy black overcoat. He had to keep it on and buttoned up to cover the Magnum he had tucked into the top of his trousers. He felt nervous and uncomfortable as the gun pressed into his well-padded stomach.

To fill in time, he had done the tour of the house on his own. What a relief not to have to follow a guide. He was able to go at his own pace – which was fast, barely pausing to look at any of the paintings or objects, though he did notice the empty display case in the Salon with its polite notice announcing that the exhibits would be put on display just as soon as they had been recovered from the thieves who had taken them.

Ah yes, thought Luigi – the robbery Mr Harry had mentioned.

Near the end of his tour, Luigi approached a guide, one of whom was on duty in each of the main rooms, and asked her a question.

'You tell me, please – is there a wedding today?'

'Oh, yes, indeed,' said Mrs Carter, the guide. 'It's Lady Sophie – the Earl's daughter. They're coming here from the church. We're all very excited!'

Luigi made it plain from the expression on his face that he did not share the feeling.

'What is this "Earl"?' he asked. 'I thought he was Lord?'

The guide put on a very slightly condescending tone. 'Well, they're all lords in a way. I mean, Earl Hooke is sometimes called Lord Hooke. But then you have Lord Wymark, his son.'

Luigi did not quite follow this but he picked up one salient point.

'So, Lord Veemark – he have a father?'

'Oh, yes.'

It was to be expected, perhaps, that he would have had, but Luigi only meant to convey his dawning realization that Lord Wymark's father not only had existed but was alive now.

'He very old, if he Lord Veemark father?'

Mrs Carter gave a little laugh and dropped her voice a fraction.

'It depends what you mean by "old"! He's over seventy, yes.' She wanted to be helpful. 'Look, there he is in that photograph.' She pointed to the wiry looking man. 'And that is Lord Wymark next to him – it's not too hard to tell them apart.'

'He with red face?'

'A little bit,' conceded the guide.

Luigi managed to tear himself away from this chat and wandered off until he reached the tea room and gift shop. He bought himself a cup of coffee, though he knew he would hate this horrible English stuff, and a large slice of chocolate cake – over which he poured one of the two tubs of cream he had taken for his coffee.

It was now four o'clock and the woman behind the cash register assured him that the wedding party would be arriving any moment now from the church. She could hardly wait to desert her till, she said, to try and get a look.

Luigi went out of the house and managed to find his way round to the front. Just then the first wedding cars from the procession were crunching to a halt on the far side of the oval green in front of the house. Everyone would have to walk across the grass to reach the door. A gaggle of staff from the castle stood nearby to greet the guests and usher them through the Salon and onwards into the marquee on the north side. But first everyone wanted to catch a glimpse of Lady Sophie. They had to wait while the guests parked in the Fair Mile, disgorged from their cars and gathered by the door. Luigi hovered as inconspicuously as he could, which was not very, but no one considered it odd that members of the public should want to catch a glimpse too. He thought to himself that if he had had a camera it would have provided perfect cover.

He felt an involuntary shiver when he first realized he was looking at his target for the first time in the flesh. Duncan, Lord Wymark, was unmistakable with his strong personality, red face, and forthright bearing. Luigi instinctively ran a hand down to the gun beneath his coat.

And then he saw the Earl of whose existence he had only just become aware. He couldn't understand these British and the peculiar names they gave themselves. He knew what a lord was. He knew what a count was – they even had them in Italy – but an '*eorl*'? He did not like the word, and could barely pronounce it.

The Bentley drew up containing Sophie and John. Luigi felt she could have had a more splendid wedding dress, a longer one, but it was of no real concern to him. He felt a vague sense of regret that he was about to spoil her wedding day, but he had his job to do and shouldn't be sentimental about the weddings of people he didn't know.

He felt a great desire to get it over with – but no, he mustn't rush it. He wouldn't stand a chance of escaping from all these people, even waving a loaded gun at them. His car was three hundred yards away in the car park on the other side of the house and it would be very easy for anyone to block his exit.

The guests began trooping into the house behind Sophie and John. They paused in the Salon for the formal photograph, in colour, the one that would end up in *Harpers*, and then the newlyweds stationed themselves at the entrance to the marquee at the end of the covered walkway that ran from the rear door of the house.

Glenellen had excelled herself in creating the row of pillars that lined the covered way. She found it hard not to keep fussing and fiddling, to make sure every vista and prospect was just as she had designed it. It was while she was binding up one of the flower displays that Duncan spoke a word of congratulation to her. Joanna was at his side and he was beaming. Glenellen looked at him a touch shyly, but realized all was well now if he could do that. She smiled. Duncan and his family stretched out their hands for glasses of champagne, orange juice for the girls, and disappeared into the tent.

Luigi Corsini had taken himself from the front of the house and made his way back round the outside to the marquee which was now humming with loud conversation and the gentle tinkle of a piano trio. He was sweating.

He was conscious of other visitors to the house clustering about in small groups trying to catch a glimpse of the bridal pair, the Earl and Countess, and the other guests. He found them very annoying. They were a distraction. He began to boil – with nerves and anxiety. Would he ever be allowed to pull this off?

It would be stupid of him even to consider going into the marquee. He would be spotted immediately and would never be able to get out again afterwards.

He remembered what he had told himself: he must do what he had to do where it would not be discovered until he had made his escape. He had a thought and went up to another of the guides who was trying to shepherd away any member of the public who drifted too close to the wedding party.

'What time the house close?' Luigi asked.

The man looked at his watch.

'Well, it's closed already really. Five o'clock officially, but last admission's four thirty, and it's just gone.'

The guide looked at Luigi with no hint of suspicion. 'Want to go round again? You been in?'

'Yes, I been in, but I missed the shop.'

'Oh, that's all right, sir. Just you go round backwards, so to speak. No trouble. You'll find it by the exit round the corner there.'

Luigi scuttled in and managed to re-enter the house without anyone stopping him. He bypassed the shop, glided past the open door of the tea room where the last visitors were just ending their meals, and was soon among the maze of downstairs rooms. He opened the first door he came to and went in.

It was pitch dark and he wondered whether he should risk turning on the light. He did so and found that he was in a wine cellar. It was a good fifty feet square and was sectioned off from wall to ceiling by racks. It occurred to him that even if someone came in and disturbed him, he would probably be able to find a dark corner in which to hide.

Luigi had a quick look at the vintages and was impressed, even if they were mostly French wines. He decided to leave the light on and hide out of sight of anyone coming through the door.

He had to think very hard now. He was in the house; he would somehow – God knew how – have to get Lord Wymark out of the wedding to come to him; he then had to get out of the house undetected and make his way to the car park. Ah, yes, that was a point. Someone was bound to notice that his car had not been driven away when the other visitors left and conclude he was still in the grounds, maybe even start looking for him. He must wait for a while, but not too long.

It was time for the speeches. John's best man, Simon, made a droll one pointing out that basically the purpose of the day's events had been to ensure the continuance of things very much as they had been for some time now. Namely, that Sophie and John would continue to live under the same roof and live their lives as hitherto.

This caused a slight *frisson* among those of Hugo and Molly's generation who, even these days, were still not quite at ease with the idea of young people living together before marriage. And even if they had been, well, perhaps it wasn't quite right to draw people's attention to it in public.

Then Hugo spoke – rather well, most people thought. He described Sophie in glowing terms, thanked her for the loyalty she had always shown to the family, and managed even to be polite about the man who had taken her away from him.

'I have read many of the things John has had to say in the papers, and I find them broadly sound,' Hugo said, pushing his thin, old voice to make it fill the tent. People noticed the qualification, 'broadly'. But then he removed all doubt and concluded that it was a beneficent deity that had caused Sophie to be thrown from her horse in Sniggs Wood and John to be there to pick her up.

Duncan laughed loudly, rather glad he hadn't got to make a speech and wondering just how long it would be before he had to give away the first of his daughters. He felt, too, that his father had come home on this day without in any way usurping his position. How good it was that all that trouble was water under the bridge now.

He accepted a second piece of wedding cake, in spite of Joanna's reminding him of his waistband, and was just about to say something unusually self-deprecating on this subject to Uncle Alec when he was interrupted by Lopez.

'I wonder if I could have a word, my lord?'

'Yes, what is it?'

Lopez drew Duncan out of earshot of his wife.

'I'm sorry, sir, but I thought it only right to tell you. I believe it is *good* news, sir, otherwise I would not have disturbed you. There's a phone call from the police. Would you like to take it in the Gold Library, sir?'

'Oh, very well. Perhaps they've pulled their finger out at last.'

'I think so, yes, maybe.'

Duncan wordlessly made a gesture to his family that he had to go and would return as soon as he could. He walked along Glenellen's colonnade and into the house. He passed through the Music Room and into the Gold Library and skipped over one of the ropes in order to get to the phone by the fireplace.

'Hello. Wymark.'

It was Detective Inspector Bennett from Craswall who had been Duncan's main point of contact over the theft of the silver. He thought Duncan would like to know, and he apologized for ringing on a Saturday afternoon, that the stolen silver had been recovered – all of it.

'Did you catch the buggers?'

'Ah, no,' the policeman said sadly. 'It's a bit of a long story. We were very close, but they slipped through our fingers due to a slight misunderstanding. But we still hope to make an arrest one day.'

'Ah, you do? Well, that's better than nothing, isn't it? When do we get it back? The stuff. Oh, I see. Well, quick as you can.'

Duncan replaced the receiver and paused for a moment in the Gold Library. Then he turned to go back to the marquee.

On an impulse he decided to find Lopez and tell him. After all, Lopez had been the first to tell Duncan about the theft, so he should be told of its recovery. But Lopez was not in the colonnade to the marquee, nor was he in the Salon.

Ah, well, Duncan thought, I'd better find him now that I've started.

He went down the servants' staircase and headed for the butler's pantry, thinking Lopez might have retreated there for a break. He was heading down the last twenty-five yards of the passage, a little tiddly, quietly humming to himself – a line from one of the hymns, as it happened – when he noticed something. There was a light shining under the door of the wine cellar. Perhaps Lopez was in there?

Duncan opened the door.

'That you, Lopez?' he called out.

There was pause and then a quiet acknowledgement, in an accented voice.

'Where *are* you, Lopez?'

There was no reply. So he walked deeper into the cellar to investigate.

He saw the man reach for a gun. In the top of his trousers. Duncan could do nothing. In a moment he had been hit three times with the silenced bullets. Blood was already coursing from the wounds.

No one could have heard, Luigi Corsini rejoiced to himself, his nerves still aflame with the surprise at having his target handed to him on a plate like this.

Alas, a fourth bullet had sped past Lord Wymark and burst into a bottle of Château Latour, spraying the red liquid about the walls until it mingled with the dark red blood of the victim.

Luigi crunched over the broken glass and wine-soaked floor, making for the door. He stuffed the still hot gun once more into the top of his trousers.

With luck, he would be away before anything was discovered.

# CHAPTER 29

It began to rain in earnest. At the end of the Fair Mile, a vivid rim of yellow sky separated the horizon from the blackest of black clouds as though the bottom of the cloud had been folded over. But John and Lady Sophie Tarrant couldn't wait any longer. The Bentley was due to pick them up from Castle Cansdale at six thirty and take them to Sophie's cottage where they would transfer to her car and set off on the first leg of their honeymoon. That was to be a night spent at a hotel thirty miles away. Next day, on Sunday, they would fly to Ireland from Heathrow.

'Well, you'd better go and change,' said Joanna to Sophie, a little distractedly. It was odd of Duncan to go off like this in the middle of a gathering. There was a time when she might have worried he was seducing one of the guests upstairs, but she hoped all that was over now.

'You know where to go? I'd better take you.'

Joanna led the newlyweds up to the Green Bedroom where their going-away things had been laid out on the bed.

It was possible that a reason for Joanna's going with them was just to make sure they didn't walk in on Duncan in bed with someone. It had happened before, after all.

But no, there was no more sign of her husband in the bedroom than anywhere else.

'See you when you're ready,' she said. 'The car's here already, I think.'

When she'd gone, John held Sophie in his arms and kissed her. It was their first moment alone together since being legally bound. And then they started to change.

Half an hour later, all the guests clustered around windows on the south side of the house, unable to go out and wave farewell because of the torrential rain.

'Thank Duncan,' Sophie said to Joanna, giving her a kiss, 'for letting us use the house. Sorry we missed him.'

291

Joanna nodded, mildly exasperated. Then with a final wave the couple dived under umbrellas and ran to the Bentley. They were driven off down the Fair Mile and people stood watching until the car was a small speck and finally disappeared from sight into the rain and darkness.

Hugo and Molly decided it was time for them to go, too, rain or no rain. The Earl felt another attack of disapproval coming on at Duncan's absence. There was really no explaining it, but he was trying very hard not to jump to conclusions. The Silver Cloud was brought closer to the door for them and then they, too, were gone.

Inevitably, there were some who lingered long after the majority had departed. Joanna rather wished they would all go; only Uncle Alec was staying the night.

'Lopez.' She beckoned the butler over. 'You said he was taking a phone call?'

'Yes, my lady.'

'In the Gold Library?'

'Yes.'

'D 'you know who it was he was talking to?'

'The police. They said they had some good news for him.'

'How very odd.'

Joanna asked Lopez to fetch her a glass of champagne. It might help get her through the exasperating situation she was in.

Josephina offered to mount a search party with her sisters, and her mother cautiously concurred. The girls scampered away; with a hundred or so rooms in the house, they would have quite a task.

'Should I take a look in the park?' asked Lopez. 'It is getting dark.'

'But it's so wet. Put the lights on and see if that helps.'

Lopez went down to his security cubbyhole and did as Joanna advised. Then he armed himself with a large golfing umbrella and walked out into the curiously glazed light that the security lamps shed round the outside of the old building.

Then he had an idea. Perhaps his master had taken one of the guests to view the restored Pantheon. Lord Wymark was quite proud of the work, even if it had been done by Miss Glenellen with whom there had been all that trouble. This check took Lopez over the grass and out of the area of the floodlighting. The bottoms of his trouser legs and his shoes soon became soaked. He tried the doors of the Pantheon, but they were locked. He knocked and called out, but there was no answer. He did not like the cold, damp smell of the stonework, and quickly turned back to the house.

Castle Cansdale glowed from this distance, with the marquee like a cake set down before it.

Lopez stopped for a moment as he crossed the grass. He thought he had heard a movement in the trees. But, if there had been anything, he had not looked quickly enough. Perhaps it was just an animal. Or the wind and the rain. He ran the rest of the way back to the house.

The caterers were already clearing out the marquee. The remains of the wedding cake were being carefully carried down to the kitchen to be kept for Sophie and John's return. Before long, the house would be free of visitors and Lopez would be able to take off his damp shoes and put his feet up.

Josephina's scream was one of the most horrible noises that he had ever heard in his life. It came welling up from the bowels of the house like some dreadful exhalation.

Lopez ran across the Salon and skittered down the stairs quicker than he had ever moved in all his time at the house. He thought that one of the girls must have had some terrible accident in the kitchen. So that was where he headed.

But he did not have to go quite that far. As he dashed round the last corner he saw Josephina and her two sisters clutching each other outside the wine-cellar door. Their lemon-coloured dresses were smeared with blood and they were crying uncontrollably.

Lopez went in, saw nothing at first, but then reached the rear racks.

And so he found the body of his master, lying in a pool of half-congealed blood and broken glass into which Château Latour was dripping from above.

It simply did not occur to Rupert that he was now the heir to the Hooke title and the Cansdale estate. For the moment, he was numbed to the point of empty-headedness by the fact of Duncan's terrible and quite inexplicable death.

He soon became conscious, though, that he was now the surviving responsible member of the family, and ought to take charge – but only in the sense that he realized his father had gone home and Uncle Alec was not exactly the man to deal with an emergency like this.

Lopez was told to summon the police and Joanna was ordered to take the children up to the flat; Jacky went with them. Uncle Alec explained to the wedding guests that they all must leave 'because there has been a terrible accident'.

While Rupert waited for the police to arrive, which would take time, he asked Lopez to show him the body. They entered the wine cellar together and crept forward, their shoes crunching the fragments of glass that lay everywhere.

'Three bullets, see,' said Lopez, helpfully.

'Yes,' gasped Rupert, hardly any sound coming out.

He had never seen a dead body before, and certainly not a murdered one. He was struck by its utter stillness, not least because Duncan had never ceased moving when he was alive. He had hummed with vitality, like some overheated engine, but now lay horribly still.

'Who can have done it?' Rupert continued to whisper his words. 'I mean . . . *why*?'

'I have no idea . . . your lordship.'

It was only then that Rupert realized. He looked at Lopez, almost uncomprehending at first. He ran a hand distractedly through his hair. 'I mean, he was pretty unpopular,' he went on, his gaze returning unwillingly to his half-brother's body, 'but not so anyone would want to *kill* him . . .'

'No.'

'Couldn't have been anyone at the wedding surely?'

'I don't think so. I don't know.'

'I suppose the police'll want to know about everybody.'

'I had better go outside and wait for them, sir. They might get lost.'

'Yes, of course, Lopez.'

Rupert climbed slowly up the stairs to the Salon and paused before the portrait of his great-grandmother – the one in which she wore the bracelet Jacky now had.

He suddenly felt very small and very alone. This vast pile would now become his. It was what he had always dreamed of. But why had it had to come to him in this way? At that moment, he could not find room for the thought that this was the only way it could have come to him. Without really knowing why, he sensed that the transition would not be an easy one.

Already he was a different person. Jacky noticed it as he came into the room. He seemed older and more authoritative. He glanced at Joanna who was being comforted by Uncle Alec. Rupert tried a weak smile and made a gesture of despair.

'Are they here yet?' Joanna asked tearfully.

'No, not at the moment. It takes time to get from Craswall.'

'Who could have done it?' she sobbed. 'Can you think?'

'I don't know, Joanna. I suppose he'd got one or two enemies, but not that bad, surely. I can only think it was an intruder of some sort. Perhaps a burglar he bumped into by accident. With the wedding on, and all the visitors, I suppose someone could have got into the house . . .'

But Joanna wasn't so sure. She could only think of all those people Duncan had got across over the years. It could be anyone. People he'd kicked off the estate. People he'd been rude to. What about the husband of

294

that woman who had the baby? God, the police would have a field day digging through all that muck!

They had arrived now. There was a crunch of gravel, a squeal of brakes, the sound of car doors slamming and urgent footsteps. Rupert went to the window, parted the curtains and looked out.

'I'd better go and speak to them.'

Jacky held out her hand for his and squeezed it. Rupert gave her a look which told her he was all right. Then he went down to meet the police.

The chief one appeared to know the house and turned out to have been in charge of the inquiry into the silver robbery. Indeed, it very quickly emerged he must have been one of the last people to speak to Duncan alive, to tell him about the recovery of the silver.

'And who are you, sir?' Detective Inspector Bennett asked.

'I'm Rupert – Lord Wymark's younger brother. We were all here for my sister's wedding. Or, at least, the reception. Duncan suddenly went missing and then he was found by his daughters.'

'Lot of people at the wedding, were there?'

'Heavens, yes. I suppose you'll want to know who they were?'

'One thing at a time, sir.'

'I'm sorry. You know what you're doing, I expect. I'll be upstairs if you want me. Lopez will tell you anything you need to know. I'd better go and make a few phone calls.'

'Er, well, I'm not sure about that, sir. Perhaps you'd wait until we've had a little think. If you'd be so kind.'

'Of course, Inspector.'

Rupert left the policeman who turned and started questioning Lopez.

'Where's he from then?'

'Mr Rupert lives in London. But it will all change. You see, Lord Wymark was the heir to the Earl – who lives at Stoke Cansdale. Now Mr Rupert is the heir.'

'I see,' said the policeman, and vaguely wondered if there had been any rivalry between the brothers.

More police arrived and started a thorough search of the downstairs area.

'There's no point in our doing the grounds till morning,' the inspector said. 'But it'll have to be done, even if it's all washed away.'

The evening went by as the police photographer, the fingerprint men and finally the undertaker went about their work. Duncan's body was removed to the police mortuary in Craswall.

Towards eleven, Rupert could stand being cooped up with Joanna, the girls, Uncle Alec and Jacky no longer. Lopez, who'd been run off his feet, had brought them all a little supper, but the claustrophobia was unbearable. He went downstairs and sought out Detective Inspector Bennett and asked if it would be all right to inform his father, at least, of what had happened. It might be better if he could sleep on the bad news rather than find out next morning. The inspector gave his assent and Rupert went to the library and dialled the Huddleston number.

Molly answered and instinctively knew something was the matter.

'It's Duncan, isn't it? What's happened?'

Rupert told her the news. 'The police are here, of course. We're a bit trapped. We were going back to London, but I expect we'll have to stay the night.'

Then Hugo took the phone from Molly.

'This can't be true,' his father shouted over the phone. 'What nonsense is this?'

It took Rupert several minutes of calm description before his father believed him. Gradually, the energy disappeared from Hugo's voice and he sounded quite deflated.

'Of course, you know what this means?' Hugo said after a long, embarrassing pause.

'In what connection?'

'This is a catastrophe as far as the settlement goes.'

Trust Father to be worrying about that, thought Rupert.

'God knows what'll happen,' Hugo went on. 'We're not two years into the seven-year term. No one thought of this. They thought I wouldn't last the course; they never thought it would happen to Duncan!'

'Well, Father, we'll just have to sort it out as best we can.'

'Doubt if there's a precedent,' mused Hugo. 'We may have to go to court.'

'Don't worry about things like that, Father. Try and get some sleep. See how the world looks in the morning.'

Hugo doubted he would sleep at all that night.

When Rupert went back up to the family flat, he found that Joanna had started worrying about Sophie and John finding out about Duncan's death.

'It'll ruin their honeymoon.'

'Where are they staying tonight, does anybody know?'

'They're going on a plane tomorrow, that's all I know,' said Joanna. 'I think they must be spending tonight somewhere not far away.'

'I suppose it'll be in the papers,' Jacky noted.

'The police want it kept quiet,' said Rupert, 'but that won't be for long.'

'I suppose they won't read papers on their honeymoon, if they're abroad, will they?' Jacky said hopefully.

'Oh yes, they will,' Rupert said. 'John wouldn't allow a honeymoon to interrupt his reading.'

Then Joanna started worrying about the funeral. She had an idea that the police sometimes wouldn't release a body if there had been a murder. And then dawned the realization that she and the girls would no longer be living in Castle Cansdale. They would have to move away. What sort of life would be left for her now?

The girls had been sent off to bed before all this kind of talk had begun. But now, as Rupert saw, the talk might help Joanna and the rest of them come to terms with the shattering experience they had all shared. The four of them drank and drank, but it didn't seem to make any difference. They remained as sober as when they'd started.

From down in the house the sound of people talking and moving about continued to rise up to them. The radios in the police cars outside on the forecourt kept up a constant barrage of flat-voiced information. They felt as though they were in prison.

Josephina came down to complain to her mother about the noise. It was obvious that no one was going to get much sleep as long as the police remained in the house. Towards midnight, Rupert phoned Molly once again and found that Hugo and she were still awake. Could they possibly manage to put up Joanna and the girls at Huddleston – Jacky, himself and Uncle Alec, too?

Molly said they would manage somehow, even if someone had to sleep on the sofa.

The girls, still in their nightclothes, were wrapped in blankets. The small, mournful procession made its way downstairs and climbed into police cars which ferried them all to Huddleston.

The household staff had been told to go back to their homes in the village and, at last, towards twelve thirty, the only occupants of the house were Lopez and Detective Constable Kenworthy of Craswall police who would stand guard till the morning. The Detective Inspector had left having decided there was nothing more to be done until daylight. Lopez went round locking all the doors and made a quick tour of inspection with DC Kenworthy. The marquee which earlier had been full of the sound of happy laughter now stood forlornly on the grass, eerily lit by the security lights. Lopez noticed that the rain had all but stopped.

Warily, with the policeman, he went down to the basement area once again, hardly turning to glance as they went past the closed wine-cellar door. Lopez ushered DC Kenworthy into the security room and gave him a flask of tea to see him through the night. Then he bid the constable goodnight, let himself out of the kitchen door and went over to his room in the Spring Lodge. The rain had suddenly started again and his feet got damp once more as he made the short dash across the yard. He had doubts as to whether he would be able to get to sleep. Even without seeing what he had seen that day – the worst experience of his life – Lopez had other worries. What would happen to his job now? Would he still be employed at Castle Cansdale when Master Rupert took over? Would he even want to stay at Castle Cansdale after what had happened?

The rain had been the last straw. Mark Moore had to admit defeat. He was cold, miserable and wet to the skin. Everything had gone according to plan until the early evening. He had moved into the wood in the late afternoon and hidden himself in the trees where they reached their nearest point to the house, near the Pantheon.

Even getting to that point had required a major effort. The lanes all round the estate were busy with cars – everyone seemed to be on the move – but he had managed to find the turn-off he had reconnoitred previously and had hidden his car in a copse near the wall of the park. He had then scaled the wall with a rope ladder which he left hanging in place on the inside. It was not an easy task getting over the wall as he had to take with him a box of electrical equipment; it was the size of a portable radio and weighed rather more. There then followed a walk through scrub and trees of about a quarter of a mile before he could take up his waiting post by the Pantheon.

Mark dug himself in and prepared for a long wait. For hour after hour he lay watching people come and go around the marquee. He was aware of the paying visitors finally departing – though one car remained, oddly enough, in the car park. Then the wedding guests, with agonizing slowness, seemed to be going away, too. Mark knew that he must continue to wait until the house had gone to bed and all was quiet.

Mark had said nothing of what he was doing to anyone, not even his father. He had conscientiously made sure his information and expertise were equal to the upgraded security at the castle and then he waited for his chance. It came when he heard, through Jacky, about Sophie's wedding reception. That, surely, would be the ideal sort of distraction to confuse people in the house. They would slip up on security. They'd get drunk. He'd be able to take advantage.

Mark had no reason to revise this view for most of the time he lay in wait. Of course, there might be more people staying overnight in the house. There might be more stragglers, more outsiders – the caterers and so on. But they could also be a useful distraction. Tonight was the night, indeed – the best night he could have settled on.

And then it had all gone wrong. First, the downpour – he had remembered to bring everything but a waterproof. Secondly, the arrival of the police. He had no way of finding out what that was all about. He heard the sirens and saw the blue lights as they shot across the grounds until they parked in front of the house. He glimpsed uniformed men moving about in the well-lit rooms. He almost picked himself up and ran back to his car beyond the wall. But something told him to sit tight. He couldn't possibly be the cause of the police activity. They must be there because of something else.

Of course, there had been that moment when the butler came out to the Pantheon and tried the doors. Had he spotted anything amid the trees? Mark didn't think so. Maybe there had been a fault in the security system? Surely not. From Mark's observations on other nights it wasn't switched on until the last person went to bed, though the floodlights sometimes came on early.

He would just have to wait and see.

The police seemed to stay for hours. Mark couldn't imagine what was taking them so long. And then when midnight struck on the church clock in the village and the police still had not gone, Mark began to have the heavy feeling that he would have to abort the whole operation. He had been sandbagged. He had been defeated by fate. His father would laugh at him, hold him up as a failure.

And then the rain started in earnest again. He listened to it as it splashed on the leaves, then felt it as it dripped down his collar and united with the damp warmth left by the earlier downpour. Once more he had to wrap the electrical equipment in the black plastic bags he had brought along for another purpose.

Then shortly after midnight the police cars went away. Mark saw the red lights come up on the security cameras but just when he thought it might be safe to start working on them, the rain increased and made it impossible. He nearly threw in the attempt once more, but then called himself back. After all this, how could he give up? He looked at his watch. He would wait another half-hour, just in case there was anyone watching the security screens.

Then he would begin his work, rain or no rain.

# CHAPTER 30

The day after the murder saw the start of the task of interviewing every one of the hundred and fifty guests who had attended the wedding reception, together with the staff at the castle and the outside caterers. An appeal was made for every member of the public who had been admitted to Castle Cansdale on the Saturday afternoon to come forward.

After the police had been to talk to the Earl and Countess at Huddleston, and to all the family who had stayed with them on Saturday night, Mrs Powers the housekeeper finally found time to contact her friend, Lopez, at the castle.

'They said you were the last to see him, you poor thing.'

Lopez made a perfunctory attempt to play down his misfortune. The worst thing, he told Mrs Powers, had been having to sleep alone at the castle last night, with but a solitary policeman for company.

'You'd better tell them about that feller in the pub, hadn't you?'

'What "feller"?'

'The one who asked you all those question. Remember?'

'Oh, yes. Is right.'

The police were interested and duly made a note of the information, though Lopez found it hard to remember anything about the man. He had had a moustache, and a ring in his ear. He hadn't been what you'd call memorable.

One of the castle guides, Mrs Carter, who knew nothing of the killing until she turned up for work at Sunday lunchtime, was more helpful. She remembered the odd-looking man who had asked her about Lord Wymark's whereabouts just before the guests came back from the church. She found it hard to describe him. He simply 'wasn't the sort who usually come here'. The police were interested in that, too, and wrote it down.

It was decided that the house would be closed to visitors for the foreseeable future and a constable was detailed to stand by the North

300

Lodge entrance and explain the reason to people. He was also told to keep an eye open for anyone suspicious who turned up.

Lopez was suffering from delayed shock by this stage and was wandering about distraught, unable to keep to his room but equally unable to go near his usual haunts, the butler's pantry, the kitchen and, of course, the wine cellar where the body had been found. He went for a walk in the park, but there were policemen combing the still sodden undergrowth for any sign of the murder weapon, and he couldn't be alone with his thoughts. So he went back into the house and sat, all huddled up, in the Salon, staring morosely in front of him.

Suddenly, he rose anxiously from his chair. There was a gap on the wall where a picture should have been. The Rembrandt of an old woman. The police would never have spotted it missing because there was no obvious sign to indicate it had ever hung on the wall – the wallpaper had been replaced as part of the renovations. But a tiny pinprick of the hole showed where there had been a nail.

Lopez quickly checked the rest of the room to see whether anything else was missing.

There was – from one of the display cases next to the one from which the earlier silver theft had been made. A gold basket, a tray and several snuffboxes were gone. They all dated from the eighteenth century and were priceless.

Lopez went first to the guides who were sitting forlornly in their room in the stables block. He brought them back with him to the house and they did a rapid search of all the public rooms until they had spotted what else was missing. Apart from the Rembrandt, all the missing items were small in size and thus easily portable.

'These things – they were here, yesterday?' Lopez asked.

'Oh, yes,' the guides chorused, no less dismayed.

'I tell the policeman.'

A detective chief superintendent was now on the scene and wanted to know whether the stolen items had been in place when the last members of the public were shown out the evening before. There was no doubt they had been. The guides always carried out a check last thing before going home.

'And you didn't notice they were missing at any time until this morning, Mr Lopez?'

The butler shook his head. He had been too upset 'by the other thing' to look very closely at the contents of the castle.

The DCS could only come to the conclusion that the thief must have lingered on after the house was closed to the public, perhaps hidden downstairs, and that Lord Wymark had come across him by chance. Even

301

so, that didn't quite fit. Most burglars didn't equip themselves with Magnum 397s – which, it had now been established, was the weapon used to kill Lord Wymark.

Still, one thing was certain. The thief hadn't got in during the night. DC Kenworthy had been keeping an eye on the security monitors and hadn't seen anything.

Once Jacky and Rupert had given their – not very helpful – details to the police at Huddleston, they had a bite of Mrs Powers's scratch lunch and then made their farewells. They were stunned by the news of the robbery, even though it might go some way to explaining Duncan's death.

Joanna, still wearing the wedding outfit in which she had even slept, was embraced silently by Rupert. There was nothing more to say. But Joanna spoke softly to Jacky and told her to look after the baby when it came.

Rupert muttered to Hugo that they would no doubt be back very soon – for the funeral.

'Oh, yes,' said Hugo. 'And we'll need to talk about the other thing.'

'The house?'

'Exactly. You know Elliot, my legal chappie? I'd better get him over to sort it out. I'm afraid it won't be easy.'

'Don't think about it, Father. There's no hurry. We'll find a way.'

'But I *do* worry!' exclaimed Hugo, thinking this was what Rupert had said. 'I mean, I don't know if Duncan made a will. And if he did, I don't know what it contains . . .'

A will? Rupert simply hadn't thought of that. Was it possible that Duncan had willed the estate in such a way that he, Rupert, could not inherit it? Or if he hadn't left a will, would that mean Joanna, as his widow, would automatically inherit it?

The new Lord and Lady Wymark drove in stunned silence back to London. Jacky, her usual optimism in abeyance, brooded on what sort of a world she was bringing their child into. It seemed to offer nothing but difficulties and disappointments. That she was now a 'lady' and would one day become a countess hardly felt like compensation at this moment. She brooded, too, on this interruption to their domestic plans. Would they have to forego the house in Castle Wharf just as they were beginning to sort it out, and move into Castle Cansdale? With all the talk of wills and tax and settlements, would there even be a castle for them to move into?

Rupert thought rather more of his title. There had always been the remote possibility he would end up in this position, but he had never allowed himself to think very much about it. At a stroke, his life had been changed. He would no longer be able to go his own sweet way with his comfortable but undemanding job, his pretty wife, and his easy-going ways. Owning the castle was what he had always dreamed of, but that would depend on Duncan's will. And then there was the transfer that Hugo had made to Duncan – how would that be affected by the death? Would Rupert have to arrange the selling off of lands to pay the inheritance tax? Would he have to sell off the family heirlooms – or, rather,those that hadn't been stolen?

Rupert rejected the idea of simply walking away from it all. He could decline to use the courtesy title; disclaim the earldom when the time came; refuse to have anything to do with the estate; parcel it up and hand it over to a trust. But that would go against the grain, deeply disappoint his father, and wipe out that sense of family obligation he found so hard to ignore.

'I'd better ring Mum,' Jacky said as soon as they reached Castle Wharf. 'I don't suppose she's heard yet.'

'No. It'll be in the papers tomorrow.'

'Better tell her.'

Jacky spelt out to her mother what Duncan's death would mean: the likelihood of their moving to the castle to take over his role; the fact that Rupert would assume his dead brother's courtesy title which would mean that she would now be Lady Jacky.

What would, under any other circumstances, have been greeted with whoops of envious, fantastical laughter was now received in more muted fashion. Her mother was pleased about the title and castle – how could she not be? – but everything was getting out of hand. Jacky had a lovely husband, a lovely house, the baby on the way – what did she really want with titles and such when it seemed that murder and theft went with them?

The phone call did not end on the usual upbeat note. Cynthia would tell Freddie – and Mark, of course.

Mark wasn't to be found. Cynthia hadn't a clue what he was up to these days. He came and went at all hours. He was working on something quite obsessively, but his mother knew better than to ask. Freddie Moore came home around tea time on the Sunday afternoon. He had been playing golf and – so he said – beating the others hollow.

'There's been trouble down at Cansdale,' Cynthia told him flatly, almost before he'd come through the door.

Freddie took a breath and had a rapid think before he reacted.

'What sort of trouble?' he asked, not looking at her.

'Duncan's been killed. Shot three times. At Sophie's wedding.'

Freddie bit a lump of flesh in his mouth, as though to steady himself. He went and sat down at the kitchen table, and almost immediately bounced up again.

'You'd like some tea, I expect,' Cynthia said.

He nodded and stared in front of him.

Was this anything to do with Mark? Had his boy fucked it up? He knew Mark hadn't been home the previous night. And, though he'd been playing his cards very close to his chest, it seemed quite likely that he'd try to pull off the Cansdale job round about the time of the wedding.

Had something gone wrong? But *shooting*? Surely Mark hadn't gone in with a steamer? There'd been absolutely no need for that. Absolutely no need.

'Where's Mark?' Freddie asked, not bothering to disguise his concern.

'Why, what's he got to do with it?'

'Nothing, nothing, just wondered . . .'

Cynthia put the kettle on and fussed with the teabags. She said to her husband, not looking at him: 'He's not been messing about down there, has he?'

'Nah, nah, of course not. Him?'

'Yes, *him*!' Cynthia turned on him. 'You're on to something, aren't you? You and him, I don't know what it is, but I can tell you're on to something.'

'Nah, nah, shut your bleedin' mouth, woman! You know I'm straight. I've not done nothing.'

'What about Mark then? What's he up to? It'd be like you to set him on to do the dirty work. That's what I think.'

'Look, you bitch, there's nothing going on. *I* don't go round killing people. Mark doesn't either. I've got nothing to do with bleedin' Duncan Wymark. I'm very sorry he's a goner – even if he was a shit. You think I'd be stupid enough to do summat like that with our Jacky in the family? Come off it, girl!'

'There's something fishy going on, I can tell – and I don't bloody like it.'

Cynthia took her tea and walked with it as quickly as she could out of the room.

'Bloody cow!' Freddie shouted and stormed out of the front door, slamming it violently.

As had been supposed, John Tarrant wasn't one to let a honeymoon interfere with his daily intake of newsprint. After flying from Heathrow to Cork on the Sunday morning, Sophie and he had checked into their Irish country house hotel. They had gone straight to bed, then out for a walk, then dined well.

Now, on the Monday morning, they were sitting up in bed having breakfast. There was porridge with thick brown sugar and cream, copious supplies of soda bread with fresh butter and honey on the comb, and lots of black coffee.

They had one or two minor quibbles. The bed was not as large as it might have been for all they planned to do in it over the next few days. There was a colony of rooks cawing away in the trees outside. But none of this really mattered. Beyond the windowpanes lay a landscape punctuated by an occasional tree and fence but otherwise completely flat. It was peaceful and reassuring. Sophie and John were as happy as they were supposed to be, lulled by Irish charm and hospitality and by their own good fortune.

John took up the *Cork Examiner* and read about Irish politics and fatstock prices. The rest of the world seemed very far away and of little importance.

And then he saw a column marked 'World In Brief'. He jumped when he saw it, just a two-sentence report:

> Lord Wymark, 43, owner of Castle Cansdale, Wiltshire, was found dead of gunshot wounds after a family wedding on Saturday. Art treasures, including a Rembrandt, were stolen from the stately home and police believe Lord Wymark must have disturbed thieves.

John stared at the paper; gripping it hard. For a moment, he actually wondered if he could conceal the news from Sophie. He sensed their honeymoon collapsing.

Later that day they were on a plane back to London. Then they drove down to Wiltshire, Sophie reading the English newspapers they'd bought at the airport. Rather more was made in them of the murder of Lord Wymark than in the *Cork Examiner*. Once more, the colourful details of Duncan's philanderings and his Uncle Alec's supposed shame were paraded before readers. Quick footwork had also meant that the last photographs taken of Duncan with the bride and groom found their way to the press. About the only thing missing from the reports was any clear indication why Duncan should have been murdered in cold blood. There were hints that plenty of people might have held a grudge against him, given the way he had carried on – but, the papers reported, the police had no firm leads to go on.

Back in Bethany Cottage – which was to be their joint home from now on – John and Sophie tried to find out what had been going on. But this was difficult. Hugo and Molly were still putting Joanna and the girls up and didn't like to discuss what had happened in their hearing. Joanna had taken up more or less permanent residence in bed and announced her resolve never to set foot in Castle Cansdale again. Uncle Alec had gone back to London.

When Sophie and John drove themselves over to the castle to collect one or two things for Joanna and the girls, and with a view to retrieving their wedding presents, they found only Lopez wandering about, still in a daze, and a solitary police constable who told them it would be quite impossible for them to take anything from the house without his getting authority from higher up.

John had to get quite shirty with the man to gain access to the girls' rooms in order to pick up the change of clothing and some of the treasured possessions they had requested. Sophie shuddered at the mournfulness of the place. There was no sign of Glenellen in the Pantheon – it was locked. All renovation work had been suspended. The marquee stood, still waiting to be dismantled, inappropriately gay in its colours.

'Come on, John – I can't bear this any more. Let's go.'

Lopez followed them to the front entrance, shadowed by the policeman. Sophie paused before the house, massive and daunting and so damnably silent. Her eyes skipped over the motto carved across the front, as they did every time she arrived or departed from the house.

' "In this hope I live",' she murmured to herself. And then she hastily stepped into the car and waited for John to drive her away.

'You'd almost think there was a jinx, wouldn't you?' he said, as they turned out of the North Lodge into the village.

'Yes,' she said in that chopped way she had. 'And yet, whatever happens, the bloody house just stands there – doesn't say a word, never gives away its secret.'

'Perhaps it won't stand for ever,' John said, full of foreboding. 'Probably have to be carved up anyway now.'

'Oh, *no!*' Sophie cried. 'That would be like blaming the house when it's only a . . . witness.'

They were on the other side of the village now, away from the castle, and felt an almost tangible sense of relief.

'Poor Rupert,' she said after they had driven a little further. 'He's been handed the poisoned chalice.'

'Yes, I know,' said John. 'He's really landed in it.'

'And Jacky. I bet she never expected any of this. Hope her baby'll be all right. That'd be the last straw, wouldn't it?'

'She'll be all right,' John said reassuringly. 'She comes from tough stock – as we very well know.'

Sophie glanced at him behind the wheel, and didn't know what to make of that remark.

Freddie hadn't been able to find Mark anywhere. In the end, his boy didn't come home to Dorset Avenue till the Monday evening. His father was beside himself. From the morning papers, Freddie learned that Duncan's murder had been accompanied by a robbery. The police naturally concluded that Duncan had disturbed the robbers in the middle of their job and they had shot him.

So, was this Mark's little job, or had he been pipped at the post by some other outfit a second time?

Mark was taken aback by his father's urgent questioning. He had anticipated announcing his triumph and receiving fatherly approval.

'Come upstairs,' Freddie said shortly, indicating the boy's mother who was sitting nervously in the kitchen.

In the den, Freddie slammed the door and poked Mark in the shoulder so hard he fell back into a chair.

'Now, what's this, boy? What you gone and done?'

'I did a job. And done it proper. All gone, and got the readies – well, most of it!'

'It was where we was thinking of?'

'The castle, right!'

'So what about the bleedin' other thing, you stupid fucker?'

'What other thing?' Mark had to push away the fist with which his father kept pummelling his shoulder.

'Don't give me that! You know what I mean. It's in the papers.'

'What is? My job? In the papers! I haven't seen – I've been busy . . .'

'Yeh, your job – and the other thing. You fixed old fucking Duncan, didn't you, you berk?'

'Howja mean?'

'Come off it! Three bullets, they said.'

Mark's jaw dropped visibly. His fingers went to his moustache as if to have something – anything – to hold on to. He went very cold, then started to sweat. His voice came out in hesitant jerks.

'Honestly, Dad – it wasn't me. When did it happen? I don't read the papers. You having me on?'

Freddie didn't give him an answer, but paced up and down, and then went to the window and looked out.

Mark felt a sick, heavy feeling in the depths of his stomach. He realized all too quickly what had happened. Some other fuckers had beaten him to it – again. That was why the police had been in the castle so long. That was why he'd had to wait. He'd walked right into it, completely unknowing.

'Dad, you've got to believe me. Listen! When was he blagged, then – Duncan?'

'Saturday afternoon, during the wedding. Jacky was there, for God's sake! How could you be such a dick-head?'

'No, hold *on*! It was during the do in the tent, you say?'

'That's what they say.'

'Well, look' – and Mark said this with more than a note of triumph – 'I didn't go in till after midnight. One o'clock more like.'

Freddie turned slowly from the window.

'You mean that?' he asked coolly.

Mark nodded.

'Then you're the unluckiest sod who ever walked this earth. If they nab you for the robbery, they'll do you for the other, too. Fuckin' hell!'

There was a long silence while Freddie returned to surveying neighbouring Brentwood through the window and Mark went back over all his arrangements of the past few months, wondering where he could have left himself vulnerable to detection.

After a while, Freddie seemed to relent. 'Did you get anything good?'

Mark told him about the snuffboxes, the trays, the basket, the candlesticks, and the Rembrandt. It had all been disposed of that morning – all except the Rembrandt.

'Nobody'll touch that,' Mark said.

'Serve you bloody right. What'd I say? You don't pick up nothing till you got a home for it. Took it on the off-chance, did you?'

'Well, yeh. It seemed small enough.'

Freddie shook his head slowly from side to side.

'Ah, well,' he said, almost smiling at last, 'everyone's got to make their own mistakes – and you've certainly made yours, chum!'

Mark squirmed in his chair.

'Where is it, then – the picture?' Freddie snapped.

'Thought you didn't want to know.'

'True. Just as long as it's not burning a hole in this house, or anywhere else of mine. Now, go on. Clear off!'

Mark stood up as casually as he could and let himself out of his father's den. He didn't say a word to his mother and left the house. He wasn't going to stay there a moment longer. He'd find himself a place of his own.

After all, he had plenty of his own money now.

A week passed before Craswall police released Duncan's body for burial. It was an acutely agonizing time for Joanna. There was something deeply unsettling about the thought of her husband's body resting in a police mortuary along with the relics of less savoury people. Until his body was returned to her, she would not be able to think straight about anything.

Even when it was, she did not see the body herself. She turned down the opportunity to view it in a funeral parlour at Craswall. It had been explained to her that one of the bullets had been fired at close range. It had blown a quarter of Duncan's head away. The embalmer in Craswall, where they didn't have much call for that trade, had been unable to render the injury presentable.

But Joanna was reassured after a fashion when she set eyes on the large coffin at the funeral in St Michael's. That it contained her poor darling, she had no doubt. She forgave him everything now. She carried herself splendidly. And she watched, stoically, as the coffin was laid to rest outside the church, below the wall of the Hooke family chapel. As Duncan had died before succeeding to the earldom, he was not buried with his ancestors. It was the last cruel blow.

Rupert took her arm and held Serena, the youngest daughter, by the hand. He cut a grave, dignified figure. There was about him, too, that new authority Jacky had first noticed shortly after Duncan's body had been found.

She wasn't present at the funeral. The birth of the baby was almost due. Just as Rupert had become next in line to the Hooke earldom, so he might be about to acquire his own heir.

Hugo was a wraithlike presence at the funeral. It was as though he had already dropped out of the race of life, become an increasingly irrelevant figure in the story of the Hooke generations. He blamed himself for all that had happened, grieved that he had ever fallen out with Duncan, and was utterly determined to make amends before he himself was taken away.

# CHAPTER 31

'No, I don't think that would be a good idea,' Rupert told Drew Elliot sharply. 'We couldn't talk properly at Huddleston. Duncan's widow's still there.'

'Yes, of course,' the solicitor replied, back-pedalling fast. 'I didn't mean to suggest . . . thoughtless of me. Somewhere else, at your convenience, and your father's, of course.'

'What's wrong with your office, or Mr Templeton's perhaps?'

'Well, I'm afraid now I'm retired I don't really have an office. And as for Sidney's, well, it'd be very cramped for the four of us . . .'

'Then it had better be the castle. It's still closed to the public, so we could have any room we liked. I'll get it organized.'

Ten days had passed since Duncan's funeral and the change in Rupert's manner had become ever more noticeable. Overnight, as it were, he had grown up. He was now not only the heir to the Hooke title but also, as he saw it, the only person who could take over the running of Castle Cansdale.

But that was not an assumption he was legally entitled to make. As Drew Elliot had already intimated to him, Duncan had indeed made a will. And as he very shortly discovered, Duncan had consciously blocked his inheritance of the estate. He had taken the decision that the estate should go to his own immediate family and not to the heir to the title. In the event of his predeceasing his wife, Castle Cansdale would pass to Joanna, and only then to his offspring, female or male – though, of the latter, of course, there had been none legitimate when he died. It was Duncan's final, capricious, spiteful gesture. The will had been revised along these lines only a month before his death – at the time when he had finally come back to Joanna.

'I can't imagine why he did it,' Hugo said. 'I mean, I thought he quite

310

liked you. And besides, he should've made sure that the title holder kept the property.'

'There might be other reasons,' Rupert suggested, with more than a trace of bitterness. 'Duncan never looked on me as a brother. He knew I was more interested in the property than he was. And I think he thought he still might have a son one day. When I got married, perhaps the prospect of my having sons and continuing the line made him feel threatened.'

'S'pose there was something in that – as it's turned out.'

Rupert was, indeed, now the father of a son. Nicholas Arthur Hugo Hooke had entered the world six days after his uncle was laid to rest. His arrival seemed to secure the Hooke dynasty for a little while longer – seemed, indeed, to make up for much that had been hanging loose even before Duncan's death – but whether Nicholas would ever inherit anything worthwhile was much in doubt at the moment.

During the second week in May, Rupert drove down to Wiltshire with Jacky and the baby. Leaving them with Molly and Joanna at Huddleston, he took his father over to Castle Cansdale for the inevitably painful meeting with Drew Elliot and Sidney Templeton.

Rupert approached the session in a pugnacious spirit. It did not help that Elliot had drawn up Duncan's will – as well as being Hugo's legal adviser of long standing. In addition, Rupert was convinced that Elliot – and Templeton – had been seriously at fault in the advice they had given over the transfer of Cansdale from Hugo to Duncan – the transfer which had enabled Duncan to cheat Rupert out of the prize he so dearly sought.

Everyone had assumed that Duncan would outlive his father. The only problem Elliot and Templeton had foreseen was Hugo's dying before the seven years of the PET scheme were up. What they had not done was to ensure the handing on of the gift to the right person beyond that. At least, Duncan's death had not triggered off tax on the PET. The success or failure of that exercise still depended on Hugo's surviving the necessary seven years – or at least a good portion of them.

As Hugo and Rupert drew nearer to the front entrance of Castle Cansdale and spotted Drew Elliot's Rover already waiting there, Rupert said, 'I think, Father, that we should definitely bring in a new solicitor at some stage. I don't believe Elliot's up to it. The trouble is, all this is going to rumble on for months, years probably, and he does know the case.'

'He's always been my adviser,' his father told him, with a sigh.

'Yes, I know. And I don't think you've been well served, frankly.'

'The accountant chappie's all right, isn't he?'

'Yes. Templeton's okay. And he's about the only person who can begin to understand the tax. Even so I think he failed to spot something vital about the PET. He didn't see that the 1987 Finance Act extended PET relief to gifts made into trust. If you'd set up a trust, Duncan wouldn't have been able to do what he liked with the estate.'

'Rupert,' his father said wearily, 'I don't understand a word you're talking about . . .'

The new Lord Wymark was about to say something very sharp to his father, but then thought better of it.

Retirement did not seem to have changed Drew Elliot. He was his old, oily self. He was hovering by the front door to greet Earl Hooke and Lord Wymark, and led them without delay to the Gold Library. Dust sheets had been tossed over some of the furniture. The room was mournful and looked less attractive than any of the four men could remember having seen it.

Rupert quickly established that he was running the meeting. He gave a short summary of the areas which he thought needed to be discussed. Elliot countered with a rather dry statement of Rupert's own position.

'If I may say so, sir – may I draw attention to one of the anomalies of primogeniture?'

Rupert nodded.

'It is this: although it requires that a title be passed to the first-born and then to the next in line, in a pre-ordained and well-established fashion, it does not require that the estate – house, lands, properties – naturally follow.'

'I don't need you to tell me that, Mr Elliot,' said Rupert.

'Forgive me, I think a summary might be helpful to all parties.' He looked at Hugo for approval and received it.

'Now, in the regrettable circumstances of recent weeks, what we have is a very interesting situation. Although it might seem natural that you should assume the responsibility for the estate, taking over your late brother's role as, shall we say, the custodian, in lieu of your father, the simple fact is that you have not inherited either the house on its own – which, of course, would need assets to support its maintenance – or anything else.'

Sidney Templeton shifted his bulk and looked sideways at the young Lord Wymark as though to sympathize with him. He sensed that Elliot was taking some pleasure in rubbing him up the wrong way, almost as though Elliot was speaking on behalf of his late client, the previous Lord Wymark.

Rupert spoke quietly, containing his anger. 'I was quite well aware of what you have just said before you said it. I think it would be more constructive if we moved on to a more telling aspect of the case. It strikes me as quite wrong that a title can be divorced from lands and property, although I am aware that it does happen quite frequently. In taking the steps he did two years ago, that was certainly not my father's intention.'

Hugo nodded.

'What you may not appreciate, Mr Elliot, is that this great house has now passed into the hands of a woman who has clearly stated on more than one occasion since her husband's death that she has not the slightest intention of ever setting foot in it again. What I would appreciate from you – and, failing it, I will not hesitate to instruct other solicitors – is constructive advice as to how I can persuade Joanna to make the whole thing over to me.'

Before Elliot could come up with any sort of reply, Hugo exploded: 'This is quite ridiculous! How did we ever get in this mess? Elliot, you've got a lot to answer for.'

The solicitor signalled desperation.

'If I may come in here . . .' Templeton swayed into action, staring at his papers, though not reading from them. 'My understanding of the situation is that what Mr Elliot says, sir, is substantially correct. But you, sir' – wagging a finger at Rupert – 'are surely on to something, too. I can't imagine, from what I know of her, that the widow of the late Lord Wymark would want to assume responsibility for the estate, even if she were inclined actually to set foot in it.'

'Certainly not,' Hugo bristled. 'She's quite devastated. I should know; she's been living with us ever since it happened. She's vowed never to come anywhere near where Duncan was killed. I can't say I blame her.'

Elliot came back into the discussion.

'Forgive me for saying so, but that may only be a temporary state of mind. She might come round in the end. And again, possibly speaking out of turn, but you'll forgive me, she may not be interested in running – or even entering – the estate, but she might very well want the revenue from it. Widows do tend to.'

Hugo glowered but said nothing.

'We'll have to ask her to make her position clear, then,' said Rupert.

'Yes. She might make it over to you, particularly as you are obviously so keen to run it. But, if I may say so, would you do that if you were in her position? We're talking of something worth seventeen or eighteen million, after all.'

Rupert brushed his hand back and forth across his nose in a gesture he had copied from his father.

'Of course, you could be well out of it, my boy,' Hugo said. 'Nothing but trouble, all this. There's a lot to be said for being one of those life peers, you know. They don't have any of this agony. Look at my old friend

Toby Blair. He got one of those life jobs for lining the Tories' pockets and he's as happy as Larry. None of these problems for him!'

Rather quietly, Rupert replied – and it was the first time he had ever expressed the view in front of this father: 'Trouble is, I don't feel that way. Now that what's happened has happened, I feel that it should go on – the title and the land together, for as long as we can make them.'

Elliot and Templeton both drew themselves up simultaneously.

Rupert cut them short before they could speak. 'You don't have to say it. Unless I can persuade Joanna to give it all up, I'll have to go to court to get what I want. I'll do that, whatever the cost. And, if I get stuck, I'll have both of you up for giving such negligent advice to my father and Duncan.'

Templeton raised his eyebrows at the threat and Elliot soothed and smoothed. Hugo was impressed by Rupert's stand.

'I think there is only one way to proceed,' Elliot said, suddenly matter-of-fact. 'Unless Lady Joanna accedes to your request – and she would no doubt wish to have ample provision for herself and her daughters were she to do so – you will have to consider forming a trust to buy it from her. Or find some very rich investor to buy it and run it as a highly commercial concern – with perhaps you as tenant and manager.'

Rupert began to look more cheerful. With his background in venture capital, this was just the sort of proposal he could understand.

After another half-hour, the meeting broke up with all participants feeling a little more positive about what had to be done, if also conscious of the problems that lay ahead.

'Well, that's an idea, isn't?' Hugo said quite cheerily as they waved farewell to Elliot and Templeton and drove back to Huddleston.

'Mmm – but let's not mention it to Joanna just yet,' Rupert cautioned his father. 'I'll have to do a bit of digging around when I get back to London. See if anyone would be interested.'

'Mum's the word, then!' And Hugo appeared to put the matter right out of his mind, there and then.

Back home, he was more intent on taking a good look at his new grandson, indeed, at his first grandson. Nicholas was a delightful little fellow, with rather chubby cheeks – not looking particularly like either of his parents at this stage – but he had a good head of dark hair and a surprisingly firm grip with his tiny fingers. The little baby made the pain of recent weeks and the strong possibility of future agonies slightly more bearable.

Hugo held the baby and at once seemed a softer person than Jacky had ever seen him before. She could see that the baby would be what finally removed any doubts her father-in-law might have had about her marriage to Rupert. She truly hoped so.

Joanna hardly said a word during the family gathering and sat disconsolate, still mourning her husband.

'Now, what are you going to do about the house?' Hugo asked suddenly. Jacky wished that he hadn't, lest it upset Joanna. Rupert was confused as to what his father was talking about.

'Which one?' he asked, not sure whether Hugo was back to Castle Cansdale.

'Your one on the Thames. I suppose you'll want to keep it, whatever happens?'

Joanna glanced at her father-in-law, aware there was something afoot, but he didn't acknowledge the look. Nicholas chose that moment to put his perfectly-formed little fingers on the tip of his grandfather's distinguished nose and gurgled delightedly.

'Yes,' Rupert replied, somewhat hesitantly, not sure what to say in front of Joanna. 'But don't you think, with all the . . .?'

'All the what, Rupert?' prodded Hugo, only vaguely sensing the tension, and with his customary single-mindedness ignoring it.

With sudden firmness, the new Lord Wymark replied, 'You're right, we will need a London house whatever happens, now that we've got Nicholas. So that's that.'

Jacky decided it was time to relieve Hugo of Nicholas, hoping that Rupert would take the hint that it was time for them to be going.

'We'll need to have a little chat,' Rupert finally said to Joanna, when the homeward move was announced. 'Please give me a ring if I can be of any help meanwhile . . .'

Molly, who had remained silent for most of their visit, kissed Rupert, Jacky and Nicholas goodbye, but did not accompany Hugo to their car.

'Can I say something?' asked Hugo, just as they were about to drive off.

Jacky got into the car with the baby, and turned towards Hugo, wondering what it could be.

Hugo swallowed and went on: 'You are a wonderful girl, Jacky. Your joining us is one of the few things that's gone right for the family lately. I really am glad. So I don't want you to feel that we don't appreciate – Molly and I, that is – appreciate what you mean to us, and to Rupert, of course. I know we get things wrong as a family. I bear a hell of a lot of the blame for the mistakes, and for the terrible things that have happened. You must sometimes wonder what on earth you've let yourself in for by marrying into us! But that's it, my dear – I'm afraid you're one of us now. Whatever misfortunes come our way, come your way, too. I do hope you understand.'

Jacky nodded, but did not have the courage to speak. She knew it was true, of course, what Hugo had just said, she had always known it, but she was touched that he had taken the trouble to express it.

'Your mummy and daddy all right, are they?'

'Oh, yes,' said Jacky, surprised that the old Earl should be interested. 'Well enough, you know . . .'

'Good!'

And that seemed to be the limit of Hugo's interest. Rupert started the car and pointed it in the direction of home.

He felt guilty about having taken a whole day off work to deal with pressing family business. Fortunately, the firm was so delighted to have a real live lord on its payroll that it had made him a director; it was busy having new letterheads printed to reflect Rupert's changed status. That was the world into which his half-brother's death had pitchforked him.

The miasma of legal, dynastic and taxation complications at times threatened to engulf the Hooke family over the following months. There was no chance of anything being resolved quickly – or, indeed, in the foreseeable future. It was as if everything was for the worst in the worst of all possible worlds.

The person who had that thought – and did not share it with anyone else, because he had no one to share it with – was Uncle Alec. Excluded from consultation on the important issues facing the family, he also had a rather more pressing worry. With Duncan gone, so presumably was any hope of continued employment as Castle Cansdale's archivist, historian, and general good chap to have about the place.

His innocent pleasure with a tart had more or less deposited him back where he started – not knowing where the next few thousand was coming from. Alec had received all kinds of assurances that his media appearances would not suffer as a result of what had happened. Quite the reverse: that sort of fame was good for business – increased the viewing figures, and all that. But the weeks passed. The invitations dried up. There was no talk now of a second series of *An Englishman's Castle*. The telephone fell silent.

And there was something else. He had lost access to his one great love: Castle Cansdale. They said it would be open to the public again shortly, but no longer would he be able to go there and potter among the papers and books in the Gold Library. With all the doubt over ownership, he did not even know to whom to apply for permission to visit and he didn't like to ask, in the circumstances. He was at a complete loose end – until, that is, he developed another obsession.

Uncle Alec knew the importance of obsessions – how life was a poor thing without them. It seemed he was no longer to be allowed his sexual obsession. His great love, the family seat, was no longer available to him. What he must do was find something else to absorb him – for what else did he have to do with his time? What other reason did he have to live?

The new obsession was ready-made – staring him in the face – and was what all his thoughts returned to now, anyway. He was going to find out how Duncan had come to be killed. Was the guilty person really a burglar? Alec found that hard to believe. There must have been some other reason. But the police were incompetent – or put on a very good impersonation of it. They hadn't found out who had killed poor Duncan, they hadn't recovered the stolen goods, and they'd made a pig's ear of solving the previous robbery. The silver had been recovered, yes, but they hadn't managed to pull in the thieves.

One evening after he had dined alone in a rather too expensive restaurant near his South Audley Street flat, Alec returned and was suddenly struck by the emptiness of his desk. Only a few months ago it had been piled with files and books. He had been in the thick of activity; now there was nothing. Then something pulled at his memory. Perhaps it was the light – the way the light fell on the table. He found that visual similarities often triggered thoughts about past times and places. But he could not work out what it was. He picked up a proof copy of the full-length book he had written on the history of Castle Cansdale. He was unspeakably proud of it and couldn't wait for it to be published. He flicked through the elegantly designed pages and experienced a warm feeling of satisfaction. Then he looked at the pictures – including ones of Hugo and Molly, Duncan and Joanna. That made him sad. He turned to Barry's plan of the house which was being used as the front and back endpapers of the book.

Then it came to him. The original of the plan, the one that had gone missing, he'd shown it to Jacky's father and brother that time they'd unexpectedly come to see him. They had shown an interest in it. Perhaps they could throw some light on its whereabouts. Yes, a strange visit – he had never been quite sure why they had taken the trouble to talk to him. Hadn't they made him some kind of promise? That if he was ever under any pressure from the press they would protect him? A preposterous suggestion, but hadn't they left him a number he could call them on?

Freddie Moore at last managed to find out where his son had been living since the impetuous walk-out from Dorset Avenue. It didn't take long for a man with Freddie's contacts to find out these things, and, as soon as he had the address, he drove straight over to sort Mark out.

The chief surprise Freddie faced was finding a woman answering the door to the maisonette in Peckham.

'Who the bleeding hell are you?' he asked.

'Might ask the same,' was all the reply he got. It wasn't so much a woman as a girl. A bit punky, Freddie thought – all matt black leather, white skin, and not very appetizing. Mark must be out of his mind.

'Is he in then?'

'Who d'you mean?'

'Don't give me that, girl. My boy – Mark, where is he? And don't mess me about.'

'I dunno.'

'Well, tell him to ring his dad,' he told her. 'It's very urgent, see. Got that? Urgent.'

Freddie went away, completely unimpressed that Mark was – in one respect at least – displaying signs of normality. Getting himself a girl at long last was a fairly natural thing to do if he had made a bit of money for himself out of the Cansdale job. But Freddie wished he'd chosen . . . well, somebody more like what he himself would have chosen.

At least she passed on his message, though it wasn't until the evening that Mark came on the phone. His father went straight to the point.

'You've left your shirt hangin' out, boy – know that?'

'How? What d'you mean?'

'That Alec geezer we went to see. Remember? Randy Uncle Alec? Well, he's been on to me. Can't find his map of the castle. Wants to know if we knows what might have happened to it. Well?'

'Well?'

'Well bleedin' what, you dick-head? You half-inched it from him, didn't you? And don't you see? If he starts gabbing you had some – let's face it – pretty unusual interest in the old place, it could lead back to you, boy.'

'No, it won't. They'll think he's ga-ga – like he is.'

'No, they won't, son. Like I said, your tail's hangin' out. Want to get done for blagging his lordship? You'd better put your skates on, sonny boy. Do something about it.'

'What, for Christ's sake?'

'That's your pigeon. You're the big-time ponce now, ain't you? You sort it out.'

Freddie hung up by chucking one part of the phone against the other.

Mark turned and looked away from the girl friend who'd been listening to him. He wasn't able to confide in her, and certainly not about this. His first thought was that he'd have to pay another visit to South Audley Street and knock old Alec Hooke about a bit.

# CHAPTER 32

Rupert and Jacky's new house on Castle Wharf wasn't quite the total delight it could have been. Rupert still felt uneasy about the amount of Freddie Moore's money there was in the property. It wasn't like having a building society loan when you could pretend the house was all yours, even if it wasn't; it was more personal than that. The money meant that the spirit of Rupert's father-in-law seemed resident inside the front door.

Apart from which, Jacky had the full-time job of looking after Nicholas, who was every bit as demanding of her attention and time as anybody else's first baby. She hadn't begun to think of making herself presentable for the cameras once more. Indeed, she wasn't totally sure she ever would be.

And then there were the builders and decorators. Although the house had had only one owner before Rupert and Jacky, almost every room needed something done to it and there was no option but to have the work done around them.

Short tempers were the order of the day. Jacky felt tied down by the constant attention demanded by Nicholas; Rupert tended to brood as soon as he returned from the office, without always saying what he was worried about. It wasn't hard to guess, however.

'Guess what's happened now?' Rupert suddenly asked on one such evening. 'Merrilee Bridgewater's back on the warpath.'

'Duncan's friend? Back where?'

'Started making waves. I thought the boy had all been taken care of. Duncan made a financial settlement on him, but now his mother's after a share of the estate.'

'Greedy old cow! What about the girls? They ought to come first.'

'Well, so they should. Duncan left the estate to Joanna with the provision that it should be shared equally between Josephina and the other two when their mother died. But the boy could have a claim. She's after a quarter share.'

'But that's ridiculous!'

'I know. I've been on to a solicitor who knows about these things (anything to avoid Hugo's old has-been) and he says the lad's in with a chance. It's unlikely he'd get a quarter. His settlement has to be taken into account. But what it all means, my darling, is that she'll probably go to court for a ruling. This one'll run for ever and ever, I'm afraid.'

'Why *did* you have to be related to Duncan?' Jacky asked only half-seriously.

'And why are you your father's daughter? Sorry, that's unkind. Duncan still manages to shaft everybody, even from the other side of the grave. Did you ever meet anyone so catastrophic?'

Jacky did not bother to respond to the rhetorical question. The bonus of marrying into a titled, landed family, as she had done, was more than balanced by its disadvantages. She was beginning to hate the whole business. And besides, being able to call herself Lady Wymark was already losing its charm. She couldn't take it seriously. She didn't *feel* like a lady.

'It's all down to Father in the end,' Rupert went on, to get it all off his chest for the hundredth time. 'If he hadn't shilly-shallied over sorting out the estate, this would never have happened. And if he'd got the proper legal advice, we wouldn't be fucked from here to kingdom come.'

Jacky carefully placed baby Nicholas in his cot and hoped he would sleep. Then she went and sat by her husband and took his hand. She hadn't anticipated this doomed tone of Rupert's. The soothing had some effect: he became less tense.

'Perhaps it doesn't matter if we don't get the castle,' Jacky ventured gently. 'After all, it's only since Duncan died there's been the possibility. Before that, we hadn't a chance.'

Rupert noticed the 'we', but didn't say anything.

'And if it's going to be such a terrible burden, we'd be better off here, in our own little place.'

'But I'd always dreamed of it! And then to have it snatched away by Duncan's deliberate act – *and* the solicitor's incompetence – it's hard to take.'

Jacky held his hand very tight.

'And I suppose the rest's a worry, too,' she suggested, understandingly.

'What rest?'

'The robberies. And the way Duncan died. I can't believe it'll ever be cleared up, can you?'

'Left to the police, no. They really are hopeless. Still, you never know what Uncle Alec'll turn up!'

'What's he got to do with it?'

'Turned detective. Thinks he's Sherlock Holmes, or something. Rang me at the office. Wanted to ask me a tricky question, so he said.'

'What about?'

'Freddie and Mark.'

Jacky coloured. A feeling had grown upon her, before this, that in the tragedies of Castle Cansdale there was something for which she was somehow to blame. She did not know what it was. But she sensed that her joining the Hooke family had precipitated these disasters.

She hardly managed to speak the words, 'What've Dad and Mark to do with Uncle Alec?'

'Apparently they went to see him – before all this happened – at the end of last year.'

Then Jacky remembered. At the family gathering after the old Countess's funeral, Alec had mentioned the visit. She'd been too upset by Duncan's taunts about her father to take it in properly. Alec had also said something about chatting to Mark and Freddie about architecture. Jacky's feeling of foreboding grew.

'As Uncle Alec tells it,' Rupert went on, 'it was just after the trouble he'd had with the papers. They seemed to be offering him some sort of "protection". If he had any more trouble from the press, they'd sort it out for him.'

Jacky coloured even deeper. It sounded all too like Freddie.

'And did they – you know – help him?' she asked apprehensively.

'He didn't ask them to, of course. But he's just realized, after they'd gone there was a plan missing from his flat. He thinks they must have taken it.'

That explained the chat about 'architecture'. Jacky felt close to tears. She asked, 'What kind of plan?' – already anticipating the answer.

'Of the castle. A very old one.' Rupert didn't look at her, and tried not to put too meaningful a tone into saying, 'Might have been useful for anyone wanting to get in.'

Jacky couldn't hold back the tears any longer; they poured down her cheeks.

'Are you thinking what I'm thinking?' she sobbed.

Now it was Rupert's turn to take her hands in his.

'I'm trying not to think at all, darling. It doesn't bear thinking about, does it?'

Jacky was still stoically refusing to use a handkerchief or a tissue, as though this would admit she was crying. The large tears dropped in spots on the wool of her dress like the start of heavy rain on a summer's day.

*   *   *

Next morning, Jacky cut a very different figure – of determination and resolve. With Nicholas safely strapped in the baby seat of the car, Jacky was driving from Docklands to Essex to visit Dorset Avenue.

Cynthia greeted her with happy surprise but as soon as the pleasantries about the baby were over, Jacky made it clear she had other things on her mind.

'Where's Dad? Is he in?' she asked.

'I think he's in his den, dear.'

'I want a word with him. Here, you look after Nicky for me.'

Freddie didn't have time even to begin his usual 'darling daughter' greetings. Jacky slammed the door behind her and parked herself on the paper-strewn desk where he was working. He was forced to give her his full attention.

'Now, look,' she began, nerves clutching her throat, 'no beating about the bush, right? I want you to tell me: what's been going on between you and Mark and Rupert's people? 'Cos, if there is anything, you've really landed me in it. I tried to keep you away from them – that's why we got married like we did. But you can never leave anything alone, can you?'

Freddie stayed seated – which was unusual enough. His way of dealing with any challenge was always to bounce up and start moving about. But Jacky's position on the edge of his desk kept him pinned to his seat. He didn't start hurling abuse either, which was his customary way of dealing with anybody who put him on the spot. For what seemed like an age, he gave no answer to the question. He looked Jacky in the eye, then looked away again.

'So, you think there's been something going on, do you?' he said at last, quite quietly for him. It was out of character for Freddie to be in awe of any woman, let alone his own daughter.

'Look, I bloody *know* there's been something going on. I don't know what exactly, but I get the stink of it, whatever it is. Trust you to start meddling, Dad – and risk spoiling all I have with Rupert and the baby. How *could* you be so stupid?'

Freddie played it very cool – and coolness had never been his primary characteristic.

'Just get off my desk, Jacks, and sit yourself down on that chair. Okay?'

Slowly, Jacky did as she was bid by her father. Then Freddie stood up and addressed her from a position of height.

'I don't know what's been going on, either,' he began. Jacky was sure it was a lie. Something had been going on – in which case he must surely know about it. After all, her father's favourite boast was that he knew what was going on, knew everyone, was always in touch.

322

'Don't believe you, Dad. You and Mark's been up to something, haven't you?'

'Thank you, Lady-fucking-Wymark,' he said, with a sneer. 'No, we haven't.' He corrected himself: 'Least, *I've* not been doing nothing. You'd better talk to Mark. He doesn't live here any more, that's why I'm not speaking for him. If I ever did.'

'Not here any more? Where is he then?' Jacky snapped.

Freddie told her about Mark's new flat. He gave her the address, as she was so insistent, and warned her about the punk girl friend she'd probably find there.

Her mother was left looking after Nicky while Jacky drove west into the real East End, clutching her *A to Z*. The chances of Mark's actually being at home when she reached his flat didn't bother her. Nor did the prospect of his girl friend – and what a surprise that was – opening the door. She was in such an indignant rage that nothing would stop her from getting to the bottom of the business, however long it took.

In fact, the door of the flat was opened by Mark himself. One look at Jacky's eyes told him what he was in for and he backed away, quite unable to deter her.

'Take no notice of that,' Mark gestured to the sleeping form of his punk girl friend. 'She's well away.'

So, indeed, she looked. Jacky wondered if she was on drugs. Whatever it was, she was dead to the world.

'Dad said I had to talk to you.' Jacky came straight to the point. 'I don't know what you've been up to, but I've got a bloody good idea.'

Mark looked as if he was going to play the sullen card, but his eyes gave him away. They swivelled, as though he was consciously remembering to act the innocent.

'What you been doing then?' Jacky demanded, never so beautiful as when angry.

Unexpectedly, Mark didn't deny anything. He took a different tack.

'One thing at a time,' he said, using his hands in a way that mirrored one of his father's favourite gestures.

Jacky noticed a gold bracelet on his left wrist. So Mark *had* undergone a big change recently. Once upon a time he would never have worn anything like that.

'You took that plan off Uncle Alec, didn't you?' Jacky persisted. 'Stole it off him, didn't you? There's no point in saying you didn't. Everybody knows about it – the police, everybody. They'll have you in in no time at all. You silly bugger, Mark.'

'That old fart,' Mark muttered. 'What's he know?'

'He knows you and Dad went to see him, took his plan of the castle, and

323

next thing it's robbed and Duncan dead. How do you think it looks? And how d'you think it looks for *me*? I'm married to Rupert, you know – if you hadn't noticed. How d'you think I feel if my kid brother's got mixed up in all that? Why did you do it, Mark? Are you nuts or something?'

Mark looked at the sleeping form of his girl friend as though hoping she couldn't hear.

'I want you to tell me straight,' Jacky insisted before Mark had had time to start talking. 'You bloody owe it me, don't you?'

Her brother made no sign of acknowledging that obligation, but started on another tack.

'I want you to know,' he said, conceding a little at last, 'that Dad had nothing to do with it. Got that? Dad had nothing to do with it. It was my show, right?'

Jacky nodded. There was a kind of relief in knowing that. She'd been a little hard on him earlier. There was no reason to doubt Mark. If he said it, it must be so.

'And the other thing,' Mark went on, 'is whatever else I done, I didn't have anything to do with . . . the dead man. Nothing at all, you hear? I didn't even set eyes on him.'

Jacky said nothing, but allowed the words gradually to seep in. This was encouraging, and she could surely rely on her brother to tell her the truth. He might have been a fool, he might have lied to his father and mother, but he wouldn't lie to her. He never had, in all their childhood together – and besides, if he did, she would know.

'You went to the castle, though. With anybody else?'

'No, no one. I did it on my own. I think I chose the wrong day . . .'

'You can say that again. And you knew I was there?'

'Yes. I got the date off you. Remember?'

Jacky gave an exasperated sigh. 'What've you done with the stuff?'

Mark looked as if he was going to clam up.

'I mean, if you've still got it, there might be a way to give it back to them . . .'

It was a forlorn hope.

'It's all gone, been got rid of.'

'Even the picture?'

'The Rembrandt, you mean? No. No takers for that.'

'You've still got it then?'

There was a long silence. Finally Mark asked, rather sheepishly, 'You going to shop me, then?'

'No,' said Jacky, and for a few seconds Mark was filled with the innocent hope that if she wasn't going to shop him, he would be all right. And then she demolished his hope with a few more words.

'No, *I* won't split on you. Don't need to. They'll be on to you without anything from me. I just had to find out for myself. Satisfy myself you'd been as bloody foolish as I thought you had. How will I ever be able to go into that family with my head up, after what you've done? How *could* you, Mark?!' The last words were delivered in a high shriek of exasperation.

Jacky picked up her handbag, turned away from Mark and stepped briskly out of his flat.

Mark saw that she was different from the 'sis' he had grown up with. Wasn't she a 'lady' now? It showed. She was one of *them* – one of that other, contemptible, lot.

Mark stood looking at the sleeping form of his crashed-out girl friend and tried to tell himself that all was not lost. There must be a way to fend off the inevitable. If only he'd moved more quickly over that stupid Uncle Alec. It should have been possible to silence the old bugger, even if he'd had to take him out.

Jacky, as she had said, didn't go to the police. She was not a member of the Moore family for nothing. But seldom can loyalties have conflicted in a person as much as they did in her.

That evening, she told Rupert what had happened – and found she had already been proved right. She wouldn't have to shop Mark. He'd given himself away.

'Well, I had a caller today, at the office,' he told her simply. 'Police-man – sent round by the Craswall lot. That's the way they seem to work – get local bobbies to make their calls for them. Anyway, it was a simple matter. There's a firm called Manorial who did the security system at the castle. When they heard about the robbery – and, after all, it's in their interest to be squeaky clean – they did a check. One of their salesman remembered a man coming in to look at cameras who mentioned Cansdale. Can you guess what his name was?'

Jacky didn't dare.

' "Rupert Hooke" – he used my name.'

Jacky's mouth fell open. 'So they came to you?'

'Yes, one of the Craswall police was, apparently, bright enough to realize who I was, and make the connection, but he knew I wasn't the man in the photograph.'

'What photograph?'

'Ah, you see, Manorial, being a security firm, know a thing or two. They have these cameras in their own offices, connected to videos. Anyone who visits the showroom gets filmed automatically. Didn't take them long to winkle out a picture of . . . well, you can guess who.'

'You told them who it was?'

'Of course.'

325

'He says he didn't kill Duncan. I believe him.'

'I'd like to believe him, too. But even if he didn't, he'll most likely get done for it, won't he?'

Joanna gradually began to get over what had happened to Duncan. She came to realize she couldn't spend the rest of her life grieving over someone she had only intermittently loved anyway. It seemed such a pointless thing to do. The girls were now back at school, which helped a lot. The temporary quarters they occupied at Huddleston were less crowded, and less of a hotbed of fetid, female emotion. Joanna was, however, still sticking to her resolve not to set foot in Castle Cansdale again. This was a curious position to maintain, Hugo and Molly felt, given that she, by fortune's whim, had become its owner.

But no, she simply could not face the thought of going back to that grim dungeon, as she perceived it, and so a plan formed in her mind to take one of the houses on the Hooke estate – a property sufficiently large to contain herself and the three girls until they left home.

Drew Elliot began to put the plan into action. Almost all of Joanna's clothes and possessions were now in store pending the completion of the deal. Nothing of her or Duncan or the girls remained at Castle Cansdale. Lopez, in his last act as butler, had supervised the retrieval of all this property. He had then relinquished his post with a pension – also arranged by Mr Elliot – and moved into a cottage which he shared with Mrs Powers who was still Hugo and Molly's housekeeper.

Joanna, although she had not taken any interest in the running of the Hooke estate before Duncan's death, now began to put her mind to it. In this she was helped by Colin Blakiston, the land agent, and by Hugo – who felt obliged to sort out some of the mess. She began to look forward to the start of the hunting season in the winter, even if it did earn her the soubriquet of the 'Hunting Widow'. She was determined not to let anyone keep her from her only remaining pleasure.

Still, there was no very clear indication from her of what would happen to the Hooke estate in the long term. Hugo, with rather more delicacy than he had used in such matters when the house and lands belonged to him, was the first to encourage her to resolve the matter. There were times during the long legal proceedings when he felt himself to be directing his own posterity. It was odd, having unburdened himself of the responsibility a year or two previously, to have the reins almost back in his hands once more.

'You know, Joanna, I'm an old man, keen on tradition – at least, when it comes to the big house,' Hugo explained. 'I respect your position, even though of course the way things have turned out the house cannot descend as it should, hand in hand with the title, down the male line.'

Joanna shot him a suspicious glance, wondering where this was taking them.

'Ideally, I'd like to see Rupert have it eventually. He'll have the title when I'm gone. And I think he ought to have the house to go with it. Besides, he actually likes the house. So, as you don't want to live there, there are two things you could do with it. You could allow Rupert to live there as what they call tenant for life. That means, he would be responsible for running it, until such time as he goes. Then it would revert to whoever else you nominate in your will. Or, and I'm bound to say I prefer this option, you could sell the estate outright to a trust or, though I'm not so keen, a commercial enterprise. Then they could nominate Rupert and Jacky as tenants. How does that strike you?'

'Who would the trustees be? They'd have to find a penny or two.'

'Rupert's into all that kind of thing. I'm sure he'd raise the money, even though it'd be millions, as you know.'

It didn't take long for Joanna to agree with her father-in-law that the idea of selling the whole white elephant, as she saw it, was by far the best thing – even if it might mean Castle Cansdale's long history in the Hooke family coming to an end. She did not want the place; she might as well have the millions for herself in her widowhood; and she sensed the rightness of providing a way for Rupert to live in a house he had always wanted – if that way could be found.

There was still the matter of the claim from Duncan's illegitimate son – or rather from Mr and Mrs Bridgewater – but no doubt a relatively small sum of money, as agreed in court, could buy a way out of that little difficulty. And so it would transpire.

The way was thus made clear for the future of Castle Cansdale, and having overcome the potential hurdle of Joanna's opposition, Hugo felt he had pulled off quite a coup. Furthermore, he had in a sense redeemed himself for the mess he had made by procrastinating on the previous occasion the future of the estate had been raised.

Rupert duly began looking in earnest for investors willing to put up the necessary millions to buy the estate from Joanna. This meant that, with luck, he and Jacky could one day be installed as tenants of the castle. It would not belong to them; they would be tenants only at the invitation of whatever trust or commercial interest bought the estate; but that was the only way.

It was during a meeting at Huddleston when Joanna was having to sign some papers under Drew Elliot's direction that Rupert raised the embarrassing subject of Mark Moore's arrest. He had been charged with committing the robbery on the night of Duncan's murder. Police hinted that other charges might follow.

'Jacky's quite devastated,' Rupert said. 'But I keep telling her, she can't be blamed for what her family gets up to, any more than I can for mine.'

'I could tell they were a bad lot,' Hugo said, 'soon as I set eyes on 'em. But I'm not going to say I told you so, because Jacky's a dear girl, and little Nicky's a dear too. We just have to close our eyes to the rest of them.'

'Thank you, Father. And I'm deeply sorry, Joanna, there's the slightest hint of Mark's having anything to do with Duncan's death. We can't believe he killed him. We'll just have to see what the police come up with.'

Joanna had clammed up at this mention of the forbidden subject. She gave a tight-lipped smile and looked away.

Hugo valiantly tried to change the subject and called for a drink. Drew Elliot continued to play a largely mute role in the proceedings and Molly, wishing to avoid calling in Mrs Powers, wheeled over the drinks trolley herself.

At the beginning of August, just over three months after Duncan's death, Hugo and Molly drove past the ornamental gates of Castle Cansdale down by the South Lodge and allowed themselves a brief glimpse of the noble pile shimmering a mile away in the rare sunlight of an English summer.

After all the gloom of the previous weeks – which might now, it seemed, be swept away – Hugo and Molly had revived their plans, long postponed, for a holiday in Sicily and were on their way to Heathrow airport.

Having all but settled, as Hugo thought, the one great issue in his life, there was still the unfinished business that drew him once more back to Sicily. As he never stopped reminding Molly, it was fifty-two years to the month since he had last set foot on the island. There were many things he had forgotten about the island – some, too, that he had chosen to forget – but he knew that it was going to be very, very hot.

# CHAPTER 33

Since being released from goal in Reggio at the beginning of the year, Benino Noto had been back home in Palermo carrying on very much as he had always done. Alvaro was far from pleased. Though making the regular trips to Reggio had been a chore, it was even more of a burden having his father back in town once more.

It was quite some time after he came out of prison that Benino demanded to know what had happened to the English contract. Messages were sent; more pressure applied.

Then at the end of April: 'I have just heard, Father,' Alvaro announced, 'it has been carried out. Lord Wymark is dead.'

There was no response from his adoptive father.

Alvaro went on: 'There was some trouble with the sleeper in London. He didn't have the experience. The English are very old-fashioned about guns. He had difficulty in obtaining one. Pietro Bonfiglioni had to find him one in the end.'

Benino gestured disbelief. 'What kind of country is it where you cannot get a gun? It is not like America.'

Alvaro shook his head. 'I believe not. But our man took him in hand.'

'Who is that again?'

'Pietro Bonfiglioni. He had to give Corsini a warning. He has a restaurant in London. He had to be told what might happen to it if he failed.'

'So, it is all done then? Honour has been satisfied?'

'Yes, Father.'

Benino gave no sign, but he felt deep satisfaction that the old score had at last been settled. His mind would be freer now to concentrate on the bloody chaos that still engulfed the West Sicilian Mafia in the wake of the 1987 convictions.

'Will you tell Mother?' Alvaro asked.

'No. You tell her. She will not understand anyway, being a woman.'
'I think she will, Father.'

Hugo and Molly were unable to fly direct from London to Palermo; they had to change planes in Rome. The couple of hours' wait at Leonardo da Vinci airport soon had Hugo restless and irritable, with Molly, as ever, doling out the soothing balm. It was a wonder she never exhausted her supply.

At Palermo airport, Hugo stood out from among the people in the small dark crowd, his aristocratic bearing and tweedy clothes unmistakably marking him out as a Britisher abroad in the ninety-degree heat. He did not like the Lancia the hire firm had provided for him, simply on the grounds that it was not the same as the car he was used to driving at home.

'It wasn't like this last time,' he rumbled. 'Brought the Alvis all the way, we did.'

'I suppose we're going to hear a lot about *last time*,' Molly commented, rather more waspishly than she usually said such things. 'Just remember it's my *first*, that's all.'

Hugo never rose to challenges like these, whoever they came from, and simply told his wife she would have to do the driving as he didn't feel quite up to it. So Molly gripped the wheel and they hurtled off along the *autostrada* in the direction of Palermo.

As they approached the centre of the Sicilian capital, Hugo unbent sufficiently to compliment Molly on the way she had adapted to Italian driving techniques. The chief thing, it appeared, was to keep moving, never to stop. If you were joining a main road or entering a roundabout, you had to keep up speed in the confident assumption that other drivers would allow you to merge in with them. Molly took to all this with alarming enthusiasm, and Hugo kept his eyes closed when he should have been reading the map.

Then they found themselves stuck in slow-moving traffic that was negotiating a fair. Molly was getting hotter and hotter, coming to terms with an unfamiliar car. Hugo was being his usual self trying to read the map. Heaven knows how he'd ever managed in the army.

At last they located the narrow road that shot up from the harbour through a rather squalid part of Palermo, and spotted the gates of the Hotel La Torre. Molly abandoned the car under the porch and all but threw the keys at the porter, telling him to park it for them.

A manager in a frock coat bowed deeply before *milord inglese* and with an imperious wave at his minions led Hugo and Molly along immense corridors towards their suite in the tower.

Little had changed since Hugo's last visit. The atmosphere, which

Molly considered Mussolini-esque, remained the same. As they followed the manager, who was gesturing incomprehensibly at features on the walls, memories dimly pricked at Hugo's mind.

Once in the tower room, Hugo went straight to the window and opened it. A noise of chuggings and bangings wafted up from the harbour below – vastly more busy than he could remember. Immediately below, he saw those half-dozen pillars held together with iron hoops – remains of an ancient civilization but now, rather forlornly providing the background for a swimming pool and drinks terrace.

Then he looked down at the garden. He knew what it meant to him. That was not why he had come back, but it was a potent memory – and not one he had shared with Molly.

They dined at the hotel that night, on the terrace, with the stars twinkling brightly above. Distantly, on the hills across the harbour, they watched car headlights flashing back and forth as their drivers twisted and turned up steep roads.

'I like it very much,' said Molly. 'I really do. Thank you, Hugo, for suggesting it.'

'Ah, yes,' Hugo replied, and gently touched her hand with his.

They spent three days pottering about, but chiefly sitting in the sun by the pool. Molly loved it. Her idea of heaven was reading a book in the sun by a pool, but Hugo – who had never been a reader, and who was always cautious about exposing himself to the sun – soon became bored.

Their next stop was the Villa Politi in Siracusa – a hotel to which Winston Churchill had come to paint and to lick his wounds after the 1945 election defeat – but it was clearly not what it had been. It came as a relief when once more they packed and transferred to the San Domenico Palace at Taormina for another few days.

At last they reached Agrigento, towards the southern coast, and booked into a hotel, the Villa Athena, which had a prime position looking across the row of ancient temples in the old city. It was here that Hugo became his brisker, younger self once more. He had come armed with maps and documents on the Allied landings of 1943. The local mayor was alerted to the presence of the eminent Englishman and, as he was unable to speak Hugo's language, handed him on to a local schoolteacher and amateur historian.

In blistering heat, Hugo and Molly were taken to the old landing grounds and to several war cemeteries. But there was hardly a scrap of evidence of what had taken place almost half a century before on the beaches; in not one of the dusty rolls of war dead was there any mention of the whereabouts of Richard Giles Cansdale, 7th Earl Hooke.

To Molly's surprise, Hugo quickly began to concede that his quest was in vain and that his father's grave, if he had ever had one, would never be found. He seemed at last to accept that he would never be able to bring back the body to Bourton Cansdale and commit it for burial in the Hooke chapel as he had always wanted.

The Sicilian schoolteacher was not going to be put off that easily, however. He said they might enlist the help of the newspapers, and a day or two later a short report of Hugo's quest, together with a picture of the '*Earl e Contessa di Hooke*', appeared. The report was picked up by one of the Palermo papers. But still no useful information was forthcoming.

It was time for Hugo and Molly to give up and drive over the mountains back to the capital, where they had arranged to spend a few more nights at the Hotel La Torre before flying home.

Benino Noto could not make it out. He stared at the newspaper, smoothed it out, strained his eyes to read it again. Still, he could make no sense of it. He sipped a coffee to clear his mind.

'My wife, come here,' he ordered Consiglia. His voice still contained the contempt he had extended to her for years.

Consiglia wearily stood up and walked over to the table where her husband sat.

'You read this to me. I cannot understand it.'

'I cannot read. You know that. Why do you humiliate me so?'

'But you can see a picture, can't you?'

Consiglia bent over the page of newspaper and stared hard. It meant nothing to her, this picture of a foreigner and his wife.

'It says this Englishman is looking for where his father was killed in the war. When the Americans and the English came here.'

Consiglia was not interested. Such matters were not for her.

'I cannot understand what this means,' Benino went on, ignoring her lack of interest. 'His name is Hooke, and yet it says he came here when he was young. In those days, it says, his name was Lord Wymark.'

Consiglia froze, looked at the picture again. Was it him? Was this the man she had known? It was impossible to tell. How could she remember what a man looked like after all these years?

And yet, and yet . . .

'If it is Lord Wymark, you know what that means?' Benino looked her in the eye – such a rare thing.

'It means Alvaro's father is still alive.'

'Yes,' her husband said, 'and it means the fool we employed killed the wrong man. I must speak to Alvaro'.

*      *      *

332

Next morning, a small blue Fiat slipped quietly into the car park of the Hotel La Torre. Alvaro Noto stepped out, his black suit creased, as ever. His information had been speedily acquired. It only took a phone call to find out where in the whole of Sicily a visitor was staying. Earl Hooke and his wife were back at the Hotel La Torre prior to flying home on the Saturday. Alvaro knew their ticket numbers, the details of their flight, and even the registration number of their hire car.

He wanted to take a look at the man for himself. Benino was right. There was no doubt about it. They had all been confused by these strange English lords and their titles. Earl Hooke was the Lord Wymark who had stayed in Palermo in 1938. He was the man who had dishonoured Consiglia and who was therefore Alvaro's actual father. That Corsini was an imbecile.

If Alvaro could understand it, Corsini had killed this Earl Hooke's son. An innocent victim, but there it was. There had been many such over the years. Now they would have to kill again to honour the code, and this time they would have to be sure of their victim.

For anyone but Alvaro, or perhaps for anyone but a Sicilian, it would have been a strange feeling to set eyes on his natural father for the first time. Like an adoptive child finding his true parent after many years, it should have produced a bewildering variety of emotions. But it did not.

Alvaro was curious about his father, to be sure, but it was as though he was deficient when it came to feeling emotion. He felt more intensely what this man had meant to his mother. How he had ruined her life, reduced her to a form of slavery in marriage to Benino. This Earl Hooke was probably totally unaware what havoc he had caused.

Alvaro walked confidently into the lobby of the hotel. He knew no one would challenge him. They knew who he was. He walked down the steps from the lobby to the garden where his mother had been ruined all that time ago. He wanted to see if he could spot the Englishman by the pool. If he could not, he would have to go to more elaborate lengths to identify him – find out his room number, knock on his door, all that kind of thing.

He was in luck. A cursory glance round the people sunning themselves at the side of the pool soon revealed what he had been looking for. An elderly, rather white, English-looking man – clearly the man in the newspaper photograph – was sitting on a sunbed reading *The Times*. Beside him was an elderly woman, perhaps not quite so old. They were the pair.

Alvaro sat down on a low wall by the pool and stared across at them. It was as if there was nothing linking them to him. Perhaps he did look a little like the Englishman. But he felt no bond. It was all a question of semen. Semen transferred from one body to another. Emotion did not come into it. He was curious – my God, was he curious! – but he felt nothing more.

For twenty minutes, half an hour, Alvaro watched the lord and his lady from behind his dark glasses. The age was about right. If the lord had dishonoured Consiglia in 1938, he must have been about twenty then. Now he looked over seventy. That fitted.

Alvaro moved nearer. Still no one around the pool gave any sign that they had noticed him although he was the only one in sight who was fully clothed – in a dark suit, too. He wondered whether the wife would go away – perhaps take a swim in the pool – but there seemed no chance of any movement. She was absorbed in a book. Maybe she was not the swimming sort.

Alvaro knew that this time he must do the deed himself. But first his mother must view the man who had dishonoured her fifty years before. There was an element of mawkishness in the idea, but only she could positively identify him, and there must be no mistake this time.

Alvaro had to pull himself away from the almost magnetic force that drew his eyes to every move that Hugo made. He wanted to confront the aristocrat, tell him what he'd done to his mother, let him know he had an Italian son and that honour must be restored. But not now. Not yet.

Alvaro left the pool area as unobtrusively as he had arrived. At the hotel desk the clerk confirmed that the *milord inglese* would not be leaving until the day after tomorrow. So the Earl was a sitting target. All was well.

Next morning, the blue Fiat once more pulled up in the hotel car park. Alvaro Noto emerged quickly, looked around him instinctively, and held open the door for his mother to get out. She was impressed, knowing how this courtesy would never have been extended to her by Benino. Then Alvaro took Consiglia by the hand and walked her through the hotel and out into the garden.

Alvaro was gratified to find that Hugo and Molly were once more installed by the side of the pool. Hugo was again absorbed by the airmail edition of *The Times*. Molly was reading a new detective novel. Alvaro did not take Consiglia anywhere near the pool. Although he might just have blended in, even when wearing his dark crushed suit, there was no way his mother could, wearing her dark Sicilian clothes – like a peasant widow. They stood instead over by the ancient columns.

'Well, Mother, can you see? The man by the sun umbrella that's open. Is it he?'

Consiglia strained her eyes.

'Yes, that is the man in the photograph.'

'No, Mother – that is not important. Is it the man who dishonoured you?'

Consiglia nodded perfunctorily. There was no doubt. The broken nose, the eyes, the bearing – everything. And she did not mind. What had happened had happened so many long years ago. What was the point of being vengeful? It was one of those things.

'Would you like to talk to him?' Alvaro asked.

'No, my child, it does not matter. I would not have anything to say.'

'But he might – you know – he might have something to say to you.'

'No, my child. If you must do what you plan, it should be done – with no more heartache for me, please.' It was apparent that Consiglia was now resigned to the killing of the Englishman.

'I understand, Mother.'

He held Consiglia by the arm and led her away, but he took her round by the pool on the Earl's side. As they passed, the Earl looked up from his paper. The sun was in his eyes and he could not see either of the two people going by. Molly's eyes were glued to her book.

'They do not know you,' Alvaro muttered.

'It is not surprising.'

'I suppose not,' said Alvaro. He guided her away, through the hotel and back to the car.

'And yet you will kill these people? Why must that be?'

Alvaro sank into the driving seat and took off his dark glasses.

'Not these people,' he told her. 'Just the man. He is the guilty one.'

'But why must it be done? He is old – like me. It will serve no purpose. It is too late. What is the point? Why must it be done?'

Alvaro rested his hands on the steering wheel and stared ahead of him.

'It is too late, that is true,' he said. 'But that is not the point. You know how we work. You have lived with our family's code and traditions for so long. It must be done. There is no arguing. *I* am not arguing – and it is I who must do the deed this time. It is I who must kill my father.'

His mother made no reply. It was useless. These Sicilian men had their own rules. It was not for her to try and change their ways.

Alvaro backed the car out of the parking space and gently nudged it into the more competitive arena of the Palermo traffic. He took his mother back home and had lunch with her, of sheep's milk cheese and figs. Not a word more was exchanged between them. It was strange, but not unusual in that country.

Benino Noto appeared unconcerned when later the same day Alvaro told him what he had done. He had confirmed beyond a doubt that the Englishman at the Hotel La Torre was the correct Lord Wymark. He also admitted that he had taken Consiglia and shown the man to her. She was in no doubt either. The lines were drawn for the execution of the contract.

What Benino neglected to say was that he had not left the matter to Alvaro to take care of. He was suspicious of his 'English' son. The incompetent arrangements in England might have been due to his son's not wanting to have his real father killed. So Benino had quietly summoned one of the lesser corporals in the family business. Vasco had long since proved his worth. In the recent Mafia upheavals he had not defected to another family. He had remained faithful to the Notos. Benino knew he could rely on Vasco.

He told him of the English lord at the Hotel La Torre. He must be eliminated. Instantly. No questions, no explanations. Smoothly, quickly, no fuss. But effectively. Vasco nodded. He had been given such orders by Benino before and he had never failed.

Benino had a further thought. 'There is a woman with him at the hotel. His wife. She must not be harmed. Neither must she see you. You understand?'

Vasco nodded and quickly left Benino's house. In his car he opened the glove compartment: the gun was there, wrapped in a towel. Without a moment's hesitation, he turned the car up towards the Hotel La Torre. It would almost be a pleasure to execute a command from his real boss. Alvaro was a failure. Benino was the true head of the family.

Evening was falling over Palermo. The music was about to begin by the open-air restaurant at the Hotel La Torre. Stars again filled the sky. It was going to be a balmy night.

# CHAPTER 34

Hugo was looking forward to his dinner. As he grew older, meals had become increasingly important as key points in his day. There was, after all, not a great deal else to look forward to. In any case, dinner at a hotel was special, and this was their last one. They were going home tomorrow afternoon.

Hugo and Molly were dressing before going down to the restaurant. They hadn't packed evening wear, that would have been too formal for Sicily, but Hugo was slipping into his white smoking jacket and Molly putting on a stole over her flower-patterned silk dress.

Hugo was also looking forward to the meal because it would be eaten *al fresco*. He had long looked upon eating in the open as one of life's great pleasures. Indeed, there had been a time when he nearly drove the Castle Cansdale kitchen staff mad during a brief craze he had for dining on the roof. The leads on the tower were accessible via a narrow circular stair and Hugo liked nothing more than to have his dinner there as the sun went down over the trees at the edge of the park. There were, however, certain disadvantages. So far was the roof from the kitchen that the food was invariably cold by the time it entered anybody's mouth. The staff hated carrying the trays up the twisting stairs. Above all, the English weather was rarely suitable. But once Hugo had made a decision to eat on the leads, it was too much trouble to unmake the decision. So he and his guests would end up pretending to enjoy the experience while wrapped up in overcoats and scarves, hands frozen round their knives and forks.

Italian nights were more reliable; they had been perfect throughout this enjoyable holiday. Molly still worried whether Hugo would be warm enough, however. Shouldn't he put his cashmere sweater under his jacket?

'Not necessary,' Hugo snapped. 'Wouldn't look right.'

Wouldn't they be better off taking a table *inside* the restaurant, but by the door?

337

'Don't be silly, dear. Much more likely to get a draught . . .'

Molly gave in as she usually did now when faced with Hugo's stubbornness – a stubbornness that waxed as his bodily powers waned. There had been a time when Molly had felt obliged to take measures to ensure that Hugo's health did not suffer. She saw it as her duty in the light of the inheritance problem. On no account must Hugo be allowed to pass on before the seven-year period was up. Then, with Duncan's death, although the gift of the Cansdale estate transferred to Joanna – and Hugo still needed to survive the seven years – the whole business came to seem quite farcical. She now took a fatalistic view of the matter. What would be, would be – and there was no point in trying to head off fate.

None of this did she express to her husband. She selflessly pampered him and put up with him. She had noticed that since Duncan's death, Hugo had begun to look his age much more, lacked his old strengths, and seemed to have lost interest in life. His unsuccessful attempt to find his father's grave was typical. It was as if he had never really wanted to follow the matter through. Through either lack of energy or lack of real purpose, it had ended up looking like an empty filial gesture. His stubbornness was selective; certainly, it hadn't extended to continuing the search after the initial attempts failed.

Molly found herself wondering, increasingly, how long she would have left with him. On some days she thought he would last indefinitely. That stubborn streak looked as if it would carry him through any number of vicissitudes; he would live as long as his grandfather and great-grandfather had done, maybe even as long as his mother. On other days, she wondered if he would even last the next two years. He wasn't a hypochondriac. He treated his doctor rather as he did the Rector, as someone to ask questions of but not necessarily to listen to. He had had a lifelong loathing of medicines and knew that there was nothing worse than dependency on them, especially when every medicine seemed to have a side effect. But he did not look strong any more. Duncan's death had destroyed something within him – probably the will to carry on the unequal struggle.

'Well, I'm ready, darling,' Molly announced brightly. 'In fact, I'm starving.'

'It's too early,' Hugo told her, tapping his wristwatch but not looking at it. 'There'll be no one else there. And you know I hate being the only people in a restaurant.'

'The bar, then. We can spend twenty minutes nicely.'

Hugo assented. They left the room and walked along the corridor until they came to the turning where the single lift was situated.

'We should walk down the stairs,' said Hugo. 'Good for us.'

'No, I want to use the lift.'

Molly won.

Of course, they had to wait an age for the machine to arrive. When it did, the doors slid back to reveal a swarthy, dark suited Italian who eyed them over and then rudely pushed past Molly, obviously intent on finding a room along the corridor.

Neither Hugo nor Molly said anything.

They made their journey down to the bar, ordered their drinks and, twenty minutes later, went out into the restaurant. They enjoyed the most wonderful meal, and afterwards were even moved to wander round the floodlit garden and down the terraces to the swimming pool – which was also lit.

The small half-circle of columns drew them and they paused for a while looking out over the harbour. They watched as a small fishing boat chugged out slowly into the inky blackness beyond the harbour lights.

There was quite a chill breeze now, and Molly tugged the too-flimsy stole about her arms and shoulders. But Hugo seemed inclined to linger. His mind was obviously bent on saying something of importance to his wife, and it took some time for him to put it into words.

'I've never told you this, Molly,' he began, 'but when I came here in thirty-eight, it was rather an important thing. We were young, of course – terribly young. Alec – sick most of the time, I remember – and Toby Blair – well, he hasn't changed much. Anyway, I remember we were desperate to – you know, do the thing. With a girl. Neither of us had.'

'By which you mean you and Alec?'

'No, not Alec, he was too young. Toby and I. We were determined not to return home until we'd done the thing. We weren't going to be very choosy, you understand. Anything would do – but it had to be done.'

Hugo stopped and Molly wondered what he was going to admit to. It was not something they had ever really talked about before. Molly had never been to bed with a man before she married Hugo. He had been married before, of course – to Kay – so she assumed he had started with her. He had been vague about it, and she hadn't pressed the matter, being of a generation and upbringing that didn't think it quite right to go into such matters. She had heard, though, of the tremendous fuss men made about the first time they did it. The traditional method had always been to get it out of the way with one of the easy girls in the village or to pay for it with a professional.

Hugo stared out to sea, then turned right round and looked at the half-lit garden. It seemed different to what he remembered. Was it smaller or bigger? He had no idea where exactly he had taken that Italian girl.

The sweet scents of the garden had prompted him to tell Molly. He wasn't sure why. It was more unfinished business. He looked at Molly and held her by the arm, seeing that she was feeling the chill.

'It was this local girl, in the end,' he began, trying to infuse his words with a lightly amiable tone.

'You mean it was a tart? You paid for it?'

At once, Hugo's resolve vanished. He couldn't bring himself to tell his wife. It seemed faintly ungracious to mention the chambermaid, and the fact they had made love in this very garden. It wouldn't be quite right.

'That's right,' he said, putting on a light-hearted tone. 'Toby and I – you ask him – we did it the same way. Never regretted since. What a business!'

Molly didn't find it easy to talk about sex, nor to subscribe to the idea that everybody was always doing it, so she tended to hoot whenever the subject came up. She laughed this time too, but it sounded uneasy.

'Time to go in, darling,' she said, tugging him away. 'Brandy with your coffee?'

Back inside the hotel, the duty manager was beside himself with apologies. He stood before the Earl and Countess and shifted uncomfortably from one foot to the other. A most regrettable – and totally inexplicable – incident had occurred, he told them. As they would find when they came to put their key in the door of the bedroom, someone – and, of course, it was quite impossible to say who, or why he had done so – had fired a bullet into the mechanism. Apparently the intruder, having failed to gain entrance to the bedroom that way, had put his shoulder to the door and burst in.

'Has anything been stolen?' Molly asked, not too concerned.

'How does *he* know?' Hugo said to her in an exasperated voice. 'Better go and check.'

'Of course, *signor* . . . *milord*. A thousand apologies. It has never happened before. We must move you to another room, immediately. A man will help you with your baggages.'

'Oh, do we have to? Rather a bore.'

When it was confirmed that nothing had been stolen from the Hookes' suite, a porter duly moved all their belongings to the one next door. Hugo and Molly retired to the bar meanwhile and had their brandies with the compliments of the hotel.

'I expect it was that rough-looking chap we saw by the lift,' Hugo observed. 'Bit unsavoury, wasn't he – don't you think?'

'I suppose so,' said Molly. 'Thank goodness we're going home tomorrow. I don't think I'd feel too comfortable after that.'

'Still, the plane's not till late afternoon. We can have a final sit by the pool, eh?'

'What's the check-out time?'

'Bugger the check-out time. After this, they owe us favour, I should say.'

The mystery of the intruder unresolved, the Earl and Countess spent a peaceful night – though Molly lay awake longer than usual puzzling (unnecessarily, Hugo would have thought) over what it could have meant. Then she picked up her detective novel and fell asleep after reading only one page.

Alvaro was furious – not only when he heard that Vasco had been fooling about at the Hotel La Torre (and doubtless frightening away the English lord and his wife) but especially when he learned that Benino had given Vasco the task of killing Hugo.

It turned into a full-scale row between Alvaro and his adoptive father.

'You had no right to do that – to give that order to Vasco. You have shown your lack of confidence in me, by calling in another to do my job. Where is the honour in that?'

Benino stared back coldly. 'Do not talk. I will do what I want. It is my right.'

'No, I *will* talk. You gave him a job to do and he made a fool of you because he did not carry it out. No! The job is once again mine. Tomorrow I will do it, and then we will have an end of the matter. There are more important things to concern us these days than settling ancient debts.'

'Yes, I agree with you.' Alvaro was taken aback by Benino's words. 'There are many more recent matters that should concern us.' Benino did not elaborate.

'I will do it myself, tomorrow,' Alvaro stated positively. 'Without fail. You call Vasco off.'

'Very well,' said Benino, with a movement of his hands as in a benediction.

Hugo was reading a copy of *The Times* which was two days old. There was something very comforting about reading of petty squabbles and goings-on back home when you were fifteen hundred miles away, you had a glass of wine by your side, and the refreshingly warm Mediterranean sun was beating down on your old head.

Molly had been in the pool a couple of times and was drying herself off a little way from Hugo. He thought it unlikely that he would swim today. What was the point, after all?

Then he became aware of a man standing a short distance off, looking down at him. He was not one of the hotel staff. Nor was he a fellow guest. He was certainly not dressed for sunbathing. He moved hesitantly towards Hugo.

'Excuse me, please,' he said. His accent was thick and he was obviously finding it an effort to speak intelligible English. 'You are Mr Earl Hooke, please?'

Hugo slowly lowered *The Times* and turned to look up at the man. Molly laid herself out on a sunbed a little way off.

'In a manner of speaking – yes, I am.'

'I speak with you, please?'

'Very well.'

Molly couldn't work out why anyone would wish to bother Hugo and turned over so her head was facing the other way, and contentedly dozed.

'My name is Alvaro Noto,' the man said.

'Really?'

'Yes. You don't know me.'

'What is it you want? I'm trying to read my paper.'

'Is important. I do not speak the English well. Not at all.'

'Well, all right. What is it?'

'I wish to explain. You will be amazed. I must tell you first, you have a death in the family soon?'

Hugo thought he saw what the man meant.

'Indeed,' he said. 'I lost my son recently. He died in rather tragic circumstances. I'm surprised you know. You are from Palermo?'

'Oh, *si, si*. I tell you why he killed.'

This was hard for Hugo to grasp. What was a man here in Sicily doing telling him about an event which was a deep mystery even back home? It was preposterous, but there was an earnestness of purpose about the man that compelled respect. He was clearly not a fool.

Alvaro Noto lowered his voice. 'I may sit, please?'

'By all means. Sit wherever you like.'

Alvaro pulled up one of the garden chairs and placed himself beside Hugo, with his back towards Molly.

'I must explain to you. You will not like. But I must explain.'

'You can tell me why my son was killed, when the English police cannot do so?'

'I do not know this English police, sir. I tell you what I know. This will make you sad. It was a mistake, an error. You understand?'

'Thought so. It was to do with the robbery we had the same day?'

'Robbery? I know nothing. I tell you only of that dead man. It was mistake.'

'But why, man, why?'

'It was for *you*!'

'Me? It should have been me?'

'*Si*.'

Hugo fell into a sombre silence. He looked at the man more carefully than he had done hitherto. Alvaro wasn't threatening, even if his eyes were hard, flat and unlikeable. Hugo did not feel frightened. He felt only puzzled by the intrusion and the bizarre news the man had brought.

'Now tell me – Mr Noto, is it? – Mr Noto: let me ask you some questions. You know who I am? You found out I was here?'

'Yes, that is right. It was in the newspaper, about you being here. And so I come to speak to you. It is important.'

'And you know who I am?'

'You are English lord, I think?'

'Yes. And what are you?'

'I am, how you say, a businessman.'

Hugo sipped his drink. 'You don't look what I'd call very *Italian* . . .'

Alvaro turned away from Hugo's stare.

'They say that. Always they say that. They say I not Italian.' He paused and cracked his knuckles. 'Is because I have English father.'

'Oh, do you? Half English, half Italian. Good for you.'

'You do not understand.'

'Yes,' Hugo answered breezily. 'I think I understand quite well, thank you.'

Alvaro looked as if he had reached an obstacle he could not get over.

Hugo turned irritable. 'This is very interesting, Mr Noto, but perhaps you could leave me in peace now.'

'You do not understand, eh?'

'All I know is, I don't like mysteries,' Hugo said flatly. 'I don't like strangers coming up to me with half-cocked stories about my son being killed instead of me. If you won't explain yourself, please go away and leave me in peace.'

'I understand,' Alvaro replied. 'It will not take minutes now. I will speak free to you.' He glanced over his shoulder at Molly, who seemed sound asleep, and then spoke even more quietly and confidentially to Hugo.

'You come to Palermo many year ago?'

'That is right.'

'You met a woman.'

Hugo looked at him, curious as to where this was leading them and at the same time reluctant to find out. He nodded slowly. Then added: 'Several.'

'She is my mother. Her name is Consiglia. She saw you yesterday. I brought her here. She saw you.'

'Did she, indeed?'

Consiglia. Hugo had quite forgotten but, yes, Consiglia had been the name of the girl he had known.

'And you are going to tell me, you are going to *claim*, you are my son?'

Alvaro inclined his head and nodded at the same time – as though to allow that there would be a challenge to the proposition. Then he stared coldly at his father.

'Who's to say?' said Hugo, after the silence had lasted for many seconds. 'Who's to say?'

'I look like you. Is it not true?'

'You might do. As I said, you don't look Italian. And you may have the nose.' Hugo tapped his, to help with the understanding. He seemed to be treating the challenge lightly, almost frivolously. But like a dark cloud covering the earth, realization of the truth was spreading through his mind.

'I think I understand,' Hugo said slowly. 'You meant to make me . . . die. For this. It's what you do around here, isn't it? For dishonouring your mother. Some such thing? And you killed my son – my real son – instead? Is that right?'

Alvaro inclined his head and nodded once again, this time as though conceding a neat point.

'You got a man in London to come and find me and kill me, but he made a mistake?'

Another nod.

'What was the mistake?'

'The names. My mother remembered "Lord Veemark". You changed your name.'

'Yes. That's right. It's a little hard for people to understand.'

Now there was a very long silence. Neither man could tell what the other was thinking.

'Tell me,' Hugo said, eventually breaking the silence, 'I want to know this – are you part of the, you know, the Mafia.'

'We not use that name. We are family. Many families.'

'But that is why you, how you, did all this – I mean with people in England, and you here? It's not just simple revenge? It's because—'

'*Si.*' The reply was more menacing than anything Alvaro had said so far. Hugo felt the first real twinge of fear.

'What are you going to do then?' he asked abruptly – loudly, too, as though he wanted other people round the pool to hear. 'Are you going to finish off the job – finish *me* off? Is that what this is about? Seems a little hard on an old fellow just for a little youthful indiscretion . . .'

Alvaro made as if to go. He stood up and hovered over Hugo's sunbed. Molly was awake again now and dimly observed that her husband was still talking to the stranger.

'I want you to know,' the Sicilian said. 'I want you to know. So you understand. You understand?'

344

Hugo nodded and picked up his *Times* in an actorly gesture of indifference.

'So what are you going to do to me now?' he asked. 'I'm an old man . . .'

Alvaro did not reply. He walked briskly away, round the pool, and went into the hotel.

Molly called out to her husband, 'Who was that, dear?'

'Nothing. Nobody.'

But Hugo could not dismiss the matter so easily from his own mind. What had it meant? Where would it lead?

And he was very, very frightened – really afraid for the first time in his long life.

# CHAPTER 35

The abandoned honeymoon wasn't the happiest start to John and Sophie's married life. By now the shock had receded, but Sophie still couldn't bear to look at the wedding photographs with Duncan appearing on them as large as life.

The couple did what they could to provide comfort and support at Huddleston, but John felt excluded from the manoeuvrings over the estate that Hugo and Rupert were involved in, and Sophie found it no more easy to deal with Joanna than before the tragedy.

The newlyweds settled into a quiet domestic routine – living together in Bethany Cottage, John using Sleepy Cottage to write in. He still managed to turn out his articles, going up to London a couple of days a week to keep in touch. Sophie continued with her design consultancy work through Waterwheel.

There, though, the death of an important client and the legal wrangles that followed cast something of a blight. While the nature of the future ownership and occupancy of Castle Cansdale was still in some doubt, it was next to impossible to plan future restoration work.

For the month of August, Joanna had given permission for the house to be opened once more to the public. Attendance figures were up on the previous year, presumably because of all the publicity. Duncan's voice could still be heard, rather eerily, as the video of the 'Hooke Experience' was played endlessly in the stables. When Sophie popped back for a look, she had to avoid that area. Nor could she face going in the 'family flat' which was now covered in dustsheets anyway, the chandeliers cocooned to keep the dust off. As for the downstairs area, nothing, but nothing, would tempt her there, least of all a cup of tea in the kitchen. The wine cellar where Duncan had been murdered was empty and the door sealed. Visitors to the house quite happily ate their sandwiches and cakes nearby.

Sophie restricted herself to looking at the public rooms, which were almost all restored now. There wasn't much left to do, except for the ceiling of the Salon (which might have to wait for another year). She naturally felt uncomfortable being in a house which seemed so much more sombre than it once had been. She concluded there would be no more work for her there.

Bill and Dickie, Sophie's co-directors at Waterwheel, had never been directly involved with the Castle Cansdale account but were well aware of the complex personal links there had been between Sophie, Glenellen and Duncan.

'I think we've got to call it a day,' said Bill at one of their weekly sessions to review progress. 'Castle Cansdale was a prestige thing – only natural – but a one-off. Jobs like that don't grow on trees. Probably have to lower our sights.'

'I don't see why we have to do that,' Sophie spoke up bravely. 'There are plenty of other houses around here, even if the other bigger ones like Badminton and Sudeley have gone elsewhere. I could have a go at them – with my connections. There's lots of special property work around. *And* we're capable of advising them about grants and all that.'

'I take your point, Sophie,' said Dickie. 'But the real bread-and-butter business is going to be much lower down the scale. We've got to be realistic.'

Sophie looked disappointed at the prospect of doing up yuppie weekend cottages and Dickie didn't come down too hard on her in case it caused a flood of tears – though it was Glenellen who specialized in those as a rule.

Out of the meeting came a kind of consensus that Waterwheel would have to tout for business around Craswall and the Hooke country villages. The Castle Cansdale excursion, however enjoyable it had been and however good it had been for their image, was now at an end.

When Sophie told her husband that evening, John was a little less sympathetic than he usually was.

'Well, it doesn't matter, does it, if your work dries up? I mean, you've got me to live off now . . .'

'Don't *say* that, love! It makes me so angry. You know we'll not go the way everyone else does. I want to pay my share.'

In fact, John would probably have been perturbed at any suggestion that Sophie might not be able to help out. He was successful as a freelance journalist but he still had to pedal hard. And it always took such a time for payments to arrive. First he had to wait for the article to be published, which might take months, and then for the payment.

'Yes, I know,' he said. 'But we don't need much to live on, do we? I mean, there's only the two of us at the moment. We've got each other, and we've got the two cottages. We neither of us want to go off on expensive holidays – I mean, look at us, spending August at home! And I suppose there's a chance of a bit when your father goes.'

Sophie frowned. 'Good God, John! Whatever made you say that? Father isn't *allowed* to pop off – for another four or five years at least! In any case, I doubt if there'll be much, if anything. All he ever had is tied up in the estate, which Joanna's got now. We can't count on anything really.'

'No, I suppose not,' John backtracked. 'Hadn't really thought.'

'And you a good socialist, too! You're supposed to be against inherited wealth.'

'Well, yes, I am, in principle – but it wouldn't half come in useful. And there's certainly nothing worth having on my side.'

'I didn't marry you for you money, John – I should've thought that was obvious.' Sophie smiled and stroked his thigh, to show she meant the remark to be taken lightly.

'I sometimes wonder why you did.'

'Because you were there. And it seemed a good idea at the time. And Duncan pushed us. Probably the only decent thing he did in his entire life. Why did you marry me, for heaven's sake? To get your own back on the ruling class?'

'Rubbish. Nothing less like the ruling class than the Hookes have I ever seen. You don't rule any more. You just sit there and have legal problems! No, it wasn't that, though I must admit to the teeny-weeny bit of pleasure I get from becoming part of your – well, your whole family circus. Even when tragedy strikes. It's so bloody different to what I grew up with.'

'I married you for the opposite reason – because you *weren't* part of all that. I also rather love you. When we got married, love in a cottage seemed infinitely preferable to any other sort I could think of.'

'Hope it still does. I don't like that past tense you were using.'

'Of course it does, darling. I've no complaints. It grows on you, don't you find? Domestic bliss. And you've been so marvellous through all the Duncan business, you really have.' Sophie touched him again. 'I don't know how I'd have got through if you hadn't been around to prop me up. I mean that, love.'

There was nothing more to be said, except for John's pious hope – 'Well, let's hope it's over. You've had enough bad luck in your family to keep most families going for several lifetimes.'

Cynthia Moore knew how to behave in the circumstances. After all, she had had some experience before of a member of the family being in prison.

That August, Mark Moore was still on remand. It was quite clear his case wouldn't come up until Christmas, or early the next year. But Cynthia couldn't abandon him. Didn't feel like going to the apartment in Puerto Banus. She stayed at home, and raged.

What he had done should have been enough to make her want to kill him. It hadn't taken anyone very long to work out the marriage connection Mark had with his victims. And it was this opportunism which had really broken Cynthia's heart. That he should have embarrassed his sister by committing such a crime was beyond belief.

But it also broke the fantasy Cynthia had woven around Jacky's life – her being Lady Wymark now, her little baby Nicholas, the prospect of them all living in a castle one day. Mark had contrived to spoil the fairy tale. It was hard to believe the Moores would ever be able to mix in company with the Hookes again.

Yet Cynthia knew how to behave. She did not blame her son when she went to visit him in gaol. She maintained an unnatural charity towards him. Mark, her outward expression said, had done nothing wrong. It was all a mistake. He would be found not guilty. She certainly felt guilty of nothing herself. This was her natural way of dealing with the world into which she had been thrust by marrying a villain like Freddie. What anger she had, she reserved for him, but only expressed it in private. She saw that his protestations of innocence and non-involvement meant nothing.

'You put him up to it, didn't you, you bastard? Couldn't lay off, could you? Took one look at that stuff in the castle and had to have a go.'

'It was the boy's job.'

'I don't believe any of that, Freddie. You didn't actually do the job, so you could say you was keeping your nose clean, but he'd never have done it on his own without you pushing him. Aren't I right?'

'Nah, nah,' Freddie said. But he didn't try very hard to convince her.

'You'll never learn, will you? As if he needed the money, or anything! It's just so ruddy pointless.'

Freddie shrank from explaining how Mark had done it to prove himself; how Freddie had pushed the lad on because of the excitement of the whole project. That was why it was so irresistible. But Cynthia – being a woman – would never understand all that.

Whenever the subject came up, as it did for most of that summer, Freddie would – as ever – bolt from the house. Cynthia was left behind in Dorset Avenue, smoking again now – what else was there to do? – and looking at the photograph Jacky had sent of herself, Rupert and baby Nicky. It was lovely. It made her cry. She had bought a silver frame and placed it on the bar in the lounge, in pride of place.

But Cynthia felt she could hardly claim to be related to the people in the picture. They were in another world. Even Jacky was not her daughter any more.

$\star$     $\star$     $\star$

'Things are coming along,' Rupert announced, smiling, rather more like his old self.

'What are, darling?'

'I've got about half a dozen people lined up ready to invest. Some quite big guns.'

Jacky was delighted to hear it, and threw her arms round Rupert. His ever more open desire to see Castle Cansdale saved for himself – if not the nation – had infected her with similar enthusiasm and revived some of the ambition she had felt when he had long ago first told her of his love of the place. It seemed only right for the heir to the Hooke title to have the castle, even if he couldn't actually own it. That way there was a chance, too, that the tenancy of the castle would be handed – in similar fashion – to Nicholas, and so on into the future. It was not a tradition in Jacky's own family, but anyone could sense the rightness of it if they tried.

'When will we have it?' she asked, her eyes bright with anticipation.

'The way things are going, we might be able to start sorting it out in a few months. Use it as a weekend place. Just as soon as the money and the legal things are taken care of – and on this one I don't think they'll take for ever.'

'We'll have to have some people, won't we? I wonder if we could tempt that butler back?'

'Hold on, hold on! One thing at a time. But I shouldn't think Lopez'd be interested. After what he went through, I think he must take a pretty Joanna-ish view of the place. But we can ask Mrs Powers the next time we're at Daddy's. She's pretty close to him, by all accounts.'

'And what'll we do about here?' Jacky gestured at the kitchen of their house on Castle Wharf – it had just been fitted at immense cost, the first major improvement they had made to the property.

'We must keep it, of course. We'll need somewhere really to call our own. Cansdale will never be that, I'm afraid. We'll always be there as tenants. Anyway, I'll still be in London for my job. There's no way I can become a gentleman of leisure or concentrate just on running the estate – as I might have done if it had really come to me. That's the reality of it, I'm afraid.'

'You'll still need to work, you mean? Perhaps I should give Maddie a ring and see if there's any modelling jobs for me. Do you think they'll still want me after having Nicky?'

'Why not? You're still in wonderful shape. All contributions gratefully received.'

One thought led to another and Rupert made the connection in his mind between Maddie Shapiro and Freddie Moore's breathing heavily behind her, and from there to Freddie's unfortunate finger in the pie of their house.

'You know what?' Rupert said, throwing himself lazily on to the sofa. 'I'd give anything to pay off the loan on this house.'

'The mortgage?'

'No, Freddie's bit. It makes me feel uncomfortable living off charity, especially' – here he lowered his eyes – 'from such a source.'

Jacky made no response.

'But there we are. We're unlikely to manage it, and that's that. But I would if we could.'

Jacky ventured to suggest that 'Freddie's bit' had not been a loan, but an outright gift.

'Well, yes,' Rupert conceded reluctantly, squeezing the words out, 'but that doesn't make it any easier to live with, frankly.'

'I'm sorry.'

Jacky came out with the words slowly, and Rupert noticed her eyes glisten. It wasn't the first – nor would it be the last – time that the sensitive topic produced this reaction in her.

'Oh, lovey . . .' Rupert leapt up from the sofa to try and console her, but now her shoulders heaved.

She was determined to say what she had to say, between sobs. 'I'm so sorry, Roo. I've let you down. My family . . . It's about the worst that could happen, isn't it? I so wanted to do the right thing – and for them to do the right thing. But they don't know any other way. I'm sorry if it's ruined . . .'

The remainder of her sentence was drowned in more tears.

'It does not matter.' Rupert emphasized each word. 'Can't you see? It does not matter. The main thing is we love each other. All the rest is neither here nor there. And my family's not complaining. They're not embarrassed. I mean, with people like Duncan and Uncle Alec in it they'd have a cheek to complain about anything Mark and your dad got up to. It's not the end of the world, what's happened.'

Jacky stopped crying but was going to take a lot more convincing. She still felt she had brought bad luck to the Hookes by marrying into the family. She'd let Rupert down, and she'd brought Nicholas into a world so much less congenial after what her father and brother had done.

The baby, who had been asleep in the next room, now started yowling, as though a party to the discussion. Jacky got off her knees, wiped her eyes with a handkerchief, and prepared to be terribly grown up with the boy.

Rupert was still following his line of thought.

'No one could have predicted what would happen. How could they? When I first met you, Daddy was still in the castle. Duncan's inheriting it

351

was years away. And I hadn't a dog in hell's chance of getting it. Everything has changed so dramatically. Your lot's behaviour hasn't brought any of this about. Merely provided a sideshow.'

'I wouldn't have any more to do with them,' Jacky ventured, 'if it wasn't for Mum. It's not her fault.'

'Quite right. I like your mum, anyway. But we're not likely to do much prison visiting.'

Jacky was shocked by Rupert's evident conclusion that Mark would get sent down. She was still trying to fool herself he'd get off.

'I expect we'll continue much as we've done till now,' Rupert went on. 'They are your parents, after all. There's no ignoring them. Though whether I can imagine them at Cansdale for a cosy Christmas round the fireside, I don't know.'

Jacky managed a small smile at this wry comment of Rupert's. Yes, Christmas would be a problem but she did so hope it could be a proper one, if only for Nicky.

She went to attend to the baby, and returned with him on her arm. He had instantly fallen silent on being given attention. Rupert waved a forefinger in front of his son's eye, in the way the child apparently liked.

'This is all that matters, you know. Stuff the rest.'

'But he's going to have to go through with it all, just like you,' said Jacky. 'Become a lord and have the castle – or not have the castle.'

'Not necessarily. He could disclaim the title if it all got too much for him. And the castle will always be looked after now by the new owners. Into the future.'

Jacky wasn't so sure. 'Well, I expect he won't disclaim. He'll go through with it, as long as he knows what it means. It's a bit like a drug, all this title business, isn't it? Anyway, we'll be dead and buried by the time he has to go through with it.'

'Well, yes – at least, I hope we will.'

Rupert looked serious for a second, and then looked happy once more. Happier, in fact, than he had done for a very long time.

The day the likely future tenant of Castle Cansdale was discussing these matters with his wife in London, the great house still stood in that baffling, mute way it had in the midst of the Hooke countryside. Of course, no one had ever heard of a building that talked, but nevertheless, Castle Cansdale had an air of resolute tight-lippedness that was quite unmistakable. It was so determinedly keeping secrets to itself, a silent witness to its own past and to the family history played out within its walls, generation after generation.

The following night, Castle Cansdale was even more mysterious. It was a chilly night for August. There were fast-moving clouds in the sky and a light breeze on the land. All that could be heard was the gentle creaking of ancient trees in the park, the rustle of a few thousand leaves. But no other sound. Not even the cry of an owl or any other animal. It was unnaturally quiet.

No light shone within the house. The blinds were down and the glass merely reflected the distant orange glow in the night sky that was caused by the streets lamps of Craswall. Near to, the only lights were the small red ones on the surveillance cameras.

But no one looked at the pictures they took; there was no one within the house to do so. It required an intruder to trigger off the floodlights, and there were no intruders that night. The rooms where treasures lay – or such treasures as had not been stolen – were watched over by sensors connected to the police station in Craswall. It would take the police half an hour to get there if any of the circuits were broken. But tonight they would not be. The house, it could contentedly be assumed, had suffered enough in the recent past. It would be allowed to slumber in peace for one night more at least.

And so it did. Next day, of course, it would be host to visitors once again as part of the special August opening. With his death, Duncan's declared aim of the house being open all the year round had long fallen by the wayside. It remained to be seen whether his target would ever be reached under the proposed new management.

First to arrive was the chief guide, Reg William, who bore the keys and knew how to disable the security devices. During the next half-hour a small procession of cars and the occasional bicycle brought up the rest of the staff necessary to maintain the house for public opening.

Miss Wardlaw, the guide who had once entertained a curious Italian visitor with tales of Lord Wymark, was the first to take up her post – still the same one in the Gold Library. How many times she had told the story of the desk made from the timbers of the *Victory*! Indeed, how many times she had passed on her anecdotes and historical trivia unasked.

She walked to her post with Mr William on a route which took them through the Salon.

'I hear that the family's likely to return,' said he. 'They're working out some new form of ownership. Would you like that?'

'Oh, of course, Mr William. Of course, I should. It's like a museum without the family. And it's been horrible with it all closed up. It'll be nice to see Lady W. and the girls again.'

'Well, it won't be that Lady Wymark, I don't expect. It'll be the new one. They're going to be "tenants by invitation", or some such.'

'Even better, then. I like Mr Rupert, whatever they say about *her*. It's only right he should come.'

'I think I agree,' said Mr William more cautiously. 'It's important for the house to be lived in. Though how much of the time his lordship will actually be here, I wouldn't care to say. His job's in London.'

By now they were in the Dining Room. At once, Miss Wardlaw saw that something was wrong. Something had been disturbed during the night.

'Goodness,' she exclaimed. 'How awful!'

Mr William bent down to pick up the fallen portrait.

'Look where it's pulled the nail out. It'll repair easy enough, though, I reckon.'

He carefully handled the oil painting which had obviously slid down the wall to the floor, then toppled forward gashing itself against the sharp corner of a foot stool.

'I do hope so,' said Miss Wardlaw, more concerned than her colleague. 'Always rather liked that one. It's such a good likeness of the Earl, even if it is a bit out of date. That's the Halliday, isn't it?'

'Yes. It'll repair. No trouble. But odd, just falling off the wall like that.'

'Glad I wasn't here in the night! I'd have jumped out of my skin.'

'We'd better not leave it here. Help me carry it down to the pantry. I'll have to type a card to say it's been removed.'

And so the torn image of Hugo, 8th Earl Hooke, was borne away, leaving a gap in the line of portraits.

Then the public was admitted to the house, and nobody thought any more about it.

# CHAPTER 36

Hugo John Stanley, 8th Earl Hooke, died by the side of the swimming pool at the Hotel La Torre, Palermo, just before lunch. Molly and he had decided that they would have a little something in the hotel restaurant to fortify themselves for the journey home by plane later in the day.

When Molly awoke from her dozing she saw that Hugo appeared to be asleep. When he failed to respond to her calls, she put it down to his usual diplomatic deafness. When she began to feel hungry, however, she got impatient and in the end touched him, gave him a shake to wake him.

Hugo's body rolled off the sunbed. Molly made a startled noise. Immediately, the pool attendant and one or two other residents who had been lying in the sun came to her aid.

It was quite apparent that her husband was dead, there was no point in pretending otherwise. Molly was remarkably composed about it.

Like his father, Hugo had died in Sicily – but not in the heat of battle, nor indeed in anything that could remotely be called suspicious circumstances. Molly was aware that her husband had been talking to a stranger shortly before, but she had no idea what that had been about, so hazy had the heat made her.

Hugo's body was carried into the hotel and up to their room. Molly felt slightly foolish walking in behind the small procession of struggling Sicilian porters and bellhops. She carried his sun hat, his *Times*, his fawn cotton jacket and one or two other personal belongings.

A doctor was called and would arrive within half an hour, even though it was the lunchtime. Molly just sat in a chair outside the bedroom where the body lay, trying hard to think straight and come to terms with what had happened.

Though she had been supportive of Hugo all their married life – supportive beyond the call of duty, everyone would agree – she had always responded to his commands. Now, for the first time, she realized she would have to extract herself from that role. They had been due to drive to the airport and catch the four-thirty plane to Rome, connecting with a flight to London. She foresaw that transporting Hugo's body back to England would prove a formidable undertaking. It would take time, and so she cancelled the plane reservations and arranged to stay on at the Hotel La Torre until the necessary arrangements had been made. She had just been about to place a call to London, to pass on the news to the family, when the doctor arrived.

He was a small, bespectacled man with a large black moustache. He spoke not a word of English, but shook the *Contessa* gravely by the hand and muttered a short speech, presumably of condolence, which she did not understand. Then he requested the hotel manager to wait in another room with Molly while he examined the body.

She twiddled her thumbs and the hotel manager looked at the floor, occasionally breaking off from this activity to tell her that everything would be all right. He would look after her. Such a terrible sadness.

After ten minutes, the doctor joined them and began to fill in an extensive form. He did it with brisk efficiency, clicking his ballpoint pen in and out of action with a flourish and concluding with an involved signature of many loops.

He conveyed to the *Contessa* that her husband had simply died – of heart failure, in all probability. Of old age, he really meant.

Well, thought Molly, at least there's nothing suspicious about that. The doctor looked almost disappointed at not having anything more colourful to say. Perhaps he spent most of his time post-mortemizing Mafia victims.

She asked if the body could be taken away and kept somewhere else while the arrangements were made for its removal to England. The doctor appeared all too eager to take it from her, as if this was more his line. With further unexpected efficiency, two porters immediately took Hugo away on a trolley, beneath a sheet.

At last, Molly was alone. She felt more than a little frightened . . . so far from home, without her companion of the past thirty or so years, and among strange people. She worried about the business of paying for the hotel bill and rebooking the aeroplane. Hugo had always taken care of that side of things. Now, suddenly and rather unexpectedly, Molly found herself landed with these responsibilities.

She had had no warning that her husband was about to die. Of course, he had been ill when they first planned their Sicilian holiday, but it hadn't been anything too serious. He had begun to look older, and behave older, especially since Duncan's death. But there had been nothing specific she could point to.

Now, as far as she could guess, Hugo had just given up the ghost. The strain of the death of his son and heir, his worries about the future of the castle and his inheritance must have sapped those vital juices. There had been no point in going on.

That was as near as Molly could get to explaining to herself what had happened. She was certainly not aware of any other reason for his death. In fact, when she thought about it, she came to see that it was rather a pleasant way for the old dear to go – sitting in the sun, by the side of a pool, even though he missed his lunch. There were many worse ways.

At last, Molly plucked up courage to go through Hugo's wallet and found his list of addresses and phone numbers. It seemed curiously efficient of him to have such a thing, but Hugo had been obsessed with what would happen 'when the time came', as he put it, and perhaps he had had such an eventuality in mind when he compiled the list. On it were numbers for Rupert, Sophie and Joanna – and the Rector, of course.

Towards the end of his life, Hugo had dropped heavy hints, not so much to Molly as to Rupert now that he was the heir, on a certain matter.

'You know to get in touch with Drew Elliot when it happens,' he had said.

'When what happens?' Rupert had asked, innocently as ever.

'When the time comes,' his father said with a knowing wink.

'Oh, that . . .'

'In my desk, in the drawing room, at Huddleston, you'll find a key. That's to my leather case. You'll find a copy of the will and one or two requests about, you know, the service.'

Rupert had tried to shut Hugo up and stop him from enjoying the thought of his posterity.

Molly wasn't aware of any of this; Hugo hadn't confided in her, as he had not confided in her about so many important matters. So she was very much on her own, and had to work things out gradually.

She dialled the number she had for Rupert, thinking he should be the first to know. He was the heir to the title, after all. Jacky answered the phone. Molly was a touch nonplussed by this. She liked Jacky, but she wasn't 'family'.

'Oh, Jacky dear – it's Molly.'

'I thought you were away.'

'Well, I am, dear. I'm calling from the hotel – in Palermo.'

'Are you having a lovely time?' Jacky knew as she said it, she shouldn't have.

'Well, dear – I suppose Rupert isn't there, is he? I don't even know what time it is with you.'

'Half past two.'

Molly sighed. That was awkward. She really didn't want to break the news to Jacky. It didn't seem right.

'I need to speak to Rupert quite urgently,' she said.

'Nothing the matter?' It was quite apparent there was, but Jacky could be relied on to make the obvious polite noises.

'Well, there *is*, actually. I need to speak to Rupert.' A shrill, almost tearful note crept into her voice. 'Have you got his office number?'

Jacky heard the distress in Molly's voice and suggested it would be much better if Rupert rang her back.

'That would be lovely, dear. Oh, and tell him not to worry . . . but I'm afraid it's bad news.'

Rupert was back to his mother within five minutes – five minutes during which Molly had sat pressing fingernails into the palms of her hands until they almost hurt.

'Oh, darling, thank God, you've rung . . . I'm afraid it's bad news . . . your father . . . I'm afraid he went this morning.'

Rupert – understandably, given the stream of alarming events that had afflicted the Hookes in recent months – jumped to the conclusion that something sinister lay behind the death.

'What happened?' he demanded brusquely.

'Nothing, dear. He just . . . died. We were sitting in the sun, waiting to catch our plane. And I saw he was . . . dead.'

Rupert rallied quickly. It did not hit him with the force he might have expected it to do. He dealt with the news matter-of-factly. He offered to fly out as soon as he could, to help – an offer his mother declined, claiming she could manage. Did she want anyone else to be told? No, she herself would ring Sophie, Joanna and the Rector.

Her son ended on a loving note, reassuring her, saying he looked forward to seeing her soon, and how he would begin to make arrangements at home, putting a notice in the paper and so on.

Rupert replaced the phone, and sat staring at the wall of his office. His first confused concern was that there was something curious about his father's death. It was just sod's law, of course, that he had been taken away when he was far from home and beyond easy reach. But Rupert was convinced that it was odd. Why so soon after the Duncan business? Why now?

Only later did it sink in, what the death meant. Rupert was now the ninth Earl Hooke. He had come into his own. He had assumed what, for so long, he never dared dream could be his.

Rupert couldn't face doing any more work that afternoon and gently broke the news to his boss who packed him off home telling him to take as much time off as he wanted. It wasn't every day a man inherited an earldom, after all.

Two weeks later to the day, Rupert, Molly, Sophie, John, Joanna and Uncle Alec walked behind Hugo's long coffin as it was carried down the nave of the church of St Michael and All Angels, Bourton Cansdale.

The church was full, as was to be expected at the passing of the one-time local landowner and landlord, but it still came as a surprise to Rupert. He had never thought of his father as a popular figure locally, but in death he was. People had a respect for the old man because of his position, if not for the unspoken fact that there was nothing that could really be said against him. Hugo had never let himself or anybody else down. He had done what he had to, as a man in his position should.

Rupert was aware of the heads half-turned as he walked down the nave. Middle-class faces, country faces, respectful, not smiling. They seemed to regard him with new eyes, now that he had the title. They seemed to be looking at Jacky differently, too – amazed at her beauty, at how transformed she was by the devastating black of her mourning.

And poor Molly, now the Dowager Countess, her face barely visible beneath the black veil.

Dutson, the Rector, stood on the chancel steps and read from the Prayer Book:

'We brought nothing into this world, and it is certain we can carry nothing out. The Lord gave, and the Lord hath taken away. Blessed be the Name of the Lord.'

Rupert appreciated the meaning in the words, as though the Reverend Dutson had chosen them especially to refer to Hugo. Molly was simply relieved that the Rector was sticking to the old Prayer Book – the one she liked. It was a comfort in her ordeal. She would listen to the music of the words, and try ever so hard not to be affected by their meaning.

They sang a hymn – it was one that the Rector had suggested. Molly had never heard it before, but she was touched by the words:

> There is a land of pure delight,
>   Where saints immortal reign;
> Infinite day excludes the night,
>   And pleasures banish pain.
>
> There everlasting spring abides,
>   And never-withering flowers;
> Death, like a narrow sea, divides
>   That heavenly land from ours.

359

When they sat down, Sophie squeezed Molly's hand, and her stepmother smiled, reassured by the solid presence next to her. And John – it was so good to have him there, how well that had turned out. So unlikely an addition to the family. How Hugo had grown to like him!

Then Molly turned to look at Rupert. It might have been the dark clothes he was wearing, but he had changed yet again since his father's death. He had acquired a bearing and an authority she had wondered if he would ever have. To think of him as a little boy just a few years ago, and now all this . . .

And Jacky. One of us, now. Nothing in her looks betrayed her origins. Nothing in her behaviour. How sad – though what a relief – that none of those Moores were in the church. Their attendance would have been impossible, of course.

The Rector was up in the pulpit now, fumbling for half-moon spectacles somewhere deep down in the folds of his cassock. This was the moment – leaving aside the actual internment – that Molly had dreaded most of all.

'Hugo Hooke was a man whom we all knew in our different ways,' he began simply enough. 'Though one might also say he was a man we all of us *didn't* know in our different ways. There was a corner of himself none of us could ever penetrate. And yet we did not mind. He was a faithful steward of a great inheritance. He was a loving husband and devoted father. There was nothing in his life which had to be hidden away. We may say he was assuredly a good man and that he led a good life.'

If any in the family pews thought these sentiments questionable, they did not show it – and they tried hard not to think it. John succeeded least well in suppressing his doubts. As the journalist he was, and could never escape being, he silently began to add footnotes to what the Rector was intoning. It's just not true, he was thinking. Hugo didn't lead a good life. He led an utterly selfish life – and he failed in the one real task he had: to ensure the handing on of Cansdale to his heir.

But most of the congregation were inclined to take the Rector's words at face value. Of course, his lordship had had nothing to hide. What could he have had to hide, someone in that privileged position?

The Rector was carrying on, unaware of doubts in any mind.

'It was, of course, the greatest of sadnesses – heartbreaking to Hugo – that he was unable to spend his last two years on earth in the great house which he so dearly loved. But with his customary resolution he put his mind to the new life he had to build beyond the walls of the great park.'

Drew Elliot and Sidney Templeton stared at the service sheet and tried not to think about the new tasks they would have to face now that God had ruled against the Potentially Exempt Transfer they had thought such a good bet.

360

*A Family Matter*

'And then' – the Rector leant his hands neatly on the brass note-plate on top of the pulpit – 'and then, great tragedy struck, as we all know, a short time ago. An incomprehensible, wicked stroke took away his eldest son. We know that there are those in St Michael's this morning who must ever live with the consequences of that most terrible tragedy.'

Here the Rector gestured in the general direction of the family – though Joanna and her daughters knew perfectly well who was being referred to. Serena, characteristically, blushed the deepest red.

'And yet, I fear, it was Hugo who suffered the deepest hurt from the loss of Duncan. It may be that he never really recovered, and when his final trial of strength came, he had been weakened by the blow . . .'

Rupert made his irritated gesture with finger against nose. He rather wished the Rector had kept off that subject. It smacked of indulgence. It was only the 'Padre' trying to show how close he'd been to the old man. It was quite uncalled for.

And then the clergyman started playing the friendship card all too apparently.

'I suppose I would not be betraying a confidence, if I was to tell you of a conversation I once had with Hugo in this very church. It was shortly before he left the great house. We stood together one summer morning just over there, in the north aisle, by the entrance to the Hooke family chapel, where so many of his ancestors lie buried and where we shall lay him to rest shortly. And he expressed to me a great sadness that his father did not lie there – indeed, had no known burial place. The seventh Earl was killed in battle and only a monument on the wall of the chapel recalls his life. And Hugo said to me he must do one thing in his life before he himself died. He would go to the battlefield in Sicily where his father had fallen, to see if there was any trace of a grave.

'Alas, Hugo did not succeed in that task – though it was the last act of his life, to go to Sicily, for that simple purpose. And like his father, Hugo, too, died in that southern land. A curious, sad coincidence. But we respect his great integrity in making that last journey . . .'

Molly was now feeling exasperated, and wished the clergyman would stop. The person he was describing was not the man she had loved, the man whose child she had carried, whose difficult character she had so nobly supported for so many years. And, frankly, she was dubious about the construction Dutson was putting on the final trip to Sicily. How, after all, was he to *know*?

There was another hymn, during which Hugo's coffin was carried from its resting place in the chancel round to the entrance to the Hooke chapel. Most of the congregation would be unable to see the burial. Indeed, only the closest relatives could be fitted into that small space, so taken up was it with monuments.

361

Three large flagstones had been removed from the floor in one corner. While most of the congregation peered through the wooden arches, the undertakers awkwardly lowered Hugo's coffin into the church floor, hard up against the wall, which meant they could not stand on each side of the grave as in a churchyard. Indeed, a scaffolding device had had to be erected to assist them in their task.

'Man that is born of a woman hath but a short time to live, and is full of misery. He cometh up, and is cut down, like a flower; he fleeth as it were a shadow, and never continueth in one stay . . .'

Dutson's voice rose from the chapel. The coffin reached the prepared resting place in the vault below. It would be arranged more carefully another day. Room was left for Molly's body to join Hugo's in the fullness of time.

'We give thee hearty thanks,' Dutson spoke on, 'for that it hath pleased thee to deliver this our brother out of the miseries of this sinful world . . .'

Rupert glanced up at the tablet to his grandfather, with its wording about his having gained the respect of the district, and wondered what words they would find to put on Hugo's memorial. That would be something to arrange on another day too.

Soon they were walking out of the church. The line of black Daimlers carried the principal mourners away – not towards Castle Cansdale – Joanna still refused to go back there – but towards Huddleston.

The wake was uneasy. For some reason, the guests did not unbend as they were supposed to do. Maybe they felt that it was not just Hugo's funeral they were attending, but the latest act in a crushing series of events after which there could be no relief.

'Well, thank you, Rector,' Molly said, unconsciously avoiding the 'Padre' Hugo had so willingly used, 'and thank you for what you said. So touching.'

'And so true, I trust,' said Dutson. 'I know it won't be easy for you, but I shall do all I can to help you.'

'That is very kind of you. Of course, I have the children. Sophie and John are wonderful, and very soon I think we shall have Rupert and Jacky in the castle.'

'Yes, I hope so. I hear that is being arranged.'

'Perhaps what's past is past, and we may be allowed a little . . . rest from all that's been going on.'

'Surely, surely. You deserve it.'

By the door at Huddleston, Molly found herself being greeted in kindly fashion by a portly-looking man she barely knew.

'Just had to say, Molly, how sad . . . how sad . . .'

It was Lord Blair of Flaxmoor – Toby Blair, Hugo's Oxford friend.

Molly recognized him at last and couldn't help recalling what Hugo had said in Palermo – about what the two of them had got up to with the girls there.

'Thank you for coming, Toby. Hugo was talking about you . . . only recently. He said what a time you'd had in Sicily before the war!'

'Oh, did he? Well, it's all a long time ago now.'

Lord Blair didn't know quite what to say next and awkwardly slipped away, relieved to see 'young Alec' beckoning to him.

Out in the garden, two young couples were talking a touch uneasily among the rosebushes. Jacky, Countess Hooke, was very tense in the presence of John Tarrant. She hadn't forgotten that it was he who had caused the disclosure of her Father's background. Unfair though it undoubtedly was, she held him responsible for Mark's foolish prank and the fact that her brother was now facing a prison term.

John Tarrant put down her remoteness to her wanting to play the Countess. That was unfair of him, likewise – but perhaps there was an ounce of truth in it. Sophie, as ever, did the smoothing over. She did not really want to say what she said, but it seemed a good way to heal things.

'There's going to be another member of the clan,' she announced.

'That's wonderful, Sophie,' said Rupert, and rather enthusiastically kissed his half-sister. 'As one goes, another comes . . .'

Rupert was anxious to get away. Sophie thought he simply wanted to escape the misery of the occasion, but when they had made their farewells, he turned the car not in the direction of the winding lanes that led to the motorway, but towards the gates of Castle Cansdale itself.

He drove to the front of the house and stopped. Without getting out of the car, he pointed up with his hands still resting on the steering wheel.

'Now it's really ours,' he said quite simply. 'Or as much of it as is left. It's been a mad ride to get here, hasn't it?'

Jacky smiled nervously, and whispered, 'Yes.'

'And even now, I think there are things we shall never know.'

Then he said it again, with more emphasis: 'I think there are things we shall never know.'

For it was true, at that moment.

# EPILOGUE

In the twelve months since the death of Hugo Hooke, a good deal of the bleak air of doubt and mystery surrounding his family had at last been dispelled.

A settlement had been reached on the future occupancy of Castle Cansdale. Hugo's death only two years after the start of the Potentially Exempt Transfer scheme meant that the Cansdale estate as inherited by Joanna became subject to very nearly the maximum inheritance tax. The substantial sum was raised chiefly by sales of land, but also by disposing of works of art and other treasures from the house.

All this took time, and only when the sale was complete could Rupert move forward with his plan to have what remained of Joanna's property bought up by a commercial combine now known as the Cansdale Trustees.

Inevitably, there was regret at the loss of the land – and slight, though unspoken, resentment that the future of so great a property had lain in Joanna's gift. After all, she had never cared for the castle, and she had not visited it since the day of her husband's death.

Even though it was reduced in value because of inheritance tax, Castle Cansdale's sale resulted in Joanna's becoming a millionairess. What she would do with the money, or with the rest of her life, was an open question. She had rather pointedly distanced herself from Hooke country and all its memories by cancelling plans to move into a house on the Cansdale estate. Instead, she purchased a substantial manor in Leicestershire. From there she planned to raise the children and ride to hounds two or three days a week with the Quorn.

At about this point, the Cansdale Trustees, in an elaborate dance choreographed, for the most part, by Rupert, duly invited the 9th Earl Hooke to accept the tenancy of Castle Cansdale. He and his family could reside there for only as long as the Trustees' invitation stood. But that was enough. Rupert had his wish. He was the master of all he surveyed, within the limits of the agreement. There was the perfectly reasonable possibility that he would be able to occupy the home of his ancestors for the rest of his life. There was also the happy thought that his heir, Nicholas, Lord Wymark, would be able to live there when he eventually succeeded to the earldom. Never mind that behind a curtain of seeming tradition and continuity there lurked a business venture in the form of the Cansdale Trustees who ran their investment as a money-making concern based on revenues from the land, from rents, and from visitors to the house. It worked, and was a reasonably happy solution to a difficult conundrum. Whether Castle Cansdale would one day have to be turned into a theme park, a funfair, or even a wildlife safari experience to survive was a question that did not need answering just yet.

And certainly not on the late summer Bank Holiday twelve months after Hugo's death. During the Saturday and Sunday, the castle hummed with the sound of car- and busloads of visitors, all of them eager to savour the 'Hooke Experience' either in the house or in the picnic spots around the park. Then in the evenings, the ropes were removed and the house became once more the home it had always been.

Rupert and Jacky did not restrict themselves to the 'family flat' as Duncan and Joanna had mostly done. Instead, they would go down and use the Music Room, the Gold Library, and the Dining Room as they were supposed to be used, not left as museum pieces.

Baby Nicholas, now one year old, adored the house – which surely boded well for the future. No need for him to have a model castle and toy soldiers. He had a real castle of his own to play with. There was company for him, too. A sister, named Cynthia after her grandmother, had been born in June. The event and the naming had brought about a reconciliation of sorts between Jacky and her parents.

Indeed, that very weekend, Freddie and Cynthia had been invited to stay at the castle. Not so long before, it had seemed unlikely that such an event would ever occur. In January, Mark Moore had been sentenced to five years for his robbery. The murder charge had not been brought. Mark managed to convince the police that he had not entered the house until the small hours of the morning after Duncan's death. It helped that Craswall police were hugely embarrassed to find that Detective Constable Kenworthy had not only switched off the alarm system but admitted having fallen asleep in front of the security monitors. Mark had used sophisticated electronic jamming equipment unnecessarily, it turned out.

Nevertheless, Mark's crime threatened a permanent rift between Rupert and his in-laws, despite certain mitigating factors. After his conviction, Mark gave information to the police on the way he had disposed of the Cansdale treasures. Remarkably, two thirds of the property had been recovered and was back once more on display at Cansdale. The Rembrandt, repaired and restored, was in pride of place in the Salon. It had proved impossible to dispose of, just as Freddie had told Mark. Together with the silver from the previous robbery – carried out by still uncaught thieves, and which had been returned at last by the Craswall police – this meant that the most important treasures of the house were back together again, much as they had always been.

It was also helpful in the reconciliation that Freddie Moore was a changed man. Not that he had renounced his old ways overnight as a result of his son's conviction. That would have been too much to expect, though he had been discomfited, to say the least, when it all came out. Freddie's bounce had been eroded by a partial stroke. It was hardly noticeable now, unless you had known him before in his perpetually restless, active days. But the stuffing had been knocked out of him. He spoke more slowly – spoke, indeed, much less than before.

Cynthia, who had weathered the storm over Mark in her customary way, now devoted herself to looking after Freddie. Sensing this change, Jacky used the birth of her second child to put the relationship with her parents on a better footing.

Freddie and Cynthia were thus quite subdued – as well as overawed by the magnificence of their daughter's home – during the weekend they were staying at Castle Cansdale. Freddie seemed frightened of admiring anything he saw, in case, somehow, it had Mark's fingerprints on it. Cynthia enjoyed herself a little bit more – delighted at her daughter's status but in fact rather more pleased that Jacky appeared to be happy with it. Her daughter had also taken to motherhood with great ease, and that wasn't something Cynthia had really expected.

This was more than could be said for Sophie. She and John now had twin boys and Sophie found them quite a handful. Jacky was aware there might be other reasons for Sophie's rather worn air these days. Money was tight, especially since, after Hugo's death, there had been a swap of houses. Sophie and John had moved into Huddleston, while Molly had taken Bethany Cottage. It was just what Molly had always wanted and she now involved herself in village life with gusto, and with more actual participation than the previous Dowager Countess.

This late summer Sunday, John, Sophie and the twins had even been persuaded to come over to Castle Cansdale and eat at the same lunch table as Freddie Moore, the man whom John had been the first to rumble. Curiously enough, John found Freddie more interesting now that he had been punished by his stroke and through his son. They fell to chatting about this and that, and John – being John – felt no compunction in asking Freddie about those aspects of life on which he was an expert.

'It's not what it was,' Freddie mourned. 'I mean, when I was operating, you knew where you were. There was a respect for the gangs. You knew your patch and you stuck to it. You didn't go messing up some other geezer's. Now, there's no . . . discipline. It's everyone for himself. It's bloody chaos, if you ask me.'

John was amused by this lament for the good old days of crime, when every criminal knew his place. But he made no comment, and just let Freddie see that he was listening and enjoying it.

'And another thing,' Freddie went on. 'It's not as simple as it was. Now it's all this computers and stuff. You need a degree in bleeding electronics to do a job these days! I can't understand it. I was born too long ago to cope with all that. It's more professional.'

'White-collar crime.'

'Yeh. That's what they call it. Of course, there's still some of the old types around. But now, it's all drugs that's at the back of it. I'm really old-fashioned, I could never understand any of that. You know what I mean? Sex, money, even a bit of GBH – I can understand why a guy could put himself out to do them, but not drugs. Can't understand it.'

'But that's all it is these days – with the Triads and the Mafia, and all that?'

'Too right, John. It's all changed. I don't begin to understand it, like I said.'

Uncle Alec sat, seemingly far away, on the other side of the Drawing Room, playing with Nicholas on his lap, and trying not to be drawn into conversation with Freddie or Cynthia. It had taken a little bit of diplomacy on Jacky's part to get him mingling at all with her parents. Uncle Alec was not likely to forget the way Freddie and Mark had tried to bamboozle him over his little spot of bother with the prostitute – and how Mark had stolen the plan of the house from him to use in the robbery.

But it was impossible to avoid a meeting. Uncle Alec now spent almost as much time at Castle Cansdale as Rupert and Jacky. When he became tenant, Rupert offered his uncle the kind of access to the castle he had enjoyed in Duncan's time. Uncle Alec had taken him at rather more than his word. Having been given his own little workroom on the first floor, he proceeded to move in, even to the extent of selling his Mayfair flat. The Cansdale Trustees paid him a small retainer as 'historical consultant'.

All day long now he could ferret among the Hooke archives and plan further historical works about his ancestors. He was no trouble, but he was there. When Rupert, Jacky and the children went up to their Castle Wharf house in Docklands, which they did for most of each week, Alec stayed in the country.

Jacky did not mind; Uncle Alec was a pleasant old thing – though there were times when she longed to have the castle just for her husband, the children and herself. The servants were never far away either. Lopez had, to general amazement, agreed to come back as butler. Mrs Powers, with whom he still lived, had moved from Huddleston as chief housekeeper. And so Jacky's dream of being occasionally, for however short a period, on her own had to take second place to the dream which had come true: being mistress of a great house.

Sunday lunch was held in the Dining Room promptly at one o'clock. At two twenty-five the family was gently eased out of it and back into the private rooms upstairs, so that the house could open as usual to visitors.

John suggested a walk in the park. Whether this was for reasons of health may be doubted. It was probably to get away from the claustrophobic atmosphere of a family gathering.

He led the way out of the house. Freddie, who had probably never taken a walk for the good of his health since he had had to do it in prison, followed in his wake, limping slightly. Uncle Alec put on a coat and muffler despite the warm weather and, unusually for him, too, stepped out of the house into the light of day. Rupert brought up the rear, still ever so slightly shy of exposing himself to public gaze.

The odd quartet of males, glad to be away from the women and the children, ambled halfway down the Fair Mile before turning to look at the view of the house – a view which never failed to please. Then Rupert prompted them to pay a visit to the restored Pantheon.

Uncle Alec, with a twinkle in his eye, insisted on showing Freddie Moore every piece of sculpture and discoursing on its importance in the history of art. Freddie retaliated by wanting to know the value of everything.

The restoration of the Pantheon was a monument to the work done throughout Castle Cansdale by Glenellen Summers. But now she, like so much else, was part of the castle's past. She had left Waterwheel and gone back to California with her little girl. She was part of that particular past of which mention was seldom made these days.

It was when the quartet was emerging from the Pantheon, intent on getting back to the house for tea and cake, that a strange thing happened. A man – a visiting member of the public, presumably – brushed rudely past and went inside the Pantheon.

He did not look like a stately homes enthusiast, and for a brief moment Rupert wondered whether it would be all right for him to be left alone in that storehouse of valuable sculpture. It was about the only room at Cansdale that visitors could see without a guide being on duty all the time.

What was especially odd about the man, who looked foreign, was that he was quite obviously distressed, and appeared to have been crying.

When Hugo died in Palermo – of shock, remorse, guilt, or simply old age, whatever the explanation – it had not closed the matter of the youthful indiscretion he had committed there so long before.

Consiglia Noto, the woman he had dishonoured, continued her unhappy existence, still treated at less than her worth by Benino and by all her sons but one. Alvaro was the exception. But then he had to be. He was the living evidence of his mother's shame and he did everything he could to make her lot a happier one.

Yet he had an impossible job dealing with Benino Noto. His adoptive father had not gone back to prison, although his appeal against sentence had been rejected. The lawyers and the system guaranteed that he would probably remain free for the rest of his life while they argued. And so Benino was firmly in charge of the 'family' business.

Alvaro, who had been relegated to a supporting role, hated it. His wife, Maria the schoolteacher, began to talk of their going away, even of leaving Sicily altogether. But it seemed an unreasonable proposition. Where could they go? To America? But Alvaro was over fifty now. Too late to start a new life on a different continent, in a young man's country.

And then the decision was made for him. Benino wasn't satisfied with the mere fact that Hugo was dead. Alvaro should have *killed* him. The man who had dishonoured his wife should not have been allowed to die of natural causes but with several bullets in him.

'I want you out of here – for good,' Benino told Alvaro coldly. 'I have decided you should go where you really belong. You are not one of us. That Englishman's blood in you has proved too strong. You do not have the spirit we need.'

Alvaro was to go to England to help run the Mafia's drugs operation there. Pietro Bonfiglioni had been caught by the British authorities and put away, and there was need for a new man to take over.

'Maybe you will do better there. You have shown that you are not one of us by your incompetence. Maybe you will do better in the land of your father. If not, you know that it is a long hand that will find you . . .'

So Alvaro was sent to England to redeem himself. It was a slow business, getting to know the country and how it worked. At least he could now speak the language a little better. His schoolteacher wife had leapt at the opportunity to get away from the narrow, wicked, mind-numbing world of Palermo. She grasped the opportunity even more willingly than Alvaro. She saw it as a way of escaping at last from the Mafia's grip. Perhaps Alvaro would finally find some legitimate work to do. And perhaps they would finally throw off all that they had grown up with in Sicily.

Maria did not accompany her husband, however, when Alvaro decided to pay a visit to Castle Cansdale. He had to see the place for himself, and on his own.

Luigi Corsini was the one to tell him all about it. The restaurant owner in Soho was one of the contacts Alvaro had been given. He turned up one lunchtime, unannounced, at La Principessa. Luigi was quite shaken when he said who he was and why he was in England. Luigi had expected to be allowed to get on with running his restaurant undisturbed after his tormentor, Pietro Bonfiglioni, went to prison. Now here was another Sicilian breathing down his neck.

A table for one was made available in the corner where Mr Harry, the fat man with the pile of newspapers, usually sat. Alvaro was told to choose whatever he liked from the menu. He liked the look of the *antipasto misto* on the trolley and piled his plate with it.

'No pasta – not at lunch time,' he explained. 'My wife, she will cook for me tonight, as she always does.'

'Very nice,' Luigi said.

Then Mr Harry arrived and had to be shunted to the only spare table, by the kitchen door. Luigi apologized frequently and promised him a free *sambuca* at the end of his meal.

'A friend of yours?' Mr Harry inquired, looking across at the grim Italian sitting at his table. 'Important is he? One of your friends from that organization I'm not supposed to mention?'

'Shhhhhhh!' Luigi hissed, darting fearful looks at Alvaro.

Mr Harry had a feeling he had stumbled upon a terrible truth. He spent the entire meal watching the man in the corner, convinced with every mouthful Alvaro took that that was the explanation for his presence.

Did the man in the corner come, as Luigi originally had, from Palermo? If so, he didn't look very Sicilian. In fact, he looked curiously English in some respects. Mr Harry wondered about him while lowering the level in his bottle of Corvo. What was Luigi up to? He had never got to the bottom of the restaurant owner's interest in Lord Wymark – the one who had been shot in the robbery.

Come to think of it, the man in the corner looked rather like one of those Hooke people. He even had the nose. How very peculiar. Perhaps there was some connection between the Hookes and the Mafia! Perhaps there was some dark family secret? Or perhaps it was the British Mafia who had robbed Castle Cansdale? Except that some young lad had been jailed for that, hadn't he?

Oh well . . .

That was where Mr Harry left it – on the edge of a solution. He wasn't an investigative journalist, after all. He wasn't even a newspaperman. He simply liked reading lots of newspapers and magazines. Luigi had never found out what he really did.

Of rather more interest to Luigi was the story Alvaro told him. When the rest of the lunchtime eaters had departed, the new arrival from Sicily sat drinking coffee and told Luigi his story: why 'Lord Wymark' had had to be killed; how – through no fault of his own – Luigi had shot the wrong man; how the actual 'Lord Wymark' was now dead anyway.

'Will you take me to the place where you killed the man?' Alvaro asked pressingly. 'I must see it, you understand?'

But Luigi argued that it would be highly dangerous for him to show his face there. He would give Alvaro instructions how to get to Castle Cansdale, but the other man would have to make the journey on his own.

And so, on the Sunday in late summer, Alvaro drove down to Wiltshire from his home in Surrey. He first went and located his real father's tomb inside the church of St Michael and All Angels, Bourton Cansdale. He stood in the Hooke chapel and looked down at the brass tablet on the floor which marked the final resting place. And then he read the simple inscription:

Hugo John Stanley Hooke, 8th Earl Hooke
Born Castle Cansdale 1918
Died Palermo 1990
'In This Hope I Live'

That was when Alvaro's tears first began to flow. He was moved as he had not been when he met the living Earl beside the pool at the Hotel La Torre. But here lay his father. The man he had been told to kill. That was unbelievable, unforgivable. How could any man, for any reason, be told to kill his father? Thank God he had not done it. That would have been the worst wrong he could have committed. God had taken the matter out of his hands, and so he remained innocent of that most terrible of crimes.

Alvaro drove to the castle, shaking with the realization of his position. It became more astonishing, the more he discovered about it.

He toured the house. He stood in the Dining Room before the portrait of his father when young – restored now after its crash to the floor the day Hugo died – and more tears came.

He saw the portrait of Duncan, Lord Wymark, whom he knew to have been killed wrongly instead of Hugo. And he saw the colour photograph of the present Earl Hooke – a young man just turned thirty, who had succeeded to the title because of what Benino Noto had ordered fifteen hundred miles away.

Alvaro felt hot, as though he would expire through the pressure of the knowledge he had on his brain, knowledge which no one here in this great old English castle shared. He felt he would burst if he did not indicate to someone, anyone, who he was and why he was there.

He looked again at the photograph of Rupert and Jacky and their two children. How odd it was to think that he, Alvaro, was just as much a son of Hugo Hooke as this young man. Indeed, this Rupert looked rather less like their father than he did. That was ironic. But his wife! Such a beautiful woman – how lucky this lord was to have married her.

Alvaro formed a desire to see these people in the flesh rather than in photographs. But how could he do this? In his still slow English, he asked one of the guides, 'Where is the Earl Hooke, please?'

The guide confided that the Earl was, indeed, within the castle at that very moment with his family and several relations.

'How I see him?'

'I'm afraid that's most unlikely,' the guide told him with a smile. 'They keep to themselves when the house is open to the public. There's security reasons, too, of course.'

'But I must see them!' Alvaro almost cried.

The guide said no more, but noted the curious obsession of the visitor.

Alvaro moved on, studying every picture and object on display with great attention.

Miss Wardlaw, the guide, recalled the last time a foreign visitor had inquired persistently about the whereabouts of the family. She shuddered, and went to tell Reg William of her suspicions.


'By Jove! Did you see that?' It was Uncle Alec who spotted the resemblance.

'Rude bugger!' said Freddie, just as he had once reacted to Duncan Wymark's public pushiness.

'What?' asked Rupert in a low tone, remembering his manners and position.

'That man,' explained his uncle, 'was the spitting image of your father. The nose, the face – the everything!'

'Father? You must be joking. Anyway, I didn't notice,' said Rupert dismissively. 'Seemed in rather a hurry.'

'Bloody foreigner,' was Freddie's further contribution.

'Yes,' agreed John Tarrant, amused at all this reaction.

The four men entered the house again by the door on the north side – just as guests had done from the marquee on the day John married Sophie, the day the whole history of the Hooke family had taken a different course.

Nothing more was said until they were back in the upstairs drawing room. The women hadn't stirred since settling there after lunch. Sophie had tried to keep the twins quiet; Jacky had chattered brightly while Nicky crawled around on the floor in front of her; and Cynthia had held her granddaughter closely. Her namesake had been asleep the whole time.

'Quite remarkable,' said John, referring not to the baby but to the odd encounter at the Pantheon. He told Sophie they had seen 'this visitor – foreign-looking, Mediterranean type in clothes and manner but looked just like your father. Had the nose and everything. We all thought the same.'

'Where?' asked Sophie. 'With the visitors?'

'Yes. He was going into the Pantheon just as we came out.'

'Looked like an I-tie,' Freddie laughed. 'Perhaps he's in the Mafia! Come to bump us all off!'

Cynthia frowned at such near-the-bone stuff from her husband.

'Father was always very fond of Italy – Sicily, especially,' Rupert murmured. 'Wasn't he, Uncle Alec? Went with you once, didn't he – as well as when he died?'

'Yes, yes,' Alec agreed. 'Very true.'

'What are you suggesting, darling?' Jacky asked pointedly.

'Oh, nothing, nothing,' Rupert quickly assured her. 'Just a thought.'

It was a thought that had also occurred to John Tarrant. The pieces all fell into place: an illegitimate son of Hugo's, a desire for vengeance, an ill-fated attempt to kill him resulting in Duncan's death. That was a possible explanation, surely?

But John could not bring himself to tell these people. He leant forward and cut a slice of fruit cake. He put it on his plate, picked up a fork and napkin, and settled back to eat it. Then he had a sip of the Earl Grey that Lopez had just handed him.

'You're Spanish, aren't you, Lopez?' John asked the butler.

'Yes sir, though I now more English than the English, so you say!'

'You're definitely not Italian?'

Lopez assured everyone he was not, and was obviously very pleased that this was so.

Uncle Alec savoured the delicious cake and tried to make a connection, too, between Sicily and the recent dramatic events in Hooke family history. Did all the elements add up to something, or was it just coincidence? He would have to think about it – indeed, would enjoy doing so. He had, after all, dedicated himself not so long ago to finding out the real reason for Duncan's death.

Rupert declined the cake, drank tea, looked fondly upon his wife and children, and even upon his in-laws. Today, he felt rather happy. He had so much of what he wanted; never mind what he had had to go through to achieve it.

He gave Jacky a smile. She thought how nice and young he looked, as though he had cast off his recent cares at last.

Just at that moment, there was the sound of voices outside the door. The ninth Earl Hooke put a finger to the bridge of his nose and looked thoughtful.

'Lopez, would you be so kind and see what that is?' he said.

The butler went out and returned after a minute or two.

'A little trouble with one of the visitors. The guides are making sure he leaves.'

'Thank you, Lopez. I think we're all ready for a little more tea, if you'd be so kind.'

Jacky couldn't help noticing how much more like his father Rupert had become since inheriting the title.

But, unlike Hugo, he was never going to meet Alvaro Noto. Nor would he ever become aware of the Sicilian's existence, now or at any other time. And the reason why Duncan had been killed would remain a secret shared by four Sicilian men and one Sicilian woman.

Not even Molly knew the nature of the revelation her husband had been given shortly before he died. It was a secret Hugo had taken to the grave.